ALSO BY NANCY THAYER

The Hot Flash Club
An Act of Love
Belonging
Between Husbands and Friends
Bodies and Souls
Custody
Everlasting
Family Secrets
My Dearest Friend
Nell
Spirit Lost
Stepping
Three Women at the Water's Edge
Morning

THE HOT FLASH CLUB
strikes again

NANCY THAYER

THE HOT FLASH CLUB

strikes again

A Novel

DOUBLEDAY LARGE PRINT HOME LIBRARY EDITION

BALLANTINE BOOKS • NEW YORK

Copyright © 2005 by Nancy Thayer

All rights reserved.

Published in the United States by Ballantine Books, an imprint of The Random House Publishing Group, a division of Random House, Inc., New York.

Ballantine and colophon are registered trademarks of Random House, Inc.

ISBN 0-7394-5005-0

Printed in the United States of America

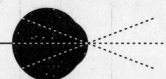

This Large Print Book carries the
Seal of Approval of N.A.V.H.

FOR

Jean Mallinson
With admiration
And gratitude for
Thirty luscious years of epistolary friendship

ACKNOWLEDGMENTS

Gallons of Godiva to the heavenly Linda Marrow and the divine Meg Ruley!

Crates of Nantucket Sweet Inspiration chocolate to Deborah Beale, Steve Boldt, Mimi Beman, Martha Foshee, David Gillum, Gilly Hailparn, Charlotte Maison, Tricia Patterson, Jane Patton, Pam Pindell, Josh Thayer, Jill Hunter Wickes, Sam Wilde, and Arielle Zibrak.

Thanks to Terry Pommett for information about videography.

And for Charley . . . all the chocolate kisses you want!

THE HOT FLASH CLUB
strikes again

1

Because Polly Lodge liked to look on the bright side, the word she chose to describe her mother-in-law was *challenging,* as in "the ferret makes a challenging pet." So when Polly's only child, David, married, Polly vowed to be the best mother-in-law she could possibly be, and the least interfering.

Sometimes, this was a struggle. But even though her son's wife, Amy, was a week overdue for the birth of Polly's first grandchild, Polly did not phone David and Amy every day. Of course they would call her when the baby was born! In the meantime, she didn't so much sleep at night as levitate a few inches off her bed in a trance of anticipation, every instinct straining to hear the ringing of the phone.

And then the phone rang.

It was the middle of the night. Polly lurched up and grabbed for the handset, knocking all her books off the bedside table.

"Hello?"

David's voice was gorgeously smug. "Hello, Grandma."

Polly shrieked. "Amy had the baby!" She switched on her bedside lamp and sat up, leaning against the headboard. From the foot of her bed, her ancient basset hound, Roy Orbison, shot her a long-suffering look, then laid his head down between his paws and resumed snoring.

"She did indeed." David's laugh was proud.

David and Amy's insistence on having the baby born at home with a midwife had worried Polly, but she'd kept quiet, and now the joy in her son's voice signaled that all was well. Polly fell back among her pillows, weak with relief. "Stop it, David! Don't torture me!" They'd also decided, when they'd had the first ultrasound, not to be told the sex of the baby, nor to discuss the names they were considering.

"Jehoshaphat Feast Piper has just arrived on planet Earth, weighing nine pounds, three ounces, and bellowing like a bull."

The string of unfamiliar syllables made Polly blink. "Jeho—huh?"

"Jehoshaphat was a biblical king, famed for his righteousness."

"Oh, David!" Tears streamed down Polly's face. "A little *boy*! Oh, darling, congratulations! How's Amy?"

"She's beautiful." Now David's voice was choked. "She was awesome, Mom."

"Oh, I'm sure she was! Please tell her how proud I am of her. Give her a hug for me. And lots of kisses for everyone! Is there anything I can do?"

"No, thanks. I think we're going to try to snatch a few hours of sleep. We're exhausted. Well, Amy is."

"I'm so happy for you all, David. I love you all so much!"

"Thanks, Mom. We'll phone in the morning."

Polly clicked off the phone and looked at the clock. Three seventeen. Her grandson had been born sometime around three seventeen on September 20. Her grandson. Little Jehoshaphat.

Little *Jehoshaphat*?

"Stop it!" Polly snapped at herself. She threw back her covers and flung herself from her bed with such energy she disturbed Roy Orbison, who, for an old dog with sagging skin, could conjure up an impressive array of expressions. Right now he resembled an exasperated hausfrau, hair in curlers, arms folded over her Wagnerian chest.

"Well, I'm sorry!" Polly told the dog. "But you're a dog, and I'm overwhelmed, and you're all I've got at the moment, so you can just bear up and sacrifice some sleep to keep me company!"

Roy Orbison sagged a bit, morphing into his Jeanne-d'Arc-at-the-stake pose, but stayed at attention.

"In the first place," Polly muttered, reaching for her silk robe and pulling it on over her nightgown, "isn't Jehoshaphat an awfully big name for a little boy? 'Stop, Jehoshaphat, don't put that raisin up your nose!'" She slid her feet into her slippers. "And what if he goes through that prepubescent plump phase David went through? You *know* his nickname will be Phat! Although"—Polly stopped tapping the top of her head as she did more and more these days when she was trying to remember something—"isn't *phat* 'cool' now? I mean, the word itself? Something I saw on television . . . But never mind what's cool *now,* it's bound to be out of style when Jehoshaphat is a preteen."

Roy Orbison fell over on his side, groaning.

"But we're *not* going to be critical, are we, Roy?" Flicking on lights as she went, Polly headed down the stairs. She wouldn't get back to sleep now. She didn't have to call Roy Orbison to join her; the animal was catatonic unless he suspected someone was headed for the kitchen, in which case he became Wonder Dog. Sure enough, she heard a thud as he hit the floor, then the clicking of his nails.

In the kitchen, she poured herself a mug of milk and popped it into the microwave. "Oh, Tucker," she said aloud, "if only you were still alive."

Her husband, Tucker, was David's stepfather, so this baby would be his step-grandson. Still, Tucker would have shared every ounce of Polly's joy. Oh, she could imagine just how he would smile! Tucker had died two years ago, and while the heart-searing grief had diminished, Polly still missed him every moment of every day.

The microwave beeped. She took out the mug and held it in her hands. So nice and warm.

Roy Orbison came waddling into the kitchen. The vets warned Polly the dog was overweight. But he was fifteen years old, for heaven's sake! He deserved a treat now and then. Instead of collapsing in his usual heap of wrinkles, he sat at her feet and cocked his head at Polly, doing his best Loyal Fido at His Mistress's Feet impersonation.

"You are such a fake," Polly said fondly. "But all right. I'll add a celebratory spot of brandy to my milk, and you can have a great big dog biscuit. Okay?"

Roy Orbison wagged his tail and passed gas.

In the morning, Polly showered, dressed, and breakfasted, and it was only eight o'clock. She wouldn't call David and Amy yet, they might still be sleeping, and she couldn't possibly sit at her desk and accomplish anything, so she phoned her best friend, Franny, to share the good news, and then she went up to the attic to dig out the boxes of baby things she'd been saving for thirty years.

By noon, Polly had not only found the various little rompers and blankets and quilts, she'd put them through the washing machine and had them tumbling away in the dryer, and still David hadn't phoned. She couldn't wait any longer. She dialed the Pipers' house.

David answered in a whisper. "Oh, hi, Mom. How are you?"

"Impatient!" Polly said with a laugh. "David, when can I come see little Jehoshaphat?"

David paused. "Amy wants you to wait a couple of days. She's concerned about strange germs."

Strange germs? Polly's jaw dropped. "Amy thinks I've got *strange germs*?"

"Not just you, Mom. Everyone."

"Oh, David, that's—"

"Humor us, Mom. Amy's exhausted. We all are."

Polly took a deep breath. "All right. What about tomorrow?"

"I'm not sure. I'll let you know."

Polly felt her lip quiver. She felt cold-shouldered, left out. "But, David, I can't *wait* to see him."

"I know, Mom. I can't wait for you to see him, either. He's beautiful."

Thank God for her garden! Polly hung up the phone, slid into her gardening clogs, and stomped outside. She'd already planted her new bulbs and put most of the outdoor furniture away, so she headed to the back of her yard to prepare her little vegetable plot for winter. She worked away furiously, thrusting her spade into the ground, turning over the lumpy soil, carrying heavy piles from the compost heap and mixing it in. Her garden would be better for this next spring. Plus, it kept her from pulling out her hair.

Relatives! No wonder Einstein had named his incomprehensible hypothesis the theory of relativity. $E=MC^2$ was easy, compared to her own familial galaxy.

Polly had grown up in South Boston, where her father was a schoolteacher, her mother a homemaker. Both parents were kind, loving, and as boring as turtles. Their lives clicked reliably through the familiar, repetitive routines of their days, and anything else made them nervous. They never yearned for adventure, wealth, or fame. Hell, they nearly broke out in a rash when they had to travel to the middle of the state to see Polly's brother, and two years later Polly, graduate from U. Mass./Amherst. Polly's father died young of emphysema, brought on by too many cigarettes, Polly's mother just two months later, of a heart attack brought on, Polly was certain, by the stress of being without his familiar presence.

Naturally, since Polly's parents never went anywhere and were totally predictable, Polly's brother became a geologist, working in Alaska, Dubai, and any other location as far as possible from South Boston, while Polly married Scott Piper, a man so fabulously interesting, Polly's mother took to biting her nails and weeping during dinner. Polly's father simply hid in his basement workshop as if it were a bunker.

Scott was older, unpredictable, and because he wrote travel books for a living, seldom on one continent for long. For a few years, Polly traveled with Scott to Mexico, where she got some great silver jewelry, to Peru, where she got dysentery, and to Newfoundland, where she got pregnant.

Scott didn't want to be grounded by a child, and Polly didn't want to lug a baby around in a basket she'd woven from banana leaves and twigs. Plus, Scott had the disconcerting habit of sleeping with indigenous women. Polly returned to Boston to be near college friends during her pregnancy, and it was her college friend Franny who stood by her side during labor and childbirth. Polly didn't even know where Scott was then, and when he got the news of the birth of his son, he sent her an African fertility statue, but didn't bother to come home or even phone. A year later, Polly divorced him.

In the early years, Polly and David lived, first, in a small apartment, and later in a little rented house. During the day, while her mother babysat David, Polly worked as a secretary for a Ford dealership on Norwood's "Auto Mile" on the outskirts of Boston. The owner had three daughters and a wife who couldn't thread a needle, so one day when business was slow, Polly volunteered to help when some of the girls' clothing was torn. If her mother had taught her anything, it was how to mend. She did it at first for no charge, because it was easy enough to do at night while David slept, but quickly the owner's wife asked for Polly to repair or alter other clothing, and *her* friends began to ask if Polly could sew just a few little things for them. The other women, busy as teachers or lawyers or accountants, didn't have the time, experience, or patience to reattach a button, take up a hem, let out a cuff, or stitch darts into a skirt. Polly agreed, but she would have to charge them and was astonished at how grateful they were to pay any fee for what came as easily as breathing for Polly. Before she knew it, she was able to leave her secretarial job, work full-time in her home as a seamstress, and live, if not in luxury, at least in comfortable financial security.

Every year or so, Scott dropped in to say hello, presenting David with a musk-ox tooth or a box carved from Siberian birch, but that was the extent of his interaction with his son. A few years ago, Scott had died in a scuba-diving accident. Scott's

parents had both died young, without seeing their grandson, so that pretty much took
care of that side of David's family tree. Because Polly felt vaguely guilty about providing her son with so few relatives, she gave
David a cat and a dog, who turned out to be
excellent substitutes.

For years, she sewed all day, spent her
nights feeling lonely, going on blind dates,
which made her feel even lonelier, or visiting
her increasingly withdrawn parents, who
seemed perversely pleased by Polly's difficult life because it proved what they'd told
her, that marrying that wandering Scott
would bring only doom. When they died,
she grieved, but she also felt an unexpected
sense of relief. Now, no matter what, she
could no longer disappoint them.

Then a miracle took place.

Polly met Tucker Lodge. They fell in love
and married and lived almost happily ever
after. Tucker loved David as if he were his
own, and David worshiped Tucker. The marriage had a truly fairy-tale quality, except
that in place of a wicked stepmother, Polly
had a malevolent mother-in-law.

During the eighteen years of her marriage
to Tucker, the only times Polly ever consid-

ered herself unhappy or unlucky were when she was around Claudia, who considered Polly deeply inferior to her son and never attempted to hide the fact. Sometimes Claudia's sheer, intentional meanness made Polly's heart cringe and jump like a beaten animal. Some nights Polly crept away from her sleeping Tucker, hid herself in the downstairs bathroom, and cried her heart out. And she swore to herself that when *she* became a mother-in-law, she would be loving, accepting, and kind.

Then, two years ago, David told Polly he was going to marry Amy Anderson, and while Polly smiled and congratulated her son, she mentally gagged like an old cat choking on a fur ball. Not that Polly looked down on Amy. She just found Amy so *strange.*

Amy was a Birkenstock, batik, and braids kind of girl, who drifted through the world in unusual garments she and her mother made on their farm, which had been in the family for generations. A strict vegetarian, Amy was so soft-spoken and gently, dreamily *healthy*, she made Polly want to swear like a sailor, smoke cigarettes, and inject ice cream directly into her veins. When Polly, David, and Amy were together, Amy said little, but stared at David with her large brown eyes, oozing a rather creepy intelligence, like some small, alert, brown bat.

The Anderson family grew organic produce—strawberries, tomatoes, and squash—on their hundred acres of land forty-five minutes west of Boston. They made jam and chutneys and bread to sell in their country store, along with handcrafted dolls and hand-knit wool caps and mittens. It was an idyllic rural life, with many charms, and Polly believed it gave David a sense of stability that had been missing from his early life, when his adventuring father had disappeared into unknown lands and his anxious mother was bent over the dining room table day and night, sewing the curtains and clothing that supported herself and her son. It was Amy's family, Polly thought ruefully, that made David feel, finally, at home.

After college, David had worked in the same bank where his stepfather had been vice president, but when he became engaged to Amy, he quit the bank to work at the Anderson Farm and General Store. Polly was surprised, but not upset. She had suspected that David had gone to work with Tucker partly to please him and partly because he had no clear idea what he really wanted to do. She knew from her own experience how children choose different lives from their parents'. She tried to be tolerant as she saw her son change.

She was just so unprepared for the changes.

At Christmas, she gave David and Amy beautiful cashmere sweaters, only to have them handed back to her, still in the box. "We make our own garments," Amy had informed her with the gently reproving righteousness of an Amish elder. "Or, if necessary, we buy them at the secondhand shops." Polly thought of all the pleasure David had taken, after being promoted at the bank, in buying several handsome suits from Louis of Boston. She stared at her son, who only smiled placidly, like a tranquilized bull. She reminded herself of Claudia and kept her mouth shut.

For David's birthday, Polly wanted to take him and Amy out to dinner at Locke-Ober's, a posh Boston restaurant. Amy had sweetly objected, "We don't eat at restaurants. We don't believe in supporting the gluttonous American consumer economy."

Polly had cleared her throat and asked, meekly, in that case, could she invite Amy and her family to her house for a birthday celebration for David?

Yes, Amy had said, that would be nice. As long as Polly understood they would eat only organic foods and no sugar.

Polly had looked at her son, who had been born with a sweet tooth as fierce as her own. David had smiled back serenely.

"I know!" Polly had offered without a hint of desperation. "Could I treat you two to a weekend on the Maine coast?"

Amy had wrinkled her forehead in gentle alarm, as if Polly had proposed sending them to a nudist colony. "Why would we want to go to Maine when we have so much beauty around us?"

David had always loved the ocean, finding physical and spiritual energy in its blue tumbling and surge. But now David sat so quietly, Polly privately wondered whether Amy had cut out his tongue.

"Okay, David," she asked in lighthearted

tones, "what *would* you like for a birthday present?"

"We need a new tractor for the farm," David told her, quickly adding, "I don't mean you should pay for the entire thing, but perhaps you could give us whatever money you were thinking of spending on my birthday and we could add it to our savings toward the tractor?"

A tractor? Her son had a degree in economics and he wanted a tractor? He hadn't even played with tractors as a child. Was he brainwashed? Polly wondered. Had he joined a cult?

Whatever had happened, he seemed happy, so she thought of Claudia and kept her mouth shut.

David and Amy were married on a sunny July day on the Anderson farm. David wore clean but grass-stained chinos and a peasant shirt embroidered by Amy. Amy wore a see-through natural-hemp garment, through which her breasts and belly showed in all their pregnant glory. Tucker's mother, David's step-grandmother Claudia, was invited, and Polly, squeezing between the Scylla of Claudia's bitter formality and the Charybdis of Amy's organic purity, offered to drive Claudia out to the farm. Claudia accepted and wore a suit and high heels, even though Polly had cautioned her that the wedding would be outside. David and Amy walked hand in hand to stand in front of the minister—a sight that brought tears to Polly's eyes—they looked so beautiful, so innocent, like Adam and Eve at the beginning of the world! Beside her, Claudia stiffened. The moment the ceremony was over, Claudia turned toward Polly.

"You didn't tell me the girl was pregnant. Nor that she's an exhibitionist."

Several people standing near them cast startled looks at Claudia.

"Oh, Claudia," Polly began soothingly.

"I'll wait for you in the car," Claudia said, and stalked away.

Let her wait, Polly thought rebelliously. She followed the party to the reception table set out in the barnyard, toasted the newlyweds with a glass of mouth-puckering homemade Anderson raspberry wine, kissed the bride and groom, and hugged Katrina and Buck Anderson. Standing alone, she surveyed the crowd, realizing only now how few of David's old chums were present. Had they not been invited? Her opinion about the wedding had not been requested, so she'd not offered, but now she felt even more strongly that her son had been indoctrinated into a strange sect.

She smiled at everyone, then, claiming that Claudia, who was in her eighties after all, didn't feel well, took her leave, feeling, as she walked away from the crowd, like an outcast.

She drove Claudia back to her home in the charming, Waspy suburb of Dover, listening in resignation as Claudia criticized the wedding and each of its participants. Polly was too tired and depressed to argue.

Finally they reached Claudia's enormous old house on Madison Street.

"Thank you for coming," Polly said to Claudia. "I know David was glad you were there."

"I doubt that very much." Claudia undid her seat belt and opened the car door.

"I'll phone you when the baby's here," Polly called out cheerfully.

"If you wish," Claudia replied. "It's of no

particular interest to me." Without a backward glance, Claudia strode up the sidewalk and into her house.

Now Polly leaned on her spade, watching
the sky turn indigo. Her back ached pleas-
antly and the outdoor labor had filled her
with a mild euphoria and a sense of accom-
plishment. A fat orange sun rolled low in the
sky, casting a benevolent glow on the earth,
and the air was sweet and chilly, with a
bracing fall tang. I'll phone Claudia, Polly
decided, to tell her about Jehoshaphat.

Why bother? she asked herself.

Because, Polly told herself, I believe in
love, all kinds of love.

She believed in romantic love, of course,
and how could she not, when she had been
married to a man she loved passionately for
eighteen years? Even before she'd met
Tucker, she'd believed in all kinds of love.
Her faith had infused her life.

Maternal love, she believed in, beyond
doubt, because her only child, David, had,
over the thirty-four years of his life, brought
her the most profound joys, even though he

also had sent her into some of her most extreme fits of insanity.

And brotherly love, or general love, whatever it could be called, Polly believed in that, too. At some point in her life she had come to a kind of bedrock belief that all life was a struggle between good and evil, darkness and light, love and hate. She firmly believed that every individual's actions tipped the balance toward good or evil, and that if there was anything she, as one individual, could do, it would be always to try to choose the good, even when she found it difficult.

So she would not let herself pout because she hadn't been invited out to see her grandchild. She would put away her gardening tools and pour herself a glass of wine and rejoice that her son had gained a wife and a tractor and a boxed set of relatives, and now a son of his own. She would be pleasant to her mother-in-law and respectful of her daughter-in-law. She would patiently wait to hold her grandchild in her arms.

2

Twenty-six years old, five feet one, and weighing, with all her clothes on, scarcely one hundred pounds, Beth wasn't the bravest person at the best of times, but tonight she was *determined* to ask her boyfriend, Sonny, about something that was driving her crazy.

She and Sonny had been dating for three months now. They'd been sleeping together for two. They read the same thrillers and discussed them over dinner at Beth's. They went to movies and Sonny took her out to dinner afterward. He phoned her every morning to say hello; he'd taken her for a week's vacation on the Cape in August and had reserved a room for them in Vermont in the fall for a romantic leaf-peaking week-end. She trusted him. She loved him. And from the way he made love to her, she could almost believe he was in love with her.

But he never asked her to do anything on Sundays, and often during the week, when she phoned him, he wasn't home. Was he seeing another woman? *Sleeping* with another woman?

She *had* to know.

———

Beth had first set eyes on Sonny one Saturday afternoon in a bookstore. Outside, rain streamed down from a sky as gray and low as a bad dream. June's welcome warmth had been washed away by the rain, leaving the air chilly, even sharp. The grass was sodden, muddy, the flowers bent nearly sideways by the downpour, the streets geysered with spray from passing cars. The forecast was for rain all day long.

Inside, the bookshop was warm, bright, and inviting, its aisles filled with other readers on the prowl for just the right book. Music softly lilted through the air, as gently tantalizing as the aroma of hot chocolate drifting from the coffee shop in the corner. Beth loved the spaciousness of the large store, the sense of an infinity of books, the unobtrusive companionship of other people, the bright, glossy lure of book jackets, the profoundly secret worlds they enclosed. This was her idea of heaven.

She was in the Thriller section, looking at the new John Le Carré, when she became aware of the man browsing nearby. How could she *not* notice him? He was *gorgeous.* Tall, muscular, lanky, in his jeans and plaid flannel shirt. Big hands. Curly black hair. He glanced her way, and she saw that his eyes were navy blue.

He smiled at her.

Blushing, she hurriedly feigned fascination with the books in front of her, even though she was so absolutely stunned with attraction she might have been in front of the bodybuilding section for all she knew.

She couldn't resist: without turning her head, sliding her eyes sideways, she looked his way again.

The man took a book off the shelf and studied it, *exactly* as Beth did, giving a moment for the cover, turning it over to read the back copy, opening it to the inside back to consider the picture of the author, returning to the inside front to skim the summary, and finally, opening the book in the middle and reading a few lines to get the gist of the author's style. His hands were large, his fingers beautifully shaped, and he wore no rings. Not married! His left thumb was bandaged, was that a clue? Perhaps he was—a chef?

As if he sensed her scrutiny, he looked at her again. And smiled that smile, again.

Beth smiled back.

"Hi," he said.

"Hi." Beth wished she'd worn something more alluring than her old jeans and blue sweater.

"Good day for browsing," he said.

Beth nodded. He was so handsome. So masculine. What on earth could she say to him?

He held out a paperback. "Have you read this one?"

Ah—*this* she could talk about. "I have. It's brilliant, his best book."

He cocked his head, studying her as if she were a curiosity. "You read a lot of thrillers?"

"I do. I prefer the older ones set in foreign places I know I'll never travel to. Hammond Innes, Gavin Lyall."

He was nodding his head in agreement. "Andrew Garve?"

"I have a collection of Andrew Garve paperbacks!"

"I thought I was the only one who knew about Garve." He held out his hand. "I'm Sonny Young."

His hand was warm, his skin slightly rough, which made her own skin tingle. "Beth Grey."

"Want to grab a cup of coffee?" He was still holding her hand.

"Sure," she said, trying to sound nonchalant, even though if he'd asked her to stand out in the rain with her clothes off, she'd have said "Sure" to that, too.

The only child of an accountant for H&R Block and a librarian, Beth was well aware that she had lived a sheltered and, some would say, eccentric life. Every weekend of her childhood, her parents took her to the library, the Museum of Fine Arts, the various museums of science, followed by dinner at the Ritz, where she sat up straight and learned to use a fish fork. Some evenings they attended a concert, ballet, or opera. Beth loved every minute of it. Only gradually did she realize that other fathers explained the games of baseball, football, and hockey to their children, rather than the plot of *Tosca*. Other mothers baked, sewed, or planted gardens rather than read.

In high school, Beth continued accompanying her parents to the theater. By then, she was used to being considered an oddball, a brain. She did have friends, a small group of quiet, intellectual geeks, who eavesdropped in the cafeteria with tremulous awe to the tales of the cool kids doing wild and dangerous things, and who sighed enviously over the popular girls with their bouncy personalities and their dramatic teenage romances. Of course, Beth's teachers doted on her, little bookworm that she was, and helped her win a scholarship to Smith College, where she earned straight A's, worked in the library, made some good friends, and finally, in her own timid way, lost her virginity to a U. Mass. physics major who went off to grad school at Stanford.

After college, Beth returned to Boston to work toward a master's and then a Ph.D. in English literature at BU. Her parents invited

her to move back in with them then, and
Beth was tempted. It would have been so
convenient—her bedroom unchanged, their
routines compatible with hers. But she reminded herself she was a grown-up and
must act like one, so she took a small apartment in Brookline, and a job in the BU library to pay her rent. She was happy with
this arrangement, until the dark winter night
when her parents were both killed in a car
accident on their way home from a lecture.
Then Beth regretted terribly every moment
she'd missed spending with her parents.
She had loved them so much. Even better,
she'd liked them. Now she was all alone.

For the first time, books did not provide
sufficient retreat or company. Most of her
college and high school friends were in grad
school, scattered all over the continent,
slaving away on dissertations that left them
little time for idle conversation. The best she
could hope for was a quick e-mail.

Occasionally she went out with some of
the other Ph.D. students for coffee or tea,
so she was developing a little group of al-
most-friends, but graduate school was, after all, such a hotbed of neuroses, rumors,
conspiracies, and cliques that friendship

with her colleagues was as risky as having tea with the Borgias.

Besides, some of them resented the plush, cushiony nest bequeathed by her parents, who, as cautious, well-organized people, had protected Beth in their death as they had in their lives, leaving behind, in their detailed wills, a substantial amount of money. When they died, she sold their house—it would have been too heartbreaking, plus kind of odd, to live in it. She put the money in the bank and considered buying a place of her own, after she had earned her Ph.D. and found a teaching position. Her parents' prudence meant she could concentrate on her academic work, unlike most of the other students, who took jobs at Starbucks and Stop & Shop to support themselves.

Sometimes, Beth thought, it might be good for her to work at such places. She knew she had a bad habit of retreating from the real world into books, especially romances, which wasn't such a horrible thing, since her field was medieval romantic literature. The fictional world was so much more satisfying, with its terrors, challenges, dragons, and magic. Often the tales had happy endings, and if they didn't—well, they were only stories.

———————

They sat in the coffee shop for four hours. Sonny told her he was a carpenter working with his father and brother, that he lived in an apartment in an old Victorian house in Methuen, that he'd been a jock in high school until he'd broken his ankle in several places. While he'd been laid up for the summer, a neighbor had introduced him to the pleasures of thrillers, and he'd been hooked ever since. Beth told him about her own life, her parents' deaths, and that she was working on her Ph.D. in medieval literature. It was nearly nine o'clock when they realized how the coffee shop and the bookstore had emptied out.

Sonny smiled wryly. "As much as I hate to admit this, I guess we're going to have to leave here, sooner or later."

Beth checked her watch. "Eeek. I should have been back at my desk hours ago." Reluctantly, she rose.

He said, "I'd love to see your Andrew Garve collection."

"Oh!" Was he asking her for a date? He could certainly find Andrew Garve books elsewhere. "Oh, well, that would be fun." *Fun,* she thought, *don't be so lame. You want to have sex with this man.* "Want to come by tomorrow?"

He shook his head. "Tomorrow's not good for me."

A wave of embarrassment passed through her. Had she seemed too eager?

"How about Monday night?" he suggested.

"Um, that works."

He took a pen from his jacket, scribbled something on a napkin, and handed it to her. "My phone number, in case something comes up."

She gave him her address and phone number. His smile was like the gentlest of kisses. They walked through the store, stopping just at the door. Rain was still pouring down.

"My car's that way." He pointed.

"I'm parked over there." It was in the opposite direction.

"Okay, then, I guess we'd better run for it." He put up the hood on his yellow slicker. "Bye, Beth."

"Bye, Sonny."

He raced off in the rain. Beth hurried to her own car through the puddles, splashing water up on her jeans, soaking her shoes, and she thought the raindrops floating around her were like diamonds, sparkling from a good witch's wand.

———

Now, three months later, Beth waited in terror for Sonny to arrive. Poor Sonny, who had no idea he was about to be interrogated like one of the heroes in his beloved thrillers. Well, not *interrogated,* but questioned. Nicely. Perhaps even charmingly. But *definitely.*

The novels she read in a white-hot blur of guilty pleasure hadn't fully introduced her to the painful way love could warp time. If she wondered whether the fictional lovers would end up together, she just kept reading into the night, until she'd finished the book. Or she could cheat and read the last page first. Real time, she was discovering, could not be hurried, and passionate love could be torture—not the gorgeous "exquisite torture" of books, but the nail-gnawing, lip-nibbling, stomach-dropping variety that made her want to crawl into bed and suck her thumb.

A truck rumbled up the street. Sonny! Racing to the kitchen, she poured herself a glass of wine, drinking so quickly she choked. She heard his knock. She opened the door. There Sonny stood, handsome and strong.

"Hi, Sonny."

Stepping inside, he shut the door, leaned against it, and pulled her to him in a long kiss.

"I made spaghetti," she told him when she could catch her breath.

"I got a video," he said. "We can watch it after dinner." He held her hips against his. "Want to eat dinner? Or do something else?"

"Actually," Beth said, forcing herself to pull away just a little, "I'd like to talk a bit, first."

She thought he'd be surprised, maybe even a little wary, but she was the one who was surprised when he said, "Good. Because I'd like to talk to you."

"Oh?"

"Let me get a beer," he said, going into

the kitchen and coming out with a bottle of Heineken.

Until Beth had met Sonny, she'd never had any kind of beer in her refrigerator. She liked seeing the bottle in his hand, so upright, rigid—masculine.

They settled on the futon she used as a sofa. Drawing her legs up, she tucked them beneath her so she could face him. "I have a question to ask you," she said.

"I have a question to ask you," he echoed. "You first."

"Okay." She took a fortifying sip of wine. "I need to know if you're seeing someone else."

Sonny looked bewildered. "Why would you think I'm seeing someone else?"

She looked down at her hands. Her face was burning. "Because you never ask me to do anything with you on Sundays. And a lot of the time, if I call you in the evening, you're not at your apartment."

"Oh," Sonny said. "Well." He let out a long, gusty sigh.

That sigh seemed so laden with import, Beth's heart nearly stopped. Sonny was married, Beth suddenly realized. Or dying.

"Look," Sonny said. "I'm not seeing another woman. I don't want to see another woman, Beth." He put his beer on the table, took her wineglass from her and set it next to the beer, then held her cold hands in his. "I love you, Beth."

Her mouth fell open. "You do?"

He nodded.

Her eyes filled with tears. "Oh, Sonny. I love you, too!"

"I want to marry you, Beth. That's my question: do you think we could have a life together?"

Amazed, Beth could only nod.

Sonny pulled her to him and kissed her on the mouth. His mouth was soft, warm, and beer-flavored. She wrapped her arms around him. He picked her up and carried her into her bedroom—she felt like a heroine in the romances she loved! Sonny laid her on the bed, gently brought his body down on hers, and kissed the hollow of her neck. All the voices in her head were stilled as her body melded with his.

Afterward, she lay against him, her face buried against his chest, breathing in the pungent smell of sweat and sex. Her legs were wrapped over his torso. She could feel his moist penis against her thigh.

"Sometimes," she murmured, "when we're making love, it seems more than physical to me, Sonny. It seems spiritual. Oh, it's ineffable."

Sonny was silent. Then, to her surprise, he said, "Sit up."

"What?"

Gently he pried her off him and pushed her up to a sitting position. He sat, too, and turned toward her. "Listen," he said, but for a long moment he didn't speak. He took a deep breath. "I don't know what *ineffular* means."

She grinned.

His face darkened like thunder. "Great. You're laughing at me."

Horrified, she insisted, "No, Sonny, *God*, no! I'm not laughing at you. I'm just smiling because you're so cute."

"No," he said stubbornly, "you're laughing at me." His face softened. "I've never felt this way about a woman before, Beth. I've only told one other woman in all my life that I loved her. I know I'm not good with words, and we might as well face that, as well as the fact that you're smarter than I am. I don't want our differences to come between us when we marry."

"I'm not—" Beth began to protest.

"You're book smarter than I am. I didn't go to college."

"That doesn't matter!"

"Really?" He held her with a steady gaze. "You're earning your doctorate. I'm a carpenter. Think about it."

She put her hands on his face, shivering a little as the bristles of his beard scraped her palms. "Oh, Sonny, I love you so much."

"Yeah, but forget the sex—"

"Like I could!"

"I'm serious. We're so different. Wait, Beth, hear me out. I've been thinking about this a lot. Like, will I bore you when you get your Ph.D.? Will your friends look down on me?" Before she could speak, he continued, "But then I think, when we have children, it might be a good thing. We'd have all the bases covered, you could help with their schoolwork, and I could teach them sports."

She was nearly swooning with love. She'd always been afraid to trust a handsome man, worried that, in reverse fairy-tale fashion, his façade would hide a toad inside. Now Sonny's earnestness, his vulnerability, were amazing and precious to her. It was like opening a rocky geode to find gemstones glittering inside.

"We like thrillers," she offered weakly. Her scholarly skills kicked in. She counted on her fingers, finding enormous relief in quantifying the indescribable. "We like the same kind of food. We share the same political views. We both go to church, but not as often as we should. We're both morning people. We hate spending huge amounts of money at expensive restaurants when we could share a pizza and a video. On the other hand, I love ballet and opera."

Sonny thought a moment. "I went to see the *Nutcracker* when I was in fifth grade." His face fell. "But I can't see myself going to ballets or operas very often."

Beth nodded. "Well, I can't imagine I'll ever get excited about football or hockey."

Sonny took her hands in his. "What about baseball?"

She'd watched the Red Sox on television with Sonny. "Well," she confessed, "I think Danny Ramirez is kind of cute."

Sonny burst out laughing. "It's *Manny*!"

Beth smiled back. She knew it was Manny. But her little error might make him feel better about not knowing what *ineffable* meant.

Good grief! She didn't know she could be devious! She buried her head in his chest, hiding a triumphant grin.

Sonny drew her against him in a bear hug. "I guess it's time for you to meet my family."

"Oh?"

"You want to know where I am Sundays or nights when I'm not with you? I'm over at their house, helping Dad with the yard. Mom fixes a great Sunday dinner. We watch baseball or football, whatever. My younger brother, Mark, and my sister, Suze, still live at home. I mean, we're a close family. They're really nice. They're just kind of over-whelming, in a noisy kind of way. I guess I was enjoying having you all to myself for a while. But it's time you met them, definitely."

Beth bit her lip. "Do you think they'll like me?"

"God, Beth," Sonny said. "How could anyone not like you?"

3

She was going to be late!

Carolyn Sperry gunned her black Mercedes off the highway onto a two-lane country road with so many bends and curves she had to brake frequently. Finally she was forced to drop her speed to a sluggish forty miles an hour. She looked at the clock on the dash, then at her watch. That damned personnel meeting had run over its allotted time.

Cursing, she almost drove past the handsome stone gates she'd been seeking. She slammed on her brakes, jerked the steering wheel to the right, and squealed through the entrance to The Haven.

Mums and impatiens bobbed from the windows of the gatehouse. Green lawns dipped and flowed gracefully from the long stone driveway into the distance. The main building, an impressive stone castle, was brightened with flower beds. Pots of hibiscus bordered the massive front door, and the cars parked near the house were all sleek and costly. Good. It looked expensive. She *liked* expensive. Anyway, she could afford anything, would gladly pay anything, if they could help.

But *could* they help?

She hurried up the steps. The stone lions reclining majestically on either side wore wreaths of fresh flowers. She frowned, trying to judge what that touch of whimsy implied about this place.

Inside, she crossed the marble foyer and gave her name to the receptionist, who immediately showed her through tall double doors into a handsome lounge. Another point for The Haven. Carolyn hated being kept waiting.

The grandeur of the white marble fireplace and the floor-to-ceiling, leaded-glass casement windows was softened by rugs, sofas, chairs, and lamps in shades of rose and cream and emerald.

A door at the far end of the room opened, and a striking woman entered. Slender, attractive, she wore violet silk slacks and a lavender top with a swirling scarf.

"Hello," she said, holding out her hand. "I'm Shirley Gold, director of The Haven. You must be Carolyn Sperry." Shirley gestured toward a sofa and took one across from her. "Someone will be bringing tea in a moment. Apple spice, no caffeine, but delicious for this time of year. It's a gorgeous day, isn't it?"

"Yes." Nervousness made Carolyn's voice crack. "Yes, it is."

"Well, now," Shirley said. "Let's talk about what The Haven can do for you. You read our brochure?"

"Yes."

"Great." Shirley slipped a purple pen from a notebook and turned to a fresh, lavender page. "Do you mind if I take notes? It will help me organize a path for you. I assure you, everything you tell me will be held in the strictest confidence."

Carolyn laughed. "In my case, that may not be necessary. I feel like everyone in the world knows about my problems." She twisted her hands together, realized what she was doing, and laid them in her lap.

"Really? Why is that?"

"Because the Sperry name is so well-known."

"Oh, yes." Shirley nodded, tapping her pen against her mouth. "I believe I have seen several pictures of you in the *Globe* and the *Herald.* You and your husband are patrons of the arts—"

"True," Carolyn interrupted, "but what matters is my company. The Sperry Paper Company."

"Is it in Sperry, Massachusetts?" Shirley inquired, naming a town thirty miles north.

Carolyn was taken aback. "The *town* was named after the *company*! Are you new to the area?"

"No, I'm not." Shirley responded quietly with a smile. "Perhaps this offers some assurance that not everyone in the Boston area knows about your private concerns."

A tap sounded on the door.

"Come in," Shirley called, and a woman entered, bearing a silver tray set with tea and gingersnaps. "Thanks, Sally," Shirley said as the woman set it on the table.

The next few moments were occupied with serving tea.

"Thank you." Carolyn accepted a cup. "I didn't mean to be abrupt. I admit I'm on the defensive these days. Sperry has become just a flea on the back of the giant paper companies, and I'm sensitive to the loss of its importance."

"That's perfectly understandable—"

"Sperry is holding its own. We've cut our inventory to focus on our signature product: elegant, personal, watermarked stationery. We still employ over three hundred people, and except for a slight dip a couple of years ago, our orders are actually on the rise, but we have to be vigilant. And I have a double whammy of responsibility."

"Oh? Why is that?"

"My great-grandmother Geraldine Sperry started the company in 1918." Carolyn leaned forward, her words spilling out in a rush. "She was widowed, with two little girls, and yet she managed to found a successful enterprise from her own interests, talents, and initiative. Geraldine Sperry intended for the company to pass from mother to daughter. But my father's mother gave birth to only one child, a boy. My father. Aubrey Sperry. I'm an only child. I'll inherit the company. I'm the vice president now. And—I'm pregnant."

"Congratulations."

"Yes, thank heavens! I'm thirty-seven years old! All the Sperry employees, as well as everyone in the town, and anyone belonging to a certain stratum of Boston society, have been waiting for me to produce this child."

"And you?"

"I've always dreamed of having a daughter someday." Carolyn placed her hands gently on her protruding belly. Her emotions brought a tremble to her voice and tears to her eyes. "We've had the amnio. It's going to be a girl!"

"I'm so glad. How far along are you?" Shirley asked.

"Just two months." Carolyn caressed her belly, and as she met Shirley's eyes, she felt her face soften with a love and vulnerability she was powerless to hide. "I'm so happy! It took me a long time to get pregnant. I was afraid I'd waited too long."

"This is your first child?"

"Yes. Hank and I were married five years ago." Carolyn laughed abruptly. "I'm still surprised *any* man married me. Most men can't deal with a woman being more successful or wealthy than they are."

"And Hank can?"

"Oh, absolutely. He's a Wellingell. His family is much wealthier than mine. The Wellingells run a private environmental conservation foundation. His mother and sisters are so strong-minded they make me look wimpy. Hank travels a lot, evaluating fragile or endangered ecosystems, helping groups set up preservation, advising on government policies."

"So he has nothing to do with the paper company?"

"Nothing. Which is good. I have to work with my father. That's enough stress."

"Tell me about your father," Shirley suggested.

Carolyn's mouth tightened. "My father is handsome, charming, and well liked by everyone at the company."

"And your relationship with him . . . ?"

Carolyn shrugged. "I love him, of course. He loves me. We work together well enough. But we've never been close, except perhaps when I was ten, when my mother died."

"Your mother died when you were ten? How terrible for you."

"It was." Carolyn looked away.

"What happened?"

Carolyn lifted her chin defiantly. "Heart attack. At thirty-seven."

"I'm so sorry."

"Anyway, my father's seventy. He's slowing down. Really, he should retire."

"Is that a possibility?"

"Oh, absolutely. It's high time he enjoyed life, kicked back, played golf, traveled, whatever."

"But then you'd have to have more responsibility for the company."

"That's what Geraldine Sperry intended."

Shirley made some notes in her book. When she returned her attention to Carolyn, she said, "Why don't you tell me why you've come to The Haven?"

Carolyn closed her eyes. "I've been warned that my high blood pressure puts my pregnancy at a risk."

"You're seeing a doctor, of course."

"Dr. Lewis. He's the very best ob-gyn in the country."

"What does he suggest?"

"I'm going on medication. But he wants me to try some lifestyle changes as well. He suggested I come here." Carolyn rubbed her forehead. "He thinks I work too hard. I've told him that I *live* to work. He said if I want to continue this pregnancy, I'm going to have to change that, at least for the next few months."

Shirley asked, "What do you normally do to relax?"

Carolyn snorted. "I've got too much to do to *relax.*"

To Carolyn's surprise, Shirley came across to sit on the sofa next to her. Softly, she touched Carolyn's arm. "You're under a lot of stress. But you're a healthy young woman, and intelligent enough to understand there are things you can do to help yourself. Perhaps it would help if you think of relaxation as part of your work."

The sheer kindness in Shirley's tone melted the imaginary rod that kept Carolyn's backbone stiff. Longing swept through her—she wanted to slump against the other woman. She wanted Shirley Gold to wrap her arms around her, stroke her hair, and say, "There, there. Everything will be all right."

She wanted her mother.

Tears stung her eyes. She sniffed them back.

Briskly, Shirley continued, "I'm going to work up a program for you. Massage twice a week. A consultation with our nutritionist and our aromatherapist. An hour a week with our counselor—"

"Do you think I'm *crazy*?"

"Of course you're not. But a counselor can help you find ways to deal with stress. Ways to calm yourself, and to believe in yourself. Also . . ." Shirley checked a list, then continued, "I'd like you to join our Friday-night quilting bee."

"But I can't quilt!"

"Perhaps it's time you learned. Quilting is a wonderful activity, after all. It's calming. And the group conversation is usually pretty fascinating. I think quilting bees were probably what women did a hundred years ago instead of seeing psychiatrists. If more women belonged to them today, fewer women would be on antidepressants."

"No quilting," Carolyn said firmly.

"Fine." Shirley picked up her lavender notebook and flipped through it to a calendar. "I'd like to have you start right away. I think you should give yourself a health day. Could you come in Thursday, from noon until five?"

"Are you kidding? Remember, I've got a company to run."

"Perhaps it's time you learned to delegate."

"I know how to delegate! But no one can do my work as well as I can."

"How do you know? Why don't you let someone try?"

"I've told you. My father is—"

"Older, yes, but can't he carry the load for a while? He is your father, after all. He wants you to have a healthy baby."

"Why, yes, I guess he does."

"Tell him about your health concerns. He'll want you to take care of yourself. Remember: it's part of your duty, your job, to take care of yourself, so you can provide the company with its next president."

Carolyn mulled this over for a moment. Her father could probably keep Sperry muddling along.

"All right. I'll talk to him. I'll try to fit my hours into whatever schedule you come up with for me."

"Wonderful. I'm sure The Haven will be good for you."

Thirty miles west of Boston, on the banks of the rushing Rock River, lay the long brick buildings of the Sperry Paper Company. Because sulfuric acid was used in the manufacture of paper, producing an unpleasant, rotten-egg-like smell, the town of Sperry had grown up a few miles east, on the other side of a rocky hill that blocked most of the stench. On the other side of the valley, looking down on Sperry, sprawled the Sperry family home, an enormous Victorian mansion.

Carolyn had lived in the family home all her life, as had her father and his mother and grandmother. Her father lived here still. It was another family tradition that worked, because the house was so large a Wagnerian opera could be performed within its walls and no one would notice. Carolyn's father lived in the south wing; Carolyn and her husband, Hank, in the north. The west wing, with its great ballroom, billiard room, and conservatory, was seldom used. Carolyn and her father met in the east wing if they decided to have dinner together, which was often, since Hank traveled so much. Carolyn and Aubrey each had kitchens in their own quarters, but they also had a wonderful housekeeper, Mrs. B., who had been with them forever.

Today her father's Jag wasn't in the drive, and Hank would be gone overnight. Carolyn entered her house through the side door, chatted with the housekeeper for a few moments to be sure everything was under control, then went down the long hall and into the living room. Stretching out on a sofa, she was ready to click on the evening news when she heard a car come up the drive. Two car doors slammed.

Two doors?

She heard the housekeeper's greetings. Someone shrieked. Someone laughed.

"Coming right up, Mr. Sperry!" the housekeeper said.

Carolyn's living-room door opened, and her father walked in. He looked unusually handsome, his silver hair brushed and gleaming, his eyes bright.

Next to him stood a plump young woman with wispy brown hair.

No, she wasn't just standing next to him. She was *holding Aubrey Sperry's hand.*

Carolyn put her feet on the floor and sat up straight. Oh, no! Was her father ill? The other woman had a nursey look about her.

"Carolyn, darling," her father said. "I want you to meet Heather. My wife."

"Your—" Her brain would not compute. *"Wife?"*

"My wife. As of the last twenty-four hours."

"And sixteen minutes," Heather added in a soft, high, little-girl voice, gazing enraptured up at her husband. She looked more like his grandchild than his wife.

"But how—When—"

Mrs. B. appeared in the doorway with a silver tray, three flutes, and a bottle of champagne.

"Thank you, Mrs. B.!" Aubrey Sperry took the tray from the housekeeper, who slipped discreetly from the room. He set it on the coffee table and, with much eyebrow waggling at his bride, manipulated the cork from the bottle. He poured three times, handed a glass to his wife, and one to Carolyn.

"I can't drink, Father," she reminded him. "I'm pregnant."

"Oh, a little sip won't hurt you. You've got to toast the newlyweds!"

Stunned, Carolyn accepted the glass.

Aubrey sat on the sofa, pulling his new wife next to him. "I'm sure you're wondering how we met."

"Um, yes."

He patted Heather's thigh, looking dotingly at her as he spoke. "I stopped in at a bank in Arlington three months ago to cash a check. Heather was the teller. Our eyes met. When she handed me my money, our fingertips touched. The next day I took her out to dinner, and we've been seeing each other ever since."

"I had no idea."

"I'm well aware of that, darling, and it's not your fault." Aubrey's voice took on a patronizing tone. "You were so preoccupied with your morning sickness, and I know how important this baby is to you and Hank. I thought it best not to intrude."

Preoccupied? Carolyn thought wildly. It was more as if morning sickness had tackled and thrown her to the ground. And wasn't this baby important to her father?

"And quite frankly, we enjoyed our little secret," Aubrey was saying, looking terribly pleased with himself. "We were able to spend time together, far from the madding crowd." He wrapped his arm around Heather, cuddling her.

Carolyn felt the room tip. When had her father become *cuddly*? He'd never cuddled *her,* not even when she was a little girl.

"We knew we were in love from the moment we met," her father rhapsodized, "and since I'm not a young man—"

"Oh, Aubrey." Heather giggled. "You act like a young man."

"That's because you inspire me." Aubrey nuzzled his bride's ear.

"So you got married," Carolyn prompted.

"Yes. We couldn't wait. I want to live with Heather. We decided to get married without any fanfare, so we organized things and were married yesterday by Judge Lawrence," Aubrey concluded triumphantly.

"Wow," Carolyn said weakly. "Amazing."

With a gentle roll of her shoulder, Heather loosened herself from Aubrey's embrace and leaned forward, her hands on her knees, which, Carolyn noticed, were plump and led straight down like tree trunks to thick ankles. "This must be such a shock for you," Heather said. "I know you must have a million questions. It's really important to me that you understand how much I love your father. I'm going to do everything I can to make him happy."

"What would make me happy right now would be to take you out to dinner," Aubrey told his wife. Rising, he said to Carolyn, "Let's coordinate our schedules and find a time you and Hank and Heather and I can have dinner together, here at the house, so we can have a nice long family evening."

"All right, Father," Carolyn agreed. She stood, too, grateful to find the floor steady beneath her feet. Her father looked at her expectantly. Usually she could interpret his slightest facial twitch, but this look was new. *Oh,* she thought, and leaning forward, gave her father's new wife a kiss on the cheek. "Welcome to the family."

"Thank you, Carolyn. I hope we'll be great friends," Heather replied.

Turning, Carolyn kissed her father's cheek, noticing how he smelled, for the first time ever, of some really terrible men's cologne. "Congratulations, Father."

He smiled, pleased. "Thank you, dear."

Dear, Carolyn thought. When had he ever called her *dear*? Obviously Heather was having a softening effect on her father. Was that a good thing? Carolyn looked at her watch, wondering if it was too late to phone her lawyer.

4

"Okay, lean mean beauty queen," Julia chanted, "let's get this show on the road."

Belinda stood quietly by the kitchen table. She was small for her age, and Julia, who was tall and made even taller by her fabulous black boots, had to squat down to be on eye level with the girl. Julia was aware of what a striking contrast they were: Julia, thirty, her short black hair sliced and shaped against her skull like a cap of raven feathers, her black eyes intense as jet, her long, lean body clad in tight black jeans and a sleeveless black tee. And Belinda, seven, a slight elfin princess with long honey-brown curls, large blue eyes, and a penchant for fuss and ruffles that would have thrilled Queen Victoria. A stranger, seeing them, would wonder what they had in common. The answer: Tim Hathaway, Belinda's father, Julia's husband.

"Teeth brushed?" Julia asked.

Obediently, Belinda curled her lips back, exposing tiny, gleaming white teeth.

"Hey, those are some sweet mini-marsh-mallows!" Julia joked. "Backpack? Okey-dokey, smiley-smokey, let's put your lunch pail in." She opened the pink plastic Barbie box and pointed to each item in turn. "Peanut butter and banana sandwich. Check. Carrot strips. Check. Apple juice and straw. Check. Two Oreos. Check." She slid the lunch box into the backpack, then, with great care, slipped Kitty Ballerina into the backpack, zipping it just to the stuffed animal's neck, so she could see out. "You okay, Kitty Ballerina?"

Julia answered in a high, squeaky Kitty Ballerina voice, "Okay!"

Belinda grinned. A major victory for Julia.

"Bye-bye, sugar pie," Julia said to Kitty Ballerina. "Here's your morning kiss." She smacked Kitty Ballerina on the cheek.

"Thank you, Julia!" Julia squeaked in Kitty Ballerina's voice. "Love you!"

"I love you, too, Kitty Ballerina," Julia said as she helped Belinda into her pink fleece jacket. Taking Belinda's hand, she led her out to their friends' big red SUV. She lifted

Belinda up to the seat and carefully buckled her in. "Buckled in, henny-pin. Here's your morning kiss." She smacked Belinda on her soft pink cheek. "Love you, Belinda. Thanks, Paula. You're good to go! I'm picking you both up this afternoon, Belinda and Sarah. I'll be waiting!" Sliding the door shut, she patted the SUV and headed back to the house.

Inside, the morning spilled before her like sunshine through the windows. Downstairs, the Burrill wedding video lay on her desk, where it had to be edited, cut, matched with music, and spliced together into one seamless perfect hour that would capture for the newlyweds and their loved ones the magic of their day. Before Julia could turn to that, though, she had to put the house in order. So much had changed in the little girl's life, *too* much, and if, by setting the chairs at familiar angles and arranging Miss Mouse perfectly on Belinda's bed, Julia could make the world seem less frightening and more stable, well, she could do that, and gladly.

But as she cleaned the kitchen and tidied the house, Julia was accompanied, as she often was, by a shadow, a gray, gloomy specter of her parents' disappointment at the way she was spending her time. Her parents, both liberal lawyers, had hoped she'd do something meaningful with her time and intelligence. She was fortunate, her parents had reminded her daily; she could—she *should*—make the world a better place.

In college, Julia had majored in political science, even though she hated it, and taken every photography course offered, because that was what she loved. She'd wanted, someday, to compile a book of photographs of the impoverished and marginalized that would bring tears of pity to the jaded wealthy, causing them to spill open their bank accounts and address the wrongs of the world. After college, she'd worked at odd jobs—Starbucks, Tower Records, Filene's—and, on her time off, roamed the darker streets of Boston, taking photographs.

Then her best friend had asked her to be the official photographer for her wedding. Julia took the formal, posed shots that would be secured in silver frames, and she also videotaped the wedding and reception, edited it imaginatively, and created such a gorgeous, effervescent record of the event that people watching laughed and cried and shouted with joy. Julia loved this kind of work, and almost at once she found herself in demand as a videographer. Her days were packed with birthday parties, retirement parties, weddings, anniversaries.

Nice, her parents thought, but hardly *significant* work.

She'd met Tim Hathaway at a party. Tim was a dentist, the nonsuicidal kind, he joked, an orthodontist, actually. As a boy, he'd had terrible buck teeth, and the skill of an orthodontist had changed his life. He enjoyed his work, how the precision of infinitely small procedures could work miracles of enormous personal magnitude. He was thirty-five, widowed, with a five-year-old daughter, Belinda.

Tim's wife Annette had died tragically young, of a swiftly moving cancer. Tim, burdened with sorrow and anxiety, was also, secretly, fraught with guilt, for only a few days before Annette was diagnosed with the cancer, he had asked her for a divorce, and she had heartbrokenly agreed. They had gotten married because it had seemed the right thing to do at the time. All their peers were getting married. Tim had finished the grueling years of school and was setting up his own orthodontic practice, and being married seemed the next logical step. Annette had finished college and tried a number of jobs, none of which had really caught her fancy. They'd been pleased when Annette was pregnant, adoring of their infant daughter. Annette lovingly performed the outward duties of homemaker. Tim came home every night to meals scrupulously made from the newest cookbook. His clothes were always clean and ironed, the house decorated to its furthest inch. But when Belinda was tucked away in bed at night and the dishes were done, Annette and Tim sat in the living room watching television with the warmth of strangers at an airport, and when they went to bed, they were both always too tired to do more than fall asleep.

Annette's illness brought them close again. They stopped speaking of divorce and spent their energies trying to make joyful memories for Belinda. They explained to Belinda that Mommy was ill, that she might have to go away for a while, that this would be hard for Belinda, but that she should know her mother would always love her, would always be there, somewhere, in the universe, like the wind or the sunshine, loving her. They did the best they could.

The day after Annette died, Belinda, who was five, stopped speaking.

For the first few months, Tim was patient. The loss was so devastating, so unfair, he seldom felt like speaking himself. Why shouldn't a child react to such injustice, such a loss, with some kind of powerful, life-altering emotion? She would speak again, he was sure, because Belinda had been a normal and, for the first few years of her life, even a slightly advanced child. Because Annette and Tim read to her so much from the moment she was born, Belinda had developed a large vocabulary. She'd loved preschool and kindergarten and had plenty of friends, including a best friend named Sarah, with whom, during the last weeks of Annette's illness, Belinda had continued to play. So the sudden muteness was obviously psychologically based. In a way, it had a rightness to it. Belinda would speak again in her own good time.

But after three months, gradually, Tim began taking Belinda to a round of child psychologists. Nothing worked, not puppets or playacting or music. The experts assured him this was not unusual, a kind of selective mutism that would eventually resolve itself. They advised him to simply give her time. After all, Belinda was continuing to attend school, where, her teacher said, she seemed alert and engaged. She could hear well and took orders with alacrity. Her penmanship was clear and firm. She did all assignments involving pen and paper. She was learning to add and subtract, and at recess she continued to join the little clique of girls she'd always been with. The other children had, during the first weeks of first grade, taunted Belinda, but receiving no reaction, quickly accepted her eccentricity and, somehow, in the way of children, included her in their games.

Tim dated Julia for months before introducing her, gradually, to Belinda, and Julia, who by nature was impulsive, gave the child the space and time to get used to her. Before long, Belinda gladly snuggled up in Julia's lap when Julia offered to read her a book. After a few months, Tim sat down with Belinda to tell her he wanted to marry Julia and have her live with them all the time. Belinda hadn't raged or cried; she'd simply nodded. At the intimate wedding at a friend's home, Belinda had been Julia's flower girl, admiring her mirrored reflection in her flouncy pink dress and flowered circlet, and smiling during the wedding.

When Tim proposed to Julia, he asked whether she might be willing to live in the house where he had lived with his first wife. He wanted to provide his daughter with as much stability as possible. Julia was so crazy in love with the man she would have lived in a root cellar if he'd asked her. She told him of course.

They married, and Julia moved into Tim's sweet little saltbox with its picket fence and wild-cherry tree. Julia, who had decorated her own apartment in cool teak, natural hemp, and ivory linen, became chatelaine of the home daintily, and in Julia's view, gaggingly, decorated by Annette, Tim's first wife. The wall-to-wall carpets Julia vacuumed were deeply plush rose-silver. The dishes she washed were white, adorned with roses, and the kitchen wallpaper had roses twining up a green trellis. Belinda's room was a symphony of lavender. Julia turned the pink-and-gold, blossom-bedecked master bedroom into a guest bedroom for Annette's parents, who lived in western Massachusetts and often visited. She redecorated the former guest bedroom for herself and Tim, stripping away the chiffon, scarf-valanced, rose curtains, brocade spread, and floral sheets. She painted the walls a warm cream and hung thirty of her favorite framed photographs. She chose a bed with a plain teak headboard, and a dresser of matching wood. Now, when she needed to catch her breath or escape from the smothering flowers, she had a place to come.

Tim cleared a space in the basement for Julia's workshop, and she did work there, but not as often as she'd intended. Running a home and taking care of Belinda took a lot of time, and she wanted to do it right. She wanted very much to help Belinda feel safe with her. She knew it was crucial to provide a nurturing, familiar environment for the child.

On the other hand, Julia mused now, as she folded Belinda's clean clothing into the drawers exactly as Belinda liked it, sometimes Julia felt she was ruled by a mute, midget tyrant who could have given Gandhi a few lessons in passive resistance.

If Belinda didn't like something, she stuck out her lower lip, dropped her eyes to the floor, and looked pathetic. She refused to leave the house unless her clothing was put on in an inexplicable order. She wouldn't eat unless the food was presented to her in a specific sequence, and vegetables she wouldn't eat at all. When Tim suggested she stop watching television and get ready for bed because she had school the next day, tears threatened, with the result that most nights Belinda fell asleep in front of the TV.

Recently, it seemed to Julia that Belinda's compulsions were increasing. This week at the grocery store, when Julia refused to let Belinda take a pack of Oreo cookies off the shelf and eat them right then and there, Belinda had burst into tears and refused to walk with Julia, slumping down in a dead weight. Julia had had to leave her loaded cart, carry Belinda to the car, drive back to the house, and return to shop at night when Tim was home. Yesterday, at the mall, Belinda had imperiously pointed at an expensive Madame Alexander doll. "Sorry, sweetie, not today," Julia had said. Belinda sagged, weeping like an abandoned angel. Again, Julia had had to curtail her shopping.

She'd been so embarrassed, carrying a seven-year-old, sobbing girl through the mall. People cast curious and sometimes critical eyes her way. Julia was terrified that Belinda would throw a similar fit in front of Agnes, Belinda's maternal grandmother, Annette's mother, who disliked Julia and watched eagerly for signs that Julia was making Belinda unhappy. One of the difficulties was that Agnes's path to complete happiness was paved with sugar—*lots* of sugar, the same nutritional monster prohibited by all the savvy moms of Belinda's peers. Whenever Agnes came for a visit, she brought a jar of Marshmallow Fluff. No matter the time of day, she'd bustle into the kitchen to make Belinda and herself peanut-butter-Fluff sandwiches. "Mm-*mm*!" she'd gloat. "Isn't this delicious!" Belinda would happily nod, slurping away at the gooey mess, while Julia kept herself busy preparing tea or coffee, valiantly keeping her mouth shut. If Marshmallow Fluff were the Elmer's glue of Agnes's bond with Belinda, Julia would not interfere, especially since Tim, a dentist, and wildly cavity-conscious, didn't try to intervene.

Fortunately, Agnes and her retired, rather

passive husband, George, lived three hours away in the western part of the state. Unfortunately, Agnes and George visited often, seldom notifying Julia in advance, but swooping down like a pair of turkey vultures hoping to spot a carcass. *Julia's* carcass.

Agnes wanted Belinda to live with them; *they* knew how to raise children. Julia, they pointed out loudly and often, had no experience. Clearly Agnes thought Julia was a snaggletoothed evil stepmother from her worst fairy tale, a judgment that could only get worse if Belinda went into one of her pathetic crying spells.

But Belinda cried when she had to go visit her grandparents. Agnes insisted Belinda spend two weeks of every summer and two or three days of every major holiday with her grandparents. During the ride to the western part of the state, Belinda reverted to infantile behavior, sucking her thumb and rubbing her cheek on Kitty Ballerina's. She had to be lifted out of the car and carried up to her grandparents' house, and when Tim and Julia arrived to bring her home, she was waiting, nose pressed against the window. Couldn't Agnes *see* all that? Julia tried to respond to Agnes's dislike with tolerance and kindness—she did feel great sympathy for this woman who had lost her beloved daughter. But it was difficult, especially since Julia's best efforts never pleased Agnes. Tim's own mother had died a few years ago, and his father had retired to Florida, so Agnes and George were really the only grandparents Belinda knew, and Julia longed for a smoother, more cooperative relationship. Julia had asked Tim whether they should see a family counselor. Tim reminded her that none of the therapists he'd seen before had helped Belinda come out of her spell of muteness. Patience, they'd all advised. Patience, and the healing powers of time.

Now, as Julia finished making Belinda's bed, pulling the Barbie doll sheets tight and tucking them, each in her exact place, she tried to cheer herself by humming a jaunty little tune.

But humming made Julia's throat burn. And her ears ached. This had been happening more and more recently, so often that she was just, slightly, worried. She went into the bathroom and took one of the sinus-relief tablets she'd bought last week. She had no fever. She felt well and full of energy.

If this was some idiotic psychosomatic trick her body was playing on her, she would—what? Well, she'd be glad; because if it wasn't, then something serious was going haywire in her head.

5

It was like being hit by a tornado. It knocked the breath out of her, turned her life upside down. She was like Dorothy from *The Wizard of Oz,* but in reverse: her life, which until today had been brilliant with color, all at once faded to black and white.

Faye put down the phone and sat quite still, just looking around her condo, trying to make sense of her life. She thought she'd done so well!

Two years ago, she'd been happy, living with her husband in the spacious home where they'd raised their daughter, Laura, to adulthood, where, in Faye's third-floor studio, she'd painted still lifes that sold often and well. Then Jack was felled by an unexpected heart attack. Suddenly alone in the large house, Faye found herself so stunned by grief she could no longer paint. She struggled valiantly to live with loss, and then menopause hit her, hard. And *then* Laura had come to her, sobbing, because she thought *her* husband was having an affair.

Thank heaven, in the midst of it all, she'd met Marilyn, Shirley, and Alice, women her age, who shared similar problems. They'd formed the Hot Flash Club, and Faye's life had turned around.

With their encouragement and advice, Faye had sold her home. She'd given half the selling price to Laura and her husband so they could buy a home, and she moved into a condo in the distinguished, old brick building housing Shirley's new spa. It was a temporary home, a kind of emotional half-way house, until she decided exactly where and how she'd like to live the rest of her life. She'd started taking classes in art therapy, and she taught classes in art at the spa. She'd gotten her life back on track. She'd prided herself on becoming, at fifty-six, a capable woman who could accept what life dished out with humor, intelligence, and hope.

She'd been a *fool.*

Now, in a kind of blind panic, Faye rose, grabbed her purse, left her condo, and hurried along the back halls of the spa and out to her car in the back parking lot. Forbidding herself to cry, she settled into her BMW and drove along the country road to the Mass. Pike east to Boston. She sped along, holding back hysteria by munching all the candy she carried in her purse, until she entered the city limits. Then she doubled back west, her heart and soul so empty, she stopped at a gas station to fill up her tank and buy more chocolate.

Caught in the stream of traffic, she turned on the radio, hoping music would soothe her, hearing instead the hourly news, which reminded her that today was Friday, when the Hot Flash Club always met at Legal Seafoods for dinner.

A few cars ahead, a battered truck's tailgate snapped, scattering the highway with household rubbish: bent aluminum lawn chairs, small electric appliances, garbage bags, an old crib. The evening rush of Boston traffic from the city toward the suburbs braked to a sludgelike crawl.

Faye didn't mind slowing down. She was

in no hurry to get to her destination. She was even glad to have a reason to be late. From her purse, she took another giant Snickers bar, tore off the wrapper, and bit off a hearty chunk, savoring the sweet chocolate. How sanguine she'd been just a year ago! Those first few months when she'd met Alice, Marilyn, and Shirley, when they'd formed the Hot Flash Club and giddily resolved to solve each other's problems, those days had been almost like the first sweet weeks of a love affair, wild with possibility.

But it *hadn't* been an illusion, Faye reminded herself, biting off another hunk of candy. The Hot Flash Club *had* changed her life, and *she* had helped change *their* lives. She'd changed herself, too, or she thought she had. Right now her self-esteem was so low, she couldn't *imagine* how she'd taken on the role of suburban secret agent she'd so blithely—and, she had to admit, successfully—adopted then.

Faye smiled, remembering what fun she'd had, how much the danger and intrigue had made her pulse race. She'd actually succeeded at her assignment—no, more than succeeded. Not only had she found out whether Lila Eastbrook was marrying Marilyn's son for his money, Faye had also discovered the secret at the Eastbrook family's heart.

Family heart. Her mood collapsed. Of the four members of the Hot Flash Club, Faye knew she was the most maternal—or she could just turn that thought around as the other three would and admit she was the most dependent on her maternal role!

Shirley, who'd been married and divorced three times, didn't have any children, and her life's dream of establishing a wellness spa had come true. She lived her dream every day.

Supercompetent Alice had managed to raise two sons as a single mother while holding down a high-powered executive position in a national insurance company. One of her grown sons was happily married, living in Texas. When Alan, her other son, showed up divorced and depressed, Alice had supported him in every way, but she hadn't been obsessive with worry the way Faye would have been. And now Alice was *opposing* Alan's happiness, all because of her stubborn ideas. Alice, whose son lived

just as close to Alice as Faye's daughter did
to Faye, seldom saw her son and had yet to
set foot in the cottage where he lived with
the woman Alice shunned. Faye could never
be like that. She'd welcome anyone her
daughter loved.

Marilyn was different, too, so engrossed
with her teaching and lab work at MIT that
everything else, including her lover, Faraday, and her own granddaughter, came second. Imagine, Faye thought, as she finished
off the chocolate bar, wanting to spend
more time with prehistoric bugs than with a
living baby!

But to be fair, Alice and Marilyn had *sons,*
not daughters. What was that saying: "A
son is a son until he takes a wife, but a
daughter's a daughter all of her life"? Who-
ever said that would understand her reaction to the news she'd received earlier today.

Her Hot Flash Club friends would probably just tell her to buck up and deal with it.
She couldn't share this news yet. Fortified
by chocolate, she'd pretend all was well
with her life. She could do it. She had to.
One good thing, they always ate chocolate

desserts at their meetings; that would sustain her.

———————

Faye arrived at the restaurant to find the other three already seated.

"Hi, honey!" Shirley rose to kiss Faye. "You're late. We were worried!"

In spite of her executive-chic, forest green suit, Shirley was still a romantic. Life had given her a lot of hard knocks, but it had also given her the good friends who had helped her start The Haven. She'd never been so happy in her life.

Now, Faye thought wryly, all Shirley wanted was for everyone else in the whole wide world to be as happy as she was.

"Sorry. I had to get gas."

Faye kept her face hidden as she took off her jacket. The others had already arranged their belongings around them and were nestled in for a good long talk. The waiter arrived, handed them their menus, took their drink orders, and went off.

"There, that's done!" Shirley beamed at her friends. "How is everyone?"

Alice, a regal African-American woman in

loose silk trousers and a gorgeous tunic top embroidered thickly in brilliant crimsons and greens, narrowed her eyes as she stared across the table, scrutinizing Marilyn. Alice's executive past made it impossible for her to mince words or waste time when she spotted a problem. "I'm fine, but may I just say that I think Marilyn's slipping."

At fifty-three, Marilyn was ten years younger than Alice, but Alice's commanding presence often made Marilyn feel much younger. About thirteen. A gawky thirteen. A zit-riddled, limp-haired thirteen with bad posture. Looking confused, Marilyn rested her arms on the table and straightened her back. But because she knew Alice meant well, she defended herself. "I don't think so. I feel comfortable."

Alice shook her head impatiently. "No, no, I don't mean you're sliding out of your seat. I mean you're letting yourself go."

Marilyn blinked. "No, I'm not! Hey, I'm wearing the clothes *you all* chose for me back when you worked at TransWorld, Alice!"

"Exactly," Alice pounced. "And that was over a year ago."

"Marilyn." Shirley leaned forward with a

conciliating smile, resting her hand on Marilyn's. "Alice means that your hair needs a touch-up and reshaping. Remember," she added, "what *I* looked like before I met you all?" Actually, Shirley kind of missed her old hippie/gypsy/country-western-singer look, but she couldn't deny that the new, improved executive Shirley, with her chin-length auburn bob and tailored suits, gave her the image she needed to impress her board of directors and staff.

Faye waited while the waiter brought their drinks and took their orders. Then, gently, she told Marilyn, "Your blouse and jacket *are* looking a bit old."

Marilyn glanced down. It was true her clothes were spotted from chemicals she used during the classes she taught at MIT, and true, too, that she needed to see the hairdresser. "Maybe I've been a little preoccupied lately," she explained vaguely, fishing the tip of her silk scarf out of her margarita. Fifty-three years old, a brilliant scientist, and she still couldn't get the knack of wearing scarves.

"What's going on, honey?" Shirley asked.

"Troubles with Faraday?" Alice suggested.

"Oh, Faraday's fine," Marilyn replied with a dismissive wave of her hand.

"I like Faraday!" Alice stoutly declared. "He's handsome, literate, charming."

"Beautiful manners," Faye added.

"And I, a 'mature' woman, should consider myself lucky to have a beau," Marilyn said, "even though he can't keep an erection longer than thirty seconds."

"Sex isn't everything," Alice reminded her. Alice's beau, Gideon, was recovering from an operation on his prostate.

"No one knows that better than I do!" Marilyn shot back. "I've only had sex with three men in my life, and it wasn't delicious with my husband and it's not delicious with Faraday." She sighed. "I just wish I could get him to talk about it. I'd love to have him see a doctor. Or try Viagra."

Faye interjected, "I read a statistic just last week, saying the American public spends more money on Viagra than it does on Alzheimer research."

"You know what that means," Alice told her. "In a few more years, all the men will have erections, but they won't remember what they're for!"

Laughing, Shirley leaned forward, lowering her voice. "That reminds me of a joke. Ancient Chinese proverb: If man with erection enter airplane door sideways, he going to Bangkok."

Faye grinned. "Mrs. Clinton went to China with her husband, and at the state dinner she was seated next to the president of China. She turned to him and asked, 'Do you have elections here?' He smiled and replied, 'Yes, every morning.' "

"Girl," Alice said, "that joke is so old!"

The waiter brought their entrées.

"Bon appétit!" Faye said to the others, and they all picked up their forks.

After a few moments of pleasurable devotion to their food, Alice announced, "Hey, we set a new record. We got to the subject of sex before our dinners arrived!"

"Well, it *is* the most fascinating subject in the world," Shirley said.

"Really?" Faye asked. "I disagree."

"Then you're depressed," Shirley announced.

"Oh, come on!" Faye laughed.

"I'm serious. I don't care how old you are, if you lose your sexual desire, you're lacking something. It's like missing a vitamin in your diet."

Alice snorted. "Don't exaggerate, Shirley! Surely sexual desire is a personal thing. Some people just enjoy it more than others."

Marilyn weighed in with her scientific point of view. "All sorts of variables must apply. One's age, for example. Nature wired us to crave sex the most during our reproductive years, so the species will propagate. So as we grow older and lose our reproductive capacity, our hormone levels flag—"

"Not to mention certain male reproductive parts," Alice added wryly.

Shirley shot back, "Nature *also* arranged things so that when we have sex, endorphins are released in our bodies, making us feel better, happier, and calmer. This, in turn, has a beneficial effect on our bodies."

"Other things release endorphins, too," Faye argued. "Nothing could make me happier than holding my granddaughter! Work can make me feel pretty euphoric, too. Not to mention chocolate!"

"But chocolate makes you gain weight," Shirley pointed out, "and sex doesn't."

Faye's face fell. "I know I've gained weight—" She smoothed her hands down over the layers of pastel silk that sheltered her rounded, buxom body.

"Hey!" Alice interrupted, leaning forward to address Shirley. "Back off! We've been over this ground before. Not everyone has an irritating little buzz-saw mosquito metabolism like you, Shirley! Since I retired from TransWorld, I've gone from a size eighteen to a size twenty-two and then some, although I'm walking and exercising more regularly than I ever did before. Never mind the competitive bridge games Gideon and I play twice a week, which are mental workouts that must burn up about a zillion calories! Faye's doing everything she can, but once you get past sixty, your body does pretty much what it wants to do."

"Well, you're over sixty," Shirley responded calmly, "but Faye isn't."

Faye lifted her chin in defiance. "*I* think everything changes when we hit menopause. After all, that's what brought all of us together. That's why we're the Hot Flash Club. And the changes just keep coming. I mean, my weight's sticking on in ways it never used to. Gosh, now I've got such a big bum you could sit on it!"

Marilyn looked mystified. "But, Faye, we

all sit on our bums. That's what they're there for!"

"No," Faye explained, "I mean *you* could sit on *my* bum." Reaching around, she patted her right hip. "It's like I've got a shelf or a ledge sticking out in back."

Shirley and Marilyn laughed, but Alice said, "I'm with you, girlfriend. I feel like I've got beanbags glued to my rear."

"You two are *so* exaggerating!" Marilyn told them. "I'd rather have your bums any day. My wrinkled bum hangs down in back like a stage curtain when the play's over."

"Yeah." Shirley nodded. "I know what you mean. That flat-bum thing isn't very sexy." She sighed. "I used to have the nicest, *pert,* little rounded bottom. Even *I* thought it was cute. But since I hit menopause, my buttocks sag like a bunch of wet laundry."

Faye laughed, relieved that even skinny Shirley had image issues. "Well, no matter what our body types are, we're all having to deal with changes. But, Shirley, I don't want to think of myself as *fat,* or dislike my body. It's nice, being comfortable, and rounded. It makes me remember my grandmother, and how good I felt being around her, how secure and loved. I hope my granddaughter feels that way with me."

Thoughtfully, Marilyn aligned her silverware. "I have a grandchild, too, and I love her with all my heart. I also find great satisfaction in my work. And I eat lots of chocolate." Blushing, she admitted, "But I still spend a lot of time thinking about sex these days. I don't try to, I just can't help it."

"That's not surprising," Shirley said. "You like to talk about variables. Well, look how your situation and Faye's vary. She was happily married for thirty-plus years. She had great sex with her husband. You were married for the same amount of time, but to an arrogant little prick who never made you feel good in bed. I'd say your body has some catching up to do."

Alice chuckled. "You make it sound like all people are allotted an equal amount of sexual pleasure at birth. But I know what you mean, and I agree. Age has something to do with it, and experience—"

"And stage of relationship," Faye cut in. "After thirty-five years of marriage, I still adored Jack. We loved being with each other, just noodling around, reading or talking. What we lost in panting, groaning, hormone-driven sexual passion, we gained in tenderness and affection."

"You were lucky," Alice said. "I really like Gideon. I really *care* for him. He's a good man, a good friend, trustworthy, loyal—we're very affectionate with one another. I can imagine living the rest of my life with him, although let me say right here, we haven't yet seriously discussed even living in the same house, and we may never get to that point. We both like our independence. Still, I must confess I often feel just a little disappointed that because of his prostate operation, passionate sex won't be part of our relationship."

"Well, I'm more than a little disappointed," Marilyn admitted. "I *really* miss the sexual component. I suppose it would be different if I hadn't had that little fling with Barton Baker—"

"That asshole," Alice spat, and for a moment the four were silent, remembering the executive secretary at TransWorld who had seduced Marilyn and betrayed both Marilyn and Alice.

"Asshole, sure," Marilyn continued, "but he was an angel in bed!"

"Here's my question," Faye asked softly.

"Why do we care so much that our men have erections? As proof that we're sexy? Or for the sex itself?"

"Excellent point, Faye!" Alice pointed her fork at her friend. "When Gideon and I were first dating, I really needed confirmation that I was attractive. I mean, since I was last with a man before Gideon, my body had changed so much, my new bra size was forty-two long." She waited for the others' laughter to die down. "When I learned Gideon had prostate cancer, I felt sorry for him, but also, I hate to admit it, secretly relieved, because I knew his failure to stand at attention wasn't because the sight of me didn't turn him on. But now he's okay, the scare's over, and we've got the rest of our lives to think about. He *tells* me he thinks I'm sexy, but I'm a little disappointed he can't *show* me. But he's so wonderful in all other ways. We have so much fun together." She nodded, agreeing with her own thoughts. "I'm lucky he's in my life. I love him," she added simply.

"Have you told him yet?" Marilyn asked.

"Does he love you?" Shirley asked.

"Oh, yes." Alice's smile signaled private pleasures.

"I'm so glad," Faye said, patting Alice's hand. "Love is the *best.*"

"Love and good sex ain't so terrible," Shirley added, grinning smugly.

Instantly, Faye, Alice, and Marilyn went from melting smiles to matronly suspicion. Justin Quayle, Shirley's beau, was twelve years younger than she, handsome, charming, and glib. He was also, in spite of his education, unemployed, and deeply in debt after investing the little money he had had in a real estate deal that fell through, leaving him behind in child support payments for three children living with two ex-wives. He'd moved into one of the condos in the expansive The Haven complex, where he paid no rent, which didn't bother the other three much, but also, no utilities, which did. Yet they'd discovered that the usually compliant Shirley was intractable on the subject of her lover. Shirley paid for Justin's expenses and stonewalled the others when they tried to discuss him. After several intense arguments, they'd reached an agreement with Shirley. They wouldn't complain about Justin if she'd promise not to marry him without telling them first.

But that didn't mean they had to listen to Shirley sing the man's praises.

"Let's get back to Marilyn," Alice suggested. "Whatever the reason for it, I think Marilyn needs another shopping spree. I mean, when was the last time you bought any new clothes for yourself?"

Marilyn thought about it. "This summer! I had to buy jeans and shirts and shoes for my hiking trip with Faraday!"

Alice and Shirley snickered, and even gentle Faye's mouth trembled with a smile.

"What?" Marilyn demanded.

"Honey." Faye put a reassuring hand on Marilyn's. "Hiking clothes don't count. We mean dress clothes. Like you wore at Trans-World."

Marilyn thought. "I bought some new underwear," she confessed, blushing. "At Victoria's Secret."

"All right, Marilyn!" Shirley laughed. "High five!"

Marilyn looked bewildered. Because of the other three, Marilyn no longer thought exclusively about the primordial Paleozoic ages during which her beloved trilobites had lived, but she still wasn't au courant with the contemporary world around her.

"Look, you all, it's not my love life that troubles me. I'm worried about Teddy and Lila. Lila's mother is a terrible strain on their marriage."

"I'm not surprised," Faye said. "When I worked for Eugenie Eastbrook, I was a nervous wreck. She's such a perfectionist, she'd give Martha Stewart hives."

Alice frowned. "I thought Lila had liberated herself from her mother. After all, Eugenie wanted a Hollywood wedding with a cast of thousands. But Lila had the guts to marry Teddy in their sweet private ceremony instead."

"Yes," Marilyn agreed, "but Eugenie has turned that to her own use. After all, Eugenie believes it was *her* day they ruined. She's angry and petulant and she expects them to make amends every single day of their lives."

"But Lila had a baby!" Faye protested. "Didn't that cheer Eugenie up?"

"For a while, yes. Eugenie got to give a mammoth baby shower, complete with a swan made from about a zillion gardenias. She's delighted that the child's a girl. I swear every day she shows up with a new Prada outfit for the six-month-old. I think what she really wants to do is to move in with Lila and Teddy and run their lives. She's agitating to have them enroll this *infant* in the most elite preschool in the area. She's always at their house, or phoning them."

"That's not good," Faye agreed. A terrible thought struck her: had her son-in-law thought *she* intruded too often?

Marilyn gave a rueful laugh. "I know. Teddy's starting to stop by my place for a drink after work, just to escape what he calls MILDEW—Mother-in-Law's Deadly Exhaust Waste."

Alice exploded with laughter. "MILDEW! That's great!"

"That's terrible," Faye protested, but pretended to laugh with the others.

"But so appropriate," Alice argued. "My mother-in-law drove me nuts. She came over every day when I'd just had my first baby. If he cried, she told me I didn't have enough milk. Or that my milk was off. She made me absolutely miserable."

"MILDEW," Shirley cackled. "Mother-in-Law Delivers Every Woe."

"MILDEW." Alice grinned wickedly. "Mother-in-Law Deserves Every Wart."

"MILDEW." Marilyn gasped with laughter. "Mother-in-Law Doesn't Ever Wash."

Faye waved her hands to get their attention. "Come on, you guys. Not all mothers-in-law are bad. Three of us *are* MILDEWs. And my husband Jack's mother was heavenly; she was one of my very best friends! And I hope Lars likes *me.*"

"MILDEW!" Alice couldn't control herself. "Mothers-in-Law Demand Eternal Worship."

Shirley chuckled. "MILDEW: Mothers-in-Law Don't Ever Wait! Your turn, Marilyn."

"Um, MILDEW: Mothers-in-Law Do Everything Wrong!"

"That's *so unfair*!" Faye lost control. She burst into spectacular tears.

The other three stared at her, astonished.

Marilyn put her hand on Faye's arm. "Faye? What's wrong?"

"They're *moving,*" Faye wailed, scrambling around in her purse for a handkerchief.

"Here." Alice handed her a clean tissue. "Who's moving?"

"Laura and Lars and—" Faye felt her chin wobble helplessly. "And Megan!"

"Where?" Shirley asked.

"Why?" Marilyn asked.

"Take a drink of water," Alice advised Faye.

"Deep breath," Shirley said.

Faye obeyed. After a few moments, she was calm enough to talk. "Lars had an offer from a law firm in San Francisco."

"San Francisco," Shirley echoed. This was bad.

Tears streamed down Faye's cheeks. "His best friend from college owns the firm. He flew Lars out, then flew the whole family out so Laura could see how she'd like living there. Who wouldn't like living in San Francisco?"

"Three thousand one hundred and forty miles away," Marilyn said soberly.

Shirley rolled her eyes. "How can you be so precise?"

Marilyn shrugged. "I have a memory for numbers."

Faye sobbed harder.

"Oh, come on," Alice said, using her bossy voice. "There are such things as airplanes."

Faye shook her head. "I want to be able to see my granddaughter every *day*! At least once a week! I've been babysitting her! Now she'll forget me!"

"She won't forget you," Marilyn promised.

"Of course she won't!" Alice agreed. "Look, use your computer—"

"I don't know how to use a computer!" Faye sobbed.

"Well, learn," Alice snapped. "You'll be able to talk to Laura and Megan every day, using the computer camera. She'll see your face, hear your voice—"

Faye buried her face in her napkin. "But I want to hold her in my arms!"

The other three sat silent, respecting her misery.

Then Shirley cleared her throat. "Maybe you'd better find someone else to hold in your arms."

"Yeah," Alice agreed. "Good idea, Shirley. Faye, we need to find you a man."

"I don't want a man!" Faye retorted. "I want my granddaughter!" Raising her flushed, miserable face to Alice, she snarled, "And don't tell me I'm too dependent on them."

"I wasn't going to say that," Alice rejoined in her best executive/queen-of-the-universe/don't-even-think-of-arguing voice. This time she turned her most daunting glare on Shirley, the counter of all calories.

"I was going to say this is so upsetting, we all need an enormous infusion of chocolate!" She raised her arm. "Waiter! Dessert menus, please."

6

At last Polly was driving from her home in the Boston suburb of Belmont out along Route 2 toward the bucolic countryside.

In her blue Subaru, she sped along a rural road beneath maples and birch dripping leaves of gold and crimson. She turned onto a pebble drive winding through Amy's family's farm, passed the renovated barn where Amy and David lived, and stopped in front of the charming old colonial farmhouse where Katrina and Buck lived. Someday Amy and David would live here, when they were grandparents, continuing the cycle.

Polly jumped out of her car. From the trunk, she retrieved the pretty wicker basket she'd filled with David's baby blankets and clothes and tied with a huge blue silk ribbon. She carried them and her own strange germs to the front door and rapped the brass knocker.

Katrina opened the door. Like her daughter, Katrina had lank brown hair, huge brown eyes, and emanated a smug vegetarian calm, like a parsnip.

"Polly, how nice of you to come."

Katrina led Polly into the front parlor with its handsome wide boards and rather uncomfortable early-American furniture. The room was hot, for in spite of the warmth of the October day, a huge fire flickered in the fireplace. Between the fireplace and the antique spinning wheel sat Amy in an antique rocking chair, and in her arms lay a small swaddled bundle.

"Oh, my," Polly breathed, tears welling in her eyes. She tiptoed close to mother and child.

Katrina, who always hovered, lurked like a shadow at Polly's left shoulder. Amy, oblivious to Polly's presence, continued to rock the baby, holding him tightly to her breast.

"Hello, Amy," Polly whispered. "Congratulations."

Amy didn't look up. "Thanks." She continued rocking.

"You look beautiful," Polly said. "How do you feel?"

"Great," Amy responded, still not looking up.

Polly waited a few moments, then quietly asked, "Amy? Could I see him?"

"All right," Amy whispered, and moved her arm just an inch or two, enough for Polly to spot a patch of pale skin and a rosebud mouth.

"Could I hold him?" Polly pleaded.

"He's asleep," Amy said.

"I'll be careful," Polly assured her.

With a slight pout, Amy rose, relinquishing the baby and the rocking chair.

Polly settled in the chair, gently drew the blanket away from the baby's face, and fell head over heels in love.

Jehoshaphat's face was as round as the moon, except for a little tab of chin and a bump of a nose. He had a full head of thick reddish blond hair and skin as pearly pink as the sheen of a slipper shell.

"He's so beautiful," Polly said. She pulled the blanket away and gazed upon the baby boy's body in its white undershirt and diaper. His tiny toes and fingers were curled like baby shrimp. His legs angled up like a little frog's.

"You'd better cover him up," Amy said. "He'll catch cold."

Not in *this* room, Polly wanted to say, for the temperature had to be over eighty, but reminding herself that this was Amy's baby, she hastened to wrap the blanket around her grandson, who snuggled against her with a tiny little birdlike peep.

"He's hungry!" Amy cried, alarm in her voice.

"Maybe he needs to be changed," Katrina said, rushing toward Polly and snatching the baby from her.

"I'll feed him, Mom." Frantically, Amy began to unbutton her flannel shirt.

"But he's not crying," Polly pointed out sensibly. "He only—"

But Amy seized her child from her mother's arms and rushed from the room.

"I'll fetch you some soy milk," Katrina called, running after her daughter.

Polly sat stunned, feeling as if her hair must be streaming straight backward, as if blown by a gale. She told herself to calm down. She'd only had thirty seconds with the baby, but surely Amy would return to nurse him. She could sit next to Amy on the sofa and stare and stare at his little pink hand.

Katrina fluttered back into the room. "Amy's settled back into bed," she announced. "I tucked a pillow under her arm, and Jehoshaphat's nursing nicely."

"She doesn't have to go to her bedroom to nurse him," Polly began.

"Oh, but Amy's so *sensitive*." Katrina clasped her hands together, beaming with munificent purity, as if she were Mother Teresa and Polly were Courtney Love. "She needs to be alone to nurse Jehoshaphat. Would you like some herbal tea?"

Polly hesitated. What she wanted was to see her grandson. Patience, she reminded herself. "I'd love some."

Polly followed Katrina into the large country kitchen with its flagstone floor, slate sink, and long pine table. It was a cozy room, and Polly respected its authenticity, even though there was something smug about it.

"How was the birth?" Polly asked as Katrina set a mug of tea and a plate of carrot cookies in front of her.

Katrina clasped her hands again. "Miraculous." Sinking into a chair, she said, her face glowing, "Amy spent much of her labor in the bathtub. Then David and I helped her out and dried her off so she wouldn't be cold. Then David held Amy by her shoulders." She demonstrated, putting a hand beneath her own arm. "I knelt next to Amy, so that she could rest one thigh on my knee, and the midwife caught Jehoshaphat as he came out!"

Something pinched Polly's heart. "You were there at the birth?"

"I was. That's what Amy wanted." Katrina's eyes filled with tears. "It was amazing. So beautiful. The most beautiful moment of my life."

"How wonderful for you."

"Yes, and I got to hold Jehoshaphat while the midwife and David helped Amy expel the placenta. He was so red! And yelling his little head off. I wrapped him in blankets and held him close. He calmed down, and it seemed he looked right at me. We *connected.* I think he'll always feel close to me because of those first few moments of his life."

Polly swallowed her envy, reassuring herself that *she* would have days and months and years to get to know her grandson.

The back door flew open. When David strode in, all of Polly's misery vanished. Her son was so handsome, strong, tall, and vigorous. He wore work clothes, weathered jeans, and a blue denim shirt. And he looked happy.

"Hi, Mom!" David grabbed Polly in a bear hug. "Have you seen Jehoshaphat?"

"Just for a second," Polly began.

"Jehoshaphat was sleeping in Amy's arms," Katrina explained, her voice buttery with tolerance, "but when Polly insisted on taking him, Jehoshaphat cried, so Amy's upstairs, nursing him."

But that's not true! Polly wanted to protest. Jehoshaphat hadn't *cried* when Polly took him, he'd only made a little peep. She bit her tongue.

"I'll look in on them in a minute." Going to the refrigerator, David took out a carton of milk and poured himself a glass. "What did you think of him, Mom?"

"Oh, darling, he's beautiful. I've never seen such a beautiful baby, except, of course, when you were born."

"Thanks, Mom." David smacked a kiss on her forehead. "I'm going up to see them."

"Take off your boots first!" Katrina reminded him.

"Oh, yeah, sure." David dropped down into a chair to unlace his boots.

Katrina rose, smiling at Polly with the noblesse oblige of someone putting change in a hobo's cup. "It was good of you to come out, Polly. We'll call you again, when everyone's feeling a little stronger."

Polly stared at Katrina. Surely she didn't mean Polly should leave now? "I've brought some gifts for Jehoshaphat and Amy," Polly said. "I'd love to give them to her."

Katrina bristled. "Those *things* in the wicker basket?"

"Yes. I brought clothes and blankets I've been saving for years. They were all David's."

"Oh. I see." Katrina's jaw set. "I'm sorry, Polly, but I'd rather Amy didn't use old things on little Jehoshaphat."

Polly gaped. "But Amy said you only wear clothing from thrift shops."

"Yes, but we know which shops are hygienic."

"Well, Katrina, I washed them all in hot water. They're—"

"Very well." Katrina sighed. "I'll check

them to see if they're all cotton. Amy was always allergic as a child, and Jehoshaphat might be, too." With her eyes still on Polly, she said, "David, wash your hands before you go up."

"Oh, yeah, right." David washed his hands, then pecked a kiss on his mother's forehead and headed for the stairs. "See you later, Mom." Off he went in his stocking feet, up the back stairs, taking them two at a time.

"I'll walk you to the door," Katrina said to Polly.

———

Polly wept as she drove back to her house. She felt helpless, frustrated, and furious. At home, she stomped through her hall to her study off the kitchen at the back of the house. She would pour herself a glass of wine and phone Franny and vent.

Familiar bumps sounded down the stairs. Roy Orbison waddled in to greet her, looking hopeful.

"Hello, old friend," she said. "I'll feed you in a minute." The message light on her answering machine was blinking.

"Polly." Her mother-in-law's ringing voice sounded loud and clear. "This is Claudia. I wonder whether you might be able to come to tea tomorrow. Anytime in the afternoon. Let me know as soon as you can."

Tea? With Claudia?

———————————

From the first moment they'd met, Claudia had made Polly aware that Claudia did not approve of her. In fact, Claudia had disliked every single thing about Polly and never hesitated to make this crystal clear.

To start, Polly was from South Boston, which in Claudia's view signified that Polly was hopelessly unsophisticated and, worse, completely unimportant. This was so embarrassing for Claudia, really it was, to have a daughter-in-law who was so *common.*

Then there was the matter of appearance. Polly should have been, as Claudia was, regally tall and slender, with straight, obedient hair. Instead, Polly was short, buxom, and freckled, with rebellious curly red hair. In high school and college, Polly's cheerful, bouncy good looks won her the position of head cheerleader. As an adult, her mature curves drew admiring glances from men and easy hugs from children. Around Claudia, Polly wore her most modest, nunlike clothes, and still the older woman's face pinched with disapproval when she looked at Polly.

"I can't hide the fact that I have breasts!" Polly had wailed to Tucker one night.

"And thank heavens for that!" Tucker had assured her.

But what Claudia abhorred most about Polly was that she was a seamstress, spending her days working on other people's clothing. Claudia's disapproval turned to bitter resentment when Polly continued with her business after marrying Tucker, though there was no financial need. Claudia could not grasp Polly's love for her work. For Claudia, it was insultingly déclassé.

Tucker's first marriage, to a beautiful young woman named Vanessa from a truly appropriate family, had pleased Claudia, for a while, but eventually Claudia found Vanessa tiresome because she was obsessed with maintaining her figure and her beauty, a mania Tucker gradually came to find as irritating as his mother did. When he and Vanessa divorced, it caused only a small glitch in his mother's life; now she had no one with whom to attend the DAR meetings. Other than that, Vanessa's family and Claudia remained on friendly terms whenever they met at the opera or the important holiday parties and lost touch when Vanessa remarried and moved to California.

Polly was forty-two when she married Tucker. She considered herself past childbearing age, a matter of some magnitude, for Tucker was Claudia's only child and his first marriage had brought no children. Tucker assured Polly he was content to be stepfather to David, then a gawky fourteen. Over the years, as the three of them melded into a comfortable, affectionate little family, Polly dared imagine that Claudia would also come to care for David, who was, after all, an intelligent and well-mannered boy. But Claudia's opinions of Polly and David ranged between disapproval and disdain.

Of course, at first, Polly had tried to please her mother-in-law. Muttering mantras about love, patience, and goodwill, she made overtures: Would Claudia like to join Polly for lunch at a new, chic restaurant? See the school play in which David was a star? Drive up to Vermont with David, Tucker, and Polly to see the fall foliage?

She would not.

You're wasting your time trying to win over my mother, Tucker assured Polly. Claudia would be satisfied only if he married Queen Elizabeth, and even then only if Queen Elizabeth gave up her corgis, because Claudia abhorred dogs. But Queen Elizabeth is too old for you! Polly reminded Tucker. Exactly why Claudia would approve of her, Tucker said, grinning. No nasty sex.

Would your father have liked me? Polly had asked. Oh, sure, Tucker told her, but he'd never have shown it. Tucker's father had been a banker, more comfortable with numbers than with people. He'd died, quietly and without fuss, from cancer, when Tucker was in his thirties. Claudia's response had been to wear black and refuse invitations to cocktail parties or charity events for six months.

After Tucker married Polly, Claudia became involved with genealogical research. She joined the New England Historical and Genealogical Society, attended lectures on genealogy, and traveled several times a year to England to visit the towns where her ancestors, one of them descended from King Edward I, had lived. As she grew older and arthritis forced her to give up tennis, sailing, and golf, she filled her time reading biographies.

Polly was grateful for this because it provided something like conversation during their hellishly long obligatory holiday meals. Dutifully Polly served Easter, Thanksgiving, birthday, and Christmas dinners with the formality Claudia required, because Claudia grew white with fury if the men wore jeans and no tie or if the women wore trousers instead of dresses. If Polly's guests didn't belong to the elite social class that mattered only in Claudia's mind, Claudia didn't bother to chat. Claudia never thought the wine appropriate or good enough, the turkey or lamb roasted properly, or the centerpieces up to her standards. All Polly's friends, and then David's friends, and finally David himself after he hit his late teens, spent holidays elsewhere.

Gradually, Polly gave up. During the later years, when only Polly, Tucker, and Claudia sat at the long table with its white linen cloth, silver candlesticks, and elaborate meal, Polly felt a kind of desperation filling her with hysterical laughter. She fantasized saying or doing something outrageous, like sticking carrots in her ears or starting a food fight with Tucker, something that would offend Claudia so terribly Claudia would never speak to her again.

But she didn't live out her fantasies. Claudia was Tucker's *mother.* These were, after all, *family* occasions. Polly *had* to invite her, and for a few days a year she tried her best to please her.

Two years ago, on a beautiful June day, Tucker had had a heart attack while playing tennis. He collapsed on the court and died before Polly could even say good-bye.

Claudia wore a hat to her son's funeral and chastised Polly for not wearing one. She berated Polly for having "Let It Be" sung at the service, though Polly told her Tucker had always said that was the song he would want. Claudia told Polly a sleeveless dress was inappropriate, though it was a hot, humid day. That David's hair was too long. That David's girlfriend Amy's dress, a rather Victorian-looking floral sundress, was inexcusably tasteless.

For a few moments, the exhilaration of battle swelled in Polly's chest as she contemplated telling Claudia off in language that would make Robert De Niro recoil. She stared at her mother-in-law, so properly dressed in black suit and black hat, so arrogant and ruthless and unkind. Then she reminded herself that this was the day of Claudia's son's funeral. Claudia now had no one on the planet who mattered to her.

"Oh, God, *Tucker*," Polly had cried. "Claudia, how will we live without him?" Tears streaming down her face, she bent toward her mother-in-law for a comforting embrace.

Claudia sniffed and stepped away. "Get control of yourself," she ordered. "At least *pretend* you've got some class."

Polly had closed her eyes and blown her nose in her cocktail napkin. David came up and put a consoling arm around Polly. Claudia stalked away, called a cab, and went home.

For three weeks after Tucker's funeral, grief enclosed Polly in its bitter grip. She didn't phone Claudia; why should she? Claudia hadn't phoned her.

But Claudia was an elderly woman living alone. Tucker had found his mother exhausting and infuriating, but as much as he was permitted, he had loved her. Polly knew *she* must live up to some basic standard of moral conduct out of respect for her husband, and her own sense of values as well.

So Polly phoned Claudia every week to chat. It was as easy as pulling her teeth out with her own hands and just about as pleasant, but Polly assumed that the very fact that Claudia deigned to spend time on the phone with Polly was evidence of some kind of bond. She felt obligated to continue to try.

That Christmas, Polly hadn't felt like buying a tree. All the carols made her cry, so instead of inviting Claudia for a full-scale Christmas feast, Polly had Claudia, David, and his fiancée, Amy, over for a low-key Christmas-night meal, after which they exchanged presents. Polly gave Claudia several glossy coffee-table books. Claudia gave Polly what she gave her every year for

Christmas and for her birthday: jewelry from a charity thrift shop. Polly knew this was the source because bits of glass were always missing, or the clasps didn't work, or Claudia "accidentally" forgot to remove the little white tag that priced the item at $1.00, the implied message being that Polly wouldn't appreciate and didn't deserve anything better.

That winter was a blur for Polly. She couldn't sew. She could scarcely dress herself. She took Roy Orbison for walks and sat up all night long watching old movies and sobbing. She slept during the day. She ate too much, or she forgot to eat. Still, she phoned Claudia once a week. Whatever else the older woman was, she was a connection to the man Polly had loved with all her heart.

By the spring, Polly had recovered much of her natural good spirits. She invited Claudia for tea at the Ritz. To her astonishment, Claudia agreed to go. Their conversation was as stilted as always, but wasn't it better than nothing? She hoped Tucker was floating around on a cloud somewhere, looking down to see his wife and his mother together.

During the past year, driven by a sense of duty and the hope that Tucker, and God, especially if She kept records, were watching, Polly had continued to phone Claudia and occasionally to accompany her out to tea.

But *Claudia* had never phoned *her.*

Why was she calling now?

Polly collapsed in a chair, dug a box of chocolates from their hiding place, and ate five in a row.

7

Sunday morning, Beth paced her apartment like a Pavlovian dog torn between a bell and a buzzer. In five minutes Sonny would pick her up to take her to spend the day with his family. His only words of advice had been "Don't dress up!" This surprised Beth, because Sonny never seemed to notice what she or anyone else wore. So he *meant* it when he said it, but still, it *was* Sunday dinner, and she *was* going to meet his family. For an occasion like this, the good manners her parents had drilled into her demanded a certain standard of "dressing up." She decided on blue jeans ironed till the creases snapped, leather loafers, and a simple blue cashmere sweater. She brushed her hair until it shone and added a blue velvet headband.

As she stood by her window, watching for

Sonny, Beth reviewed what Sonny had told her about his family. Sonny worked with his father, Merle, and his younger brother, Mark, in their carpentry business, Young's Construction, in Methuen, Massachusetts, where Sonny and his parents and his grandparents had all grown up. His mother, Bobbie, was the bookkeeper. His sister, Suze, coached high school sports. Sonny had moved out of his parents' house when he was twenty, into an apartment only a short walk away, but far enough to provide him some privacy for his adult life, by which he meant, Beth could tell by his sheepish expression, sleeping with lots and lots of women.

Sonny's white pickup pulled up to the curb. Beth grabbed her jacket and ran outside. The autumn air was crisp, but Sonny wore no coat, only jeans and a tartan flannel shirt with the sleeves rolled up. He smelled of leaves and sunshine and tasted, when he drew her to him in a kiss, of apple cider.

"Ready?" he asked.

As they drove along toward Methuen and his family's home, Sonny listened to a pre-Patriots-game radio program. Beth leaned her head against the window and tried to let her mind drift, but it wouldn't *drift.* Like a record stuck in a groove, her thoughts constantly replayed her fears: what if Sonny's family didn't like her?

But Sonny *loved her,* she reminded herself. He'd told her so.

But he'd told another woman he loved her, too. He'd told *only one other woman* in all his life that he loved her.

Gently, Beth tapped her head against the window. How could being in love make her so euphoric one moment, and so miserable the next?

"Here we are," Sonny said, pulling into a double driveway, behind a black pickup, a tan SUV, and a red Corvette.

The Youngs' home sprawled before her, a hodgepodge of architectural styles and materials, set on several acres of land loosely separated into particular areas. Behind the house, the workshop loomed. Nearby were heaps of metal and piles of wood waiting, Beth assumed, to be recycled. She could glimpse a small apple orchard blending into a dark forest, and between the orchard and the house lay a vegetable garden, fenced against deer and rabbits. A few bright orange pumpkins shone like lights from the brown earth.

Beth followed Sonny up the steps to the long porch, each step set with a pot of orange mums or a colorful gourd. The door Sonny pushed open was hung with Indian corn.

"Hey, everyone!" Sonny shouted. "We're here!"

Immediately, Beth was blasted with sensory overload. Here in the living room a television blared, while from another room a woman called, and Sonny was pulling Beth through the living room into an enormous kitchen smelling of roast beef and pumpkin pie. A woman turned from the stove, wiped her hands on her apron, and said, "Beth! I'm Bobbie, Sonny's mom! It's so nice to meet you!"

"Nice to meet you, too," Beth said, just as a shaggy overcoat exploded from the other end of the room and galloped toward Beth, emitting a noise that was half-bark, half-yodel.

"Tinkerbelle!" Sonny said.

The dog threw herself on Sonny, who fell to the floor with her. Back and forth they rolled, wrestling, until Sonny tickled the dog's stomach, which made Tinkerbelle lie on her back with her hind legs kicking the air spasmodically, as if she were pedaling a bike.

Beth stared, fascinated. No one in her family had ever thrown themselves on the floor. They never even *sat* on the floor.

"All the girls do that for Sonny," Bobbie joked fondly. She was a large, vigorous woman, wearing jeans and a flannel shirt beneath her apron. Her black hair, salted with white, was chopped in a short, sensible cut. She wore no jewelry or makeup, which would have been unnecessary, because she had large, beautiful, dark blue eyes like Sonny's, and like Sonny, an irresistible smile, which shone full force as she watched her adorable son.

"Hey, dinner's just about ready," Bobbie told Sonny. "You go out and round up the others. I'll show Beth the house."

Sonny jumped up and went out. Beth followed Bobbie from the kitchen.

"This place is a do-it-yourself dream." Bobbie gestured as she led Beth through a maze. "The original three rooms were once a farmhouse when we bought it thirty years ago. Merle added rooms whenever he had the time. I guess it's still a work in progress. We enlarged the upstairs when Sonny and Mark and Suze were born. Then we turned the little dining room into a large family room and enlarged the kitchen, because every-body's always in the kitchen, anyway. When Sonny and Mark got into their teens, Merle turned the garage into a weight room, then built on a garage."

Beth thought the Young house had the wandering rectangular coherence of a game of Scrabble. "It's great," she said.

Bobbie stopped in the family room with its huge television. One wall of shelves was crammed with trophies and photographs. "Our rogues' gallery," she announced with pride.

A pictorial history of the Young family spread out before Beth, who leaned for-ward, genuinely interested.

"Is this your wedding picture?" Beth asked, gazing at a photo of a younger Bob-bie in a short white dress, next to a man who looked almost exactly like Sonny.

"Yes." Bobbie's voice warmed as she spoke. "We couldn't afford a proper big wedding. We couldn't even afford a honeymoon. But we couldn't have been any happier if we'd spent a week in the Bahamas."

"Is this Sonny? Gosh, wasn't he a cute baby!"

"All my babies were."

"Look at Sonny in his baseball uniform!" Beth gushed. "He's adorable!"

"Nine years old. The best hitter in his league."

"Did he ever think of playing professional ball?"

"No, I don't think he did. He always wanted to be like his dad."

"And is this Suze?" Beth nodded toward a picture of a girl with pigtails, matching snowflake mittens and cap, spinning on an ice rink.

"Yes. For a while we thought she might become a professional skater, but she had a nasty fall when she was fifteen. Broke her ankle. Ended *that* career."

"Oh, how terrible." Beth studied the next few pictures. "Is this Suze, playing field hockey?"

"Yes. She was able to play her junior and senior years in high school. Developed a taste for it, and now she's the girls' field hockey coach at Methuen High."

"Good for her!" The next photo drew Beth closer. Squinting, she studied the color photograph of Sonny in a powder blue tux with a gorgeous, buxom blonde in a pale blue, strapless gown. Sonny's arm was around the girl's slender waist, his hand resting possessively on her hip. Their faces shone with the gloss of young love.

"That's Sonny and Robin just before the junior prom," Bobbie said, adding matter-of-factly, "Sonny must have told you about Robin."

"Um," Beth murmured uncertainly.

"They were high school sweethearts. Man, were they in love!" Bobbie sighed. "They were so adorable together. Here they are, king and queen of the senior prom. And here they are when Sonny was captain of the football team and Robin was head of the cheerleading squad. Isn't she beautiful?"

"She certainly is," Beth agreed.

"That was taken after Robin helped me paint the family room." Bobbie pointed to a photo of Robin and Bobbie, both in overalls, both spattered with paint, holding up brushes and laughing triumphantly at the camera. "She hung out here so much as a kid. She idolized Merle and used to beg him to let her help him. She got to be a pretty good little carpenter. We were so thrilled when Sonny was dating Robin. Thought they'd get married and take over Merle's business eventually."

Beth stood frozen in uncomfortable silence, unable to think of a response.

"Hey!" someone yelled. "You must be Beth. I'm Sonny's father. Call me Merle." Merle Young strode into the room, bringing a burst of fresh air with him. He was bald, with hazel eyes, and he was just Sonny's height, but stockier. His hand, as he shook Beth's, was hard and calloused.

"And I'm Mark." Sonny's brother was a stocky, brown-haired, hazel-eyed copy of his father. Bits of leaves poked from his old wool sweater. "Nice to meet you, Beth."

"And I'm Suze." Sonny's sister looked just like her photos, only healthier. Her skin glowed, her black hair shone, and she carried her strong body with the ease of a natural athlete.

"Dinner's ready," Bobbie told the gang. "Let's go in the kitchen." Over her shoulder, she said to Beth, "I gave up the dining room to have a family room, but now I want Merle to build us a real dining room we can use for holidays and birthdays."

"No dining room," Mark protested, throwing an arm around his mother's shoulders. "You'd make us sit up straight and not belch in a dining room."

"Please!" Suze rolled her eyes at Beth as they followed the others.

"Mom!" Sonny was at the stove, stirring a pan. "You let the gravy get lumpy."

"I did no such thing," Bobbie protested, taking the spoon from him. "Put the roast on the platter," she told him.

Everyone else grabbed bowls and carried them to the long pine table.

"Can I help?" Beth asked.

"Sure," Sonny told her. "Get the platter out of the cupboard and hold it for me while I get the roast from the oven." He pulled on a pair of oven mitts.

Beth opened a cupboard door. Glasses. She opened the next door. Mugs. The next cupboard was crammed with Tupperware.

"It's on the lower shelf," someone said silkily.

Beth turned to see a beautiful woman laying silverware on either side of the plates.

"I'm Robin." Her voice poured out like honey.

Beth almost whimpered. Robin was more beautiful than in the photos. Clad in jeans and a white, long-sleeved tee that showed her spectacular figure, her blond hair pulled up in a high ponytail, she looked like every man's dream.

"Hi, Robin." Beth forced herself to smile. "I'm Beth."

"Oh, yes, I've heard all about you." Robin picked up a pile of paper napkins.

Beth lifted up a white ironstone platter that must have weighed twenty pounds. "Is this the right one?"

"Perfect." With two enormous forks, Sonny hefted a roast the size of Texas onto the platter.

Beth staggered at the combined weight. Bobbie chuckled, "Oh, honey, you're going to drop that!" and took it from her.

Sonny put his arm around Beth's shoulders. "Robin's helping Mom try to slap some sense into this house."

"Robin's a painter," Bobbie proclaimed proudly as she set the roast on the table.

"Oh? An artist?" Beth asked.

Everyone laughed. "Robin doesn't have time for sissy stuff," Mark said, punching Robin lightly on the arm. "She paints houses, and makes a good bit of money doing it, too."

"She's got her own scaffolding and her own crew," Bobbie added. "Come on, everyone, sit down."

Bobbie took her seat at one end of the table, Merle at the other, Beth and Sonny on one side, facing Mark, Suze, and Robin, who had to squeeze together to fit. It was clear Beth was sitting in Robin's usual place.

"It's grab, root, and growl in this family," Merle informed Beth as the others reached for bowls, helped themselves, and passed the food on.

"Take bigger helpings," Merle ordered Beth. "You're too skinny."

"Dad," Sonny objected.

Gorgeous Robin laughed, showing perfect white teeth. "Better get used to it," she warned Beth. "One thing about this family. They're not shy."

"Now what is it you do?" Merle asked.

Pleased to be asked, Beth said, "I'm

completing work on my Ph.D. in English, and working in the BU library."

"I almost went to BU!" Mark told her.

"Yeah," Bobbie reminisced fondly. "Back in his rebel days." She poured gravy over her food.

"Decided to work for Dad instead," Mark said.

"Sonny wanted to be an architect." Robin smiled warmly across the table at Sonny, who was focused on his food.

"Really?" Sonny hadn't told her this. She turned to look at him. "Why—"

"College just costs too much," Bobbie remarked.

"Anyway, they *had* to put *me* through college," Suze piped up. "I'm the smart one in the family."

"Just because you go to college doesn't mean you're smart," Merle grumbled. "I know lots of morons with college degrees." He glared at Beth's plate. "Don't you like the food?"

Beth quickly lifted a fork of potatoes and gravy to her mouth, just as Tinkerbelle knocked Beth's arm with her eager, wet nose. The fork flew from Beth's hand onto the floor, leaving a trail of gravy across Beth's cashmere sweater.

"You'll get wise to old Tinkerbelle's tricks," Robin assured Beth.

But will I get wise to yours? Beth wondered, forcing a smile.

8

The newly enlarged Sperry family had their first meal together in the vast formal dining room with its glittering chandeliers, elaborately carved and inlaid mahogany sideboards, velvet drapes, and antique oils whose frames gleamed softly in the candlelight. The table itself was seven feet wide and twenty feet long.

Carolyn had decided to roll out the good silver and china for this intimate family celebration. She wasn't certain how she felt about her father's new wife, but for her father's sake, Carolyn was determined to be welcoming. She'd personally arranged the centerpiece of baby roses and white irises, which she'd suggest that Heather take back to their wing, and she'd had a wonderful triple-layer cake made with the words "Congratulations, Heather and Aubrey!" written in white icing as a surprise for the newly-weds.

Now the housekeeper set a crystal goblet of milk at her place at the linen-swathed table. "Thank you, Mrs. B.," Carolyn said.

"You're welcome, dear." Mrs. B. quietly left the dining room.

"Our first meal together!" Carolyn's father said from his place at the head of the table. He raised his glass, filled with wine as rosy as his face.

"Here's to many more," Carolyn toasted, and her husband, Hank, and Aubrey's new wife, Heather, echoed her words.

When, over twenty-seven years ago, his wife had died unexpectedly from a heart attack, Aubrey Sperry had mourned deeply and in his own peculiar way, engrossing himself in his work and shutting out anything that reminded him of his wife. Unfortunately, that included Carolyn. Her father had sat at the dinner table with her every night, inquiring about her homework and other school activities. He'd attended her recitals and high school and college graduations. He'd even taken her out to dinner occasionally. But though they lived in the same house, an emotional distance stretched between them. When her father started dating, Carolyn felt both relief and jealousy. She knew it was good for her father to have a life away from the company, she even under- stood, intellectually, that her father might be happier if he remarried, but she worried that any woman replacing her mother might eclipse Carolyn in his heart. Ashamed of such thoughts, she kept them to herself.

Over the years, Aubrey Sperry had squired a variety of elegant Bostonian social swans. How odd that he would marry this plain little partridge, Heather. As Aubrey lifted the heavy silver carving knife and fork to the roast, Carolyn studied her father's face, thinking what a mystery people are to each other, for here was this man who shared her DNA and her daily life, and there sat his new wife, someone Carolyn would never have expected Aubrey to so much as glance at.

Whatever the reason for his choice, Aubrey looked happy with his new wife, seated wide-eyed on his left. The candle- light illuminated Aubrey's hands with their age spots and ropy veins and his wrinkled, jowly face. Her father was aging. The years had reversed their roles; now she was the one who should protect him.

For her part, Heather looked rather cowed by the silver candlesticks, thick damask napkins, and gold-rimmed Limoges bowls of rice and vegetables. In a high, little-girl voice, she tittered, "This is an awfully big table."

"Too big for comfortable modern family meals," Hank agreed. Rising, he went around the table, serving the food with the panache of a butler. "I don't want to ask Mrs. B. to do it," he explained. "It's enough that she had to cart all this stuff in here."

"The house was built by my grandmother," Aubrey explained to his new wife, "back in the days when people had lots of help. Cooks, maids, young boys to do the heavy work."

"It's a beautiful room." Carolyn glanced around the grand chamber. "But impractical. We usually eat in our own dining rooms, or in the kitchen, with Mrs. B."

"Does she live here?" Heather asked.

Carolyn answered, "Mrs B.'s got her own home just a short drive away, down in Sperry, where her husband lives. He's retired from the post office, a classical-record fanatic. She loves working here in the day so he can play his music full blast. She goes home in the evening, unless the weather's terrible or we have a big party that runs late. There's a small bedroom off the office, between the kitchen and the family room, which is hers."

"You know, we haven't had a party for years," Aubrey remarked.

"Let's have one," Carolyn suggested. "Hey! How about a gala cocktail party to announce your marriage and introduce your new wife?"

Heather looked round-eyed with terror.

"We'll discuss it," Aubrey said, patting Heather's hand.

Hank finished serving the roast, potatoes and asparagus and returned to his place at the table. "So, Heather, tell me about yourself."

Heather replied meekly, "There's not much to tell."

Hank kindly prompted, "Did you grow up around here?"

Heather nodded. "In Arlington."

"That's a nice suburb," Hank said encouragingly.

Heather bent her head and concentrated on cutting her meat.

"Heather's parents are both dead, unfortunately." After Heather's shy utterances, Aubrey's voice seemed to boom. "Her father was a plumber, her mother a housewife. Heather and her brother, Harry, inherited the house and lived in it together until our marriage. Haven't met Harry yet."

"You're lucky to have a brother," Carolyn told Heather. "I always wanted one."

Heather smiled but said nothing.

"Is he older or younger?"

"Older."

"*Much* older?"

"Two years."

This was like trying to fill a bucket of water drop by drop. Carolyn thought of all the women her father had dated, women with enormous charm and easy eloquence.

It was Aubrey who elaborated. "Heather went to Brighton Community College. Worked as a teller at the Arlington Citizens Bank, part-time. Then she decided to work there full-time, and she's been there for twelve years." Reaching over, he patted his young bride's hand. "And I'm lucky she worked there the day I needed some extra cash. Otherwise, we never would have met. Now," Aubrey boomed, "Hank! Tell me about what you've been up to!" Turning to Heather, he explained, "Hank's an environmental activist. Always saving one forest or another."

"Actually," Hank said, "I'm trying to save an entire hillside in western Massachusetts. Developers want to turn the land into a minimall." Always passionate about his work, Hank held forth for the rest of the meal.

Later, in the privacy of their own living room in their own wing, Carolyn collapsed on the sofa, lifting her feet into Hank's lap so he could massage them.

"Ahhh," she sighed. "If I'd known you were so talented at this, I would have married you sooner."

"And here I thought you were captivated by my sexual magnetism," Hank chided.

"I was," Carolyn said, grinning. "I am." She closed her eyes, adjusting a pillow behind her neck. "What do you think of my father's little bride?"

Hank rubbed the ball and then the arch of her left foot. "She's an odd one. I never would have guessed she was Aubrey's type."

"I know." Carolyn placed her hands on her belly. She hadn't yet felt the baby kick. She couldn't wait! "She's so shy and she doesn't seem very smart! I just don't understand what Dad sees in her."

"Maybe she's restful for Aubrey. Maybe he's exhausted by strong women. Strong women have ruled his life. His grandmother. His mother. You. Maybe he enjoys having a submissive, sweet little woman at his side."

Carolyn studied her husband. "Do you find me exhausting?"

Hank lifted her foot and kissed it. "I find you *stimulating.* Exciting. Arousing." He licked her toes.

"That tickles." Carolyn giggled. Shifting on the sofa, she said, more soberly, "Heather certainly doesn't fit the image of a gold digger. But, Hank, this marriage just doesn't feel right to me."

"Maybe it's just the shock. It happened so fast. Without *your* control or even your knowledge. And look at Aubrey. He's got a bounce in his step and a gleam in his smile."

"True. And I want him to be happy. But it almost seems as if Heather's playing a part. Oh, hell! I don't want to talk about Heather anymore. She's interrupting my foot massage." Carolyn relaxed against the sofa, deciding to enjoy the moment.

Monday afternoon, Carolyn and Aubrey sat at a conference table at the Sperry Paper Company with Frank Mooney, the head of personnel, going over the new changes in the governmental health plans and the impact they would have on the company's health policies. Outside, the wind howled, splattering hard pellets of rain against the large plate-glass windows. The turgid governmental prose, the dizzying sheets of numbers, and the unremitting storm set Carolyn's nerves on edge.

"Carolyn, are you all right?" Frank asked.

Carolyn fished a handkerchief from her purse and blew her nose. "I'm fine, Frank."

Frank eyeballed her skeptically. "You

don't look so hot. And that's the third time you've sneezed."

"Frank's right," Aubrey said. "Why don't you go home, Carolyn. Take the day off. Grab a nap. You don't want to come down with a cold."

Carolyn gazed at the stack of papers before her. The pie charts seemed to bubble and contract like cells under a microscope. "I think I *will* go home," she conceded, putting her calculator, pens, pads, and glasses into her briefcase.

"We'll leave the list of changes for your approval," Frank told her.

"Thanks." At the door, Carolyn turned back. "Is Heather at home?" she asked her father.

"She told me she's driving to Arlington to pack up a few of her belongings," Aubrey said. "We're meeting at Il Bocce for lunch."

Good, Carolyn thought, driving out of the factory lot and through Sperry. Someday soon, she'd spend a few hours sharing girl talk over hot chocolate with Heather, but today she wanted to crawl into bed and sleep.

No. She wanted to cut a huge wedge from the leftover cake, eat it in bed while watching an old black-and-white movie, and *then* fall asleep.

She drove up the hill toward the old Victorian, which today, in the pouring rain and darkened air, was looking rather like the set for *Psycho.* Parking in the porte cochere, Carolyn let herself into the side foyer and walked into the main hall. She'd always loved the paintings here and had developed the habit of chatting to the memorialized women as if they could really hear her.

"Hello, old dears." Her mother, Elizabeth Carolyn, her grandmother Helena Elizabeth, and her great-grandmother Geraldine Helena smiled down at her from the boundaries of their heavy gold frames. "I've got to give little Elizabeth Geraldine her nap."

She was about to open the door into her wing when she heard a slight noise from the direction of Mrs. B.'s office between the family room and the kitchen. Then, another noise. A clicking. She thought Mrs. B. had taken the day off. Oh, God, did the house have mice?

Or was it just the rain?

Another noise, a kind of snap. Well, if

Mrs. B. was here, perhaps she wouldn't mind popping a hen in the oven for tonight, and making her famous apple/onion/walnut stuffing. The very thought warmed Carolyn.

Passing through the large drawing room and the smaller family room where she and her father celebrated Christmas, she moved through the shadowy house toward Mrs. B.'s office, where all the household accounts were kept. The wind rattled the windows and sent shadows scuttling into the corners, while a draft made the hem of a wall tapestry lift and fall in a ghostlike curtsy.

The office door was open. Carolyn stepped into the room.

"Mrs. B.?"

Seated at the desk, tapping away at the computer, was Heather, who shrieked when Carolyn entered. Carolyn's heart jumped.

"Oh!" Heather gasped, fluttering a hand at her chest. "You startled me!"

"You startled me," Carolyn countered. "Aubrey told me you'd gone to Arlington for the morning."

"I thought you were at work," Heather rejoined. In her fleecy yellow cardigan embroidered with flowers, with her flushed face and nervous mannerisms, Heather resembled a chubby adolescent who'd been caught sticking a plastic tattoo on her arm. Still, Carolyn noticed that, shocked as Heather was, she was busily clicking and dragging the mouse, no doubt closing a file.

"This is Mrs. B.'s desk." Carolyn walked around the desk to look at the screen, which, sure enough, now showed only the blue screen saver.

Heather cleared her throat. "This house is *so* complicated. I thought I might be able to find a chart here about which rooms are used, where the linens are, that sort of thing. Also, I'd like to start cooking for Aubrey. Does Mrs. B. have any special vegetarian recipes on her computer?"

"Best if you wait and ask her when she's here," Carolyn said coolly.

"Of course." Heather chewed her lip.

Carolyn sat on the edge of the desk. "I had to leave work early today," she explained, trying to be friendly. "I think I'm coming down with a cold."

"Oh, dear. Can I get you something? Some aspirin? Or, perhaps, make you some chicken broth? I've read that Harvard scientists did a study that *proved* chicken soup has healing qualities."

"That's kind of you, Heather," Carolyn said sweetly, noticing as she spoke that the household ledger was open on Heather's lap. "But I think I'm going to cut myself a slice of the chocolate cake."

"It's delicious, isn't it?" Heather clapped her hands like a child. "That was so thoughtful of you, Carolyn, to surprise us with a cake. It makes me feel so welcome." Then she noticed Carolyn looking at the open ledger. With the swiftness of a Jekyll and Hyde, Heather's face hardened. Her voice was harsh when she demanded, "Who has signatory powers for this account?"

The sudden change of subject surprised Carolyn and affronted her. What right did this little interloper have to question her about personal financial matters?

The right of a wife, Carolyn realized with a jolt.

"Mrs. B. does," Carolyn told her. "And I do. And, of course, my father."

"I'll have to be able to use this account, too." Now Heather was matter-of-fact, even official. "I'm going to start cooking all of

Aubrey's meals. I'm going to be sure he gets more salads and vegetables."

Carolyn laughed. "Good luck getting him to eat them."

"Oh, he'll eat them if I fix them," Heather said confidently. "I want him to live a long time, after all."

Carolyn met Heather's eyes. The little-girl meekness was gone, replaced by defiance . . . even a glint of menace.

"I want him to live a long time, too," Carolyn agreed mildly. "I hope you can get him on a healthy régime." She moved away from the desk, toward the door. "I'll talk to Mrs. B. tomorrow, to tell her to have your name added at the bank."

"Oh, please, don't trouble yourself," Heather sweetly protested, adding firmly, "I'll tell her myself."

Dazed, Carolyn wandered back through the halls and into her private wing, so disconcerted she forgot the chocolate cake. As she passed through her living room and dining room, she drew her hands over the backs of the sofas and chairs, grounding herself in a blessedly familiar reality. In the kitchen, she turned on the kettle and took a packet of chamomile tea from the cupboard. An invisible pressure pushed against her skin, as if her body were a balloon being inflated, making her edgy, uncomfortable. High blood pressure, she thought, closing her eyes and leaning on the counter. Heather's unexpected metamorphosis had unsettled her.

But why?

Think it through, Carolyn told herself. She was a sensible woman, capable of comprehending that the last few moments with Heather had caused her suspicions to flare up, jumping from Point A, Heather's transformation, to Point X, which was—what, exactly? What did the most neurotic side of her fear?

Could a dumpling like Heather have designs on the ownership of the Sperry Paper Company! Carolyn laughed at the thought.

Still, she needed to sit down with her father to discuss all the legal ramifications of his marriage. She had to find out if there was a prenuptial agreement. How would Aubrey alter his will? Was he giving any of his shares of the company to Heather? Did they plan to have children?

Children.

Carolyn's heart boinged like a jack-in-the-box. She forced herself to breathe deeply, but she was so light-headed, she collapsed in a chair.

What if young, round, sweet, nurturing Heather had a baby? A little girl, who would rival Carolyn for her father's love, and for control of the company?

Now she was being ridiculously paranoid. Wasn't she?

9

"Oooh, isn't it delicious, lying naked like this," Julia crooned to her husband as they lay side by side Sunday morning. They'd just finished making love with the kind of blissful abandon that can happen only when a child isn't within hearing distance. Belinda had spent the night with her best friend, Sarah, and for once they had the house to themselves.

Tim gave a jaw-cracking yawn. "I don't know whether to fall back asleep or go make breakfast."

"Breakfast, I think," Julia said. "I'm starving. Let's eat in bed, and read the papers, and then nap."

"I have a better idea." Tim pulled her hips against his. "Let's have breakfast in bed, read the papers, make love again, and *then* sleep."

"Brilliant." Julia nuzzled him, curling her fingers in his chest hair.

"You stay in bed," Tim told her. "I'll make omelets."

"With peppers and onions and cheese?"

"Absolutely." Tim rolled out of bed and stalked, naked, out of the room.

Julia stretched like a cat and licked her lips. God, how she'd been craving this spell of grown-up pleasures! She hoped someday she and Tim would have children of their own, and she truly didn't resent the way her life was ordered by Belinda's needs. But these moments of satisfaction of her adult desires lent a lusciousness to her daily life, like bands of velvet on a cotton quilt.

Belinda accepted only the sweet breakfasts her mother had prepared for her: pancakes drenched in syrup, cinnamon toast sagging under the weight of butter and sugar, or cereal containing more glucose than grain.

Tim, always rushed, usually grabbed a cup of hot coffee and swigged down a glass of orange juice before leaving for work. Julia drank green tea and nibbled a PowerBar as she got Belinda ready for school. Their evening meals centered around cajoling Belinda to eat the foods Julia found repellent—macaroni and cheese, tortellini, fish sticks. Occasionally Julia prepared something just for her and Tim—beef simmered in red wine, linguine with clams—but Belinda felt left out when Julia and her father ate different foods, so very much rejected that she lost all appetite for her own meal. Usually, it was simply easier to eat what Belinda ate.

But couldn't they change things just a little? Julia wondered as she lay naked on the stirred, warm, sex-scented sheets.

For now, she'd indulge in the food whose aromas now drifted tantalizingly from the kitchen. Next, she'd get out of control with her husband. *Then,* she'd plan ways to incorporate grown-up meals into the food that pleased Belinda.

Tim raced into the room, looking frantic. "Can't you hear? Someone's knocking on the door!"

"I'll get it." Julia's limbs felt warm and heavy as she rose from bed and slipped into her black silk robe.

"Thanks. I've got to get back to the kitchen or the omelets will burn."

Julia sauntered down the hall to the front

door, wondering who would be knocking on a Sunday morning. Kids selling magazines for Little League?

She opened the door.

"Oh! It's *you*!" Belinda's maternal grandmother, Agnes, stood there, looking offended. "You gave me a fright! I've been knocking for *hours*! I'm just longing to see little Belinda."

Julia found herself backed against the wall as Agnes stormed into the house. Clad in yellow sweatpants and a matching sweatshirt adorned with a faux needlepoint rendition of a basket of kittens, her white hair bobbing around her chubby face like a bunch of bubbles, Agnes was a living Trojan horse, hiding beneath her grandmothery surface the heart and mind of Vlad the Impaler.

"Tim?" Julia's voice cracked with tension. "Darling, Agnes's here!"

Agnes was set on charging down the hall to Belinda's room, which would have taken her near the kitchen, where Tim was preparing breakfast in all his naked glory.

Julia had to stop her.

"Agnes!" she cried, and with a desperate smile, threw her arms around Tim's first wife's mother, hugging her tight. "It's so good to see you." Gripping Agnes's shoulders fiercely, she chirped, "But you look different. Let me see now. Is it the hair? No, I don't think you've changed it, it's the same beautiful color. I know! You've lost weight. Come on, confess, you've been dieting, haven't you?"

Agnes preened, looking down at her pumpkin-size belly. "No, dear, I haven't been dieting. I'm so busy, I just work it off." Returning the assessing glance, she arched her eyebrows. "Did I wake you? I didn't think I could. It *is* almost eleven." Translation: *Aren't you a little slut, not dressed at this hour of the morning like a decent woman should be!*

Tim came down the hall. He'd pulled on chinos and a white polo shirt, but he was barefoot, and his hair stuck up all over. "Agnes. How nice to see you. Sorry to say, Belinda's not here. She spent the night at Sarah's house."

"Spent the night?" Agnes's hand flew to her chest as if she'd been stabbed in the heart. "She's only seven years old!"

"She's spent the night at the Fergusons' before, many times," Tim reminded his for-

mer mother-in-law, adding, "All the therapists we saw said it was good for her to do
this, to live like a normal child."

Agnes slumped. "Oh, well." Then she
brightened. "She'll be home soon, won't
she? I'll just wait! After all, I've driven for
three hours." Her piggy nose quivered.
"Something smells good!"

Tim looked at Julia, who looked back
helplessly. "I was just making breakfast for
Julia and me. Would you like to join us?"

"I suppose so." Agnes's eyes raked Julia.
"I'm so afraid you'll catch cold, dear, wear-
ing only your robe and no slippers like that.
I'm sure we can wait to eat until you've had
time to pull yourself together." Translation:
Trollop.

A protest bloomed on Julia's lips. Who
was this person, telling her how to dress in
her own home?

But as Julia opened her mouth to speak,
Agnes performed one of her brilliant whip-
lash maneuvers. "I've always wondered
whether Annette would have gotten ill like
she did if she'd taken better care of herself.
If she'd taken a daily vitamin or worn
warmer clothing. I always made her wear
warm clothes when she lived at home, but

after she got married, well, she just didn't seem to take care of herself." Agnes's face sagged with genuine sadness.

Gently, Tim reminded Agnes, "But Annette didn't die of pneumonia. She didn't die of anything we could have prevented. Remember, we asked the doctors what caused her cancer, and they told us nothing she did or ate or wore or thought caused it. These things just happen, and no one knows why. Now, come on to the kitchen, and let me fix you a nice hot breakfast."

"That's very kind of you, Tim."

"I'll just dress," Julia muttered, heading for the bedroom.

Quickly she pulled the duvet up and set the pillows against the headboard, so the room would look tidy if, or more likely *when,* Agnes peeked in. Honestly, the woman had the instincts of a dope-smelling DEA dog! Julia pulled on a pair of black jeans and a baggy, black cashmere sweater. Sliding her feet into moccasins, she checked her image in the mirror and rolled her eyes at herself.

How could Agnes sense this was the first time she and Tim had had alone for months? The more important question was, why wouldn't Agnes want Tim to be happy?

In the kitchen, Agnes had settled at the table. Tim hurriedly whisked eggs.

"Can I help?" Julia asked.

"Please," he said, busy with a frying pan and bread. "I'm making Agnes French toast—"

"I can't believe you're eating onions and peppers for breakfast." Agnes shook her head. "You'll get terrible indigestion from all that hot, spicy food. It's so *foreign*." *Probably what terrorists eat.*

"I'll rescue the omelets." Julia lifted the eggs from the pan with a spatula and carefully scraped off the burned bottoms. She melted more butter, set the pan on low heat, and covered it. While the omelets were reheating, she said to Agnes, "Would you like some juice? Coffee?"

"Both, please." Agnes watched with glittering eyes as Tim and Julia moved around the kitchen. When they were all served and seated, she said, "Thank you, Tim. This looks delicious." She took a bite, then patted her mouth with a napkin. "Oh, my. You're still using *paper* napkins." She glared at Julia. Translation: My daughter *always used cloth napkins, and I've suggested— politely, of course—that you use them, but* you *obviously don't care about the finer things in life, so you'll probably turn my grandchild into a tattooed drug fiend.*

Tim spoke up. "I prefer paper napkins. It saves on laundry, and neither Julia nor I have time to iron."

"Yes, I realize that." With a grimace, Agnes applied herself to her French toast.

This woman has lost her daughter, Julia reminded herself. *Be nice!*

"Another thing I've been meaning to mention, Julia," Agnes said suddenly, laying her fork on her plate and skewering Julia with a deadly look. "And this is the appropriate time to bring it up, I think."

"Yes?" Julia kept her voice light.

"Must you wear black all the time? It's so *gloomy.*"

Julia laughed. "Agnes, just about all my clothes are black. I like black."

Tim added, trying to be helpful, "It's chic, you know, Agnes. It's urban. It's artistic."

"It's funereal," Agnes shot back. "I'm sure it makes Belinda think of death."

Julia's jaw dropped. "Oh, I don't think—"

"If it's a matter of money, I'd be glad to buy a few things for you," Agnes offered.

"That's very generous of you, Agnes." Julia strained to be kind. "But I can pay for my own clothes." Desperation broke out all over her body in a kind of invisible sweat. She wanted to cry: I've changed *so* much for love of this man. I'm trying so hard. I keep the house in perfect condition for Belinda. I eat the food Belinda likes. I never make noise when I have sex with my husband. Do I have to start wearing butterfly-embroidered sweat suits to make everyone happy?

Tim reached over and touched her arm. His lips moved but no sound came out. He frowned. "Julia? Can't you hear me?"

Julia put a hand to her temple and shook her head like a dog coming out of water. "Sorry, no. That sinus headache's come back. I think I'd better go lie down. Excuse me, Agnes."

In the bedroom, she shut the door against Agnes's pain-filled voice and lay down on the bed, where she curled into a fetal position. Her hearing wavered, then disappeared. A white rush of noise like a waterfall filled her head. Right now, this was a relief.

10

When the monthly meeting of The Haven ended, most board members packed up their briefcases and left the handsome boardroom, heading out to their cars. Shirley, Alice, Marilyn, and Faye remained around the conference table. The formal board meetings dealt with the hard facts, mostly the finances of the spa. The relaxed, more intimate sessions were for brainstorming, casual discussion, letting new ideas drift by. They were, after all, the original founders of the spa; they knew it was their openness to new ideas that had helped them achieve this thriving business.

Alice slipped off her shoes and plopped her feet on a chair, smoothing her silk trousers over her legs. "I'm really happy about the treasurer's report."

Shirley nodded. "We haven't broken into

the black yet because of the cost of renova-
tions, purchasing equipment for the weight
rooms, and advertising, but few businesses
do the first year, and we're almost there."
She tapped her lower lip with the end of
her pen to hide a smile—sometimes she
couldn't believe she was the president of a
functioning, profit-making business!

"The spa's reputation seems to be
spreading by word of mouth!" Faye spoke
with forced gusto. Her daughter had moved
two weeks ago, but she was going to be
cheerful if it killed her.

"I know!" Shirley unbuttoned the jacket of
the boring boxy suit she had to wear to
these meetings, letting her lavender silk
shell show. "It's fabulous. We're adding a
few new classes in yoga, spinning, and Pi-
lates. The Jacuzzi's a great success, and
we're getting estimates for an indoor lap
pool."

Marilyn took a sip from one of the bottles
of water set around the table. "Any problems?"

Shirley took a moment to consider. "Not
problems, no. More like challenges. Most of
our clients are fairly easy to serve. They
want to lose weight, gain muscles and flex-

ibility, learn to relax, reward themselves for tough days at the office or home with special treats. But just last week I did intake interviews on two women with slightly more complicated problems. One young woman has an intermittent hearing problem. She's seen specialists who can find no physical cause. I referred her to a psychologist and explained that The Haven is a wellness spa. If the cause of her hearing loss is some deep trauma, she needs the help of a trained therapist. I went through our brochure with her, suggesting beginner's yoga, aromatherapy, and massage. I want to track her progress."

Faye leaned forward. "I know the woman you mean. Julia something. She seems happy enough. Married, gorgeous, energetic, a bit severe. Her field is photography. She's in my art therapy course."

"Good." Shirley made a note. "Then you can help me decide whether we need a full-time shrink on our team for clients who have more serious problems."

Alice looked worried. "Good thing we've got plenty of malpractice insurance."

"Yes," Shirley said, "but aside from the legalities, I want to be sure we can actually

help our clients. Another woman, for exam-
ple, has a more serious medical problem."
She shot a stern look around the table.
"This, as you know, is in confidence."

The other three nodded.

"Since you're on the board, I can tell you
her name. A woman in her late thirties
joined last month. She wants help keeping
her blood pressure down and relaxing in
general, because she's pregnant, and she
already has high blood pressure. Her name
is Carolyn Sperry."

"Sperry Paper?" Alice asked.

Shirley nodded.

"She's famous," Faye said. "What a plum
for The Haven!"

Marilyn cleared her throat. "I'm not sure I
know who she is."

"Sperry Paper Company is one of the
state's oldest businesses," Alice told her.
"An entire town's grown up around it over
the last century. Aubrey Sperry, the current
president of the company, shows up at all
the best society functions, plus he's extremely generous to local charities."

"Carolyn is Aubrey's daughter," Shirley
continued. "The founder of the company
was a woman, and it's been handed down

from mother to daughter until Aubrey's mother had only one child, a boy. But Carolyn is the heir apparent, so she's got to remain involved with the daily running of the company, while at the same time being sure she carries her child, which is a girl, to full term. Plus, her father's just brought a new wife into the family constellation."

"And she has high blood pressure?" Faye asked. "She's got a lot on her plate."

"I know," Shirley agreed. "This is the sort of client who makes me lose sleep. I can only advise her. I'm not her boss, her parent, or her doctor, so I can't insist or enforce."

"What have you suggested?" Marilyn inquired.

"Beginner's yoga, weekly massage and aromatherapy. And I tried to get her to join the Friday-night quilting class, because I think it would do her good to build a community, friends with their own problems who will make her feel not so neurotic, friends she can laugh with. But she wasn't very keen on the quilting group."

"Maybe she'll make friends on her own," Faye suggested. "After all, the four of us met at a party."

"Maybe." Shirley shrugged. "Maybe not. She's pretty standoffish."

"Speaking of making friends . . ." Alice's grin had a touch of mischief. "Have we all completed our HFC assignments?"

"Oh, please," Faye groaned. "Seriously, please, let's not do this."

"Too late," Shirley announced. "It's already done!"

"Shirley," Faye said, "I'm grateful for your concern about my health and my happiness, but what the three of you are suggesting is only making me miserable."

Marilyn looked across the table at Faye. "It really will make you feel better."

"Don't even think about the sexual side of it," Alice advised her. "Just think of what fun it is to make new friends."

"I don't need any new friends!" Faye protested, hugging her silk jacket against her protectively.

"But you'll *like* them!" Shirley insisted. "Let me tell you about my candidate. Teddy Timlin. Actually, he goes by 'Tank.' He's a friend of my old boyfriend Jimmy, and he's a totally good guy. And—"

"I'm not going out with a man who calls himself Tank!" Faye said.

"How old is he?" Alice asked.

"Does it matter?" Shirley shot back. "We're not talking marriage here! We're just trying to give Faye some dating experiences, a little fun in her life, and believe me, Tank's fun."

"I think my candidate's more appropriate," Alice said.

Shirley shrugged. "Okay, fine, who is he?"

"Glen Wells. Just retired from the accounting department at TransWorld. Glen's a completely reliable, stand-up kind of guy. I'd trust him with anything. He's divorced, got two grown children, likes art museums and the symphony and so on—you'd really like him, Faye. You two would have a lot in common."

In reply, Faye leaned her elbows on the table and buried her head in her hands.

"Who's your candidate, Marilyn?" Shirley asked.

"Roger Munson. Ph.D. Works in my department at MIT. In his fifties, divorced, absolutely brilliant."

"Good." Alice rapped her pencil on the table. "Three good possibilities. Did you come up with anyone, Faye?"

Faye lifted her head wearily. "I. Did. Not. Please. I don't want to date!"

"But you have to agree with us in theory," Marilyn argued.

Faye sighed. "In theory, yes, I suppose I do. Meeting new people is good for us, and dating *can* be rejuvenating. But not always. For example, I was chatting with a young woman in my yoga class, Beth Grey, and she's just fallen in love, which is wonderful, but her boyfriend's family's sending *her* self-esteem into a nosedive."

"Let's get her together with Julia and Carolyn," Shirley suggested. "They've all got relative problems."

"What a good idea!" Faye said. "Now, how should we do this?"

"First," Alice remarked drily, "we should finish our discussion about *you,* Faye. Stop trying to wriggle out of it."

"But I really don't need a man in my life!" Faye contended.

"What's the harm in trying?" Marilyn coaxed. "It could be fun. If nothing else, it could be interesting."

"Yeah, well, it could be *humiliating,* too," Faye grumbled.

"Hey!" Alice pointed an admonishing finger at Faye. "Remember the first rule of the Hot Flash Club. *Don't let fear rule your life.*"

Faye shook her head. "I'm not afraid."

"Then *do* it," Shirley said. "Start with Tank. I can personally vouch for the guy, he won't rape or murder you—"

"Be still, my heart," Faye muttered.

"—and you already know he's not the kind of man you'd match up with long term, so this is just kind of a fun experiment."

"We're not letting you off the hook," Alice said.

With a desperate sigh, Faye capitulated. "All right. I'll go out with Tank."

"Great! I'll phone him tonight to set something up. You're free every night, aren't you?"

Faye snorted. "Thanks for reminding me."

"Speaking of boyfriends." Alice skewered Shirley with a look. "How's Justin?" When Shirley flushed, she increased the pressure. "Has he found another job yet? I mean, he's been unemployed for, um, how many months now?"

Shirley glared. "He's *looking* for another job." Shirley sat up straighter, running a hand over her already smooth hair. "Actually—"

Alice narrowed her eyes at Shirley suspiciously.

Shirley bit the bullet. "I want to hire Justin to teach at The Haven."

"You're shitting me," Alice said.

Shirley's lips thinned in anger. "No, Alice. I am not *shitting* you. I think a course in journal writing and one in poetry and one in creative writing would be an excellent addition to our programs. I mean, come on, Faye teaches art therapy at the spa—"

Alice interrupted, "May I remind you she does it for no pay?"

"That's her choice," Shirley snapped back. "She likes doing it. Besides, Faye's one of the investors, and she'll eventually get a profit on her shares, so it behooves her to help The Haven be successful!" Shirley paused, stunned that she'd actually said *behooves* and wondering if she'd used the word correctly.

Alice turned to Faye and Marilyn. "You're both on the board. What do you think of Justin teaching at The Haven?"

"I think the courses he offers sound interesting," Faye told her. "And he does have a Ph.D."

Marilyn agreed. "And whatever salary

he'd make would be minimal. As a part-time employee, he wouldn't be eligible for health benefits. It wouldn't hurt to give him a trial run." She gave Alice a level stare. "The Haven was Shirley's brainchild. She should have creative control."

Gritting her teeth, Alice gave in. "Fine."

Shirley was eager to change the subject. "Hey! I know how to get our three new kids together. I'll invite them to try, for free, a special course combining Jacuzzi with aromatherapy. The three of you can be there, too, you can get them started talking and, when the time's right, diplomatically slip away."

"That's not a bad idea, Shirley," Alice said.

"I like it, too," Faye agreed. "Although Julia knows I teach art therapy here . . ."

Shirley said, "So what? Teachers should help judge what works."

"Plus, I won't say no to the Jacuzzi and aromatherapy," Marilyn put in.

"Let's do it," Alice said.

Shirley checked her calendar. "Next Friday evening good for you all?"

The other three looked in their appointment books and agreed on the date.

"What a productive meeting this was!" Shirley looked around the table, beaming. "And we didn't even eat chocolate!"

Alice had the final word. "Yet."

11

About twenty miles southwest of Boston lay the tree-lined, money-groomed, wealth-cushioned enclave of Dover. In the heart of this suburb, on Chestnut Street, in a brick Georgian mansion on a three-acre lot enclosed by wrought-iron fences, lived Polly's mother-in-law, Claudia Lodge.

Polly parked her car on the driveway, then stepped out into the bright autumn day. The trees burned like flames in the crisp air, and she wished she could take the time to enjoy the day, but she was a woman on a mission, one she dreaded but knew she must complete, so she dragged her reluctant body to the front door and knocked.

Her mother-in-law opened the door instantly. "Good. You're on time." Claudia's tone implied that she'd spent most of her life waiting for clueless Polly to show up.

"Hello, Claudia," Polly said. Entering the beautiful old home, with its family portraits, antique furniture, thick Persian rugs, and well-polished wooden floors, Polly had the illusion of stepping back into time, or into a book by Henry James. She handed Claudia her light jacket, revealing the beautiful hunter green corduroy dress she'd made herself. She seldom wore dresses, preferring jeans or trousers and shirts, but she'd learned to dress as Claudia preferred.

"You're looking well," Polly dutifully complimented her mother-in-law.

"Don't be ridiculous," Claudia commanded. "I look ill, and I am."

Polly blinked. Now that her eyes had adjusted to the light, so dim in this hallway after the glare of the sun, she could tell that, yes, Claudia had lost weight. "You're ill, Claudia?" she repeated cautiously. Claudia hated anything verging on personal.

Claudia hung Polly's jacket in the hall closet. "Let's do wait until we've had some tea," Claudia said, her tone of voice implying that Polly had done it once again, committed yet another social blunder.

But *you* brought it up first, Polly wanted to retort, and swallowed her remark. She hated how Claudia reduced her, in minutes, to an infantile state of mind.

Obediently, she followed the other woman into the drawing room, sinking, at Claudia's imperious gesture, into the indicated armchair. On the table between them sat the sterling silver tea service that had been in the family for generations. Polly waited while Claudia poured the smoky Hu-Kwa into thin china cups and handed one to her, without asking whether she wanted cream, sugar, or lemon. There was, in Claudia's point of view, only one way to drink tea. Her way.

Claudia was immaculately dressed, as always. She wore a plaid wool skirt, wool sweater and matching cardigan, and a string of pearls. Her hair, once dark, was now white, but shaped as it had been all her life, in a pageboy, folding under just at her ears, to accentuate her pearl earrings. In her youth, Claudia had been a great tennis player and sailor, strong, nimble, and tanned, and now in her eighties the creases and folds of her skin bore testament to all those days in the sun. Nearly six feet, and always slender, she did not try to disguise her height but wore handsome three-inch heels. Although Polly had often rued Claudia's arrogance, she'd always envied her posture, so straight and regal.

Polly sipped the smoky tea. The silence speckled in the air around them, like dust motes. Polly couldn't wait to share her news. "I'm a grandmother now, Claudia! Amy—"

Claudia waved at the air as if dismissing a gnat. "I've asked you here to discuss something important."

Polly swallowed her anger. Claudia had said she was ill—

"Some tests indicate the possibility that I might have ovarian cancer."

"Oh, Claudia," Polly cried, stunned by the news. "I'm so sorry."

Claudia sighed, exasperated. "I didn't ask you here for you to go into a sentimental fit. You can't be any help to me if you're going to be maudlin."

Polly's face flushed, but she straightened. "All right, then. How can I be of help to you?"

Claudia took a sip of her tea, settled the delicate cup in the saucer before replying. When she spoke, she kept her eyes on her tea. "I'm not able to drive any longer. Nothing to do with my illness; my eyes are not good enough for me to renew my license. I need someone to take me to the hospital."

"Well, Claudia, of course, I'll be glad to drive you."

"Good. I have an appointment for Friday afternoon, at three o'clock, at Mass. General, with Dr. Monroe. It would be convenient if you drove me and accompanied me there. The hospital is large, and I'm not as robust as I once was."

"All right," Polly said. "I'll pick you up at two."

"You'll pick me up at one. The traffic might be bad, and the registration procedure is lengthy."

"All right." In a way, it was a relief that Claudia remained her normal prickly, officious self. "One it is."

"Also, I want you to know I have my legal affairs in order."

Polly nodded and waited.

Claudia aimed her dark eyes to a spot just to the side of Polly's left ear. "You will be my executor. I'm leaving everything to the New England Historical Society. Robert Gershong is my lawyer. He has a draft of the will, and I have one, as well, in my safe-deposit box. As executor, you will receive a slight fee, and if there's any particular item you'd like to have—a painting, this silver tea service, whatever—you may choose something. Everything's in order."

"Well," Polly responded carefully, "that's good. That you have everything organized."

"I have written explicit instructions for my burial. My plot is in Forest Hills Cemetery, next to my husband's. I do not want a memorial service of any kind. Simply a few words read at my interment. I've already arranged that with Reverend Alexander."

"Goodness, Claudia, don't you want *some* kind of ceremony? You have so many friends—"

Claudia interrupted, "If you feel unable to carry out my wishes, I'll find someone else to do it."

"Of course I'll carry out your wishes, Claudia."

"Very well. Thank you." Claudia's face was as haughty as marble, but an odd little sound escaped her—a burp?

Polly felt her lips twitch and squelched a childish desire to giggle.

Claudia touched a damask napkin to her

lips. "I'll see you at one on Friday," she murmured.

This was her signal to leave, Polly knew. "Claudia, before I go, can I get anything for you?"

"I'm quite all right, Polly. I'll see you Friday."

"Would you like me to carry the tray into the kitchen?"

Claudia hesitated, then shook her head. "Pearl can deal with it tomorrow."

"Well, then. I'll see you Friday." As she rose to go, Polly yearned to perform some act of consolation, to offer comfort in some way. Since Claudia did not like to be touched, Polly simply said, "Good-bye," and went down the long hallway and out of the dark house.

Polly had always thought people who were comfortable with silence held some kind of power over those who weren't. Were they, perhaps, higher up on some evolutionary scale? Conversation seemed to Polly a normal, basic, universal human need. And there was always so much to discuss—fall fashions, movie-star marriages, politics, even the weather, for heaven's sake. Friday afternoon, as Polly drove Claudia to the hospital, she attempted to converse on these neutral topics, but was met with stony silence.

And yet, Claudia could have asked someone else to drive her to the hospital. Her "friends," were, Polly thought, social acquaintances, the sort of people with whom Claudia *would* discuss fall fashions, charity functions, and politics. Perhaps Claudia didn't want to expose any weakness to them. Still, Claudia could have phoned a limo service or even a cab. Instead, she'd commanded Polly. Which meant what? Nothing that Claudia would ever articulate, not even the simple, obvious fact that Polly was Claudia's only surviving relation.

Once inside, winding their way through the endless hospital corridors, without turning even slightly in Polly's direction, Claudia began to speak, allowing a few syllables to fall from her lips, as if her words were bits of gold she was certain Polly would rush to catch. "The gift shop here is actually rather nice," she said as they passed it. In the elevator she announced, "My primary physi-

cian here went to the same private preschool as Tucker." Polly understood that
this was cocktail-party patter, a pretense of
conversation performed for the benefit of
others in the general vicinity. "Oh, really?"
was the only response required of Polly, and
she duly provided it.

The reception area was large and attractive, with gorgeous silk-screen prints of
flowers and a wall of windows overlooking
the Charles River and Storrow Drive. A bank
of receptionists and secretaries murmured
as they processed the patients who docilely
sat waiting their turn. As they took their own
seats, Polly longed to be her normal chat-
tering self with her mother-in-law, wished
she could relieve the tension by saying what
she felt: "Isn't this scary! Isn't *cancer* the
creepiest word? Don't you want some Valium, or an antidepressant, or at least an
enormous box of chocolates? I do!" But
Claudia took a paperback Edith Wharton
from her purse and began reading. Polly
had also brought a book, so she settled her
glasses on her nose and pretended to read.

"Mrs. Lodge?" A nurse, clipboard in
hand, approached. "Will you come with
me?"

Claudia slipped her book into her purse and rose.

Polly smiled up at her mother-in-law. "Good luck."

Claudia arched a brow. "Come along, Polly, don't dawdle."

Polly blinked. "Um, what?" As a flush reddened her face, she sensed others looking over at her.

"I said," Claudia said in a voice edged with ice, "come along."

Confused, Polly half-rose. "You want me to accompany you?"

Claudia nearly snorted with exasperation. "Of course." Abruptly she turned away, head high, striding along on her elegant heels after the nurse.

"Well, all-righty then," Polly muttered under her breath as she hurried to follow.

The waiting room had been spacious. Back here, physicians in scrubs and stethoscopes surged through a warren of cubicles and offices. The nurse ushered Claudia and Polly into what seemed like a cupboard and helped Claudia up onto the examination table. Claudia allowed Polly to help her remove her mink. In her teal blue suit with the diamond pin on the collar, Claudia looked as if she were on a throne.

"I'm Jane," the nurse announced with a friendly smile as she unrolled the blood-pressure cuff and fit it over Claudia's arm.

"Hello, Jane, I'm Polly." Polly's voice came out high and squeaky. Damn! She was hyperventilating. She hadn't told Claudia she was terrified of doctors and all things medical. This common phobia, called the white-coat syndrome, caused Polly to gulp down a glass of red wine before her own annual physical. The best she could do now was squeeze herself into the farthest corner of the tiny room, where she stood surreptitiously stroking the mink as if she were reassuring a pet.

The door flew open and in strode a hand-some, robust man in a white lab coat. He extended his hand.

"Mrs. Lodge. Nice to see you again."

Claudia briefly touched her perfectly manicured claw to his large hand. "And you, Hugh."

Dr. Monroe turned. "And this is?" He smiled at Polly. He had beautiful blue eyes, a clear and intelligent gaze.

Claudia announced, "Polly Lodge. She'll be assisting me."

As if Claudia were preparing to perform surgery on Hugh Monroe, Polly thought, with a slight touch of hysteria. Polly moved to meet Dr. Monroe's outstretched hand and tripped over her mother-in-law's purse. Fortunately, the physician caught her by the elbow.

"Steady as you go," he said, smiling.

Aware her skin was now a radiant crimson, Polly murmured, "Thanks," and shrank back into her corner, feeling as suave as Jane Eyre on her first day at the orphanage. Claudia glared at her, indignant at Polly's clumsiness. At times like this, Polly was flooded with sensations so powerful she was sure they were engraved into her DNA: embarrassment at being the descendant of Irish peasants who fled, starving, from their green country to the wild Boston shore where they scrubbed the floors and waited on people who looked like Claudia. So potent, so compelling, were these emotions, they were almost like memories, paralyzing her. She reminded herself that Tucker had found her beautiful, that her generous curves had brought him joy.

"Now, Mrs. Lodge." Dr. Monroe set his blue-eyed gaze on the older woman. "How are you feeling?"

"I feel fine." Claudia spoke it as a challenge.

"I'm glad to hear that."

Nurse Jane folded up her blood-pressure cuff and scribbled in a folder.

"I'll just have a peek at your abdomen," Dr. Monroe said.

Nurse Jane pulled the curtain on its track, shutting Polly out for a few moments of blissful solitude.

The curtain opened. Dr. Monroe stationed himself on a stool while Claudia sat on the edge of the table and the nurse waited at her elbow.

"Blood pressure's great, Mrs. Lodge," the doctor announced. "Your heart's in good shape, your lungs are clear, you're generally a fit, healthy woman, which is all for the good." The nurse handed him a folder. Setting glasses on his nose, he scanned some papers, then peered over them. "However, as we said at your last visit, the CA125 blood tests indicated ovarian cancer. Now we have the results of the ultrasound and the biopsy. You do have a malignant tumor."

"Oh, dear," Polly whispered. Those had to be the ugliest words in the English language. She felt her own body shrinking back from the doctor's words, but Claudia sat with majestic, implacable rigidity.

"The ultrasound and biopsy indicate that the tumor began in an area in a cul-de-sac between the vagina and the rectum known as the pouch of Douglas."

"Ridiculous," Claudia sniffed. "I've never heard of such a thing."

She's never heard of the vagina or rectum, either, Polly thought giddily.

Dr. Monroe nodded. "No, not many of us have. It's a spot rarely mentioned. I haven't encountered it since medical school."

"Since Claudia has it, perhaps it should be named the evening bag of Douglas," Polly offered. To her surprise, Claudia's mouth twitched with the ghost of a smile.

Dr. Monroe laughed. "Not a bad idea." He gave Polly an appreciative smile. Turning back to Claudia, he said, "You and I have discussed the possibility of surgery, which you say you do not want."

"Absolutely not. I have no intention of letting some idiot nurse turn me into a vegetable."

"Well, that probably wouldn't be the result," Dr. Monroe informed her evenly. "But your tumor is wrapped around your organs in such a way that it would make an operation impossible, anyway. You could have a few rounds of chemotherapy to shrink the tumor. This might provide several more months of good-quality life for you—"

Claudia interrupted. "But would it also have negative effects?"

The doctor nodded. "It might."

"I'd experience nausea? I'd lose my hair?"

"Not necessarily. We have medications to control nausea, and the kind of chemo I'm thinking of for you would be very mild."

"Then why bother?"

Patiently, Hugh Monroe explained, "Because, as I said, it might provide you with a few more months of good-quality life—"

"Or it might not, correct?"

"We never can be absolutely certain about the results of chemo, but statistics are on the side—"

Claudia shook her head. "No. No chemotherapy."

"You don't have to decide right this moment," Dr. Monroe reminded her. "Think about it for a few days."

Claudia shrugged. "With or without the chemo, what can I expect to happen?"

"Over the next few months, you will probably experience weakness, constipation, and loss of appetite. But you shouldn't worry about pain. We have medications that will take care of that. The tumor is quite advanced. You must have experienced some symptoms, Mrs. Lodge. I'm surprised you haven't been to see me before now."

"I don't believe in making a fuss over matters."

"Yes, that's the good old Yankee way." The physician moved closer, putting his hand on Claudia's. "Fairly soon, I'd like you to get in touch with Martha Wright, who's in charge of hospice—"

Claudia withdrew her hand. "I won't need hospice."

"Perhaps not for a while, no. But you will need someone to get your groceries and perform other errands—"

Claudia shrugged. "Polly can do that."

Polly can? Polly thought with surprise. Okay, but how about asking Polly?

"Now, Mrs. Lodge, tell me, how are you feeling?"

"I'm fine."

"Are you eating?"

"Of course."

"Yet you've lost weight." When Claudia didn't reply, the doctor continued, "Are you living alone?"

"I have a housekeeper."

"And she lives with you?"

"No," Claudia admitted sullenly.

"You might want to consider having her move in with you. Since you don't want hospice. I don't mean immediately, but eventually. And now is the time for you to get your legal affairs in order."

"My legal affairs are already in order."

"Excellent." Dr. Monroe stepped away from the bedside. "Do you have any questions?"

Claudia nodded. "Are you planning to attend the Clarks' cocktail party?"

"Oh!" His eyebrows rose in surprise. "Um, I'm not sure."

"You ought to, you know. It's probably the best party of the fall. Phyllis Clark told me they're having the Guarrancia Quartet play."

"Well, perhaps I'll see you there. Nice to

see you again, Mrs. Lodge. Great to meet you, Polly." With a swift smile all around, he left the room.

The nurse helped Claudia from the table. Claudia gathered her things, and they returned to the reception area to schedule her next appointment. Claudia's back was straight and her head high, but Polly noticed how the older woman seemed to sway slightly with each step, as if working hard to keep her balance.

As they walked back through the corridors, Polly racked her brain: What would Claudia like right now? Could anything provide momentary pleasure? "Why don't we have some tea before I drive you home?" Polly asked.

"Here?" Claudia looked as if Polly had just spit on the floor.

"Sure. They've got some great little restaurants in the basement. I ate there when my friend—"

"I have no intention of eating in a hospital."

"Okay, then, let's go to the Ritz. My treat."

"No, thank you, Polly. I'd prefer to go home."

Polly knew better than to discuss private

matters in the public corridors of the hospital, but once they were settled in the car, she turned to her mother-in-law. "Claudia. I'm really upset about this diagnosis and your decision. I think you should reconsider having chemotherapy—"

"Please do not tell me what to do, Polly," Claudia snapped. "And would you be good enough to stop dawdling and drive me home? I'm tired."

To placate her, Polly put her key in the ignition and started the car. Then she tried again. "I know you're a private and independent person, Claudia. But I do want you to know I'm more than ready to do anything I can to help you."

"I'm sure you are," Claudia replied, sounding bored.

"I have a friend who's a nurse—"

"I have every confidence in Dr. Monroe."

"Of course. That's good. But this is such an enormous matter, Claudia. I could find you some books on the subject—"

"Polly, you're becoming tiresome. Let's have no more discussion of my so-called imminent death, please. In fact, I'd appreciate some silence right now."

Polly nodded and didn't speak again until

they reached Claudia's house. "Would you like me to come in with you now?"

"Don't be ridiculous. I intend to take a nap."

"Very well. But Dr. Monroe said you'll need someone to fetch groceries and do errands for you."

"True. But I'm perfectly capable of dialing the phone to ask you when I need something, Polly. I'm not that far gone."

"I didn't mean to imply—"

"And another thing. I'd appreciate it if you'd keep this information to yourself. I don't want anyone gossiping about me."

"Of course, I won't say a word—"

"Not that you run in the same crowd I do, of course, but rumors always spread somehow." Claudia opened her car door.

"Claudia, let me help you up the steps," Polly volunteered.

"Don't fuss so!" Claudia shot Polly such a venomous glance, Polly cringed.

When Polly entered her own home just after five, she was tired and a bit freaked-out. She wanted a good stiff drink. She wanted a pint of chocolate ice cream. She wanted to kick something. She felt so sorry for Claudia, and so trapped by her—

The phone rang.

"Mom?" David's young voice was like balm to her soul. "How are you?"

"I'm fine, darling, how's Jehoshaphat?"

"Fat and happy. Amy thought you might like to come out for a visit."

"Oh, I'd love it!" Polly felt like a wallflower being asked to the senior prom. "You have no idea how I'd love to see that little baby, David! I've just been driving Claudia to the doctor's. She's got ovarian cancer!"

"That's terrible! Poor Claudia," David said. "I'll send her some flowers."

"That's sweet of you, David. Oh, I'm so glad I'm going to see the baby. It makes me feel like the sun's about to shine!"

"Look, I've got to go, Jehoshaphat needs changing. Can you come tomorrow about eleven?"

"Wild horses couldn't keep me away!" Polly hung up the phone, her exhaustion forgotten. David's loving voice, the promise of seeing her grandson tomorrow morning, oh, how this made her soul soar!

The phone rang again.

"Mom?" David's voice was apologetic. "Listen, I've just been talking with Amy."

Polly could hear Amy in the background, chirping away. "Yes?"

"Amy feels"—*chirp chirp chirp!*—"and *I* do, too, we *both* feel, that while you're taking care of Claudia, it would be better if you didn't come near the baby. He's so vulnerable, you know, and germs are so easily transmitted—"

"But, David!" Polly gasped. "Honey, I won't be coming to you right from Claudia's! And of course I'll shower and change clothes—"

"Sorry, Mom. Amy just doesn't"—*chirp chirp chirp!*—"Amy *and I* just don't want to take the chance. Let's wait until things are resolved with Claudia before you see Jehoshaphat again, okay?"

"Resolved?" In spite of herself, Polly's voice became shrill. "You mean, wait til! Claudia dies?"

"Well, yeah, I guess," David answered meekly.

"But David, that could be *months,*" Polly protested. "It could be a year!"

"I'm sorry, Mom. I've got to think about

my family's health. I just don't want to take any chances."

"I'm so disappointed, David," Polly said, hating herself as she spoke those words. She had never wanted to be a *disappointed* kind of mother. Rallying, she forced cheer into her voice. "But I do understand, and of course I want your son to be healthy and free from any kind of possible threat."

"We'll send you photos," David promised.

"Oh, *lovely,*" Polly gushed. "And give him a kiss for me."

She said good-bye, hung up the phone, and burst into tears.

12

To say that Sonny had relatives was like saying lasagna had calories, Beth thought, as she and Sonny arrived at his cousin's home for the annual Halloween party. The driveway and street on both sides were crammed with sports cars, trucks, and motorcycles. A double row of jack-o'-lanterns, each carved with a ghastly grimace from which candlelight flickered, lined the sidewalk to the ranch house, which was hung with enough bats, cobwebs, witches, and ghouls to frighten Dracula.

Holding Sonny's arm, Beth stepped with care over the curb and along the walk. Her white, plastic, four-inch high-heeled boots were not only uncomfortable, they were hell to walk in. She prayed she wouldn't turn her ankle and fall.

Was she a fool to try to look glamorous?

Last year, Beth had gone to a Halloween party at another grad student's house, where her costume had been a great success. She'd put rocks in the pockets of an old raincoat, woven twigs into her hair, and gone as Virginia Woolf after she was dragged out of the river. That wouldn't work with this bunch, she knew. When she'd tried to get suggestions from Sonny, he'd been hopeless.

Then she'd mentioned her dilemma to Sonny's mother. Even now, the memory of her premarriage bonding moment with her incipient mother-in-law warmed Beth like a cup of hot cocoa.

It had been a weekday night at the Youngs'. Sonny was in the den, watching a baseball game with his father. Bobbie was in the kitchen, making cupcakes for the community bake sale, and Beth was there in the heart of the family, helping. It was her job to ice the chocolate cupcakes with silly faces. Beth was so thrilled to be included in a family production and so nervous about doing it right that every mouth on every face had a wavery squiggle. Fortunately, Bobbie thought that was deliberate.

"What are you wearing to the Halloween party?" Bobbie asked.

"I'm not sure," Beth answered. She'd thought of Cinderella and Prince Charming, but that was way too gooey. Heathcliff and Catherine? Anthony and Cleopatra? Beth couldn't help thinking of famous lovers, but she was too timid to suggest them. She and Sonny *were* lovers, though, and she did want something cute and clever and also something that made it clear as sun on snow that she and Sonny were a couple. "Sonny says he hates dressing up."

"How about Sonny and Cher?" Bobbie suggested. "That way, Sonny can come as himself." She'd laughed her wonderful laugh. "All my other children loved wearing costumes for Halloween, but not Sonny. When he was a little kid, he'd insist on sticking a paper bag with three holes in it on his head."

Beth forced herself to ask, "What about when he was a teenager?" She might as well bring up the days when Sonny had dated the peerless Robin, since it was Sonny's mother's favorite topic in the entire universe.

Sure enough, Bobbie beamed. "Oh,

Robin made him dress up, that's for sure. Let's see, one year they went as Joe DiMaggio and Marilyn Monroe . . ."

Just kill me now, Beth thought, intimidated by any woman who had the self-esteem to impersonate Marilyn Monroe.

"Another year," Bobbie continued, "they went as Beauty and the Beast. Sonny hated that, the costume was so elaborate and he got all sweaty behind the mask."

"Well," Beth mused, wondering how to discuss the image thing without entirely humiliating herself in front of the other woman, "I can see Sonny loving the Sonny part, but I don't know if I could pull off Cher. For one thing, she's so tall." Not to mention drop-dead gorgeous, glamorous, fabulous, amazing, stunning . . .

"You could wear high heels," Bobbie said. She studied Beth a moment. "Go to a costume shop and rent a wig of long black hair and some outrageous costume. Lots of glitter, jewelry, lots of makeup. You could pull it off."

"I could?" Beth squeaked.

"Sure." Bobbie waggled her eyebrows at Beth. "Show Sonny your wild side."

So Beth had gone to a costume shop,

and now here she was, in this slinky, little silver lamé dress that didn't quite fit, with a neckline plunging low enough to expose exactly how small her breasts were. She had a feeling she was going to spend most of the night arranging the waist-length black hair of her wig to fall down her shoulders and over her bust. Sonny told her she looked great, but Sonny *always* said she looked great.

The cousin's house was packed with an array of characters who might have delighted Beth if she hadn't been so overwhelmed. Gandalf whispered to Queen Elizabeth, Elton John had his arms around Bigfoot, Harry Potter danced with Cleopatra. A panoply of ghouls, ghosts, and gremlins swarmed through the room, drinks in hand, or lounged against the walls, which were hung with spiderwebs and bloody heads. From the fireplace flue hung a leg dripping with fake blood and gore. Dance music, punctuated with ear-shattering screams, throbbed. The air smelled of booze and chili.

Sonny plunged into the mêlée, and Beth followed, plastering a smile on her face as she squeezed through the crowd. In the kitchen, Sonny poured Beth a beer, at the same time yelling introductions to his cousin Saradyne, who was emptying nacho chips into a basket. Seconds later, Sonny was in a deep conversation with a vampire about a manifold.

Saradyne was plump, pregnant, and rosy-cheeked, as likable as a puppy. Beth asked, "Can I help you?"

"Sure, honey!" Saradyne shouted. "Take these out to the living room and put them on the table with the salsa, okay?"

"Okay," Beth agreed with a great big smile, but walking away from Sonny, the one face she knew in this mob, felt like setting off on a paper raft into a sea of sharks. It didn't help that she was about as steady on her heels as a cat on an ice rink. Her metaphors were getting mixed, she knew, but nothing to compare with the jumble of backs, fronts, arms, tusks, horns, and tails she had to dodge as she carried the enormous basket of nachos through the crowd.

Everyone she passed was laughing, dancing, talking, flirting. The table, draped in orange plastic, centered with a huge jack-o'-lantern, was laden with plates, napkins, spoons, a hot pot of chili, platters of fresh veggies, and bowls of salsa. Beth squeezed between a Martian and Liza Minnelli, set the nachos down, then turned to study the crowd. People were crushed together. Even in her four-inch heels, she was shorter than everyone else. A man in a Freddie Krueger mask glanced at Beth and walked away. Even Freddie Krueger dissed her! Beth flushed. She felt like such a wallflower.

Then she saw a clown coming toward her. Clowns are nice, Beth thought desperately, and forced herself to look inviting. The clown leaned toward her—she thought he was going to say something and leaned toward him. Taking a deep breath, she said, "Hi!"

"Hi," the clown said. He reached past her, grabbed a handful of nachos, and walked away, spraying crumbs as he shoved the nachos into his mouth.

So much for nice clowns. Beth began to shove her way through the crowd back to the kitchen to find Sonny. She'd just stick by Sonny's side all evening, pretending she was part of his group. Maybe he'd even introduce her to someone who didn't belong to his enormous family. She would be brave and she would persevere, and—

And then she saw Sonny, leaning against the dining room wall, grinning, and talking to—to—*Cher*? A knockout, drop-dead, amazing-looking woman tossed her long black hair and laughed. Her long, sleek legs were accentuated by high heels and black fishnet stockings fastened to a garter belt. A long black corset pushed her stunning breasts up. The costume made her seem more naked than if she'd worn nothing at all.

Beth felt, in her ill-fitting silver lamé, like Peter Pan in drag. Still, she forced herself forward, until she was at Sonny's side, or as close as she could get to him.

"Oh, hi, Beth!" said Robin with a dazzling smile.

Of course it would be Robin, Beth thought. Of course Sonny's old love would be dressed as Cher.

"Hi, Robin!" Beth answered with pretended warmth.

"Let me guess who you are," Robin suggested, cocking her beautiful head. "Um, let's see. Morticia Addams? Anjelica Huston?"

Beth smiled through gritted teeth. "Cher!"

"Cher?" Robin blinked. "But *I'm* Cher,

honey. I guess Bobbie didn't tell you. I always come as Cher. Every year. Ever since Sonny and I won Best Costume Couple, back in high school. Not that it matters. I mean, Cher has so many different looks. Next year I want to have a long blond wig like she wore in her last video."

Beth looked at Sonny. "You didn't *tell* me . . ."

Sonny shrugged. "Sorry. Never even thought about it."

Robin continued to babble while Beth processed that Sonny's mother had purposefully embarrassed her. Bobbie was a one-woman Robin Fan Club, so she had to know, *of course* she knew, that Robin always came as Cher. Bobbie probably had photos in one of her zillion albums of Robin as Cher in every variation. The question was, why would Bobbie sabotage Beth? Did she really want to run Beth off? Did she really believe that would clear the path and make Sonny fall back in love with Robin?

Hot tears of anger burned in her eyes. She had to get out of here. She couldn't let anyone see her cry. Confused, humiliated, and angry, Beth made an abrupt turn and strode away from Robin and Sonny.

Or tried to. The hem of her silver dress caught in one of her heels. In a hellishly drawn-out moment, she fell, reaching out with both hands to catch herself, wrenching her back painfully. Sonny grabbed at her arm, but that twisted her spine even more. His hand slipped away as she crumpled to the rug, where she lay in agony among a crowd of feet. Well, *now* she had everyone's attention.

"Are you all right?" Robin asked.

Beth tried to push herself up, but her back, like a fiery rope, restrained her. "My back," she managed to gasp.

Sonny swooped down like a hero, lifting her up in his arms. "What happened?"

"I caught my dress in my heel and twisted my back."

"Do you want to go to the emergency room?"

"No, no," Beth protested. "Let me just go lie down on a bed for a moment."

Sonny shoved through the crowd and down the hall to a bedroom, where he settled her gently on the bed. "I'll get some aspirin." He went away.

She closed her eyes, trying to relax, to release the pain.

Saradyne appeared in the doorway. "Someone said you fell? Are you okay?"

"I'm fine," Beth assured her. "I just twisted my back."

"I'll get you a heating pad. It will do wonders."

"You poor little thing." Suddenly Robin was there next to the bed. In her sleek Sex Queen black, she oozed health, sensuality, and superior genes. "What can I do for you?" she asked sweetly.

Beth closed her eyes again and groaned.

13

In the late afternoon, Carolyn sat at her paper-strewn desk in her office at Sperry's, scanning documents and signing them, although her body begged for a nap. As much as she would have liked to turn all directorial tasks over to her father, it was out of the question. Aubrey was absentminded these days, too busy with his new wife to focus properly on his work.

And this was good, Carolyn reminded herself. Her father was obviously invigorated by his marriage. He looked younger and happier. Certainly the food Heather prepared him was healthier than the heavier, more traditional meat-and-potato meals Mrs. B. had been serving for years. Once a week, when Carolyn and Hank and Aubrey and his wife ate together, Heather insisted on preparing the dinner, and Carolyn was impressed by the delicious, low-fat, high-fiber food Heather served. Aubrey had begun taking daily walks, too, with Heather at his side, the pair of them in matching navy blue jogging outfits. They looked pretty cute together, actually, so Carolyn was doing her best to suppress her anxieties.

After all, she had done what she could to satisfy herself that Heather was not a gold digger. Recently, when Carolyn had finally found her father in the company office alone, she'd summoned enough courage to ask him whether Heather had signed a prenuptial agreement. Yes, Aubrey had assured her, Heather had. In the case of divorce or death, Heather was to get a lump sum of $100,000. She'd also signed a statement waiving any rights to stock in the Sperry Paper Company. Aubrey made it clear that he found Carolyn's concerns about his sweet new wife insulting.

Carolyn had been sorry to give him reason to be angry with her, but glad she'd asked. Her suspicions were allayed.

Although . . . she could not forget the moment when she'd found Heather prying into the household accounts, how Heather's mask of sweetness had fallen away, how threatening, almost feral, Heather had looked. Carolyn had discussed this with Hank, but he thought that Carolyn had over-reacted. Wasn't her pregnancy making her more emotionally volatile?

Perhaps. Carolyn asked her private sec-retary, in strictest confidence, to check out Heather Grinnell online. The secretary re-ported that Heather was exactly whom she appeared to be: a thirty-two-year-old woman who'd grown up in Arlington, Mas-sachusetts, the daughter of a plumber and a housewife. Heather had, as she'd said, one brother, Harry, thirty-four years old, who had taken over his father's plumbing busi-ness. Both parents were deceased. Accord-ing to the online white page directory, the address of both adult children was their parents' house.

Next, Carolyn decided to get to know Heather. She offered to take Heather shop-ping for a dress for the company's upcom-ing annual Christmas party. Before their shopping expedition, Carolyn treated Heather to lunch, and afterward, to tea. During their girls-together day, Carolyn made several subtle attempts to probe beneath Heather's girlish surface, but Heather had remained all sweetness and light.

On Carolyn's desk, the clock's hands clicked to five o'clock. Everyone else was going home; she should, too. She wasn't accomplishing anything here.

The towering old house was silent as she let herself in. Hank was out of town overnight on an environmental fact-finding visit. She hurried down the hall to her suite of rooms and collapsed on the sofa, not bothering to take her coat off, instead pulling it over her as a cover as she curled on the sofa and slipped gratefully into sleep.

A knock at her door awakened her. Yawning, she opened her eyes and checked her watch. She'd slept for over an hour.

"Come in," she called, sitting up and stretching.

"Carolyn?" Mrs. B., their housekeeper, looked in. "Do you have a moment?"

"Of course. Come in. Sit down." Too hot

now, Carolyn tossed her coat aside and smoothed her hair.

"Thank you, dear." Mrs. B. entered, taking care to shut the door tightly behind her. She settled in a chair. "My, look how big you've gotten! How are you feeling?"

"Slothful," Carolyn said wryly. "What's up?"

The frown line between Mrs. B.'s eyes deepened. "Perhaps you already know this. I just feel that it's my responsibility to mention—you're aware that there's a line of guaranteed credit on the household account."

"Of course."

"And also on your father's personal checking account."

The baby seemed to be pinching her bladder with her toes. Carolyn changed positions. "I didn't know about my father's account. I've never had occasion to use it. Now that you mention it, I'm not surprised. We all have lines of credit, it's standard. We set it up for the household account for emergencies—fire, the roof falling in, whatever."

"The thing is, Carolyn, the bank statements came the other day. I balanced it against the checkbook. Your household account has had fifty thousand dollars drawn on its credit line."

"Really?" Carolyn frowned. "I can't imagine why."

"So I took the liberty, because, you know, I open all your father's personal mail for him and sort it—he gets so many requests for charitable donations, so many invitations. I opened his bank statement. His personal checking account just had one hundred fifty thousand dollars withdrawn from the personal credit line."

A cold wave of dread clutched Carolyn.

"I don't mean to cause trouble. You know I don't want to overstep any boundaries." She leaned forward, peering at Carolyn. "Carolyn, are you all right?"

A mysterious force boiled inside her. This must be how a volcano feels just before it blows, Carolyn thought. She put one hand on her belly and the other over her eyes. "Just a bit dizzy."

"Oh, dear. Oh, I'm so sorry." Mrs. B. looked stricken. "I shouldn't have—I didn't mean—perhaps I should have waited—"

Carolyn shook her head briskly. "Mrs. B.,

it's all right. Please, don't worry. You absolutely did the right thing, coming to me."

Mrs. B.'s voice broke. "I care so much about you and your father."

"And you know we couldn't keep this house going without you." The housekeeper was getting old, Carolyn realized with a shock. She assured her, "You were right to come to me. I'll talk with Father and let you know what's going on. In the meantime, don't fret."

"Thank you, dear." Mrs. B. rose and went away.

Carolyn's heart surged, agitated and alarmed.

———

That evening, Carolyn made herself a grilled-cheese sandwich to eat with the enormous salad and ratatouille Mrs. B. had left for her. She ate in bed. It felt so good to put her legs up! She wondered whether she ought to have a bed, or at least a recliner, moved into the office for the remainder of her pregnancy.

Yet as tired as she was, Carolyn knew she'd never sleep tonight. Anxiety pulsed through her like a breaking news broadcast on a television screen.

Aubrey had probably bought a *fabulous* car for his new wife, Carolyn decided. Except there was no new car in the garage. All right then, a fur coat, and tickets for a cruise around the world—it was easy to spend $200,000.

It was almost eleven o'clock when she saw headlights flash in the driveway. Ready for battle, Carolyn headed down the hall.

"Oh!" Heather peeped as she and Aubrey entered. "Hello, Carolyn! I didn't expect to see you up so late!"

"Did you have a good evening?" Carolyn asked conversationally.

"Wonderful," Heather cooed. "I've never had such delicious food before in all my life."

Aubrey helped his wife slip out of her coat—it *was* fur. "What's up?" he asked Carolyn.

"There's something I need to discuss with you. Won't take a moment." Forcing a smile at Heather, she added, "It's just business, Heather."

But Aubrey squinted his eyes suspiciously at Carolyn and wrapped a protective arm around Heather. "I want Heather to learn about our business, Carolyn. She's welcome to sit in on any discussion."

"Fine." Carolyn led them into the living room, flicking on a few of the lamps. Carolyn claimed the best armchair. Heather settled on the sofa, with Aubrey close by. Aubrey looked dashing in his expensive suit, his cheeks ruddy from the cold air, his eyes sparkling. He looked like a happy man.

"Father, I'm sorry to do this now, but I won't sleep if I don't get it settled." Carolyn clenched her hands and straightened her back defensively. "Mrs. B. came to me today, terribly concerned about the money you've withdrawn on your credit line from the household account and your own private one."

Her father's face reddened dangerously. "I hardly think this qualifies as an emergency."

Carolyn leaned forward. "Please, Father. I don't want a detailed accounting. Just a brief explanation."

"I won't have you accusing me of mishandling my own funds!" Aubrey snapped.

"I'm not *accusing* you, Father," Carolyn replied, stunned at his sudden anger.

Aubrey's voice shook. "You have no right—"

"I have every right—"

"Oh, dear!" Heather burst out. "I never meant to cause trouble between the two of you!"

Aubrey stared at Heather, amazed. "You aren't causing us any trouble, darling."

"I only wanted to make you happy, Aubrey." Heather wrung her hands together. "I tried using the housekeeping funds, but there wasn't enough money, and besides, Carolyn was so angry when I looked in the housekeeping computer! I wanted it to be a wonderful surprise for Christmas! I had such plans! My brother was going to come help me set everything up. Now it's all spoiled!"

"Darling girl, nothing's spoiled," Aubrey promised soothingly.

"What's spoiled?" Carolyn demanded.

"New f-f-f-furniture," Heather stammered. "Your place is so masculine, Aubrey, so cold. I wanted to surprise you with a more r-r-r-romantic bedroom. I bought a b-b-b-beautiful new bed. I know you like nice things, Aubrey, so I scoured all the antique shops in the area. I was going to have the new things set up Christmas Eve day."

"What a wonderful thing to do," Aubrey said.

"But wait," Carolyn said. "That still doesn't explain how the money—"

"I gave Heather my passwords and protocols for transferring funds from those accounts." Aubrey was still red-faced, and his voice was stern as he spoke to his daughter. "I gave her free access to my funds. After all, she is my wife. It's only natural she'd want to change our part of the house for our own comfort. How much is Mrs. B. worried about?"

"Two hundred thousand dollars."

"Well." Aubrey paused, then regrouped. "That doesn't seem exorbitant for new furnishings."

Carolyn disagreed, but kept silent.

Heather's lower lip quivered.

"I think you owe Heather an apology," Aubrey told Carolyn.

"What for?" Now Carolyn was angry. "I didn't accuse her of anything. I only asked you for an explanation."

Heather sat up straight, sniffing, blinking back tears, the perfect picture of the brave little soldier. "I wanted to buy furniture that was really elegant. *Important* furniture. It's not like Aubrey is just starting out in life, after all."

The implication lay unspoken before them: Aubrey's old. This furniture will be the last he has until he dies. How heartless of you to deprive him of joy.

"Are you satisfied?" Aubrey asked curtly. Before Carolyn could reply, he stood up. "This is all the time I want to spend on this unfortunate interrogation. I'm taking Heather to our quarters now where we can turn our thoughts to happier matters."

Carolyn sighed. "Good night, then, Father. Good night, Heather."

"Good night," Aubrey and Heather replied in sync.

Carolyn watched the pair leave the room, so closely entwined they moved as one. She was exhausted, vaguely embarrassed, and still not entirely satisfied. Her pulse hammered in her throat.

14

Agnes and Belinda were on the living room
sofa, watching *Wheel of Fortune.* Agnes
had her granddaughter sitting on her right,
and her enormous pocketbook stationed on
her left, right next to her thigh, as if she were
in a train station and needed to protect it
from theft. Julia would have bet $500 a new
jar of Marshmallow Fluff was hidden inside
the purse.

Julia squatted in front of Belinda, who
clutched Kitty Balierina with one hand. Belinda still wore a pink leotard and ballet slippers. When, after the Halloween party last
week, Belinda had refused to take off her
ballerina costume, Julia had had a genius
idea. She'd enrolled Belinda in ballet class.
Belinda loved it.

"Okay, curly girly," Julia said brightly, tugging on Belinda's toes, "Dad and I are going

out to a movie! You get to have Grammy for the whole evening!"

Belinda looked sullenly at Julia and stuck her thumb in her mouth.

"Can I kiss Kitty Ballerina good-bye?" Julia asked.

Belinda shook her head and clutched her doll tightly to her chest. Agnes smiled.

Fine, Julia thought. *Embarrass me in front of my archenemy, you little traitor.* Rising, she leaned forward and quickly pecked Belinda on the top of her head. "Later, gator."

Tim ruffled his daughter's hair and kissed her unresponsive cheek. "Have fun, Belly."

At the door, Julia turned. Although Agnes had made frequent Gestapo Stealth Raids, this was the first time she'd babysat for Belinda since Julia and Tim had married. "Agnes, I've left the phone numbers of the restaurant and movie by the kitchen phone. We've got lots of tea and cookies in the cupboard, and Belinda's nightie—"

"I believe I know my way around my daughter's home!" Agnes bristled, insulted. "I helped her decorate Belinda's room!" *You thoughtless bitch!*

A soft answer turns away wrath, Julia reminded herself. "Yes, and it's a beautiful room."

"We'd better go or we'll be late," Tim cut in. "Thanks, Agnes. See you both later."

During the ride to the restaurant, Julia felt smothered by the thick venomous cloud of Agnes's dislike. She wanted to roll down the car window and stick her head out, like a Newfoundland on a hot night. But once they were seated in the restaurant, with a glass of ruby red wine in her hand, Julia relaxed. Tim relaxed. They stopped talking about Belinda and Agnes. Tim talked about work, and as Julia listened, she felt her spirits rise. She loved him so much. She'd almost forgotten that.

During the movie, Tim held her hand. In the car afterward, he pulled her against him and kissed her so thoroughly, Julia nearly melted into the seat.

"My, my," she whispered. "We'll have to have Agnes babysit more often."

———

The autumn night was brisk, slapping their cheeks with cold as they hurried from the car to the house. Inside, it was like the Sahara. Clearly Agnes had changed the thermostat. Agnes was in the same spot on the sofa, watching television.

"How did it go?" Tim asked.

"Oh, we had a wonderful time!" Agnes stood up, clutching her purse against her chest, no doubt hiding the Marshmallow Fluff. "We watched television, and I made her a snack, and then I gave her some little prezzies. An adorable baby doll. I made a dress for Belinda just like the doll's dress, pink with white lace, so sweet! Belinda liked the dress so much she went to sleep in it!"

Julia laughed. "She does get attached to her clothing. She wore her Halloween ballerina costume day and night until she had the flu and barfed on the net."

Agnes's face fell. "You mean the dress *I made* for her is nothing special."

"Oh, no, Agnes, not at all!" Julia protested. "I'm sure the dress you—"

"I know what you meant." *Nothing good, that's for sure, you sadistic slut!* Agnes turned to Tim. "She went to sleep at nine thirty, Tim." Head high, Agnes went to the hall closet. "And I did all the dishes and cleaned the kitchen."

"Thanks, Agnes," Tim said.

"It was nothing." Agnes pulled on her gray down coat.

"Agnes," Julia said, "you're not leaving! We thought you'd spend the night here."

"I'll sleep better in my own bed." *Away from you, you heartless bitch.*

"But Agnes," Tim said, "it's a three-hour drive back to the Berkshires."

"Well, I know that, of course. But I've got my gospel tapes to play, and a nice Thermos of hot chocolate to keep me awake on the way." She patted her capacious bag.

"Please don't go," Julia begged. "I hate the thought of you driving all alone through the night. Stay here. Sleep in your room."

With a martyred expression, Agnes said, "I wouldn't feel comfortable."

"But you've stayed here before," Tim reminded her.

"True, but George was always with me. No, I'm leaving. I had a lovely time with my granddaughter, and six hours of driving here and back is a small price for me to pay for the pleasure of seeing my daughter's little girl." Slump-shouldered, she left.

Julia and Tim stared at each other, half-amused, half-depressed.

"Will I ever be able to win with that woman?" Julia asked.

"Just don't take it personally," Tim said. "Agnes would behave the same way toward any woman who took Annette's place." He pulled Julia against him. "But don't let her spoil our mood. I'm feeling relaxed and just a little bit amorous." To prove his point, he nuzzled beneath her ear and kissed her throat.

"Mmm." Julia leaned against her husband, giving herself over to the rush of lust.

"I'll check the doors and shut off the lights," Tim said. "You get ready for bed."

"Lovely." Julia trailed her fingers down his torso, then went down the hall to their bedroom, taking a moment to peek in at Belinda. The child was tucked in bed, sound asleep, Kitty Ballerina next to her.

Not bothering to turn on the bright overhead light, Julia crossed her darkened bedroom and flicked on the bedside lamp. Dreamily, she undressed, thinking this might be the night to wear the red lace teddy Tim had bought her last Valentine's Day. Naked, she strolled into the bathroom.

And stopped dead, every hair on her body bristling like an animal scenting danger.

She scanned the room. Next to the sink she kept a tray of lotions, creams, and bath salts. Everything had been moved.

Well, Julia thought. Well, okay. Perhaps Agnes used her hand cream. So what? But Agnes always used the other bath that served the guest bedroom and Belinda.

She opened the cupboard where she kept her tampons, pads, potions, creams, and powders. Here, too, everything was just slightly in the wrong place.

Feeling slightly sick to her stomach, Julia returned to her bedroom and turned on the overhead light. In the bright glare, she opened her chest of drawers.

The top drawer held her serviceable everyday cotton undies and sports bras, as well as her few bits of sexy lingerie. Hidden beneath, Julia kept several pair of old cotton panties, the stains from menstrual blood washed and bleached to pale taupe blotches, ready for the first day of her period, when she often, in spite of all precautions, bled through everything. Now these stained garments lay on top of her other lingerie. The sight was like a kick in the stomach.

In the other three drawers, her T-shirts and sweaters had also been rearranged. Obviously Agnes had gone through her clothing. Either she didn't care whether Julia knew or wanted Julia to know and was daring Julia to confront her.

Sick at heart, Julia opened Tim's drawers, hoping to find them in similar disarray. No, everything here was as neat as it had been earlier today, when Julia had folded his laundry and put it away.

In the closet, Tim's jackets, shirts, and trousers hung in their usual places, but Julia's clothes had been moved around. Because most of her clothes were black, she'd developed a kind of ranking system, putting her best black slacks and shirts at the far end of the closet, because she used them the least, and hanging her everyday jeans, trousers, and shirts at the front, where she could grab something in a hurry. Now her expensive black crêpe Ralph Lauren pants were mixed in with the ordinary clothes. Her little black knit Prada shirt was balled up on the floor, beneath one of her good high-heeled shoes. When Julia retrieved it, she found the shoulder seam ripped.

Moaning, she backed away from the closet.

Tim came into the room, pulling his tie from his shirt collar. "Belinda's sleeping like a—what's wrong?"

"My clothes," Julia gasped. "Agnes went through my clothes."

"What are you talking about?"

"This." She held her shirt out to him. "She went through my things. She ripped my shirt!" Her lip trembled. "I f-found it on the floor."

"Oh, Julia, how can you be sure?"

"Look!" She thrust the shirt toward him. "It was on the floor! It was torn! My most expensive shirt!"

Tim shut the bedroom door. Taking the shirt, he let it hang limp from his hand as he inspected it, noting how the seam had been ripped from neck to armhole. "It can be sewn back up."

"That's not the point!" Julia cried.

"I know." He sank onto the bed.

"Tim, this is *creepy.* This is *sick.*"

Tim looked miserable. "Oh, Julia—"

"What? You don't think it's *sick*? That crazy old bitch goes through my things, ruins my best shirt, and—"

"I'm sure she didn't know it was your best shirt. I'm sure she doesn't even know what Prada is."

"And that makes it okay?" Julia was so angry she had to pace the room.

"No, of course it doesn't. Calm down, Julia, or you'll wake Belinda."

She turned on him. "Is that all you care about? That I might wake Belinda?"

"No, of course it's not. I'm just as appalled as you, Julia."

"I doubt that very much. Tim, she went through my lingerie. She handled my personal-hygiene things, my *tampons*, for God's sake." Julia shuddered with revulsion.

"I'm sorry." He ran his hand over his forehead.

"You don't need to be *sorry*." Julia strained to keep from shouting. "You do need to help me decide what to do!"

"What on earth *can* we do?" Tim was ashen.

"I don't know." Julia collapsed on the bed next to him. "I don't know. Except we've got to agree right now that she'll never be alone in this house again."

Tim nodded bleakly.

"I won't call her." Julia was thinking aloud. "I won't give her the satisfaction of letting her know how angry she makes me. She's such a manipulative, convoluted old cow, she'd be *thrilled* if I got angry with her. She'd use that somehow, to prove I was a bad stepmother." Julia hit her pillow. "But it's not fair! I try so hard, and this is what I get, all my things grubbed around with, her nasty cooties over every single thing I own and wear!"

Tim tried to put his arm around her, but Julia jerked away. "Don't think you can make this okay with a little jolly snuggle, because you can't!"

"I wasn't trying to make it okay," Tim protested. "I just want to help you, somehow. We were having such a good time. I thought we were going to make love."

"Oh, right, like I could enjoy that! Agnes probably spat on the sheets." Julia stormed to her dresser and began to dump her

clothes into a wicker basket. "I'm not sleeping there until I wash the bed linen. I'm not
going to be able to change my clothes until
I've washed everything."

"Julia, please."

"Please, *what*? Please don't feel violated
by your mother-in-law's invasion of all my
personal things?"

Tim raised his hand, palm up. "I just—I
don't know, Julia. I don't know what to do. I
don't want Agnes to come between us."

Hefting the heavy wicker basket, Julia
went out of the bedroom, down the hall,
through the kitchen, and out to the utility
room. Her rage was making her illogical.
She wanted to dump the entire contents of
the Tide container into the washing machine. She needed to do something huge
and reckless that would use up her anger.
She wanted to kick something, tear something, she wanted to throw back her head
and howl with rage. She turned the dials on
the washing machine, then stood there,
gripping the cold white metal. Her fury
roared through her head, blocking her ears
with white noise. No way could she calm
down enough tonight to sleep, and the

thought of making love with Tim was repulsive right now.

So Agnes had caused discord between them. Tonight, Agnes won.

15

"Hello," Faye said eagerly, expecting to hear Laura's sweet voice.

She hadn't spoken with her daughter for three days now, and *she* had been the one to call her. Faye didn't want to be a pest, but wasn't it only natural for a mother to be concerned about her only child and grandchild when they'd just moved clear across the continent to a city where they knew no one? Lars would be fine, of course, he'd spend his days working with one of his best college buddies, but Laura was a stranger in the city, a young woman with a new baby, not to mention a history of postpartum depression.

"Is this Faye?" growled a gravelly voice.

"Yes?" she squeaked.

"Faye, this is Tank, Jimmy's friend. Shirley Gold told me to call you."

Oh, Lord! For days she'd rehearsed a polite but unambiguous refusal, but now that this strange man had actually gone to the trouble of dialing her number and making himself vulnerable, she didn't want to be rude. It was like high school. She was weak with embarrassment for both of them. A hot flash raced through Faye's body. Beads of sweat popped up beneath her breasts, under her arms, along the back of her neck.

"You still there?"

Faye forced a laugh that came out in a trilling high soprano. God, she sounded like a neurotic aging belle, like Blanche DuBois in *A Streetcar Named Desire.* Cringing, she shakily replied, "Still here."

"Shirley thought we should meet for a drink," he said in his gravelly voice.

Faye could only imagine how this man lived, his apartment littered with beer cans he'd smashed against his forehead, his sheets stained and dirty, his underwear not washed for days at a time—*why was she thinking of his underwear?*

"Faye?"

"Oh," she gushed, hideously ill at ease, "that Shirley! She's such a good friend, so protective and kind and wanting to help, but

I'm a widow, you see, and very, very, *very* happy with my single state, but Shirley's a bit of a romantic, and she's worried because I've been just a bit despondent because my daughter's moved to California, but really, I'm absolutely fine!"

There was a moment of silence at the other end of the line. Then: "So. Do you want to get a drink sometime?"

Faye closed her eyes and leaned her head against the wall. "You really don't have to do this, you know."

He let out a brief, rumbling laugh. "It's just a drink."

The man *was* persistent. With enormous effort, Faye pulled herself together. "Yes, Tank, I would enjoy meeting you for a drink." Now her clothes were completely damp with perspiration, but at least she'd made it clear she wasn't inviting him to her condo or agreeing to go to his place.

"You live out near Acton, right?"

"Right."

"I live in Revere. Let's split the difference and meet at O'Malley's in Arlington."

Of course. A bar. She'd prefer the coffee shop of a bookstore, but would that sound too prissy? No doubt he'd be uncomfort-

able there. "I don't believe I know O'Malley's."

"It's right on Mass. Ave. Easy."

"Fine. What time?" She sounded almost
like her old self.

"Seven? This Friday?"

"All right." A thought crossed her mind:
what does a middle-aged matron wear to a
bar? "How will we recognize each other?"

His abrupt, crashing laugh interrupted
her. "Well, Faye, I think I'll be able to pick
you out in the crowd. And I look like someone from ZZ Top."

"ZZ Top?"

"The band."

"Ah, of course." She didn't want to seem
utterly clueless. She'd go to a record store
and check out the album cover.

"If the weather cooperates, I'll give you a
ride on my Harley."

Faye pressed her hand to her heart. "Well.
That would be nice." *I'll pray for rain,* she
thought.

———

Friday night, terror gripped her by the back
of her neck with a lock like a tiger's jaw.

How could *she* walk into a bar? She'd been raised to believe that a lady *never* went into bars, especially not alone. And she looked like such a *lady,* with her white hair in a bun, her grandmotherly body, her breasts like two bags of flour propped on the counter of her stomach. People would laugh when she entered the bar. People would *snicker.*

The phone rang. Faye raced to grab it up, hoping it would be Tank canceling their date, but something held her back, and she simply stood over the answering machine, listening.

"Faye?" Shirley sounded bossy. She was probably in another part of the building, in her office or condo. "Good, you're not there. You'd better *not* be there! I'm going to see if your car's in the lot, and if it's not gone, I'm going to come to your condo and drag you out to that bar myself. So I hope you're on your way to your date with Tank right now. Call me when you get home, I want to hear all about it!"

"Oh, leave me alone!" Faye told the answering machine. She hadn't been this frustrated since she was an adolescent being ordered around by her parents. If this was how it felt to be young again, she could do without it, thank you very much!

The November night was cold and crisp. Faye was glad she'd worn her tweed trousers, glad, too, that the frosty air meant she had to wear her bulky camel-hair car coat, and beneath it, a thick wool sweater, all of it hiding her fat.

She drove slowly toward the lights of Boston and Mass. Ave. O'Malley's was on the corner. It had a green-and-white-striped awning, a massive oak door, and handsome gold lettering. Through the window, she spotted a table with people laughing— young people, a man and a woman.

Not so bad, then. She could do this. She pulled her car into the lot behind the bar and turned off the engine. Quickly, automatically, she pulled the visor down. Did she have lipstick on her teeth? Was her hair okay?

Oh, God. The small rectangular mirror reflected the face of a chubby old troll. Maybe she wouldn't do this after all. She didn't *have* to go out on dates. She didn't have to do what the Hot Flash Club told her to. She could, well, *move*! She could move to Florida, find a nice little town where everyone was old. Really old, in their nineties. It would be sunny in Florida. She could teach art classes there.

It was getting cold in the car. The thing was, she didn't want to move to Florida. She'd been so brave when she'd pulled off her disguise at the Eastbrooks—couldn't she be that brave now? It would take only one hour. One painful hour.

She left her car. Straightening her spine, holding her head high, she walked around the corner, found the front door to O'Malley's, and entered.

The smoke-free air smelled like whiskey and beer. Well-polished wooden floors and a long mahogany bar made the room dark and masculine, but pockets of light glittered on the bottles and glasses behind the bar and at the back of the room over the Exit and Rest Rooms signs. Rock music throbbed beneath the chatter and laughter.

The place was packed, a good sign. The barstools were crowded. Faye looked around the room. All the tables seemed occupied. A few men at the bar glanced over at her, then looked away.

"Faye?"

She was grateful for the social instincts that made her smile. The man standing before her *was* a tank—tall, big-boned, meaty—but most of all, he was *old.* The beard hanging down to his chest was white, as was what was left of the hair on his head, most of which he'd gathered back into a low ponytail. Bifocals rested on a giant strawberry nose. Over his jeans, his denim shirt hung, barely managing to stay buttoned across the expanse of his gut.

"Hello." She extended her hand. Funny, how she'd expected someone younger somehow.

"Nice ta meetcha." His hand was rough and calloused. "I've got a table in the back."

She followed him through the crowd. If it was hard for her to get old, how much harder must it be for someone like this macho action-figure kind of fellow?

They reached a small table crammed into the corner. With a jerk of his head, Tank indicated her chair. "I'll go get you a drink. If we wait for the waitress, we'll wait all night. What'll you have?"

"A glass of red wine?"

"Sure." He went off.

Faye sat down, draping her coat on the back of her chair so it wouldn't touch the floor. Settling back, she pulled her sweater down to her thighs, at the same time glancing around the room. No one was looking at her. She relaxed a little.

Tank returned with a glass of red wine and a basket of popcorn. He set both on the table. To her surprise, he pulled his chair right next to Faye's before sitting down.

Slightly alarmed, Faye started to scoot her own chair away a few inches, but Tank leaned over first. "Sorry. Deaf in one ear, not so hot in the other."

"Oh." Faye smiled in sympathy. "The joys of getting older."

"In my case, the joys of Nam. Shell exploded, been deaf in one ear ever since."

"Oh, that's too bad." Her mind began a demented rendition of Deborah Kerr singing "Getting to Know You."

Tank leaned closer, extending his arm along the back of her chair, encircling her in a bouquet of beer, onions, and tobacco. "Yeah. Took some shrapnel in my thigh, too." He glanced downward.

Faye's eyes followed his, lighting on a jean-encased thigh the size of an adolescent rottweiler. "Well," she said perkily, "you must have recovered well enough, if you ride a motorcycle."

"True. But I'm sure that's why I've got such terrible arthritis."

"Oh, dear." Faye took a sip of red wine.

"My tackle's intact, though, in case you're wondering."

It took her a moment to interpret this. Realizing she was still staring at his thigh, she wrenched her eyes away so fast they nearly left their sockets. Faintly she said, "Well, that's good." Desperate to change the subject, she asked, "So, what kind of work do you do, Tank?"

"Any kind I get offered. Used to work on construction crews, but my back's all twisted up, so physical labor's pretty much out these days." He raised his eyebrows suggestively. "Certain kinds of physical labor I'm still good for."

Faye fastened her eyes on the TV above the bar. "Do you follow the Red Sox? My husband used to be a fanatic."

"*Yeah,* I follow them. Even used to spend money for seats at Fenway. These days I'm happy to watch from the comfort of my recliner. My hemorrhoids make it a bitch to sit on those bleachers." His hand moved to her shoulder. "I got a big TV. You ought to come over and see it sometime."

One good thing, Faye thought, she was no longer nervous. Oddly, she was having a good time. She'd never met a man quite like this one. He seemed to be hitting on her, and she took another swallow of wine to keep from giggling.

"Have you ever been married, Tank?"

Tank grunted. "Twice. Shoulda known better the first time."

"Any children?"

"One son. Lives down in Arizona."

"Oh, too bad, you must miss him."

"Not really. Never really knew the kid. His ma went off with another guy and wasn't good about keeping in touch, less she wanted some child support checks."

"Oh. That's too bad."

"You?"

"One daughter. Laura. She's married and has a little girl, the sweetest little child, my granddaughter, Megan. Laura's husband just took a job in California, so they moved a few weeks ago."

"Sucks for you."

"Yes," Faye agreed, "it does suck for me. I miss them terribly."

He pulled her against him, his mouth so close to her ear his whiskers tickled. "I know something could cheer you up."

Faye bristled. "Look, Tank, we've just met—"

His *har-har-har* laugh exploded like a jackhammer. "I wasn't referring to that, although when you're ready, I'll be only too happy to oblige. What I meant was, you oughtta come have a ride on my cycle."

Faye choked on her wine. Wiping her mouth with her paper napkin, she said, "Maybe another time."

"Why not now?" Tank pressed. "It's Friday night. You got an appointment?"

"Well, no, but—it's so cold outside."

"Ah, that's nothing." He looked her over. "You've got a coat, hat, gloves."

"To be honest, Tank, I'd really rather not. I guess I'm just a little afraid of riding a motorcycle."

"Ever been on one before?"

"No."

"I've got an extra helmet. How about if I

promise I won't go fast?" Tank belched, exuding a hot breath of onions and beer.

Well, Faye thought, *if we ride the motorcycle, he'll be facing the other way.*

"We'll just go around the block a few times."

Faye finished off her wine. It would be fun to tell the Hot Flash Club she'd been on a motorcycle. And she didn't feel afraid; certainly this arthritic, shrapnel-thighed, hemorrhoid-troubled man wasn't going to drive her into an alley and rape her.

"All right."

Tank slapped her hard on her back. "Excellent!" He rose, jerked his black leather jacket off the back of his chair, and put it on.

"Just around the block."

"Absolutely." He pulled back her chair and held her coat out, then took her hand in his and pulled her through the bar and out into the cold night air.

His motorcycle was parked by the curb just down the street. Tank handed her a helmet.

"Put this on."

She obeyed, as visions of accidents danced through her head. Tank smoothed on his leather gloves. Faye imagined Laura getting the phone call, hearing the news that her mother had died in a motorcycle accident, crumbling in a heap of grief—

"Now." Tank swung his leg over the leather saddle. "You just climb on and hunker yourself down right behind me." He patted the seat.

There was no ladylike way to do this. Putting her hands on Hank's shoulders for balance, Faye swung a leg over and settled down behind him. The seat was comfortably cushioned, but she could feel the cold through her trousers.

"Keep your feet here. Keep your arms around me." He chuckled. "Oh, I do love the feel of a woman's arms." He kicked the starter, and with a roar and a shudder the machine came to life beneath them.

Across the street, a crowd stood in line to enter a movie. A few glanced their way at the sound of the cycle, but no one stared in amazement. The tilt of the seat made her belly push forward, pressing against Tank's back, and in an instinctive act of vanity she didn't know she possessed, she wriggled and changed position, so that her breasts rested against him instead.

"That's good," Tank yelled. "I'll run inter-ference on the cold air for you."

His gloved hands twisted the handlebars and they took off, pulling away from the curb, slanting to one side, then straighten-ing. Faye felt as if someone had put a hallu-cinogenic in her wine—everything was so vivid, so intense! It was like riding naked, Faye thought, everything was frighteningly close. She was so unprotected. Tank turned a corner. The cycle leaned like a sailboat heeling in the wind.

"All right back there?" Tank yelled.

"Yes!" she yelled back. It *was* just a little bit exhilarating. The cold air stung her eyes and slapped her cheeks. Lights, shop win-dows, cars, pedestrians, streaked away in a kind of dream. Between her legs, the ma-chine throbbed like a purring animal.

"Little more?" Tank yelled, or she thought that was what he said.

"Okay," she yelled back, and Tank rounded a corner, heading along a residen-tial street leading to Route 128.

Faye's breath caught in her throat. Not Route 128! It was eight lanes of traffic rac-ing like the Indianapolis 500. He *had* to turn around, take her back to the bar . . .

Faye clutched Tank tighter, closed her eyes, opened her mouth to scream, and she felt a change in the wind. She opened her eyes. They were on the highway, with cars on either side of them. Without the insulation of a car to protect her, the noise was astonishing. It was like being in a coliseum with a roaring mob, or on a runway with a 747 coming in for a landing. Her exhilaration turned to fear. Only inches away, hundreds of pounds of hard metal sped past. The cycle was like a gazelle caught in a stampede of elephants. Her stomach turned. She gagged.

"Enough!" she shouted.

"Hell, yes, it's *fun*!" he yelled back.

Great, she was trapped on the back of a motorcycle with a deaf man.

Which ear was his good one? "Stop!" she yelled. "Tank! Stop! I'm scared!"

He lifted his hand in a thumbs-up sign and she nearly fainted to think only one arthritic hand was keeping them on track.

She burrowed her head against his back and began to pray.

Soon she felt the cycle tip sideways. Terrified, she waited to feel the impact, the scrapes along her skin, the breaking of her bones—but they straightened. They went down an off-ramp and were back on the sane streets with their blessed speed limits. Faye relaxed a little. Now she didn't have to throw up. But she really had to pee.

The ride back to the bar took forever. The reverberations of the cycle between her thighs shook her bladder so hard she felt like a washing machine about to overflow. The only good thing about it was, she had to concentrate so hard on not leaking, she didn't have a chance to be afraid.

Finally they were back in O'Malley's parking lot. Tank steered the cycle to a stop and turned off the engine. The machine quieted, then slept. Faye unclenched her hands, surprised they hadn't hardened into claws from her fierce clutching.

"Have to use the bathroom!" she said urgently, ripped the helmet off her head, thrust it at him, and rushed to the back door of the bar without waiting to see whether Tank followed.

Her legs were trembling. Her entire body was trembling. The bar bathroom was not the most hygienic one she'd ever been in, but she sank gratefully onto the commode. Not only did she have to pee like Niagara

Falls, her body also responded to the ride with a gush of diarrhea.

Well, maybe she'd lose some weight.

She washed her hands and nearly screamed at her reflection in the mirror. The helmet had mashed her hair flat against her head, pushing it into pads on either side of her face. She took her hair down, fussed with it, stuck it back in a sloppy bun. Her hands were still shaking.

Back in the bar, she found Tank at a table with another glass of wine waiting for her and his own mug of beer already half gone.

"How'd you like that?" he asked.

"It was wonderful until we got on the highway," Faye said truthfully. "Then I was terrified."

"Yeah, it's a rush, isn't it? Like flying."

"Have you ever been in any accidents?"

"Oh, sure." He rolled up the sleeves of his denim shirt to show off a long, jagged scar. "Broke this arm, one time. Another time, broke my back. Another time—"

Faye gulped her wine. She was glad she hadn't asked him about accidents before he offered her a ride. As she listened to his litany of injuries, she decided he was the oddest combination of daredevil and cry-baby she'd ever met.

"... gonna be needing a woman in my life," Tank was saying.

His hand was back on her shoulder. His face was coming close to hers. His onion-beer breath hung in a mist right in front of her nose; she had to inhale it or stop breath-ing.

"A nice little woman who likes to cook, and clean, and be a nursemaid, but the kinda nursemaid that wears those cute little short skirts, you know what I mean?" He nuzzled her cheek. "You'd look good in one of them."

The good news was he found her attrac-tive enough to proposition, if this was what he was doing. The bad news was, he'd ob-viously proposition anyone.

She pulled away. "Tank, listen, I got cold on that ride. I need to go home, take a long hot shower, and get in bed."

Tank's eyes lit up. "Well, all right, then, let's do it!"

Faye's jaw dropped. "Oh, I didn't mean with you. I just met you!"

Tank tilted his head playfully, reached out, and tickled Faye under her chin. "Come on, honey. Shirley told me you've been without a man for a long time."

Faye jerked her head away. "And I like my solitary state just fine!" For the second time that evening, she pulled on her coat and gathered up her gloves and purse. "Thanks for the drinks and the ride, Tank."

"Sure thing, doll. You take care of yourself. I'll call."

16

"How was your Thanksgiving?" Faye asked the other members of the Hot Flash Club after they settled at their Legal Seafoods table and ordered their drinks.

Alice was the first to answer. "Bizarre, thanks for asking. Gideon and his daughter and her family came to my house. The kids got bored at the table after two minutes and threw fits until they were allowed to watch television, Gideon had terrible heartburn which gave him the hiccups, and all I wanted to do was play bridge."

Shirley laughed. "Sounds like a typical Thanksgiving."

"What did Alan do for Thanksgiving?" Marilyn asked.

Alice kept her eyes on the menu. "He and Jennifer went to her family's house on the Cape."

"Do you think Alan and Jennifer will get married?" Faye asked.

"I really couldn't say." This was a touchy topic for Alice.

"They should!" Shirley said. "They're in love! And their bakery is taking off, they can't keep up with the orders!"

"It would be kind of nice if Gideon's daughter married your son," Faye mused. "Then you could both be grandparents of the same children even though you and Gideon never had children together."

Alice laughed. "Oh, Faye, you think the world begins and ends with grandchildren."

"You mean it doesn't?" Faye joked. She turned to Marilyn. "How's it going with Teddy and Lila?"

Before Marilyn could answer, Alice cut in, "MILDEW: Mother-in-Law Daily Exercises Wrath."

Faye flinched but kept quiet.

Marilyn smiled wryly. "You're right about that, Alice. Eugenie's like someone out of a Greek tragedy."

"So who got the baby for Thanksgiving?" Alice asked Marilyn.

"I did," Marilyn said. She brightened. "Want to see some photos?"

Of course they did. After the baby had suitably been admired, Marilyn slid the photo album back in her purse. "They were at my house for three hours, during which time Eugenie phoned twice, missing 'her little family on this special day.' We all felt miserable. But it seems fair to me. Teddy, Lila, and little Irene are going to spend both Christmas Eve and Christmas Day out at the Eastbrooks'."

"You won't get to see them, even for an hour?" Faye asked.

"No. And, yes, I am disappointed. But I can tell they're feeling pressured by Eugenie. In spite of all our joking, I feel sorry for Eugenie. Why would Eugenie be so involved in their lives if she were happy with her own?"

Alice laughed. "I'm not sure *happiness* always comes into it. It's like there's some kind of bizarre emotional mathematics in families. *Einstein's* wife's *theory of relativity!* I know with Gideon's grandchildren, it's as if each day has a symbolic weight. One Christmas is worth slightly more value than one Thanksgiving. Birthdays are almost equal to Christmas. Next on the scale comes summer vacation, followed by weekends. If the grandparents aren't able to see the child for two weekends because the child was sick or something, does that mean they deserve a week during summer holiday? We need a computer to figure out how to divide up grandchildren's time fairly."

"It's not the time I'm concerned about," Marilyn said, "as much as the, well, *influence,* I suppose is the word I want. I'd like to see my granddaughter interested in ideas, science, literature, music. I don't want her swept up in Eugenie's superficial world." Suddenly she glared at the others. "Don't start snorting and smirking!"

"Well, it *is* funny," Faye contended, "how different you and Eugenie are. All she cares about is appearance, and you scarcely realize you have one."

Alice cocked her head. "Is there a word for what the parent of your child's spouse is? I mean, they're not in-laws, are they?"

"Outlaw?" Marilyn ventured. "I'm Eugenie's mother-out-law."

Shirley chewed her eggplant parmigiana thoughtfully. "You can't be an outlaw, Marilyn. Your children are married, you're legally part of the family. I'm not a mother, aunt, grandmother, I'm not even a stepmother yet. *I'm* the outlaw! Certainly Justin's ex-wives and children think I am. I'm trying my best to please everyone, and they still think I'm an intruder."

"Who did you spend Thanksgiving with?" Alice asked.

"Now don't freak out," Shirley warned, shooting a look around the table before answering. "No one."

"No one!" Faye cried. "Shirley, that's awful!!"

"No, it's not. I got a lot of paperwork done. I celebrated Thanksgiving the day after, when I took Justin and his three kids out to dinner at the Ritz."

"The Ritz?" Alice was shocked. "That must have cost you a ton of money."

"It did. But it was the first time we've all eaten together. I wanted to make it special." With a little shrug of embarrassment she said, "I wanted them to like me."

"And did it work?" Marilyn asked.

Dismally, Shirley shook her head. "No. They're all teenagers, two girls from the first wife, the boy from the second, and they all seem to hate each other and their father, and they hate me because I'm connected to him. They were sullen. They were rude. At least the boy enjoyed all his food. The girls just took tiny bites and made faces."

"Okay," Marilyn conceded. "You win the title of outlaw."

"I think you need to be careful," Alice said. "Taking everyone to the Ritz—won't that give Justin the idea you're wealthy?"

"Here we go again!" Shirley sighed. "Alice, Justin is *not* after my money! He knows I don't *have* any money."

Alice pushed her plate aside and folded her arms on the table, a sure sign of imminent battle. "Justin Quayle probably thinks you have a lot of money, Shirley. He knows you're the founder and president of The Haven, which is becoming a *very* lucrative business. If nothing else, the land and buildings are worth a lot. Plus, you get a nice fat salary."

Marilyn diplomatically changed the subject. "Faye, what did you do for Thanksgiving?"

"I went to the Dawsons'. They were good 'couple' friends—when Jack was still alive, we used to do a lot with them. They had a buffet dinner, about twenty people. It was fun, I got to see a lot of old acquaintances."

"Meet any new men?" Marilyn inquired.

Faye shook her head. "The only other single person there was female."

"Par for the course," Alice said. "Face it, the statistics are not in our favor."

"Never mind the statistics," Shirley said, "we're creating our own good luck, right?" She focused her gaze on Faye. "Which brings us to the topic of your date with Tank."

"Oh, right!" Marilyn beamed. "Did you meet Tank? What's he like? Are you going to see him again?"

"Oh, yes, I met Tank." Faye hesitated, enjoying their expectant looks. "He's very nice. We met at a bar called O'Malley's on Mass. Ave. We shared a couple of drinks, and he took me for a ride on his Harley."

"No!" Alice was amazed.

"You actually got on his cycle?" Shirley raised her hand to give Faye a high five. "All right! You go, girl."

"Weren't you frightened?" Marilyn asked.

"Terrified. We even went on 128. We must have gone sixty miles an hour." She smiled at the memory. "You know, it's one of those things I'm really glad I did, but I don't want to do it again."

"So what did you think of Tank?" Shirley asked.

"He's very nice." Faye knew she had to be cautious criticizing any of the men her friends fixed her up with. It was kind of a "Love me, love my dog" situation.

"So are you going to see him again?" Alice asked.

"I don't think so. He was pleasant, in his own way, but let's just say he lacked a certain je ne sais quoi."

"You mean he's not good enough for you?" Shirley asked.

Faye shook her head. "I didn't say that at all! But come on, Shirley, his world and mine really are different. He wouldn't enjoy attending an opera any more than I enjoyed riding his bike."

"I understand," Shirley conceded.

"The sex thing wasn't there," Marilyn decided.

Faye lifted an eyebrow. "What?"

"You weren't physically attracted to him. If you had been, the rest of it wouldn't have mattered."

Faye looked skeptical. "Perhaps."

Alice was pondering something. "I wonder—if someone in his seventies dates someone in her twenties, it's called a May-December relationship. What do you call a hookup between someone who's classy like you, Faye, and someone who's more, let's just say, earthy?"

"I don't know—a caviar-Chee•tos romance?" Faye offered.

"Well," Shirley said, getting them back on track, "we'll see how you like the man behind Door Number Two. Have you spoken to your candidate, Marilyn?"

Marilyn nodded. "He's ready to roll. His name is Roger Munson, he's about fifty-five, and divorced. He's had tenure at MIT forever, he's a genius."

"Does he study bugs, too?" Alice asked.

"No, he does not. His field is quantum mechanics. Quarks are his specialty."

"Oh, yeah, I have one of those," Alice said.

Marilyn did an eye roll. "Quarks are tiny particles inside atoms."

"I knew that," Faye joked.

"He's not going to quiz you," Marilyn reminded her. "He's just going to take you out for coffee, or dinner, whatever. He's a bit quiet, Faye, perhaps a little shy, but when I brought up the subject of a possible date

with a friend of mine, he seemed very interested. I think he might be a little lonely."

"I wouldn't be surprised," Shirley said.
"We're in the holiday season now. Prime
time for loneliness."

"I read in *AARP* magazine the other day,"
Faye said, "that loneliness is the greatest
fear of both men and women when they get
divorced later in life."

"Is that why you're being so malleable
about these dates?" Marilyn asked Faye.

Faye cocked her head, considering. "Perhaps. Though I certainly wouldn't be putting
myself out there on the line if the three of
you weren't behind me, metaphorically
shoving me out the door. I really don't know
what's more frightening, trying to date
again, or facing a solitary life, and I *like* solitude. But you know, I kind of enjoyed my
date with Tank. I don't want to see him
again, but I'm really glad I met him once."

"He made you feel attractive?" Shirley
asked.

"Mmm, kind of. Certainly he made a few
suggestive moves. But he has so many
physical ailments, which he spoke about often, I'm not sure whether he was interested

in me as an object of sexual desire or as a nursemaid-slash-housekeeper."

"What else is new?" Alice asked, laughing.

"The thing is," Faye continued, "it was a positive experience for me. If nothing else, the entire evening was something completely new, and I know I need that at my age. I don't want my world to get smaller because I'm afraid to leave what is familiar and safe."

"I'll drink to that!" Shirley said, lifting her glass of seltzer.

Marilyn said, "So I'll call Roger and give him the green light?"

"Fine."

"Speaking of experiments," Alice said, "has anyone here thought any more about Project Relative Insanity? I mean, getting those three women together for a session of Jacuzzi and aromatherapy?"

"Oh, I still want to do it, definitely," Shirley said. "But we've got Christmas coming up, everyone will be too rushed. Let's do it right after the first of the year."

"I agree," Marilyn said.

"Me, too." Faye's face lit up. "Laura phoned to invite me to fly out for a week, so

I'll get to spend Christmas with my grand-daughter."

"Oh, that's wonderful!" Shirley said.

Faye smiled. "I know. So what are you doing for Christmas, Alice?"

Alice looked cranky. "I'm spending it with Gideon and his family."

"You're not going to see Alan and Jennifer?" Shirley asked.

"Don't start!" Alice snapped. "It's not my fault. They have plans to spend a week in Tortola."

"So did you buy Jennifer a Christmas present?" Faye asked.

"No, I did not, and I don't expect her to give me one. She knows I don't approve of this relationship. We never see one another, anyway, so how can I know what she likes?"

Marilyn changed the subject. "Will you spend Christmas with Justin, Shirley?"

"No, he's flying to Ohio to be with his mother. She's widowed, and Justin and his brother take turns spending holidays with her."

"If you're going to be alone," Marilyn suggested, "let's spend Christmas together."

"Good idea!" Shirley agreed. "But I don't want to cook, I want to totally relax, and you don't like cooking, either, Marilyn. Let's do something completely different."

"I know," Marilyn said. "Pizza and an old-movie marathon!"

"Don't make me jealous," Alice said.

"And don't talk about anything important when we're not there!" Faye added.

"And we'll all meet again in the New Year!" Shirley said.

17

Polly was sorry when the Friday-night yoga class at The Haven ended. The room quickly emptied. Some women yanked on coats and raced out to their cars. Others headed into the locker room, and Polly followed. She'd take her time showering and dressing—why not? Outside, the January night was black and cold. She had nowhere to go and nothing to do.

The women's locker room rang with noise and laughter. Polly stripped off her tank top and sweatpants, quickly wrapping a towel around her plump body. Her self-esteem was at an all-time low right now, especially where younger people were concerned. Some days it seemed her heart ached so fiercely, missing her son, longing to see her grandson, her body wanted to curl around the pain like an empty nautilus shell, washed up on the beach.

She sidled toward the showers, found an empty stall, and hurried inside. The hot water relaxed her, enclosing her in a world of warmth. She took her time washing her hair and soaping her body and rinsing off, but she couldn't stay in there forever.

Just as she turned off the water, she heard a woman call, "See you in there!"

Polly stepped out onto the tiles, towel around her, body dripping. She'd been in for a long time, and now the locker room was empty. But the door to the Jacuzzi room was just closing—the Jacuzzi! What a good idea! More warmth, more water therapy, and perhaps she'd strike up a conversation. Summoning her courage, she hurriedly pulled on her ancient green bathing suit, strode across the floor, pulled open the door, and stepped inside.

An unexpected fragrance took her senses by surprise. For a moment, she stood stock-still, inhaling the wonderful scent. The light in the room was less bright than usual, but she could still make out the tiles painted with beautiful images: flowers, birds, stars, planets. The air was warm and hazy with steam. Wide steps led into a deep indigo blue tub of swirling hot water.

The Jacuzzi was almost full. Six women were taking their places around the rim of the tub, and the rising steam gave them a conspiratorial air.

"Oh." Polly stopped, suddenly shy. "Is this, um, private?"

She thought she caught a glance exchanged between two of the older women, but a third woman, one she'd seen before—Polly thought she was the art teacher—spoke up.

"Not at all. Come on in, the water's fine."

Polly smiled gratefully and stepped down into the swirling liquid. Three of the women were younger than she, but three seemed about her own age, so she wasn't the class crone.

"Ahh," she sighed, sinking back into the warmth. "This feels great."

"Smells wonderful, too," said the pregnant woman, whose belly floated up out of the water like a mini beach ball.

"Good," said the art teacher. "It's something they're experimenting with, combining aroma and water therapy."

"I'll take all the help I can get," said a

young woman with a cap of striking black hair. "Christmas just about did me in."

The black woman chuckled. "Tell me about it."

"All right, I will! I've been married for a year to a man I adore, but his daughter lives with us, and she won't *talk,* and her grandmother clearly thinks I've got the nurturing abilities of Attila the Hun."

"So you're nervous and stressed?" asked a sweet-looking girl in a pastel pink bathing suit.

"Nervous and stressed?" The woman snorted. "I have killer headaches and my hearing's wonky. I've seen specialists, had an MRI, and no one can find anything physically wrong with me. A nurse suggested I try The Haven."

"Any improvement?" asked the black woman. "I'm Alice, by the way, and happy to say I'm divorced. I lost contact with my hellish old mother-in-law long ago."

"I'm Julia. I haven't been coming long enough to tell. I started in November, and then the holidays got in the way. But I made a New Year's resolution to come at least twice a week. I've got to do something or I think I'll really lose my mind."

With a wave of her hand, the art teacher said, "I'm Faye, and I have a question! Is the problem your husband's mother?" She looked worried.

"No, Tim's mother's dead, unfortunately." Julia leaned forward. "Look. Here's the deal: Annette, my husband's first wife, died two years ago. Cancer. Very sad, very difficult for everyone. Their daughter, Belinda, was five when her mother died, and she's seven now, and she hasn't spoken a word since."

"Poor little girl," murmured the slender woman with auburn hair. "I'm Marilyn."

Julia smiled hello, then pressed on. "Belinda goes to school, but doesn't talk. She has one good friend she plays with, but I think she sort of lives in a fantasy world."

The petite brunette perked up. "I can relate to that." She gave a quick shrug of shyness. "I'm Beth."

"Probably we all can relate, in one way or the other," Julia agreed. "Belinda isn't the problem, though. I think eventually she'll come out of it. Tim has taken her to lots of psychologists and child experts, who have assured him all she needs is time. No, my problem isn't the little girl. She's sweet, actually, and I think we've developed a pretty

nice relationship. It's her maternal grandmother." Julia wrinkled her nose. "*Agnes.*
The only good thing about her is that she
lives hours away, in the western part of the
state. But she makes her presence known,
believe me. She's invasive and divisive. She
really dislikes me."

"Would she dislike any woman Tim married?" Polly asked.

Julia thought about it. "Maybe. Yes, that's
a good point. It's not me she objects to so
much as anyone taking her daughter's place
with Belinda. Agnes wants Belinda to live
with her. And of course the longer Belinda
doesn't speak, the more proof Agnes feels
she has that the child is unhappy living with
Tim and me."

"That's a pretty complicated problem,"
Alice observed.

"Yeah, and it's not just an unpleasant-
feeling-in-the-air kind of thing. Before
Thanksgiving, when Agnes babysat so Tim
and I could go out, she pawed through all
my clothes. Left them in a mess." Julia
shuddered, remembering. "Like an animal
peeing to mark its territory."

Beth shuddered. "Creepy!"

Alice frowned. "Did you ask her about it?"

Julia shook her head. "I decided I didn't want to confront her. She's looking for a fight, clearly, and for Belinda's sake, I want to keep the peace." Julia's face fell. "The terrible thing is, since I can't take my anger out on her or Belinda, I take it out on poor Tim, who's perfectly innocent." Soberly she added, "It's a strain on our marriage."

"Well," Polly said philosophically, "marriage is about better *and* worse."

"Oooh," Beth moaned. "They didn't mention that in the Cinderella story."

"Come to think of it," Julia observed, "I don't believe the prince's mother is even *alive* in the Cinderella story, is she?"

"I guess that's why it's a fairy tale," Beth said. "No mothers-in-law."

Faye climbed up out of the Jacuzzi. Her face was flushed, her eyes moist, but she smiled over her shoulder. "I'm off." To the pregnant woman, she added, "You know, pregnant women shouldn't stay in the Jacuzzi too long."

Carolyn nodded. "You're right. Shirley Gold mentioned that, too." Looking disappointed, she made her way out of the water.

"Don't go," Alice said. "Why don't you get in your robe, then lie down and enjoy the aromatherapy. Put that towel under your head for a pillow."

Carolyn, appreciating Alice's authoritative tone of voice, did as she suggested. After she made herself comfortable, she smiled at the others. "I'm Carolyn."

Faye left, the others waving lazy good-byes.

"I hope I didn't say something to offend her," Beth said.

"She's fine," Alice assured her. "Go on with what you were saying."

"Okay." Beth took a moment to gather her thoughts. "Well, you can tell by just looking at me that I've got all the strength and athletic grace of a penguin, right? And my fiancé"—just saying the word made her blush crimson—"and his family are all jocks and hearty jokers. When they slap me on the back, I almost fall over."

"Why do they slap you on the back?" Julia asked.

"Because that's what they do. It's like being around a football team or something, they all sort of go around in a *herd*. I mean, they are so healthy and athletic, I get intimidated. I've always been weak and clumsy, but when I'm around them, my body goes into a kind of hyperklutziness."

"Oh, God," Polly groaned. "I can relate to that. My mother-in-law's so formal and meticulous, she makes me feel like a little Hobbit running around picking my nose."

The others laughed.

Encouraged, Beth continued, "Well, my fiancé's name is Sonny. Actually, his name is Merle Junior, he was named after his father, and he's the first son, so they call him Sonny. Bobbie, Sonny's mom, *adores* Sonny's high school girlfriend, Robin. She's plastered the house with photos of Sonny and Robin as king and queen of the prom. *Plus,* Robin is always at Sonny's parents' house. She's there for meals. She watches football games. She helps work in the yard."

"That's tough," Julia sympathized.

Beth nodded. "I've been trying so hard to make Bobbie like me. And she pretends to, in front of Sonny, but I swear she undermines me every chance she gets."

"For example?" Marilyn asked.

"Well, Sonny has a big family, and even though the kids are in their twenties, two of them still live at home. The father's a carpenter. They're all carpenters. They all eat humongous amounts of food, and Sonny and I always go there for Sunday dinner. So one Sunday I offered to bring something, it seemed only polite. I made a wonderful beef bourguignonne with wine and mushrooms, a huge pot of it. Spent hours on it. Well." A red glow spread up her neck as she remembered that day. "We showed up at his parents' house, and I gave the pot to Bobbie, who acted so thrilled to have it and put it on the stove to heat up. I went off and watched TV with the others. But when we sat down to eat, my stew had this really terrible taste to it, a kind of *fishy* tang. It didn't make you want to barf, but it gave the whole thing a weird, disgusting flavor. Everyone pretended it was delicious, but no one ate very much. What could I say? I was so confused! Later, when I was helping do the dishes, I saw several cans of tuna in the metal recycling bin. I think Bobbie skimmed the tuna water into my stew, gave the fish to Tinkerbelle—that's their dog—and sabotaged me."

"Wow." Julia whistled. "Either you're really paranoid or that mother's psycho."

"Plus, there are a lot of little things. They're always doing repairs on their buildings, or working in their garden. I'm finishing up my Ph.D. in literature, and I work in the BU library, so I admit I'm hopeless about tools and stuff. But like, once, Merle, that's Sonny's father, asked me to go get a bow saw, and I went back to the workshop, and told Bobbie what he wanted, and she gave me a pruning saw! When I took it to Merle, everyone laughed at me."

Carolyn spoke up. "Have you tried to talk to Sonny about this?"

Beth shook her head vehemently. "I don't dare say negative stuff about Sonny's family, especially about his beloved mother! He thinks they're all perfect."

"When are you getting married?" Polly asked.

"We haven't set the date yet. We started talking about marriage in the fall. He gave me this ring at Christmas." She held out her hand, showing off the tiny diamond. Her face softened as she looked at it. "I love him so much. I know he loves me. But once, for example, when we were carrying boxes into the den to decorate the family Christmas tree, Bobbie gave me a box to carry that was so heavy I could scarcely lift it." She lifted her chin defiantly. "So I'm coming here, and I'm going to get some muscles, and I'm going to get in shape."

"That's the spirit!" Alice said.

"Speaking of dates . . ." Marilyn waded across the tub and climbed the steps. "I've got one and I don't want to be late." She looked back at them with a rueful smile. "I wish I could stay."

The others waved good-bye, and then there were five in the room.

"She's about my age," Polly murmured wistfully. "And she's got a date."

"You want a date, too?" inquired Alice.

"I don't think I'm quite ready for that just yet." Polly hesitated. Claudia would hate to be talked about, but in this steamy, warm room, swirling with mysterious scent, Polly felt so safe, so included.

"Don't stop now," Carolyn urged.

"Well," Polly confided, "my husband, Tucker, died two years ago, but I've still got to deal with my mother-in-law. She's eighty-six, and ill with ovarian cancer." As the others moaned in sympathy, Polly said, "Yes, I know, it is too bad. But she's making it worse. She's very formal, patrician, re-mote. She doesn't want to go into the hospital, and she refuses to allow hospice or any strangers into her house. She does permit me to come once a day to bring her groceries and do a little cleaning in the kitchen. But she won't let me get close to her, physically or emotionally. I'd like to hear about her youth, or my husband's childhood. But she freezes me out completely."

"She's probably afraid," Beth suggested. "She probably feels embarrassed."

"Oh, no, I'm sure that's not it. Claudia's always looked down on me. Way down. She's always made it clear that her son married beneath him, and she won't change her mind just because she's dying."

Alice hauled herself up out of the tub. "Sorry, ladies, but I've got to get home."

"Bye," said the four remaining women as the door shut behind Alice.

"I should go, too," Carolyn said reluctantly.

"Darn," Polly said. "I've had more fun in this Jacuzzi tonight than I have in months!"

Julia leaned forward. "Me, too. I feel so much more, oh, I don't know, optimistic. It feels so *good* to be frank, to complain about my stepdaughter and her grandmother instead of mincing around pretending everything's rosy. But I can't bitch to Tim or I'd feel like some kind of monster."

"I like this aromatherapy," Beth said.

"I do, too, but I'm hungry," Julia said. "Want to grab a bite to eat at the restaurant down the road?"

Beth's eyes widened. "What fun!"

Polly agreed. "Dinner, yes, brilliant idea."

They all turned to look at Carolyn.

She hesitated. It wasn't as if she were signing a legal contract. It might actually be pleasant, never mind helpful. "I'm starving," Carolyn admitted. "Let's go!"

18

On the third floor of the spa building, the Hot Flash Club gathered in Faye's condo. Faye was making mimosas for them all— one without alcohol for Shirley.

Shirley lifted Saran Wrap off a plate of bluefish pâté and crackers and another from a bowl of sliced vegetables. "So you think it went okay? Tell me every single thing! Oh, I wish I'd been there!"

Alice and Marilyn leaned against the window, looking down into the parking lot. "You were right not to go," she said. "Everyone knows you're the director of the spa. They wouldn't have talked as easily in your presence."

Shirley panicked. "Did they criticize the spa?"

"No, not at all," Faye assured her. "They

love it. They just criticized mothers-in-law," she added bitterly.

"Not *just* mothers-in-law," Marilyn amended.

"Actually," Marilyn told Shirley, "we had a stowaway. One of the yoga students, a woman named Polly, wandered into the Jacuzzi room, and we couldn't really tell her to leave."

"And I'm glad we didn't!" Faye said. "She's very nice, and everyone seemed comfortable with her."

"But she's old," Alice said. "Our age, I mean."

"Still," Faye pointed out, "that didn't seem to stop the younger women from talking."

"Did they bond?" Shirley asked.

Faye turned to Alice. "You were the last to leave, what do you think?"

Alice reflected. "I think so."

"Look!" Marilyn called. "There they go."

Faye and Shirley hurried to join Marilyn and Alice at the window. Three floors below, four women got into four different cars and drove out of the parking area and down the drive.

"They're all leaving at the same time," Faye said. "That looks encouraging."

"Well, they would, anyway, wouldn't they?" Alice asked.

"Maybe not. Maybe one would leave while three stayed in the Jacuzzi."

"They've all turned right," Marilyn reported. "That's a good sign."

"Well, we've done what we can to get them together," Alice said, stepping away from the window to grab a cracker spread with pâté. "Now it's up to them."

The others left the window and settled around Faye's coffee table.

Alice looked cranky. "I just hope the older woman didn't spoil it."

"Why would you assume she would?" Faye asked.

"I certainly couldn't have talked about a lot of intimate subjects with my mother around," Alice answered.

"Me, either," Marilyn agreed.

"Nor I." Faye tucked her legs under her, curling up on the sofa. "But Laura has always been very open with me about everything. Actually, she's told me more than I wanted to know about her sex life."

"I think that's probably true of women our

age," Shirley said. "We went through the sixties, we became more comfortable saying words like *penis* and *orgasm,* and we passed that along to our children."

"That reminds me," Alice volunteered. "MILDEW: Mother-in-Law: Dastardly Evil Witch."

"Hey," Shirley snapped. "No picking on witches."

"And that would be because?" Alice prompted.

"What's a witch look like?" Shirley asked them. "An old woman on a broomstick, right? A *crone,* right? Well, in ancient times, crones, old women, were worshiped for being wise. They were considered goddesses, with mystical powers, which I for one think women still have, except in our society we've been trained to fear and disparage them. Think of the woman riding a broomstick—it's such a phallic image, right? It represents power, and men are still afraid to let women have power. Especially old women, wrinkled and warted from age. I think MILDEW should be Mothers-in-Law: Divine, Enchanting Women!"

"Shirley's right," Marilyn said. "We don't give older women enough respect in our society. It's tough on them, but we're the ones who lose out. We could learn so much from older women, even at our age."

Shirley said, "You all know Nora Salter, one of my first massage clients to invest in this spa. She's in her late seventies, had to have open-heart surgery a few months ago and knew there was a good possibility she wouldn't come out of it. I stayed with her the morning of the operation—her heart attack happened so suddenly, her children couldn't get to Boston, they live all over the world—so I went in to be with her. Okay, so the nurses come to wheel her off to the OR. She's getting IV Valium, but still it's got to be frightening. Here she is, this little, frail, old partridge lying on a stretcher with tubes in her arms being wheeled off to have her chest cracked open. I thought she might clutch my hand, look terrified, so I was prepared to be encouraging. But she just waved good-bye at me and said, "I'll see you soon!" And as they wheeled her into the elevator, I heard her say to the nurses, "Well, if there were a fourth in here, we could play bridge."

"Good for her!" Faye said.

"That's how I'd like to be when I'm elderly," Marilyn said.

"I'll drink to that!" Shirley said, and raised her glass of sparkling seltzer to the other three.

Red-and-white-checked tablecloths, candles in Chianti bottles, and Dean Martin singing "That's Amore!" gave Leonardo's Restaurant a cozy, slightly old-fashioned atmosphere perfect for a night and a group like this. Carolyn, Beth, Julia, and Polly slid into a padded red leather booth, accepted menus, and ordered drinks.

"How do you feel now?" Polly asked Carolyn. "Blood pressure feeling all right?"

Carolyn nodded. "I'm fine. In fact, I feel better than I have in a long time. I think that aroma-water-therapy thing might have done some good."

The other women nodded.

"I feel better," Beth said shyly, "because I finally got to whine about Sonny's mother. Somehow it all seems more manageable now. I think I was spending way too much time obsessing about her."

"I wonder whether it's a universal law," Polly mused, "that the one we love comes with at least one toxic relative."

"It's true in my case," Julia said.

"What about you, Carolyn?" Polly asked, looking at her expectantly.

They're all strangers, Carolyn thought with a twinge of anxiety. She shouldn't be gossiping about private family business. On the other hand, they seemed nice, straight-forward, and practical. They might even have some advice to offer. It wasn't as if she had her own clique of close female friends, or even one close friend. Her involvement with her work had kept her too busy for friendship.

"My mother-in-law lives in another state," Carolyn began. "My father is the problem."

"He's Aubrey Sperry, right?" Polly asked. "I've seen his photo in the papers for years. Handsome man."

Carolyn nodded. "My father and my husband and I live in the same house. It's, um, kind of large, and we have separate wings, plus a few common rooms for company occasions."

"How does your husband like that?" Julia asked.

"Oh, he's fine with it. Hank's wonderful about most things. Besides, he travels a lot. He's a kind of environmental trouble-shooter."

"Is your house that fabulous Victorian at the crest of a hill in Sperry?" Polly asked.

Carolyn nodded, pleased by the compli-ment. "That's the one. Anyway, my father just got married." Carolyn absentmindedly stroked her swollen belly. *This* was what mattered, this new life she was carrying. Here in the restaurant with the waiters qui-etly padding around bringing them drinks and bread and little bowls of olive oil, Car-olyn felt relaxed. She was even enjoying herself. What a concept! With a slightly paranoid expression, she looked around the room. No one was within hearing distance. "His new wife—this is all very private, of course."

"Our lips are sealed." Polly drew an imag-inary zipper over her mouth.

"Little *Heather.*" Carolyn was astonished at how good it felt to say the name aloud. "A blue-eyed blonde, a good five years younger than I am." She felt like a pot with the lid lifted, the pressure evaporating.

"I can see her now." Julia grinned. "A gorgeous sexpot?"

"Strangely enough, no. Heather's short, dumpy, and wears matronly clothes. Perhaps my father likes her because she makes him feel nurtured. But I don't trust her."

Julia made a "move along" sign with her hand. "And that would be because . . ."

"It's complicated. We have a housekeeper, Mrs. B., salt of the earth, wonderful woman, who runs the house for us, mostly, because my father and I work pretty much full-time at the paper company. Mrs. B. has been with us forever, and I trust her completely, so when she came to me with her concerns, I took them seriously." Carolyn paused suddenly, looking as if she'd just heard a message on a frequency the others weren't tuned in to.

"Baby kicking?" Polly asked.

"Yes." Carolyn shared a smile with Polly.

"Don't stop now!" Beth urged.

"Anyway, Mrs. B. pays all the household bills, groceries, electricity, and so on out of a housekeeping account that she, my father, and I all have signatory powers for. My father, naturally, arranged for Heather to be able to withdraw money, too, and did she ever withdraw money! You know how you can have a line of credit at a bank, in case of some kind of emergency? We have that on our household account for things like broken pipes, tree limbs falling on the roof, whatever. Well, within a month, Heather had withdrawn fifty thousand dollars from that credit line. So Mrs. B. got concerned and checked my father's private checking account—she has access to it, though no signatory power—and almost one hundred fifty thousand dollars had been drawn from *that* line of credit."

"Wow!" Julia, Beth, and Polly spoke in sync, like an astonished Greek chorus.

Beth's eyes were wide. "What did you do?"

Carolyn closed her eyes for a moment, as if shutting off the memory. "I confronted my father."

"That's brave," Polly said.

"You're right. It was hard. My father and I aren't close, but we've always been friendly, never adversarial. It turned out that Heather had taken the money out without mentioning it to anyone."

"What for?" Julia asked.

Carolyn touched her neck, feeling her pulsing artery. "Heather said she was buying new furniture for their bedroom."

"That's perfectly reasonable," Julia said. "I think a new wife ought to be able to furnish the house the way she wants."

"I know you're right. But the way Heather went about it—"

The waiter set their meals before them, and for a few moments everyone focused on her food.

"Look," Carolyn continued. "Maybe I sound nuts to you. Maybe I *am* nuts. But something about Heather just feels *off* to me. All my instincts warn me she's up to no good. And I've always been able to trust my instincts, which, after all, I can't control." Awkwardly, Carolyn shifted her weight on the leather seat. "I'm thirty-seven years old, and I've tried to get pregnant for years, and now, *finally,* I *am* pregnant, with a daughter, who will carry on my great-grandmother's heritage. I'm thrilled about this baby. I don't *want* to feel suspicious and anxious and on edge! But what can I do about it?"

Polly reached over and put a friendly hand on Carolyn's shoulder. "Why not let us help you?"

THE HOT FLASH CLUB *strikes again*   289

Carolyn cocked her head. "What do you mean?"

"Well, we could check Heather out, for one thing."

Carolyn shrugged. "My secretary did that. Heather's just a sweet young thing who worked as a bank teller and lived in her deceased parents' home with her older brother."

"Yeah, well, we might be able to come up with some things your secretary didn't think of," Julia said confidently.

Carolyn looked at her. "Like what?"

Julia narrowed her eyes, thinking. "Let's start with the money."

"Right," Polly agreed, nodding as she thought. "Heather said she was buying new furniture?"

"Yes. For their bedroom."

Julia whistled. "Two hundred thousand dollars seems just a tad excessive, even for people as wealthy as you are. Where did Heather get the furniture? Have you seen it? Is it hand-carved by giant Siberian wood-workers?"

Carolyn laughed and felt her blood pressure drop. "I see your point."

"Did Heather sign a prenup?" asked Julia.

"She did."

"Okay, then." Polly was on a roll. "What does her brother do? How often does she see him? Is he dependent on her for money?"

"I haven't met Harry yet. I think he's a plumber."

"Maybe *he* builds furniture, too," Beth suggested shyly.

"Good idea!" Polly told Beth. She turned back to Carolyn. "What's the furniture like?"

Carolyn shrugged. "I don't know. I haven't been into my father's wing for months. Our housekeeper, Mrs. B., cleans it, and the common rooms are between his wing and mine, so I seldom go there." She patted her belly. "I'm not sure I even want to go into his wing now that he's married. Just the thought of being accused of snooping makes me nervous."

"Well, *I* have nerves of steel," Polly said. "I'll check out the furniture. When does Mrs. B. have a day off? Maybe we can find a time when she's gone and Heather and your father are out as well. I'll stop by to 'visit' you and we can take it from there."

Feeling a bit overwhelmed, Carolyn hesitated. "It's nice of you to offer. But to be honest, I don't understand why you'd want to spend your free time doing this sort of thing."

"Oh, *drat!*" Polly slapped her forehead. "Am I being overpowering? I guess it's just your problem sounds like fun to me. Not to make light of it, but it sounds like something I could do something about. I'm so shut out of my own life."

"What do you mean?" Carolyn asked.

Polly grimaced as a familiar pain sliced into her chest. "Because while I've told you about my mother-in-law, I haven't men-tioned my son and his wife. They had a baby five months ago, and I've only been able to see him once."

Beth asked, "Do they live far away?"

"Just outside Boston!" Tears sprang to Polly's eyes. "Amy, David's wife, is very controlling. She won't allow me to see the baby as long as I'm spending any time at all with Claudia. Amy believes I'll somehow transport Claudia's germs to Jehoshaphat."

"Jehoshaphat?" Julia echoed.

"Weird, right?" Polly grimaced. "They wanted to choose a name no one else would have."

"Well, they succeeded," Julia said wryly.

"I spend so much time longing to see my grandson," Polly continued. "And so much time doing errands for my bitchy old ice queen of a mother-in-law. Oh, I do see my clients—I'm a seamstress—but that's not the same at all. My husband's dead and my best friend moved to Tucson last year. God, I sound pathetic," she finished with a laugh.

"You're not pathetic at all," Carolyn assured her. "Look at us, we've all got problems with relatives."

"And talking about it makes me feel optimistic," Beth added. "Talking about it makes me feel like I can *do* something about it."

"Let's meet again, then," Polly suggested. "Every Friday night, after yoga class. In the Jacuzzi."

"Followed, I propose," Julia added, "by dinner here."

Beth's eyes widened. "What fun!"

Polly agreed. "Dinner, yes, brilliant idea."

They all turned to look at Carolyn.

"I'll need to check my calendar," Carolyn said slowly. She wasn't used to spontaneity. Hell, she wasn't used to friendship and fun. "But I think I can manage it."

19

A shrieking wind blasted pellets of snow against Polly's face as she struggled to lift the bundles from the backseat of her car. Arms full, feet slipping in the slush, she shoved the door shut with her hip, then set off toward Claudia's house, feeling every bit like a peasant in some obscure Tolstoy novel as she trudged through the knee-high snowdrifts. It was the time of day Polly usually loved, when evening dropped veils of lilac, smoke, and slate over the sky, while lamps in houses glowed golden, offering warmth and light. But this January day had passed without so much as a glimpse of the sun, and now, not even five o'clock, darkness fell over the city like a lid shutting on a coffin.

Coffin. Argh.

Polly did what she often did to cheer herself up: she burst into a chorus of "Cock-eyed Optimist" from *South Pacific.* No one else was near enough to hear her, even if they could over the howling wind, and she needed to buck up her spirits.

Since Dr. Monroe's diagnosis three months ago, Polly had become her mother-in-law's errand girl, escort, and emotional cheerleader. In December, she missed several parties thrown by her own friends so she could squire Claudia to her society affairs. She'd set up a tree in Claudia's living room, bought her presents, wrapped them with flair, roasted the Christmas turkey in Claudia's oven, and served Claudia at her own table with her own beloved crystal, silver, and china. On New Year's Eve, she'd brought champagne and Russian caviar to enjoy as they watched the countdown at Times Square. Claudia had been gracious enough to allow Polly to clink flutes. She'd even wished Polly happy New Year.

Since the first of the year, Claudia had not left the house except for doctor's appointments, but she still refused to discuss her health with Polly. It was just so damned weird! Polly often felt like grabbing her mother-in-law's bony body and shaking her.

She knew Claudia hated to discuss bodily functions; she knew Claudia needed to be regarded as a woman of elegance and dignity. But come on! Polly wanted to cry. There's more to being a human being than elegance and dignity! There's affection, anxiety, humor, sorrow—there's love in all its many guises.

You must be so *lonely,* Polly wanted to say to Claudia. Don't you want someone to hold your hand now and then? Perhaps Claudia allowed herself to be cosseted a bit by Pearl, Claudia's housekeeper, who came every morning. Polly hoped so. What else could she do? She came every afternoon, bringing Claudia books, little treats of chocolates or a soft chenille throw, and during the last month, something hot for dinner. She sat docilely in the living room as Claudia dictated lists of errands.

Last week, Claudia had given her a front-door key. Thinking this might be an implicit admission that she was becoming too weak to walk down the hall to open the door, Polly had ventured, "Claudia, perhaps you should think about having hospice or home health—"

Claudia had cut her off. "I told you, I want

no strangers in my house." And she'd picked up a *New Yorker* and fastened her attention on that.

When Polly asked Claudia how she felt, Claudia always replied, "I'm quite well, thank you."

Well, it was Claudia's life, and Claudia's dying, and Polly wanted to respect her wishes and help her do it the way she wanted. Control was crucial to Claudia, and it had to be awful for her to be unable to control the cancer transforming her body. Polly would do what she could to help Claudia maintain some control of these last days and weeks of her life.

So, hoisting a bag onto her left hip, she unlocked Claudia's front door and let herself in. She took off her snow-covered outerwear and entered the living room.

"Hello!" Probably she sounded disgustingly perky, like a drunk Doris Day, but she'd read that smiling made you feel better, so she tried to get Claudia to smile. What was the option? To lament, wring her hands, and tiptoe around speaking in sepulchral tones?

"Hello, Polly." Claudia was ensconced in her usual place, reclining in royal state on her damask chaise longue. A table on her right held a pile of books and magazines; the one on her left was laden with telephone, television remote control, and a tray with a teacup and a croissant. At Polly's entrance, Claudia clicked off the TV, which was tuned to CNN. The light vanished, letting dimness settle over the room.

Through the gloom, Polly tried to assess Claudia's state. Claudia wore a wool skirt, a wool twin set, and pearls. But her hair, usually coiffed to perfection, hung lank. Not for the first time, Polly thought of suggesting she give Claudia a shampoo. Claudia's face looked thinner, too, skeletal really, with the ridge of brow standing out starkly and her eyes sunken into bony sockets.

"Let's turn on some lights!" Polly reached for a lamp.

"Let's *not.*" Claudia put a hand to her forehead. "I need to rest my eyes."

"Okay." Polly always walked a tightrope between Claudia's comfort and Claudia's vanity. "I made a wonderful chicken casserole for your dinner tonight. I'll pop it into the oven to heat up, then I'll be back with a glass of sherry. How does that sound?"

"Fine," Claudia said.

As Polly passed through the gloomy

rooms, the fading twilight through the windows provided the only illumination. On the dining room sideboard and from the high kitchen cabinets, Claudia's silver candlesticks, carafes, and tureens gleamed in tarnished splendor, like retired armor. Polly wondered why they hadn't been polished lately.

In the kitchen, Polly turned the oven to three fifty and slid her casserole inside. She unpacked the groceries, grateful for the friendly gleam of the refrigerator light each time she opened it. Now and then as she moved through the kitchen, an odd smell floated past her nostrils. She sniffed—but the smell was gone.

She set out two dainty crystal glasses and the bottle of sherry, filled a small bowl with salted almonds, and placed two small cocktail napkins on the tray. Claudia didn't drink more than a sip of sherry these days, but she seemed to enjoy continuing her familiar ritual. It seemed to Polly that the level of cranberry juice was the same as it had been yesterday, that the butter dish had not been moved from last night. The sink was empty and clean, the countertops tidy. Polly made a mental note to ask Pearl how much dinner Claudia was actually eating. And how much breakfast, for it was Pearl who prepared that for Claudia.

There that smell was again! Polly stood still, like a rabbit, only her nose twitching. The pungent, slightly rank, aroma seemed to be coming from the white metal trash bin next to the sink. On a whim, Polly lifted off the lid and looked in. The bin, neatly lined with white plastic, was full of food Polly had brought over during the past week. What was odd was that it was also full of Claudia's daily china and silverware. Last night's lamb stew was on top, in its handsome gold-rimmed bowl. Beneath it, on a gold-rimmed plate, was an intact mass of macaroni and cheese. Beneath that—Polly put on a rubber glove, reached in, and checked—a plate of salmon mousse.

Polly could understand that Claudia might not want to eat some or any of Polly's culinary offerings, especially when she didn't feel well. She could understand Pearl throwing the food out untouched. But why would Pearl throw out the heirloom plates and silver? That made no sense at all.

Unless Pearl was no longer coming. Unless Claudia, too weak to put her dishes in the dishwasher, was simply throwing them away.

Polly stripped off the rubber glove, dropped it on the counter, and stormed into the living room. Without asking first, she switched on a lamp.

"Claudia, isn't Pearl coming anymore?"

Claudia looked offended and didn't answer, which was answer enough.

Polly demanded, "Why isn't she coming?"

Claudia's voice was icy. "I let her go."

"Good grief! Why?" Claudia had never been able to keep help for long. Perhaps Pearl had broken a dish or said something Claudia considered impertinent.

"It's none of your affair." Claudia's eyes were holes of acid.

"Claudia, you need household help more than ever, now that you're sick."

Claudia sniffed. "*Sick* is such an unattractive word."

"Oh, Claudia, for heaven's sake, *cancer* is an unattractive word, but you have it, and you need help."

"I told you I will have no one prying into my life."

"But washing and cleaning aren't prying," Polly protested.

Claudia averted her eyes.

Immediately Polly understood. Of course washing and cleaning *were* prying, if they allowed the cleaner to see how sick Claudia was. Polly sank onto a needlepoint stool at the end of Claudia's chaise. "Claudia, you're losing weight. Are you eating *anything*?"

Claudia glared at Polly, rage steaming from her. Polly glared back. Claudia closed her eyes. When she opened them, her face was bland, her tone serene. "Has the mail arrived?"

Polly blinked. "I asked if you were eating."

"And I asked you whether my mail has arrived. I've been expecting several important letters."

"Yes." Polly kept her voice polite but cool. "I brought in your mail."

"May I have it, please?" Claudia held out her hand.

No way could Polly out-ice the ice queen. Polly acquiesced with a sigh. "Of course."

Polly went to the entrance hall, picked up the mail that had been slipped through the brass mail slot, gave it to Claudia, and returned to the kitchen. With trembling hands, she knocked back a slug of dry sherry, then, determined, went back to the lion's den.

Taking her usual seat across from Claudia's chaise, she said in a mild, conversational voice, "Claudia, let's talk about your health. Have you told Dr. Monroe you're not eating?"

Claudia looked at Polly as if Polly were a puppy who had just soiled the rug. "There's no point in my eating. I can't keep anything down."

"Oh, Claudia. How"—seeing Claudia's face, she tried to temper her words— "*uncomfortable*! Look, there are medicines to help with that. And could we please discuss getting hospice involved? They're professionals, they know how to help you, and I'd—"

Claudia whipped an arctic gaze at Polly. "*Do* you think I'm of unsound mind?"

"No, of course not, Claudia, but—"

"Then I'll thank you to keep your opinions to yourself."

"Claudia," Polly said, allowing some of her exasperation to show, "I'm only trying to help you."

"And you *are* helping me." Claudia's voice shook. She touched her fingers to the bridge of her nose, as if pushing something back. Perhaps, Polly thought, tears. Sounding profoundly tired, she continued, "And I'm grateful for the food and the errands."

"Claudia, you could be more com—"

Claudia pulled herself up straight. "But the rest of it, all these words, it's simply tiresome. Why won't you just allow me to get on with this as I choose? I know what I'm doing. Please respect that." By the time Claudia had finished her speech, her entire body was trembling. She subsided, sinking back into her cushions, a puddle of shapeless, loose wool, the only force left in her burning from her dark, angry eyes.

Polly cringed, berating herself for having driven the proud woman into a corner. *How do I do this?* Polly wondered frantically. *I don't know the rules. I don't even know the guidelines.* "All right, Claudia." She spoke her way through this as if walking on a swinging bridge in total darkness. "I'll try not to intrude, if you'll agree to tell me when you're uncomfortable, or when you need anything."

The slight downward wobble of Claudia's head could have been a nod of agreement. "Right now I need my evening aperitif."

"Right. Sherry coming up."

Polly fetched it, set the tray on the table next to Claudia, sat back down, and raised her glass. "Cheers."

"Indeed." Claudia raised the glass to her lips, then lowered it. "It's snowing again. The Weather Channel says we might get several more inches." She was rewarding Polly by conversing with her.

"It's terrible out there. I don't think the city can keep all the roads plowed."

"When has the city ever been able to do anything correctly? And I hear there's a flu epidemic."

"Yes, I guess it's terrible. A huge percentage of children are missing school because of it. Oh, I worry so much about my little grandson. When David was a baby, he got terrible ear infections, they caused him so much pain, I hope that sort of thing isn't genetic."

Claudia picked up a book and began to read.

Oh, Polly thought. *I forgot. You have no interest in me and mine.* "Shall we turn on the evening news?"

"Good idea." Claudia put the book down.

"I'd like to see how Martha Stewart's faring."

Carolyn told her secretary she was going to slip home for a little afternoon catnap. What she really intended was more like cat burglary. Not that she would steal anything, except, she hoped, some information.

She'd only just brought her car to a stop at the porte cochere when a blue Subaru pulled up behind her and Polly stepped out, looking chic in an emerald green cape.

"James Bond, I presume," Carolyn greeted Polly.

"More like Inspector Clouseau, I'm afraid," Polly joked, following Carolyn into the house. "My god, this place is a *pile*! And I mean that in the nicest possible way."

Carolyn laughed as she led Polly down the main hall. "That's great-grandmother Geraldine Helena, who started it all," she said, pointing to a painting. "The others are all ancestors, too. It's rather Addams family, I know, all this dark wood, but somehow we're always so busy with the company we never have time even to think of changing things here at home."

They stopped in the doorway to the shared living room. Taking in the massive Empire furniture, the Victorian settees, the velvet love seats, and the stodgy oils of hunt scenes and landscapes, Polly said, "It does seem a bit *Masterpiece Theatre* in here."

"True. Probably why Hank and I chose to furnish our part of the house in simple modern lines. I'll show you, but first, let's go check out my father's wing while we know he and Heather are gone. Just toss your cape here," she directed Polly, draping her own coat over the banister of the main staircase.

They went back down the hall, through the kitchen, and into the housekeeper's office. "This is where I found Heather snooping through Mrs. B.'s accounts." Out of breath, Carolyn sank for a moment into the leather swivel chair behind the desk.

"Hey, are you okay?" Polly's forehead wrinkled with concern.

"I think so. I just like to sit down whenever I get the chance."

"When is your baby due?"

"April twentieth."

"Are you getting any regular exercise? I mean, steady, gentle exercise. Are you taking a walk every day, that kind of thing?"

"Well, I do yoga," Carolyn reminded Polly.

"That's good. But you should probably be doing some walking every day for twenty minutes or so. I mean, ask your doctor, of course. But I know you're concerned about your blood pressure, and routine exercise can help with that, as well as get you in shape for labor."

Carolyn rubbed her belly with her fingertips. "I'm pretty sure I walk enough, just around the office."

"But that's not steady exercise, and it's not relaxing. You probably have employees rushing up to talk to you about work matters."

"You're right, I suppose." Polly's concern brought an unexpected lump to Carolyn's throat. Struggling to sit upright in the leather chair, she said fiercely, "My great-grandmother did it *all*! Had her baby and began the paper mill and built this house!"

"Yes, but probably not all at the same time. I'll bet your great-grandmother was younger than you when she had her first baby."

Carolyn nodded. "She was eighteen."

"There you are. Almost twenty years younger. She did it all, but not all at the same time, right? Besides, you might have some of her genes, but remember, you're your own person."

Carolyn lowered her eyes. "I don't want to be weak."

Polly laughed. "Who does? You know, Carolyn, one of the lessons having a baby taught me was that I had to cooperate with life, not try to rule it. That never works. Have you ever sailed?"

"Of course."

"Well, having a child is a lot like sailing. You do your best to stay on course to achieve your destination, but you've got to learn to work with what nature throws your way. You can't fight the strength or direction of the wind, you have to be flexible, ready to come about, tack, and trim your sails. On your best days, you'll harness the wind. On your worst days, you'll be lucky to keep from capsizing." Suddenly Polly blushed. "Sorry about the metaphor. I don't mean to lecture."

"No, no, please," Carolyn said hurriedly. "I like what you have to say." It was unusual for her to have an attractive, admirable older woman, with her lovely face and wise eyes, bossily giving advice to Carolyn. Polly wasn't holding back because she wanted to date Aubrey or gushing and flattering because Carolyn was Carolyn *Sperry.* "Did you get tired when you were pregnant? Or irrational?"

Polly's tinkling laughter spilled through the air like bubbles. "Oh, you have no idea! Look, let's finish up with this Heather business so we can go relax over a pot of herbal tea, then I'll tell you all about it." Back on task, Polly asked, "Did Heather have a reasonable explanation for snooping through the desk?"

"Yes. Said she wanted to find a map of the house and a list of Mrs. B.'s recipes, which does make sense, except that she had the household accounts ledger open, and when she saw that *I* saw, oh, man, she gave me a look that would straighten Medusa's hair! She recovered immediately, morphed right back to sweet, innocent Heather, and said she wanted her name added to the account, so she could start buying food for herself and my father, which is reasonable. But that momentary glimpse of pure malice I saw in her eyes chilled me to the bone."

"Did she act that way when you confronted her about the missing funds from your father's credit line?"

Pushing with both hands off the desk, Carolyn raised her bulk back to a standing position. "Not at all. She was like a sweet little kitten with an injured paw, heartbroken by my callousness. All she wanted was to turn my father's wing into *their* place. I certainly can't fault her for that. I had to apologize. And really, all I have to go on is that one look she shot me, so perhaps I'm overreacting. I hope so."

While she talked, she led Polly from the kitchen through the family room, down a hall, and into her father's wing. At the door, Carolyn paused. She put a hand over her beating heart.

"You know, Polly, I can strike terror into the hearts of brilliant executives who earn a quarter million dollars a year at Sperry Paper Company. I'm a whiz at public speaking, which most people fear more than death. But if you weren't here with me right now, I don't think I'd have the courage to enter my father's quarters, not now that he's married to Heather, not now that I feel like I'm their enemy."

"Well, I am here," Polly reassured Carolyn. "Plus, you are not your father's enemy. You are his daughter, taking the normal precautions anyone would."

"What if they come home while we're in here?"

Polly had already thought about this. "You'll simply say I'm a new friend, a seamstress. I want to branch out into home décor, slipcovers, upholstered chairs, and so on. You're showing me around the house so I can get a feel for design possibilities."

"All right." Carolyn took a deep breath. "That makes sense." She shot Polly a trembling smile. "Why do I feel like such a guilty little child?"

"We never stop feeling that way around our parents. Now go on. Open the door."

Carolyn put her hand on the knob and turned. They stepped inside.

"Oh, my."

"You can say that again."

The living room was crammed with furniture from every possible period. A plasma television hung over an elaborate gold table carved with gargoyles, lions, and fleur-de-lis. A plush new sofa in stunning gold and magenta brocade was centered between two marble and gilt tables. An Italianate gilt chair and a painted Regency armchair completed the seating arrangements. From one wall an enormous painted chinoiserie-style bureau loomed, while from another wall an ormolu-mounted marquetry French commode supported a large porcelain vase filled with silk flowers.

"Let's check the bedroom," Polly urged.

Carolyn hesitated. "Oh, I don't know, I think I've seen enough."

"Just a quick peek." Polly grabbed Carolyn's arm and pulled her into the adjoining room.

Every inch of the bedroom was crowded with furniture, all of it draped, swagged, carpeted, and decorated in velvet, heavy silk, gilt, and chiffon. The centerpiece of the room was a white canopy bed, its headboard carved with cherubs, hearts, and flowers, all painted in shades of gold, pink, and blue. The mirror of a white and gold French-provincial vanity table reflected back its clutter of crystal perfume bottles, the damask vanity stool, and the elaborately inlaid regent bombé chest. A chaise longue with carved, scrolled, gilded feet and vivid magenta-and-white-striped cushions sat beneath the window, framed by more chiffon curtains.

"Shades of Marie Antoinette," Carolyn whispered.

Polly snorted. "Marie Antoinette on acid."

Carolyn shook her head. "Oh, dear, oh, dear, I don't know whether to laugh or cry. I think she's tried to out-antique us. She's got every kind of possible period all jumbled together. She's bought so much stuff, I can see how she spent two hundred thousand dollars."

"Yeah, because she bought two hundred thousand pieces of furniture," Polly jested. "Okay, let's beat it, kid," she said in her best Humphrey Bogart voice. "Before they come home."

They hurried through the house to the safety of Carolyn's own wing. Carolyn collapsed on the sofa while Polly made herbal tea for them both. She brought a mug to Carolyn, then settled on a chair nearby.

"So. Are your fears allayed?"

Carolyn looked into the rosy depths of the

herbal tea. "Yes, I suppose so. I still don't like her. I still don't trust her, even though I can't exactly explain why." Impatient with herself, she waved a hand in the air, as if brushing her anxieties away. "Enough of that! I appreciate this, Polly. It was kind of you to take the time to assist me in my neurosis."

"Don't give it another thought," Polly insisted. "I'm having fun." Her eyes misting slightly, she confessed, "You have no idea how much I love being around someone young and pregnant. Even if my son's wife hadn't exiled me because she thinks I'll transmit Claudia's germs, I still wouldn't be seeing much of my son and grandson. Amy just plain dislikes me, and I don't know how I can change things."

"I don't understand how anyone could dislike you!" Carolyn proclaimed stoutly.

Polly laughed. "I don't, either! Anyway, Carolyn, it's a real gift to be around you, watching your belly get bigger every day."

"Polly?"

"Yes?"

"Would you tell me the truth about labor? Is it really so very painful?"

Polly cocked her head, remembering.

"For me, yes, it was. But you know what, I love remembering it, and every other woman I've ever talked to about it does, too. And it doesn't have to be painful. Lots of my friends have had epidurals, and it hasn't made the experience less amazing or the bond between mother and child any less powerful. The main thing, Carolyn, is the baby. You want the baby to be born healthy. And you want to be as strong as possible, to take care of the baby. Do you trust your doctor?"

Carolyn nodded. "I do."

"That's important. And you'll be in a hospital, right, because of your blood pressure?"

"Yes." Carolyn shifted on the sofa. "I've read quite a few books on childbirth, but sometimes they make me anxious."

"A little anxiety is just part of the process. You know, your experience will be unique. It is different, special, every single time."

"Like snowflakes?"

"More like volcanic eruptions," Polly jested. She took a sip of tea. "Now! Is that a wallpaper book on the table?"

Carolyn grinned. "Indeed it is. I'm trying to choose a pattern for Geraldine's room."

"Yummy. Let me see your choices." Polly scooted her chair closer.

Carolyn opened the book. The two women bent side by side, smiling at pages of sweet pastels, primary colors, ducklings and teddy bears, and the air in the room sweetened around them like a spring breeze, chasing despondent thoughts away.

20

On this January Sunday, the temperature hovered around zero. Each breath of frigid air stabbed the lungs like sabers. Frost snapped at fingers, noses, and toes. Most of the roads were empty of traffic, and in the country the deer were tucked away in their dens. Even the birds refused to come out in this cold.

So of course Sonny and his family decided to go ice skating at a local pond.

When Robin suggested it as they were gathered in the Young house, eating their Sunday dinner, Beth's spirits had plummeted like the thermometer. She didn't want to inform this bunch of jocks that she'd never been able to stand up on the ice, but she did think she'd wriggled out of going when she said, honestly, that she didn't have any ice skates.

She should have known the Youngs would have all kinds of ice skates, and certainly a pair that fit Beth.

So they piled into their various SUVs and trucks, skidded along snow-lined country roads, and slogged through the snow down to a glassy, irregular oblong of ice surrounded by bushes and dried brown grasses shivering in the breeze.

"Here." Sonny plopped down on a fallen log. "I'll get my skates on, then help you lace up yours." His teal blue wool cap made his eyes seem as blue as a summer's dream.

"Okay," Beth agreed, sitting next to him. The leather of the skates was stiff and cold against her socked feet. She'd only begun to work the lace between the metal hooks when Sonny knelt to help her, completing the task with swift, practiced movements.

"Now," he said, holding out his hand. "Let's teach you to skate."

Everyone else was already on the ice, twirling past in a carousel of color. Merle and Bobbie glided along arm in arm, legs swinging together like a pair of pendulums. Sonny's sister, Suze, his brother, Mark, and Mark's girlfriend, Barbie, raced, screaming with glee, arms pumping, legs scissoring, toward the far end of the pond, while Robin, graceful as a ballerina, wove a figure eight in a stunning arabesque, her arms extended wide like wings. Her long blond hair hung in a thick braid down the back of the gorgeous handmade wool sweater, sprinkled with white snowflakes, matching a blue wool hat. Her tall, slender perfection seemed lifted from a music box.

If Robin was Snow White, Beth felt like the Eighth Dwarf as she toddled, hanging on to Sonny, her balance precipitous, her legs weak, her ankles threatening to buckle.

"Like this." Sonny left her to stand alone while he demonstrated the technique of gliding.

Beth tried to mimic him. She staggered and flailed like a female Charlie Chaplin. Sonny put his hand on her waist, took her other hand in his, and slowly brought her along the ice with steady, even steps. Ignoring the way the wind shoved her backward, defying her quivering ankles, she concentrated on the rhythm Sonny was attempting to show her. To her delight, gradually the separate parts of her feet, legs, pelvis, and shoulders warmed into a kind of unity as she relaxed into Sonny's lead.

"Good!" Sonny encouraged. "You're do-ing great!"

She smiled up at him, stumbled, and al-most took a tumble.

He righted her, steadied her. "You just hit a bump. We all do."

Concentrating so hard she bit her lip, Beth started over. Push, glide, push, glide.

"Look, we've done a circuit of the pond!" Sonny held her as they coasted past the tree where she'd put on her skates. "Want to try it by yourself?"

"Okay." Terrified but determined, Beth re-linquished Sonny's support and lurched away, feeling as coordinated as Keith Richards on a good night. Bobbie and Merle sped past her, giving her the thumbs-up. From the corner of her eye, she saw Robin going into an Olympic-class spin, bringing her arms into her chest as she whirled, ice spurting from her slicing skates.

Focus, Beth commanded herself. Her torso jerked back and forth as she struggled to remain upright, but her legs seemed to have achieved a regular pace, and she felt her entire body soften just a little as she began to skim, faster and faster, over the ice.

Now that she was moving, she realized she had no idea how to stop.

Sonny flew past her with the bulky speed of a hockey jock. Robin floated past her, grace incarnate. Beth tried to slow down, but somehow it just wasn't working. Legs locked together in a fearful paralysis, Beth rushed along toward the far end of the pond at a speed that made her breathless. She wasn't certain she could negotiate the turn. Perhaps she shouldn't even try. The snow piled along the border of the pond looked soft enough to make a safe landing spot. Then she saw the gray of protruding sticks and rocks and fear gripped her chest.

Suddenly she felt an arm around her waist. Sonny's mother took her hand and steadied her as they looped around the end and headed back.

"I'll show you how to stop," Bobbie said. "Watch me." She whipped off, checking over her shoulder to be sure Beth was watching, then executed an elegant maneuver, pointing the toe of one skate down into the ice, bringing her body to a halt.

She did it a few more times, then skated back to Beth. "Take my hand. I'll help you."

Beth wanted to trust Sonny's mother— she had no choice right now. She clamped on to Bobbie's hand.

"First, we'll slow down. Good. Then we'll draw our skates in toward one another. Good." Bobbie skated backward, weaving her feet in and out, slowing their speed.

Beth tried to duplicate Bobbie's movements, but when her feet dug into the ice, her upper body kept going forward. Suddenly Bobbie pulled Beth forward, then jerked her hand away fast, and in that unexpected release, Beth fell with a bone-shuddering crash onto her bum.

"Oh, dear, are you all right?" Bobbie asked, her dark blue eyes dancing with laughter.

Everyone else skated up to her, laughing. Beth didn't know which hurt more, her butt or her pride.

"Hey, babe, you okay?" Sonny crouched next to her, trying to peer into her face.

Beth sniffed back her tears. The others soared away over the ice. In the silence, Beth confessed, "I feel like an idiot."

Sonny laughed. "Oh, it happens to us all. Just part of the learning experience. You know, you were doing great. It's my fault, I should have taught you how to stop." Extending a hand, he yanked her up onto her feet. "Come on, I'll help you work on it."

A hot pain shot up her ankle. "Ouch!" She couldn't stand on her right foot without wanting to shriek. "I think I twisted my ankle."

"Here, lean on me and I'll take you back to the log."

Sonny put his arm around her, leading her as she limped off the ice.

"Do you think it's broken?" he asked, looking worried.

"No, no, I think I just twisted it." Plopping down on the log, she bent over her skates, undid the laces, and rubbed her sore ankle. "Go back and skate, Sonny. I'll be fine. Really."

"Want to go to the car to keep warm?"

"No, no, I'm warm enough here." *She* might not be able to skate, but she didn't want to deprive him of his pleasure, and she could tell by his face as he returned to the ice how much he enjoyed skating.

Leaning back to catch her breath, she watched the others fly over the ice. They were all so athletic, nimble, and swift, while she was as athletic as a damp dishcloth. Beth gave herself a mental shaking. *Toughen up, you wimp!* When she took off the skate, she saw that her ankle was swelling.

Bobbie came duck-walking on the points of her skates and hunkered down on the log next to Beth. "How are you?"

"Twisted my ankle." Beth couldn't look up at the other woman, afraid she might see triumph in her eyes. "Just a little."

"That's too bad." Bobbie looked genuinely concerned. "Want to go home?"

"No, I'm fine," lied Beth.

"Well, I'll drive you home when you're ready." Bobbie gave Beth's knee a sympathetic pat. "We don't want you catching cold out here, and the others will be skating for a long while yet."

Beth looked out at the pond in time to see Robin glide up to Sonny, taking his arm. They skated side by side for a few moments, then Robin skated backward, holding Sonny's hands in hers, and they went into a waltzlike routine of figure eights and

twirls and spins that flowed as easily between the two of them as music.

"They look good together, don't they?"
Bobbie's voice was warm.

Beth couldn't deny it.

"Well, they both like skating, so they
make a real good team." Bobbie sighed.
"They just fit together perfectly."

Now Merle, Mark, and Barbie sped up to
link hands with Sonny and Robin as they
whizzed over the ice, playing crack the
whip, the colors of their scarves, sweaters,
and gloves as dazzling as their laughter.

"I'll drive you home," Bobbie offered.
"You should probably put that ankle up and
get some ice on it."

Beth couldn't get her boot over her ankle.
"You're right," she conceded.

"Want some help?"

"No, thanks." Awkwardly, Beth stood, the
pair of skates dangling from her hand as
white and grounded as a downed gull. She
took one look back at the pond. "I'm sorry
to take you away from the skating."

"That's all right," Bobbie said. "They
won't miss us."

Julia and Belinda were making sugar cookies when the knock came on the front door.

"Goodness!" Julia exclaimed, opening
the door to find a scarlet-faced, swollen-
eyed Beth leaning there, her mouth screwed
up in pain.

"Are you busy? I should have called, but
Bobbie just drove me home, and I'm so upset, I knew I just couldn't stay there all
alone!" She started off brightly enough, but
the last few words came out wobbly.

Julia pulled the door wider and ushered
Beth in. "Hey, what happened to you?
You're limping!"

Julia's sympathetic tones made Beth's
lower lip quiver. "I twisted my ankle ice skating with Sonny and the rest of that hyper-
steroid circus troupe!"

Eyes wide, Belinda tugged on Julia's
black trousers.

"No, honey." Julia smiled down at her
stepdaughter. "Beth hasn't really been with
a circus."

Beth sucked back her tears, arranged her
face in a smile, and squatted to Belinda's
level. "Hello, Belinda, I'm Beth."

Belinda scrutinized Beth carefully in silence. The child's winsome face, sprinkled

with pale freckles, nudged some of the black ice from Beth's heart.

"Oh, my gosh." Beth touched Belinda's curls. "You are the prettiest little girl I've ever seen! Look at your beautiful hair!"

Belinda smiled shyly, exposing a gap where her first baby tooth had been just days before.

"We're making cookies," Julia told Beth. "Come in the kitchen and I'll brew some tea."

"Sounds wonderful." As Beth made a move to rise from her crouching position, a hot pain clamped her back, paralyzing her. "Oh!" she cried. "I can't stand up!" Quickly, she reassured Belinda, "Don't worry, I'm okay. I just fell while ice skating. Hurt my back. I'll be okay in just a minute." The pain made her pant.

"Let's help her," Julia told Belinda. "You take that arm, I'll take this one. On the count of three, heave ho!"

Julia's strong grip hoisted Beth's shoulders while Belinda, trying to help, clutched her chubby little hands around Beth's arm. Beth staggered to her feet, doing her best to stifle a groan, but pain dropped her stomach down an elevator shaft and discharged pinwheels of color before her eyes. "You know, I think I'd better just go home."

Julia shook her head. "I'm not letting you drive when you can hardly stand. You're getting into bed with a heating pad, aspirin, and lots of TLC."

"I can't do that!" Beth protested weakly.

"Of course you can. Tim's at a dental conference in New York. Belinda and I are all alone and terribly bored with each other. We need some company."

"Really, Julia, I didn't mean to interrupt your day."

"You probably didn't mean to fall on your bum, either, but you did, and I'm not letting you go home alone until you feel better. Come on now, hobble along, old thing, and we'll play hospital."

In the guest room, Julia folded back the puffy comforter and sheets and plumped the pillows. "Here, let me help you get those clothes off."

Beth carefully lowered herself to the bed. "Sorry to be such a wimp."

"You're not a wimp." Julia knelt on the floor. "Belinda, you untie that boot and I'll do this one. Egad! This ankle's swollen twice the size as the right one! We'll have to elevate it and put some ice on it. First, let's get you lying down. Lift your arms." When Beth obeyed, Julia gasped. "Double egad! Beth, you have a bruise on your back the size of a watermelon! Belinda, run into my room and bring me my long nightgown, the one with the birdies you gave me for Christmas." By the time Belinda returned, Julia had tugged off Beth's trousers. She undid Beth's bra, then dropped the cotton nightie over Beth's head. "Now. Legs up. Lean back. Pillows okay? I'll get the heating pad, aspirin, and ice. Belinda, you gather some other pillows to put under Beth's leg. We'll need to keep her ankle elevated."

"I'm sorry to be so much trouble," Beth quavered. "I feel like such a spaz!"

Julia bustled around, propping Beth's left leg upon pillows, wrapping ice in a hand towel and fastening it around Beth's ankle. "Everyone falls when they're ice skating."

"Well, it *was* my first time. But, Julia, Sonny's mother was skating with me, she was holding my hand, then suddenly, she just *let go*! I don't think I would have fallen if she hadn't yanked her hand away so fast. The terrible thing is, I think she might have done it on purpose!" Beth yanked her hair wildly. "I just don't understand why she doesn't like me!"

"Doesn't matter whether she likes you or not," Julia stormed. "Her son loves you, and in any case, she ought to behave like a decent human being! Is that heating pad too hot?"

"No, it feels wonderful." The warmth spread through Beth's body. She felt herself relax. "I think I'm going to fall asleep."

"That's exactly what you need to do," Julia announced with satisfaction. "When you wake up, Belinda and I will have some warm sugar cookies for you."

It was dark when Beth opened her eyes, and for a moment she had no idea where she was. She realized the sound of knocking had awakened her. "Come in!" She tried to sit up, but a vise of pain held her fast.

"It's after five." Julia entered the room. "You've had almost two full hours of sleep. Feel better?"

"Much." Beth might not be able to move without screaming, but her spirits were restored.

"Great. Look what we've got for you." The tray Julia set on the bedside table held indigo mugs steaming with tea.

Belinda approached the bed, holding a plate carefully with both hands. She presented it to Beth with an expression of such pride on her face she might well be offering a six-tiered wedding cake.

Beth smiled. "Wow! Snowman cookies! With M&M's buttons!"

"Want to sit up?" Julia grasped Beth's shoulders. Together they strained to get Beth propped up against pillows. Gingerly, Julia seated herself on the side of the bed and handed Beth a mug. "Chamomile tea. Later, we'll have red wine with dinner."

"Oh, I can't stay for dinner," Beth protested.

"Why not? I've already told Belinda you don't have anyone to go home to, and I'll bet Sonny's not the best nurse in the world. Why not let Belinda and me spoil you? We like doing it, don't we, Belinda?"

The little girl nodded.

Beth studied the child a moment, then patted the free side of the bed. "Come sit up here by me. And bring those cookies!"

Belinda ran out of the room.

"Oh, no." Appalled, Beth turned to Julia. "Did I frighten her somehow?"

"I don't think so. I'll go—"

Before Julia could finish, Belinda raced back into the room, clutching several books to her chest. She put them on the bed next to Beth, then clambered up on the bed, snuggled up close to Beth, and looked at her expectantly.

"Aha." Julia grinned. "She wants you to read to her, don't you, Belinda?"

Belinda nodded.

"Cool." Beth reached for the books. "I love to read."

"Don't let her exhaust you," Julia warned. "If she has her way, she'll have you reading until you lose your voice."

"There's nothing I'd rather do," Beth said, and picked up the first book. "*Cinderella.* One of my favorites." She put her arm around Belinda and pulled her close.

"I'm going to clean the kitchen," Julia said. "If you need anything, just call."

———

They were all gathered together on the guest bed, munching a casual, delicious

dinner of grilled-cheese-and-tomato sandwiches when the pounding came at the
front door.

"Who could that be?" Shrugging and licking her buttery fingers, Julia hurried down
the hall and opened the door. Agnes stood
there, the hood of her quilted, gray parka
pulled tight, compressing the fat little fea-
tures of her face so much she resembled a
character from Dr. Seuss.

"Hello, Julia. I was just passing by, and I
knew Timmy was out of town this weekend,
so I thought I'd come by and keep you company." Agnes shoved her way inside the
house. "I see there's a car in your driveway,
and judging by the way the snow's covered
it, it's been there for some time, so obviously you already *have* company. I hope I'm
not *interrupting* something." Agnes's eyes
shone with eager malice, she was almost
licking her lips in anticipation.

"I'm surprised you're out driving in this
weather, Agnes."

Agnes's eyes darted down the hall and
into the living room. "I wanted to catch a
sale at the Bedford Marshalls. They have
such excellent sales. I'm stocking up on

birthday presents for Belinda. Where is my little darling?"

"In the guest—" Julia began, but Agnes was quickly waddling away.

"*Aaah!*" Agnes shrieked. "Who are you? What are you doing in my bed!"

Julia rushed after her. "Agnes, this is my friend Beth."

Beth lay against the pillows, the covers drawn over her lap, a picture book open in her hands, Belinda cuddled up against her.

"Why is she here? Where am I going to sleep?" Agnes demanded.

"Beth hurt her back ice skating," Julia explained. "Belinda and I are taking care of her tonight."

"Hello," Beth said politely, extending her hand.

Agnes recoiled as if it dripped snakes. "She's spending the night?"

"Yes," Julia said firmly. "She is."

"She's sleeping *here*?" Agnes seemed to puff up like a toad.

"It's the *guest* bedroom," Julia pointed out quietly.

Agnes turned on Julia, teeth bared. "You *planned* this. So I couldn't spend the night and be with my granddaughter."

"Agnes, of course I didn't plan this, how could I, when I had no idea you'd be in the area? Not to mention, I had no idea Beth would hurt her back."

Wanting to placate the older woman, who was trembling in a rather terrifying way, Beth pushed back the covers and turned around, hiking up her nightgown. "Does the bruise look any better, Julia?"

Beth's back flashed like the sunset over mountains, purple, red, black, and blue.

"It looks worse, actually," Julia informed her. "But bruises usually do as they heal."

Disappointed by this proof that Julia wasn't lying, Agnes spotted the three plates with half-eaten sandwiches tilting on the bedcovers and pounced. "You're eating in bed?"

"Beth also twisted her ankle. We didn't want her to have to get up," Julia explained reasonably.

"I see." Agnes's mouth crimped. "I guess I wasted my trip."

"Not if you found some good bargains at Marshalls," Julia coolly replied.

"I suppose I'd better drive back to the Berkshires," Agnes said grudgingly.

"You're welcome to sleep on the sofa."

Julia crossed her fingers behind her back and sent a silent prayer to the heavens.

"No, that would hurt *my* back." Agnes held out her arms. "Come here, Belinda. Give Grammy a hug, then I'll leave you all to your little party."

Obediently, Belinda went to her grandmother, who clutched the child to her as if she'd just been rescued from the *Titanic.* "You've lost a tooth!" She shot an accusing glare at Julia. "You didn't tell me she lost a tooth!"

"We took Polaroids," Julia told her. "We mailed them off to you two days ago."

Agnes snorted. "You're far too trusting of the postal service. I probably won't see that photo for a week." Genuinely sad, she said, "I wish you'd phoned me."

Julia folded her arms over her chest. "You know, Agnes, Tim's been wanting to come out and set up a computer for you so you and Belinda could e-mail each other. We could have scanned the photo and e-mailed it to you if you had a computer."

Agnes shook her head violently. "All this modern stuff is the work of the devil. It will never find a place in my house!" With that, she spun on her heel and left the room, slamming to a halt as another thought occurred to her. "Did the tooth fairy come?"

Belinda nodded, a big grin on her face.

"Yes," Julia added. "The tooth fairy left Belinda a dollar!"

"What a stingy tooth fairy you have in this town," Agnes said with vinegary hauteur. "In our town, *our* tooth fairy always leaves *five* dollars!" Satisfied at having scored this point, Agnes nodded briskly and went away.

Julia stood in the open doorway, waving at Agnes until her big Buick turned the corner and disappeared. Then she shut the door and locked it.

After Beth read Belinda a few more storybooks, Julia gave Belinda a bath and got her ready for bed while Beth phoned Sonny to tell him where she was spending the night.

"Now!" Julia entered the room with a bottle of red wine. Settling at the foot of the bed facing Beth, she handed Beth a glass. "The final portion of Dr. Julia's Medical Therapy!"

Beth socked her pillows into shape and

shifted her leg into another position. "This is the best ER I've ever been in."

Julia stretched over to tuck a blanket around Beth's elevated foot. "What did Sonny say?"

"They're all watching a football game. He said I did a great job for my first time on ice skates, and I shouldn't feel embarrassed because I fell, that everyone falls at first, and"—she finished with exaggerated perky good cheer—"maybe next weekend we can all go out to the pond again!"

Julia laughed with Beth. "Seriously, though, I doubt if your ankle will be healed enough to put that kind of stress on it by next weekend."

"Seriously, though," Beth echoed, "sooner or later I've got to learn to ice-skate."

Julia cocked her head. "You really think you can fit in with this family?"

"Well, in the first place, I'm not marrying the family. I'm marrying Sonny." Beth sat a little straighter, in spite of her aching back. "I really love Sonny. And I know he loves me. When we're together, not with his family, we're perfect. I don't mean just sex," she added with a blush.

"Honey," Julia interrupted, "there's no such thing as 'just sex.' "

"Right. Okay, then, the sex is amazing. And it's part of our love, a huge part, but not the only part. Sonny's really intelligent. He reads as much as I do, but he never finished college, so in an odd way I know he's trusting me to not make fun of him intellectually. So I don't mind being such a spaz in front of him. It's just his family that makes me feel all humiliated and dorky. His mother, really."

"Would it help if you talked to her?" Julia asked. "What if you took her out to lunch and had a good heart-to-heart?"

"What could I say? 'It hurts my feelings that you want Sonny to marry Robin instead of me, that I suspect you tamper with the food I bring over, and after skating with you I think you'd probably kill me if you could!" Beth shook her head angrily. "No cozy talk with Sonny's mother. She wants me to disappear."

"Have you talked with Sonny about this?"

"Oh, vaguely, but I always end up sounding paranoid and as if I'm fishing for compliments. I haven't told him I think his mother put tuna water in my casserole. I mean, Sonny's mother is his *mother,* she's sacred territory. I don't think he'd believe she did anything wrong even if a panel of witnesses testified to it."

Julia pulled her knees up to her chin and wrapped her arms around her legs, digging her chin into her knees as she thought. "Your case is tougher than mine. Agnes is a pain in the butt, but you've got to feel sorry for her. She's lost her daughter, and here I am, a strange woman, taking care of her granddaughter. She drives me nuts, but she drives Tim nuts, too. Tim and I are on the same side. You've got Sonny's mother right in between the two of you."

"And I *won't* feel sorry for her!" Beth said with spirit. "I mean, Sonny's old girlfriend is beautiful and a great jock, but Sonny didn't marry her! He loves me, and he's going to marry me!"

"Right. So we've got to cook up some kind of plan to get Sonny's mother off your back."

Readjusting the pillows behind her, Beth said, "My back and I thank you!"

21

Even in a hospital bed, naked from the waist down except for her silk tap pants, Claudia managed to look more regal than Queen Victoria.

Obviously she felt that way. "I don't understand," she said to Polly in a voice iced with contempt, "why this room doesn't have a closet. It won't do my skirt any good simply to be tossed over the back of a chair like that when it should be properly hung."

Polly smoothed the skirt with her hand. She would have liked to sit down in the chair, but if she did, she might wrinkle the skirt. Then Claudia would really have a fit. "It's an outpatient room, so I suppose there's no need for a closet."

"I just pointed out the need for a closet. Are you *deaf*?" snapped Claudia, rolling her eyes in exasperation.

She's afraid, Polly reminded herself. She's about to have a long needle inserted into her abdomen, and she's frightened, not to mention dying of cancer and probably constipated and hungry, too.

"Would you like a sip of water?" Polly asked. "Or maybe some juice? The nurse said Dr. Monroe will be right in, but we might have a little wait."

"I don't think Hugh will keep *me* waiting," Claudia retorted, just as the physician walked into the room.

"Hello, Claudia!" Exuding health, confidence, and the scent of cinnamon, he strode to the bed and grasped Claudia's hand in a firm clasp. "You're looking well!" With a nod toward Polly, he said, "Hello, Polly. Nice to see you again."

"Nice to see you." He'd remembered her name! Polly felt herself blush. She'd forgotten how attractive the man was, how sexy. Oh, Lord, she was developing a crush on him. Probably every woman did; women did get moony over doctors.

"We're doing a paracentesis today," Dr. Monroe informed them. "It's a simple procedure. We'll be draining some of the fluid from your abdomen, which will provide you some relief from the pressure and might allow you to eat more."

A nurse wheeled in a stainless steel cart laden with bottles and boxes. As he spoke, Dr. Monroe pulled up a chair, opened the boxes, removed gloves and needles and other paraphernalia, and deftly arranged everything at Claudia's side, chatting away the entire time as if he were at a summer luncheon.

"I don't understand why I have this fluid," Claudia complained.

"It's a reaction to the tumor," Dr. Monroe told her. "It's called ascitic fluid, and it will continue to accumulate. Now, the ultrasound you just had indicated that we've got a nice little pocket of fluid right here on the left side, so I'm going to put a needle in— sorry, this will sting a bit—then we'll just attach this drain. Nurse, if you would get the first bottle ready, please—and here we go. I saw your photo in *Boston* magazine, Claudia. You looked smashing in that red hat."

Claudia looked pleased. "That was at the Penrods' Christmas party. I'm surprised I didn't see you there."

Fluid the color of tea trickled from the long tube into a glass liter bottle. The physician adjusted it so the flow increased. "Comfortable?" When Claudia nodded, he said, "Well, you know Carol and I divorced a few years ago, and when we did, we sort of divided our friends between us, and Carol got the Penrods."

Polly's ears pricked up like a retriever at the quack of a duck. Glancing at Hugh Monroe, she saw him smiling at her, and she blushed again.

"Also, I have to admit, I'm not thrilled about going to social occasions alone." He pressed a clip, momentarily halting the flow. "New bottle, please, Nurse."

"I'm surprised you're alone," Claudia told him. "You must have any number of suitable women who would be only too glad to be your companion."

"I suppose the sticking point is the definition of *suitable*." Now he looked at Polly quite openly.

Claudia noticed. "Polly, I would like a ginger ale."

Polly gave herself a mental kick. There poor Claudia was, stuck like a dilapidated automobile having its oil changed, while Polly and Hugh Monroe, still, by comparison, relatively young and hearty, flirted with each other.

"I'll get it for you right away."

Polly hurried down the long corridor and into an elevator to the basement and the food court, lecturing herself silently. Dr. Monroe probably flirted with every woman, as a therapeutic service. It certainly got *her* blood pumping. Spotting a restroom, she darted in to check her appearance in a mirror. Her green eyes, enlarged by the eyeliner Julia had suggested she try, sparkled, and a becoming flush brought color to her milky skin. Carolyn had told her she looked a little like Julianne Moore—of course, Carolyn was just being kind. *Enough!* Polly scolded herself, and dashed off to get the ginger ale.

By the time she returned to the room, Dr. Monroe was gently removing the tube from Claudia's abdomen. With a square of gauze, he patted antiseptic ointment over the small wound.

"You should be fine now. This will heal quickly, and you should have quite a few good days with a good appetite. Eat as much as you can, to buck up your strength."

"Thank you, Hugh." Claudia awarded him a brief, regal nod.

He took one of her hands in his. "You promise you will call me if you have any symptoms that make you uncomfortable."

"Very well." She looked away, as if he were being rude.

The nurse wheeled the cart with its three liter bottles from the room.

Dr. Monroe pressed his case. "Constipation, indigestion, pain, even if it's minor. We've got all kinds of palliatives to help you. We want you to enjoy every day as much as you can."

Claudia pulled her hand from his. "Good of you."

"At some point, you'll want to check into the hospital."

Anger molded her face into a cold mask. "Never."

Dr. Monroe folded his arms over his chest and considered his patient. "Never?" he asked genially.

"Absolutely not. I abhor hospitals. I intend to die in my own home."

"Even though we can make you more comfortable in a hospital?"

"Nothing could make me comfortable in a

hospital. I intend to spend the last remaining moments of my life surrounded by my own things."

He nodded. "I can understand that, Mrs. Lodge, certainly. Many people feel that way, actually. That's why we have such an excellent home health and hospice program. That way nurses can visit you—"

"No. No strangers."

Hugh Monroe bent close to Claudia and lowered his voice, as if calming an injured animal. "We know you don't want strangers in your house. But please consider it. You might need pain medication, for example, or help bathing—"

Claudia shuddered visibly. "Hugh. If you continue like this, I shall either consult another doctor or refrain from taking any medical advice at all."

The physician studied her face. "Very well." He straightened, shot Polly a look laden with rue, then became, once again, brisk and hearty. "I'll leave you, then, Mrs. Lodge. I'll be glad to hear from you anytime."

"Must I stay here now?"

"If you want. You might want to rest a lit-

tle. Or, if you'd like, you're free to leave anytime."

"I'll leave now. This is not the most attractive room."

He laughed. "I agree. Good-bye then,
Mrs. Lodge." To Polly's delight, he crossed
the room and took her hand in his. "Nice to
see you again, Polly."

She knew she was flushing like a schoolgirl. "Nice to see you."

He seemed about to say something else.
Then a nurse came in, and he gave everyone another nod and left the room.

It was as if all the lights went out.

"Polly?" Claudia was impatient.

"Here," Polly said, rushing forward with
Claudia's woolen skirt. "Let me help you
dress."

———

Polly and Claudia walked back out of the
hospital through halls streaming with patients in wheelchairs, on crutches and walk-
ers. The parking valet brought Polly's Subaru around. Polly helped Claudia into the
passenger seat, then settled behind the

wheel. "Is there anywhere you'd like to go before I take you home?"

"Don't be ridiculous. I want to go straight home. I'm tired."

"All right, then. Would you like to hear some music?"

Claudia shrugged. "I suppose."

Polly clicked on the radio, tuning it to the classical station. Vivaldi spun into the air. Claudia leaned her head back against the car seat. Polly drove to Dover, grateful for the music filling the silence.

At Claudia's house, Polly stopped the car and unfastened her seat belt.

"Don't fuss, Polly. I'm quite capable of walking into my own home without your assistance." Claudia gathered her purse up and opened the car door.

"All right, then," Polly answered brightly. "I'll be back this evening with some dinner for you, and perhaps a nice little dessert. I'm meeting Carolyn Sperry for tea, and maybe we'll find one perfect cake—"

Claudia's head whipped around like a cobra's. "Whom? Whom did you say you're meeting?"

"Carolyn Sperry. She—"

"Carolyn Sperry of the Sperry Paper

Company?" Claudia's eyebrows rose so high they nearly melded with her hairline.

"Yes."

"How do *you* know Carolyn Sperry?" Two spots of red bloomed on Claudia's pale skin.

Polly swallowed her exasperation. Trust Claudia to assume Polly wouldn't be of interest to someone of Carolyn's vaunted social value. "I met her at The Haven, out near Concord, and we've become friends. She's—"

Crankily, Claudia cut her off. "But why would she be your friend? You're closer to her father's age than to hers."

"True. But her mother's dead. And her father just married a young woman whom Carolyn doesn't—" Polly slapped her hand over her mouth. "Oh, I suppose I shouldn't gossip." She didn't mean to be ingenious, but as she spoke, she realized nothing could have whetted Claudia's appetite more. Claudia froze like a retriever who'd just flushed out a quail from the underbrush.

"Well." Claudia presented Polly with an impressive imitation of a smile. "Run along to your little tea. I'll see you this evening."

Polly watched Claudia as she slowly, with

great deliberation, made her way up her sidewalk to her house. Claudia did not like to be touched, and she did not like to seem to need assistance, but Polly was amazed that the older woman didn't collapse, so bone-thin were her legs. Perhaps she ought to phone Dr. Monroe to discuss Claudia's state and what could be done to help her.

But if she phoned Dr. Monroe, would he think she was just flirting with him?

Damn! Was nothing ever plain and simple?

Later that day, after the early winter dusk had fallen, Polly let herself into Claudia's house, stamped the snow off her boots, hung up her coat and handbag, and went down the hall to the gloomy living room where no lights, not even the television, glowed.

"Hello? I'm going to turn on a lamp, Claudia, I want to show you what I've brought."

"*Mmmfh,*" Claudia replied, sounding slightly disoriented. No doubt Polly had awakened her from a nap. She suspected Claudia napped a lot these days.

The light came on just in time for Polly to see Claudia, slumped in a thin, sunken curl on the chaise, trying to maneuver her false teeth into her mouth.

Oh, jeez, Polly thought. Old age is so hard on our vanity! Quickly she turned away and busied herself setting a new plant on a table. To give Claudia more time to compose herself, she went into the kitchen and began dinner preparations. She poured two glasses of sherry, put them on the tray, and carried it into the living room.

Claudia had her teeth back in and was sitting up straight in her chaise. She'd patted her hair into place, although the back of it stuck up like a cockatoo's comb, detracting from her dignity as she said in plummy tones, "The azalea is lovely, Polly, thank you."

Polly nearly dropped the tray. Compliments from Claudia? "I'm so glad you like it." Setting the tray on the table, she handed Claudia a glass. "It's six o'clock. Shall we watch the news?"

"Of course." On her own, Polly paid little attention to the news, but Tucker had been a news junkie who would no more have missed the six-o'clock news on Channel 5 at the end of the day than a priest would have skipped Sunday-morning mass. So Polly relaxed in her chair, sipping her sherry and only halfheartedly listening to the commentators, instead, remembering how cozy her evenings had been with Tucker, how he'd made her laugh with his editorial comments on the news. Now as she sat with Claudia, she felt even lonelier than she would have felt if she'd been alone, because Claudia insisted on absolute silence, even during the commercial breaks, which was probably a good thing. Claudia was conservative, Polly liberal. They already had enough to disagree about. Tucker had always—

"I think Natalie Jacobsen's new hairstyle is quite attractive, don't you?"

Claudia *speaking*? Polly was so surprised she almost tossed her drink across the room. "Yes," she agreed weakly, not having thought much about the anchorwoman's hairstyle.

Claudia said nothing else, and Polly was floating back in her memories when, during the weather forecast, Claudia announced, "Dick Alpert annoys me sometimes. I wish he'd be a little less *perky*."

Polly snapped to attention. "I suppose he's trying to jazz up the weather."

"Perhaps. Although you'd think all these new graphics would be sufficient for that."

Good golly, Polly thought. *We're having a conversation!*

She had a pretty good idea why. Now that Claudia knew Polly was friends with Carolyn Sperry, Polly's social value had jumped several levels in Claudia's mind. Well, Polly was grateful for anything that would make her relationship with Claudia a little smoother.

Claudia switched channels to CNN while Polly prepared a plate of beef and rice casserole, which Polly had made using her richest recipe, because, unlike Polly, Claudia needed all the fat she could get. As she dished it up, Polly tried to think of a way to broach the subject of arranging new household help for Claudia. She wanted to do it tonight, while Claudia was in a receptive mood.

Back in the living room, she set a tray over Claudia's lap. The pungent aroma of gravy, wine, onions, and beef rose in the air. Polly poured a glass of merlot for each of them, then curled up in a chair across from Claudia, and prepared to stare at the television as she had every other night for the past few weeks.

Claudia flicked the remote and the screen went blank. "How was your tea?"

Oh, Polly thought. *Of course!* "It was fine. We met at the Ritz."

Claudia's eyes brightened. "The *only* place for tea."

"Yes, and it's near Carolyn's doctor's office."

"And how is her health?"

"She's got slightly elevated blood pressure, which has her doctor concerned, but she's doing what she can to manage it, even though it's hard when she has a company to run."

"Her husband, Hank, is an excellent man. Went to Andover and Williams. Involved with many conservation societies."

"Yes, and he's a wonderful husband, from what Carolyn tells me."

"You mentioned earlier something about Aubrey Sperry's new wife."

Polly hesitated. Carolyn had given Polly the okay to discuss her private life with Claudia, but Polly wanted to stress the necessity for discretion. "This is in confidence, you understand."

Claudia looked insulted. "Of course."

"Carolyn doesn't like her at all. Doesn't trust her. She's much younger than Aubrey, and she feels just a little *off* to Carolyn."

Claudia's eyes gleamed. She was almost smiling.

Thrilled to be the source of such pleasure, Polly elaborated, "Heather—his new wife's name is Heather—has withdrawn, over the past month or so, over two hundred thousand dollars from Carolyn's father's personal credit line."

Claudia elevated one eloquent shoulder. "Certainly he can afford it."

"True. Still. Carolyn's worried that Heather has some kind of scam going."

"Really?"

Polly had Claudia's entire attention. "Heather did sign a prenuptial agreement, so that's not the worry. And, yes, they can afford two hundred thousand dollars' worth of furniture—that's what she spent it on— but he certainly can't afford two hundred thousand dollars flying out of his account every couple of months."

"What sort of furniture did she buy?"

"Oh, dreadful antiques. Claudia, you ought to see them! Carolyn and Aubrey each have private wings in the old Sperry family mansion. Heather's filled Aubrey's rooms with a hideous mishmash of styles. Lots of painted, gilded, dainty-legged stuff mixed in with heavily carved Gothic monstrosities."

"Where did she buy the furniture?"

"We don't know. Carolyn has access to the joint household account and also to her father's personal checking account, but no way to get into Heather's personal financial statements. It doesn't matter, anyway. We've seen the furniture. It's obvious she spent the two hundred thousand dollars on the furniture."

"I wouldn't be so sure."

Polly cast a look at Claudia. "What do you mean?"

Claudia fingered the pearls at her throat. "People from the very best of families have occasionally found themselves in a temporary financial pinch. One of the solutions for this problem has been to find an antiques dealer who has, shall we say, *flexible,* policies?" She glanced over, saw that Polly was completely rapt, and continued, "Let's say that someone, let's call her Heather, needs access to liquid funds. She writes a check for ten thousand dollars cash at the bank. She takes the cash to her friendly antiques dealer and buys a nice little Chippendale chair. She takes it home, tells her husband she paid ten thousand dollars for it. In fact, she gave the dealer seven thousand, and slipped the extra three thousand into her private safe-deposit box."

"How fascinating! But doesn't the dealer have to keep records for tax purposes?"

"Of course. But these dealers buy entire estates, with masses of furniture, collectibles, antiques. They can record most of their purchases and sales for the IRS and still have a few pieces set aside for this kind of easy money. It works the other way around, too, of course. Heather might bring in a piece of furniture, sell it to the dealer for, let's say, five thousand dollars, and tell her husband she was given only three."

"My God. We never even thought of that. I mean, we never even considered where all the old furniture from Aubrey's wing went. Claudia, may I use your phone?"

"Absolutely." Claudia gestured with one languid wrist to the phone on the table next to her.

Polly punched in Carolyn's home phone

number. "Carolyn? . . . Polly here. Listen, I've just been chatting with Claudia, and she told me something really interesting." As Polly outlined the moneymaking scheme, Claudia's attention hovered near her like a hummingbird near a flower. "Yes, well, I didn't think of that possibility, either," Polly told Carolyn. "No, sorry, I can't think of a way for you to get into Heather's check-book. I assume it's in her purse. I suppose you could sneak into her room at night while she's sleeping, but *you* can hardly *sneak* in your present condition. . . . Oh, I don't know, Carolyn. I'm not that graceful. . . . Yes, all right, I'll think about it."

With a sense of trepidation, Polly clicked off the phone. Claudia had always been so quick to criticize every little thing Polly did, what would her reaction be now, having heard that Polly might stoop to sneaking around someone's private quarters in the middle of the night?

Deep breath, she told herself. She turned to her mother-in-law. "Carolyn wants me to thank you for telling us about this little cash-and-carry scheme. I'm not sure what the next step will be. Carolyn wants to think about it and talk it over with her husband."

"Excellent idea." Suddenly Claudia was looking a little green around the gills. She put her napkin to her mouth and turned her head away from Polly.

Polly tried not to show alarm. "Are you all right, Claudia?"

"A little indigestion, that's all, Polly, don't fret!" Claudia closed her eyes and leaned back in her chaise, patting her chest gently.

"Is there anything I can get you? Some soda water? An antacid?"

Claudia shook her head carefully. A moment later, she opened her eyes. "As you may have noticed," she said, all the starch back in her personality and her voice, "I'm not as strong as I was. I'm not managing to keep up with matters around the house, and I do seem to have these little emetic spells from time to time. Also, to be candid, climbing the stairs to bed at night has become somewhat of a challenge for me. I don't need assistance, but I must say the possibility of falling has occurred to me."

"Then we need to find someone to stay here in the house with you. We could hire—"

"I've told you, Polly," Claudia interrupted sharply, "I dislike having strangers in my house, and I certainly don't want them touching me."

"All right." Polly waited.

Claudia said nothing but fussed with the stems of her reading glasses.

"Oh," Polly said, suddenly realizing what Claudia wanted. "Would you like me to come stay with you, Claudia?"

"It might not be a bad idea. *If* you thought I could be of more assistance to you and Carolyn Sperry."

"Oh, well, you certainly provided invaluable help tonight." Polly's mind raced. "Could I set up my sewing machine in the dining room? I have some commissions to finish."

"Of course."

The reply came so quickly, Polly was stunned. "Would you like me to sleep here tonight, Claudia?"

"I think that would be best, don't you?"

"Of course. Well, then, I'll just run home and pack up a few things."

"I believe the guest bedroom needs dusting," Claudia said.

"Not a problem. I know how to dust."

"I'm sure you do." Her tone of voice put Polly promptly in her place.

Polly removed Claudia's dinner plate—
the older woman had eaten perhaps three
bites—and brought in a dessert plate with a
few tea cookies and tartlets from the Ritz.
She told Claudia she'd be back soon, then
hurried out through the cold winter night to
her car. Driving to her house, she found her
body trembling with the emotions she'd
been stifling in Claudia's presence—pity,
dread, and a weird kind of love that made
her burst out laughing and crying at the
same time.

22

"I'm just as concerned about this as you are."

Hank's forehead was clenched in the adorable little frown he wore when he was all worked up over saving the wetlands or the Alaskan wilderness, and to have him frowning this way now because he was worried about *her* was so cute, Carolyn could hardly focus on the problem. Sitting across from her husband at their chrome-and-glass kitchen table, finishing the hearty stew Mrs. B. had made for their dinner, Carolyn felt warm, full, and optimistic.

"But asking your friend to crawl around your father's private quarters in the middle of the night is not the solution." Hank sounded so *manly*. Carolyn felt a surge of lust, immediately followed by a twinge of guilt: how much of her mother's thoughts and sensations could a fetus experience?

She forced herself back to the subject at hand. "Then what is?" It was a reasonable question. "All I want to know, Hank, is the name of the shops where Heather bought the antiques, and the price she paid for them. If she wrote those checks to cash, we've got grounds to suspect she's pulling the kind of scam Polly's mother-in-law suggested."

"You could simply *ask* Heather where she bought the furniture," Hank pointed out.

"True. But I can't ask her how much she paid. Or I *can* ask her, but I'm not sure I'd believe her answer. I want proof, and the proof might be in the checkbook."

"Well . . . ," Hank said slowly, talking it through, "doesn't your father have the same kinds of checks we all use, with an attached transfer sheet that automatically makes a copy of all the information as you write the check?"

"Of course. Saves the time of writing everything twice."

"So where does he keep his checkbook?"

"From what I've seen, Heather has it now.

She keeps it in her purse, and her purse is always with her."

"Except when she's asleep." Hank grinned. "I wonder what she does with it at night. Whether she takes it into the bedroom or leaves it in the living room."

Atta boy, Carolyn thought. Once Hank committed to a problem, he carried through. "It would help to know that, I suppose."

"Yes. That would be a start." He looked at his watch. "It's eight thirty. Why don't we drop in for a friendly little nightcap? We used to do that occasionally, before Aubrey married Heather."

Carolyn grinned. "True. And you've been out of town. It's really just a friendly thing to do, isn't it?"

"Are you up to it?"

She held her face up for inspection, smiling. "No nervous tics. No jumping eyelids. Calm as a cucumber."

"Well, then, let's pay a little social call."

———————

Carolyn freshened her makeup, slipped her feet back into her shoes, and went hand in hand with her husband through the various halls and corridors to her father's wing. Hank knocked on the door.

Aubrey answered, looking handsome in a red velvet smoking jacket and a silk ascot. "Hank! Carolyn, my dear! What a nice surprise."

"I've been out of town most of the week," Hank explained, "and it seems like I haven't had a chance to see much of you, Aubrey, you and your lovely wife, Heather, so I thought we might drop in for a neighborly chat. If you're not too busy."

"Capital, my dear man! Come in, come in. Heather, look who's here for a little nightcap."

Heather was curled up on one end of the pink-and-gold-tasseled sofa, wearing a filmy, pastel negligé that accentuated her curving bosom and hips. Now Carolyn understood how her father might find this woman a pleasure to be around, with her soft, sink-into-able body. As Carolyn and Hank entered, Heather plucked at the plunging neckline of her negligé, her little blue eyes darting nervously. "Oh! Hello! Goodness, we weren't expecting company!"

"We can come back another night," Hank quickly assured her.

Aubrey quickly intervened. "Nonsense, we're all family here."

"Please don't get up," Carolyn hastened to persuade Heather. "You look so comfortable there. We'll just stay awhile."

Aubrey was at the drinks table, his hand on a crystal tumbler.

"Aubrey," Heather said bossily, "remember, you're supposed to limit yourself to one drink a day."

"This will be just a small one, my dear." Aubrey turned to Hank. "What would you like?"

"A little Scotch would hit the spot."

"Great. I've found a new single malt I've been wanting you to try." Aubrey poured the drinks and handed one to Hank.

"I'm not drinking these days," Carolyn said. "If it's all right, I'll make myself a little cup of tea."

Heather rose in a sherbet symphony of nylon. "I'll make it for you, Carolyn, please sit down."

"Heavens, Heather, I can walk to the kitchen." Carolyn followed before Heather could object. "What kind of tea do you have?"

The kitchen, small, modern, and efficient, was the only place in the apartment that hadn't been overwhelmed by froufrou, rococo, and gilt, although a tapestry of noblewomen in satin gowns hung above the small breakfast table. No purse in sight.

Heather opened the cupboard. "Chamomile, red zinger, licorice, and mint."

"Mint would be great." Carolyn continued to scan the room. "You keep so much fruit around. Good for you."

"I'm doing my best to keep him healthy."

"I'm so glad. Mrs. B. makes delicious meals, but they do tend to rely on red meat and white flour."

"Too true." Heather opened the refrigerator and took out a container of skim milk, poured a little into a pitcher, and set it on a tray.

"Hey, Heather. Is that a steak in there?" Carolyn asked with surprise.

Heather turned on a dime and planted her hands on her fat hips. Suddenly her voice was tinged with prissy venom. "Am I supposed to be accountable to you for every single thing I keep in my kitchen?"

Carolyn drew back. "No, of course not, Heather. I just was surprised to see what looked like a steak, because we'd just been discussing nutrition."

Heather calmed down. "We do eat red meat from time to time. And I need to eat it these days because—"

The teakettle whistled, interrupting her.

The hair on Carolyn's neck stood on end. "Because?" she prompted.

"Cups, milk, spoons, napkins," Heather murmured, pretending to be completely focused on the tea things. "Ready," she muttered, and fled from the kitchen, carrying the tray before her.

Aubrey and Hank were comfortably seated in a pair of hysterically patterned and painted chairs, looking like a pair of elks among primroses as they sipped their Scotch. Heather set the tray on the rosewood footstool with brass hoof feet that served as a coffee table. She sank back into her place on the sofa and gestured for Carolyn to sit at the other end, then busied herself pouring the tea.

Carolyn gingerly lowered her bulk, her pulse slamming in her throat. She could think of only one reason for Heather's need to eat red meat.

"It's serendipitous, your dropping in like this tonight," Aubrey informed them, gently swirling his drink as he spoke. "Heather and I were just discussing the right time to tell you our news."

"Oh, yes?" Hank looked eager.

Aubrey looked rosy with pride. Heather looked absolutely triumphant.

Carolyn held her breath. Her heart was skittering around so wildly it made her nauseous. *Don't let her be,* she prayed, *don't let her be.*

"It's a little earlier than we planned to tell you. We just found out ourselves," Aubrey said. "So we want to keep it a secret a while more, just among the family. I'm absolutely delighted to tell you that my dear little Heather is pregnant."

Carolyn felt the room spin and dim, and she fainted.

"Elevate her head!"

"No, elevate her feet!"

Carolyn opened her eyes to see three

worried faces staring down at her. She was stretched out on the sofa with pillows beneath her head and feet, a slightly awkward position for someone as pregnant as she.

Pregnant.

"Are you all right?" Hank knelt next to her, clutching her hand.

She struggled to raise herself on the soft cushions. "I'm fine. My blood pressure just goes wacky now and then. I'd feel better if I sat up." Hank put his hands beneath her arms and hoisted her up.

"Here, dear, have some tea." Heather held out a cup of pale pink liquid.

"Thank you." As Carolyn sipped the bland brew, she mentally composed herself, so that when she looked up again, she was smiling. "Father, Heather, I apologize for fainting just when you presented us with your marvelous news. I guess I'll have to eat more in the evenings and stop worrying about my weight." All the years she'd learned to be diplomatic with her employees and executives now helped her exhibit a delight she certainly did not feel. "You're pregnant, Heather? That's wonderful."

"Yes." Hank seconded Carolyn's congrat-

ulations. "Grand news, Aubrey. Felicitations,
Heather."

Heather simpered. In a breathless little-
girl voice, she said, "Our children will be
able to play with each other!"

Carolyn felt her stomach heave. The floor
turned to liquid and rolled beneath her feet.

Hank came to her rescue. "That's right!
But for now, I think I'd better get Carolyn
into bed. Thanks for the Scotch, Aubrey."

"Thank you for dropping in." Aubrey put
an arm around his wife's shoulders, and
there they stood, a united front.

———

Back in their own quarters, Carolyn undressed, Hank hovering anxiously at her
shoulder the entire time. Once she was
tucked comfortably in bed, he sat down
next to her and took her hand in his.

"Carolyn. Listen. I think we ought to give
up this idea of catching Heather in some
kind of scam. Especially if—"

"No!" She kept her voice low but urgent.
"Hank, while I was lying on the sofa, I saw
Heather's purse! It's on that French-provin-

cial secretary painted with shepherds, right next to the door to their bedroom."

"Carolyn—"

"All you have to do is wait until they're asleep. Take the flashlight, open her purse, look in her checkbook, find out the name of the antiques shops."

Hank rubbed his forehead. "What if she or your father wake up and catch me?"

"Tell them I lost an earring when I fainted and you were trying to find it. Hank, do this for me, please."

"But, Carolyn, haven't things changed now that Heather's pregnant?"

Carolyn narrowed her eyes. "If Heather was brazen enough to swindle money from my father's account, she might be lying about being pregnant."

Hank set his alarm for three thirty. When he rose, he tried not to wake Carolyn, but she was a light sleeper these days, and tonight she was especially on edge. Plumping up her pillows, she watched Hank pull on his robe and slide into his slippers. He took the flashlight from their bedside table and kissed her on her forehead.

"Tonight," he whispered, "zee eagle will lay zee egg."

She grinned, grateful for his good humor.

He left. Carolyn waited, heart pounding. The profound silence of the house in the dark of night closed in on her like melancholy, and she wondered why she was so intent on finding out about Heather. Was she selfish? Didn't she want her father to be happy, to be loved?

Of course, she answered herself, she did want her father to be happy. She liked the idea of his being married, being loved and cared for in his golden age. But she felt an equal, if not greater, obligation to the women from whom she was descended, not only to keep the governance of Sperry's in the hands of the direct-blood female descendants of Great-grandmother Geraldine, but to keep Sperry Paper Company a viable, flourishing enterprise.

Still, she reminded herself, if Heather had a child, that child would be as much a Sperry as Carolyn herself, and if it was a girl, that girl would have as much right to lead the company as Carolyn's daughter. Carolyn needed to be less rigid in her thoughts. She should remember the lessons she was learning at The Haven about letting go, letting things flow. She should try to think differently, creatively, she should turn puzzles upside down and see them from another perspective.

For example, what if she gave birth to a healthy baby girl who grew into a wonderful, intelligent young woman named Elizabeth, and what if that young woman had no interest whatsoever in taking over the company or continuing the matrilineal line? What if the new Elizabeth wanted to be a lesbian living in a commune raising dogs? Carolyn would love her just as much, and she would want her child to be happy. Yes. She would want her daughter to be happy more than she wanted her daughter to take over Sperry's.

In that case, Carolyn reasoned, would she be able to pass the reins of the company to Heather's daughter, assuming Heather had a daughter? Carolyn sat quietly for a moment, listening to her heart, and her heart responded—yes, of course. Carolyn didn't like Heather, but she might adore Heather's child, and how nice it would be, as Heather said, for Carolyn's daughter to have a friend to grow up with. Carolyn had hated being an only child, she'd felt so alone, and she knew that both she and her father were slightly warped, a little too set in their own ways, a tad bit more possessive and fussy than they would have been if they'd had siblings. Carolyn hoped she'd be able to have another child, perhaps even two more children, so that little Elizabeth wouldn't be alone, but she'd had such trouble getting pregnant this time around, and the pregnancy was so delicate, the possibility of a second and a third child was uncertain at best. So she should stop this suspicious fretting, relax, enjoy her pregnancy, and be glad for her father's happiness. Damn it, she would relax!

She heard a slight shuffling noise, and then Hank came back in the room. His hair was tousled in all directions, as if he'd been standing on his head, and he was smiling.

"Got it!" he whispered gleefully.

"Yes?"

"Found the purse, found the checkbook, which has the copies of all the checks written out over the past month, for ten, twenty, thirty thousand dollars at a whack."

Carolyn leaned forward. "And?"

"All the checks were made out to cash."

Carolyn couldn't get back to sleep. She tossed and turned all night, rising in the morning with a head full of lead and a heart full of dread. She and Hank had discussed what to do, and Carolyn had insisted they do it as soon as possible. This anxiety was killing her. Well, that was what people said, that things were killing them. But she was afraid that for her this might not be just a figure of speech. Her heart raced, flip-flopped, and chugged. Her vision swam. Her daughter nudged around inside her belly as if unable to find a comfortable position. Just when she wanted to fill her mind with tranquil thoughts and send only loving emotions through her blood to her unborn daughter, she was cursed with misgivings.

She dressed slowly, taking her time, although her fingers trembled. In the kitchen, she drank some orange juice and took her vitamins with warm milk while she brewed a pot of decaffeinated coffee. When Hank returned to their quarters, she was psychologically geared for battle.

"They'll be here in just a moment," Hank said. The frown had returned to his face.

Carolyn set the sterling silver coffeepot on the tray and began to carry it into the living room, but her husband intercepted her.

"Let me carry that." Taking it from her, he added, "And remember, I'm doing all the talking. You just try to keep calm."

Carolyn settled in a wing chair when her father and his wife tapped on their door and entered their living room. Aubrey was dressed for the day in a navy turtleneck and a navy cashmere blazer. Heather wore a pink, flowered skirt and matching sweater.

As soon as they were seated, Aubrey took command of the room. "It's lovely to see you both again, of course, but I don't see why we needed to break into our schedule. What's so urgent?"

Hank rested his elbows on his knees and steepled his hands. "Aubrey, the last thing I want to do is to offend you. Please believe that. But I'm very concerned about something, and I'd like to put my worries to rest."

"Go on," Aubrey ordered.

"Having been in your quarters several

times now, I have to say I find it unbeliev-
able that you and Heather spent two hundred thousand dollars on the new furniture
there."

Aubrey reared back, his face flushing.
"Hank! What the hell? How *dare* you med-
dle in my private affairs? It is my money, let
me remind you—"

"Yes," Hank agreed mildly, "that's right.
But Carolyn and I are both aware of the general state of your finances. We know more
or less how much money you have, just as
you know how much Carolyn and I have.
We're afraid that if you continue spending
like this, you'll soon be wanting to draw
money from Sperry's reserves."

"That's ridiculous," Aubrey snorted.

Hank looked totally unflappable. "What I
would like to know, Aubrey, is exactly where
you and Heather bought your new furniture,
and how much you paid for it. I want to be
sure some dealer didn't take advantage of
you."

How clever Hank is, Carolyn thought,
warm with admiration, to make it sound as
if Aubrey and Heather bought the furniture
together; this way it wasn't a direct attack
on Heather.

Aubrey frowned. "Good God, man, I didn't buy the furniture. Heather did. Such a tempest in a teapot. Heather can give you that information."

Hank turned expectantly to Heather.

Heather avoided their eyes. "I can't remember the names of the dealers."

"That's all right," Hank assured her. "Just show me the canceled checks. Or the transfer record of the checks you wrote. Should be in the checkbook."

Heather's face darkened, her lower lip pleating like a child's before a tantrum.

Aubrey looked at his wife. "Heather?"

"I—I-I got cash at the bank," Heather stuttered. "The dealers said they preferred it that way."

"Never mind, darling." Aubrey smiled indulgently at his wife. "Just show them the receipts."

Heather looked trapped. "I d-d-don't have any receipts. I didn't think to get any."

The four of them sat in solemn silence for a moment.

"I'll get the yellow pages," Carolyn offered. "We can read the names of the dealers to see if you remember any—"

Heather's face flushed. Her eyes filled

with tears. "You're all so mean!" She hit her thigh with a clenched fist. "So so so so *mean*!"

Aubrey looked thunderstruck. "Heather?"

"I'm sorry!" Heather sobbed. "I didn't know what else to do!" Tears spilled down her cheeks. "It's for my brother, I did it for my brother."

"Did what?" Aubrey asked, confused.

"I paid cash for the furniture, but not as much as I said, I wrote the checks for cash, and I thought if I got enough furniture, you'd believe I spent it all on the antiques, but I didn't, I gave some of the money to my brother."

"How much of the money?" Aubrey asked, his voice quiet.

Heather wailed, "Maybe a little over fifty thousand dollars. Maybe more."

Aubrey leaned back against the sofa and closed his eyes, pinching the top of his nose as if to halt the beginning of his own tears.

"Why does your brother need the money?" Hank's voice was mild.

"He's an invalid," Heather told them.

"I thought he was a plumber," Carolyn said.

"He was! But he was injured on the job and he's in a wheelchair now, and he's terribly depressed and he needs money for groceries and nurses and stuff."

Aubrey sounded tired when he said, "But why didn't you just tell me about this? Why didn't you ask me to help?"

Heather lifted a pitiful face. "Because *you're* all so elegant," she said, quivering, "and my brother isn't. He hasn't been to college. He has a tattoo. He drinks beer in his undershirt." She wept as if her heart were breaking.

Even Carolyn was moved. "Oh, Heather. I'm so sorry if we've seemed like snobs. If your brother's injured, we want to help."

"Carolyn's right," Hank added. "You should have simply told us the truth. We want to help your brother, of course. In fact"—he hesitated for just a moment—"why don't we all go over there now and meet him and figure out how we can help him."

Heather's eyes rolled around like billiard balls. She gulped noisily. "Bathroom." She coughed. "Morning sickness."

Aubrey put a supporting arm around his

wife and led her to the guest bathroom in Carolyn's suite.

As Aubrey stood waiting in the hall, Hank turned toward him. "I'm sorry, Aubrey, to have upset you and Heather."

Aubrey waved a weary hand. "It's all so disconcerting." He managed a weak smile. "It seems every woman I've ever dated has had a difficult, complicated family, either her own children, or her ex-stepchildren, or her siblings. Whatever. I thought when I met Heather, here is someone with whom my life can be simple."

Carolyn touched his arm. "I hope you're not angry with us, Father, for bringing up the issue of the money and the antiques. You were always so cautious with anyone *I* dated. *You* always warned *me* to beware of men who might marry me for my money. I suppose it was just natural that I'd be concerned in the same way for you."

"I know. I understand. Don't think I'm not grateful. There's no fool like an old fool and all that." Aubrey looked sad as he spoke, and in the past few minutes he seemed to have aged several years.

"You're not a fool, Aubrey," Hank assured him.

Heather came out of the bathroom, pale and shaky. "Sorry. I think I need to go lie down."

"Of course." Aubrey took her arm.

Heather looked at Carolyn and Hank. "I do want you to meet my brother. But I don't want your first impression of him to be when he's unshaven and rumpled. I'd like to give him time to have the house tidied and himself spruced up, just a little." She shrugged apologetically. "He's bound to be intimidated by you."

"We understand," Hank assured her, his voice kind. "Why don't you phone him. Ask him when it's convenient for him for us to come over and say hello."

23

Faye stood in front of her bedroom mirror, inspecting herself one last time before her date arrived.

Roger Munson. Marilyn's candidate. He had a nice voice on the phone, and he was taking her to dinner and a concert. Very promising.

She smoothed her indigo silk jacket over her turquoise vest and the pale lime silk shirt beneath. Beautiful colors, but they couldn't disguise the weight she'd gained. She could barely squeeze into the largest size of clothes in her closet, and *they* were so tight, she felt like a watermelon in a grapefruit skin. Not long ago, she'd cheered herself up by naming the rolls of fat beneath her breasts Honey and Bunny. Now she had a new roll. She thought she'd call this one It's Not Funny.

She'd just had her annual physical, and the results were alarming. Her blood pressure was too high and her cholesterol was off the charts. She'd started taking Lipitor, and she hated taking medication. Worse, she was borderline for late-onset diabetes. She had to face it: she was getting to the age where what she ate wasn't just about how she looked, it was about how long and how well she was going to live.

Now she was glad her friends had encouraged—all right, *compelled*—her into dating. If nothing else, it gave her something to do at night. She'd let herself become too solitary, and since Laura had left for the Coast, she'd eaten too much in the evenings. How ironic that all that comfort food ended up making her feel uncomfortable.

So she'd begun a diet and was considering joining an exercise group at the spa. And she was dating, which did help her feel, if not young, at least foolish.

The buzzer for her condo droned. She hurried down the stairs, into the small side foyer of the spa building, and opened the door.

"Faye?" A tall, lean, *handsome* man stood there.

She managed to act normal. "Yes. I'm Faye. You must be Roger."

They shook hands, he helped her slip into her coat, and they hurried out to his car, which was—*Oh, gosh,* Faye thought—a Jaguar! She settled into it feeling absolutely giddy.

Faye hadn't expected Roger to be so good-looking. His Cary Grant dark hair (he must use Grecian Formula) fell over his forehead, and his rectangular, wire-rimmed glasses gave him a kind of hip, urban, cybergeek look.

On the ride into Boston, they discussed the weather, Boston traffic, Marilyn's work at MIT, neutral topics. Roger seemed cool, reserved; his pace of speaking was just a few beats slower than Faye's. Was her excitement making her babble? She forced herself to speak more slowly.

In the restaurant, as they ordered, she felt Roger studying her. Her body responded with such a spectacular hot flash, it was all she could do not to fan herself with the menu.

They settled back with their drinks.

"Marilyn tells me you're a physicist," Faye said. The old rule she'd learned about dating—ask him about himself—came easily to mind because she really was curious. "Tell me what you do."

Roger gave a bashful smile. "Oh, you'd find it awfully dull."

"No, I wouldn't, truly. I'm fascinated with the new science."

"Well . . ." Roger explained his field. He spoke clearly, deliberately, trying to make his points precise, and when Faye asked questions, he answered without making her seem like a complete fool. He talked about quantum mechanics, atomism, particles, and quarks. All the while, Faye ate her delicious dinner and nodded as if she understood. Really, she was simply enjoying looking at the man.

When the waiter came to take their order for coffee and dessert, Roger said, "Enough about science. Faye, tell me about yourself."

"Well," Faye began, "I'm an artist, and I teach art. My husband, Jack, died two years ago. I have one daughter, Laura, who is happily married and has a little girl.

They've all just moved to California, and I miss them very much."

"You're lucky your husband died," Roger said bluntly.

Faye blinked. Had she heard correctly? "I beg your pardon?"

"I mean, you're lucky you're widowed rather than divorced. I got divorced last year, and it's the worst experience imaginable."

"Death is no picnic," Faye assured him.

"No, but at least you're allowed to keep your good memories." As he talked, his handsome face grew bitter. "With divorce, the other person is still around, a constant reminder of unhappiness, plus a present and continual misery."

"I'm sorry," Faye began faintly, not sure how to turn their conversation back onto a more pleasant track.

"Now," Roger continued, "your friend Marilyn took a big bite out of Theodore's bank account when they got divorced. But his work is more lucrative than mine, so Theodore's okay. Plus, his money attracted a real sizzler of a young woman."

"Yes, but that relationship didn't last," Faye reminded him.

"You're right. Michelle screwed Theodore, *literally*. She got knocked up, and Theodore's got to pay child support. I guess you could call *that* a lasting relationship." He laughed grimly. "But old Theodore will be just fine. His money's a babe magnet. And Marilyn is one of a kind. She doesn't hassle him at all."

The waiter arrived with their coffees and desserts. Faye had virtuously ordered a fruit cup, but now she wished she had chosen something chocolate, to sweeten this evening, which had so suddenly gone sour.

"My ex-wife took me for every penny I had," Roger continued, carefully stirring sugar into his coffee. "Our two sons have grown, thank God, so she can't get to me that way, but that doesn't mean she's going to extricate her fangs from my neck. Oh, no. She has the house, the furniture, all our savings, and she's still after me for more."

"Weren't all financial matters legally settled in the divorce?" Faye asked.

"Sure. But she *claims* her arthritis makes it impossible for her to work, which is ridiculous. The woman *needs* to work. She was a real beauty. Now she just sits around doing nothing. She's let herself get fat, fatter than you, and the more she sits, the less she can do. She expects me to keep shelling out for more treatments."

Roger continued raging, describing in detail medications and therapies his ex-wife needed. Now he spoke rapidly, as if he couldn't get it all out fast enough, this scalding stream of anger, but Faye's mind had stalled on the words, "she's let herself get fat, fatter than you." What a horrible thing to say to someone on their first date! Well, Faye thought, their first and *last* date.

Roger only stopped his rant when the waiter discreetly deposited the leather billfold with the check inside on their table.

"We'd better go," Roger said. "Don't want to miss the concert."

It was a pleasure Faye had forgotten, entering the concert hall in the company of a handsome man. She noticed several admiring glances cast their way from gaggles of single women. She imagined their envy when Roger leaned over to whisper something for her ears alone. Little could they guess that he was saying, "And another thing, she started eating herself into her so-called arthritis right after the kids were born. Everyone knows sugar's a toxin, but did she resist sugar? Hell, no."

The music—Mozart and Haydn—was lovely. For entire minutes at a time, Faye forgot that the man sitting next to her had called her fat, and as they left the concert hall to drive home, it seemed the music had soothed Roger's savage breast as well. He discussed music during the ride home.

When they arrived at the spa, he asked, "Want to invite me up for a nightcap?"

Not really, Faye thought, but not wanting to be rude, said, "Of course." She led him into the side foyer and up the stairs to the third floor and her small condo.

"It's temporary," she told him as he looked around. "Just until I decide where I want to live the rest of my life."

Roger studied her books and bits of art while she poured them both brandies. When she sat on her sofa, he sat, to her surprise, next to her. Putting one arm up on the sofa behind her back, he leaned toward her and clicked his glass against hers. "Here's to the rest of our lives," he toasted.

"Chin-chin," Faye responded.

Roger tossed back his drink, set it on the coffee table, and moved closer to Faye. He took her glass from her hand, set it on the table, and pulled Faye against him. Slowly, with great deliberation, he kissed her.

Stunned, she allowed herself to be kissed. His lips were warm and soft, his breath a mixture of coffee and brandy. *Hey!* She wanted to scream. *I thought you think I'm fat! At least he's not complaining about his ex-wife,* another part of her brain pointed out.

He continued his kiss, and now he brought his hand to rest just against her collarbone. Faye tried to move away—this kiss was a little intense for a first date.

"Roger," she said, but her word was muffled against his mouth.

Slowly he lowered his hand to rest on her breast.

Faye pulled back. "Roger. Please. I—"

"Don't stop now, baby," Roger murmured, pressing his lips against hers.

Oh, Lord, this man had more personalities than Sally Field in *Sybil,* Faye thought. With both hands, she shoved Roger away.

He kept his hand on her breast. In fact, he

moved his hand lower and pinched her nipple.

"Don't tell me you don't want this," he
said.

She grabbed his wrist and removed his
hand. "I don't want this," she said firmly.

"Sure you do," Roger assured her, and
dove toward her for another kiss.

"Roger, stop this, please," Faye said in
frustration. "We hardly know one another!"

"Oh, don't be a tease." Roger grabbed
her hand and put it on his erection. "Look
what I've got for you."

His erection squirmed against her hand
like a live gerbil. Slightly fascinated—it had
been a long time since she'd touched a
man's penis—but more angry, she wrenched
her hand from his. A hot flash—a searing volcanic explosion—tore through her body,
making her legs weak, her mind blank. Awkwardly she pushed herself up off the sofa.

"I think you should go now."

He rose, too. "Oh, come on now, Faye."
He looked amused. "We're adults, after all.
We've had a nice evening together, haven't
we? Didn't you enjoy your nice meal and the
concert?"

Before he could say another word, Faye

snatched her purse, took out a fifty-dollar bill, and thrust it at him. "Here. My share."

"Fine." With two fingers, he took the bill from her hand. "I thought someone like you might be grateful to have a little romance in your life, but if you say no, I'm not going to force you. Good night, Faye."

Faye bolted her door behind him and collapsed on her sofa, so overwhelmed with conflicting emotions she didn't know whether to laugh or cry.

On a Friday night in early February, after The Haven board meeting, Alice, Marilyn, and Faye joined Shirley in her condo for drinks and dinner, then relaxed over coffee while Faye entertained them with a detailed account of her date with Roger.

Because Shirley was director of the spa, she'd chosen the condo on the top floor, at the opposite end of the offices, so she'd have the illusion of distance between her private life and work. The rooms of the various condos were of similar sizes and shapes, since they'd been created from the classrooms for which the building was originally built, but Shirley's space had an ambience like no one else's. The walls, painted lavender, were hung with eagle feathers, dried roots, and paintings of naked goddesses.

Marilyn said, "I'm so sorry, Faye. I had no idea Roger was such a boor."

"No problem," Faye assured her. "He wasn't a monster. And he phoned to ask me out again, which made me feel that even if I'm fat, at least I'm not a *dog.* I declined, however."

"Good for you for trying," Shirley said. "We've got to take some risks now and then if we don't want to curl up like dust bunnies in the corners of our lives."

"Hear, hear," Alice agreed.

"Anyway," Faye continued, "his insults only reinforced my determination to make some changes. I started dieting after the first of the year, and I've lost four pounds!"

"I'm impressed!" Alice said. "How'd you do it?"

"Basically, I torture myself," Faye admitted. "No fats. No sweets. Just fish, chicken, veggies, and fruits. Plus, I've started using the stationary bike down in the workout room, three times a week."

"And you've only lost four pounds in one month?" Marilyn asked.

Faye nodded. "It's the whole metabolism thing. I could probably survive on air and lettuce."

"It's the whole depressing over-sixty thing," Alice said.

"Sixty isn't depressing!" Shirley contended hotly.

"Oh, come on," Alice snorted. "Get real."

Shirley stood firm. "Getting older doesn't have to mean getting tired, bored, and lethargic! People of our generation live differently from the way our parents did. We're more active—I'm speaking in general, here—we're more willing to try new things, learn computers, learn tai chi, whatever— and as long as we keep active, we can have a couple of decades of great-quality life!"

"Yeah," Alice said, "except we still look old."

"Not necessarily," Shirley shot back. "If we control our weight—"

"No matter what we do," Alice argued, "we still have creepy old veins sticking up like worms on our hands and bulging out of our foreheads! And fat? My naked backside would give Stephen King nightmares! Plus, get real, Shirley, most of us have some complication like arthritis, like I do, or mild incontinence. *Something.*"

"I'm not saying we can look like we're twenty," Shirley began.

Alice interrupted. "Twenty, hell, I can't even look like fifty!"

"I don't mind looking my age," Faye began.

"Well, I do!" Alice snapped. "I think it really sucks that older men look sexy enough to attract young women, but older women have trouble getting dates. Mother Nature is *such* a bitch! Do men have periods? No! Do they have to worry about getting pregnant when they have sex? No. Do they have to swell up and lumber around for nine months and then go through hellish labor to have a child? No. Are their bodies stretched and sagging from having children? No. Men can make more babies after fifty, and they can still look sexy enough after fifty for a woman to want to have their babies! Who dreamed this system up, anyway!"

"But you know what, Alice," Faye said, "I'm still glad I'm female. If I could have *cho-*

sen, at any time in my life, I would have chosen to be a woman."

Alice frowned. "I have to think about
that."

"*I'd* choose to be a woman," Marilyn said,
"especially *because* I got to have a child. I
liked being pregnant. I loved giving birth. I
loved nursing my son and caring for him.
I know Theodore didn't receive half the
pleasure of parenting that I did."

"Yes, well, Theodore's an asshole, let's
not forget that," Alice reminded her. "I think
some men can enjoy fatherhood as much
as women do motherhood."

"Not to change the subject, but he called
me, by the way," Marilyn announced.

"Who?" Shirley asked.

"Theodore," Marilyn told her. "Ever since
he left me for Michelle, and then Michelle
dumped him, he phones every few months.
He says he misses me, and I'm sure he
does. I used to be his general factotum, taking care of his every need."

"Another reason I'd choose to be a
woman," Faye said. "Women know how to
make their homes into comfortable nests for
body and soul. Most men don't."

"True," Marilyn agreed. "Theodore told

me he missed living with me, and I don't doubt it for a minute. I kept his house clean, cooked delicious, nutritious meals, and I gave him oral sex whenever he wanted it. He actually had the audacity to say he misses 'making love' to me."

"Girl," Alice said, "I hope you told him you weren't biting on that limp old lure."

Shirley said thoughtfully, "As you all know, I didn't get to have children. And I'd still vote to be female."

"Why?" Alice asked.

Shirley counted on her fingers. "I think we have more fun. I think we have a stronger connection to the earth. Statistically, more men commit suicide than women. Their testosterone causes them to be more combative than women. Women can have multiple orgasms. Women live longer than men. Plus," she added with a grin, "men don't enjoy shopping as much as women."

"Men are less significant creatures," Marilyn added. "For the species to continue, we need lots of females and, theoretically, only one male."

"Yeah," Alice said wryly, "and every male dreams of being that one."

"So, Alice, what about you?" Faye asked.

"If you *had* to choose, which would it be, male or female?"

"I suppose it depends on what stage of my life I was at. When I was young, first working for TransContinent, I'd have switched genders in a minute. It was just too hard back then, being a female in a male-dominant world. I'd love to know how far I would have gotten, given my same performance, if only I'd been a man. Besides, ever since I was a little girl, I always wanted to pee standing up."

Marilyn laughed. "I did, too! I wanted to write my name in the snow like my brother!"

"When I was three years old," Shirley told them, "my mother found me standing by the toilet squeezing my bare foot. I didn't have a brother, but I'd been at a friend's house that day, and I saw her older brother standing at the toilet. I thought he took his big toe out of his pants to pee with, and I was trying to do the same thing."

"Isn't peeing a male territorial thing?" Faye asked. "Marking their space?"

"Well, that would explain why guys don't care when they spray the walls and floor," Alice said. "Women think they're slobs. Men think they're conquerors."

Faye sighed. "You know? Women are all Meryl Streep, living in a Beavis and Butt-head world."

Shirley held out her hand like a stop sign. "Okay, enough about that. How are the new kids doing? I mean Carolyn, Julia, Beth, and, um, the older one?"

Faye supplied the name. "Polly."

"Right. Polly. Do you think they bonded?"

"I'm sure they did," Alice said. "On the Friday nights we don't have our board meetings, I've been using the Jacuzzi, and right after yoga class they all come in together, yakking sixty miles an hour."

"Cool!" Shirley said. "Good for us! We'll have to keep our eyes open for others who might need to have a little club."

"I'd like to bring up some spa business," Faye announced. "I'd like the spa to hold an art exhibit in May. I've had so many students doing really great work in my art classes. It would be nice for them to be able to show their work off."

"Good idea!" Shirley said. "Maybe Justin's poetry class could read some of their work?"

"Yes, that would be fun," Faye agreed.

"We'd have some munchies, wine, maybe a little music . . ."

"Yeah." Alice nodded her head enthusiastically. "We could write the costs off as advertising. We could have the spa open for tours, have Star available to discuss her yoga—"

"A spring fling kind of thing!" Shirley took out her lavender notebook. "Okay! Let's make plans."

24

Monday morning, Polly sat at the dining-
room table in front of her sewing machine,
mounds of fabric piled on either side. Claudia didn't rise until nearly noon these days.
Polly woke at six, dressed, and tiptoed
down the stairs, and had a good chunk of
quiet time for her work.

She'd adjusted fairly easily to life here,
except she missed Roy Orbison terribly.
Claudia wouldn't allow animals in her
house, so Polly had taken him to a neighbor's to live. Ten-year-old Willy Peck loved
the dog and enjoyed getting paid for the
pleasure of caring for him. Polly had left her
dog with the Pecks before, so she knew
Roy Orbison would be fine. He was even allowed to sleep with Willy.

It was Polly who slept alone, who longed

for his comforting companionship, his nose on her foot as she sewed or read.

She'd just finished the final alterations to a handsome linen suit when the buzzer from the intercom Polly had set up sounded.

Polly pressed the TALK button. "Good morning, Claudia. I'll be right up."

First she went into the kitchen to start the water heating for tea. Then she climbed the stairs and waited outside Claudia's bedroom. A moment later, Claudia opened the door and stood before Polly, dressed immaculately in wool and pearls, hose and high heels.

"Good morning." She made it sound like a command.

"Good morning, Claudia." Polly went to the stairs and down a couple of steps. This was the routine they had established. Claudia did not want to be assisted as she climbed up or down the stairs. She wanted Polly to be just beneath her, to catch her in case she fell; she had admitted to a slight weakness in her legs.

As always, Polly was humbled by the ease of motion she took for granted as she watched Claudia move stiffly, with obvious effort, the few feet across the hall to the top of the steps. Today the odd smell Polly had noticed before was stronger, clearer, and a lightbulb blinked on in Polly's head: was Claudia becoming incontinent?

Claudia put one skeletal hand on the banister. Carefully she set one foot on the first step down, testing to be sure it held her weight. This was the major effort of Claudia's days, this and climbing back up the stairs at night. Satisfied that her leg would hold her, Claudia brought her other foot down one stair. As she did, her wool skirt slithered down her wasted hips and fell in a puddle around her ankles, leaving Polly staring at Claudia's ivory silk slip.

"Oh, dear!" Polly bent forward, grabbing the skirt and pulling it up to Claudia's waist. "Claudia, you've lost so much weight!"

"I wore this skirt in college." Claudia clutched the waistband with her free hand. "It's the smallest size I have."

"I'm too fat and you're too thin!" Polly babbled, trying to make light of Claudia's emaciated frame. "What a shame I can't run a line between your body and mine and siphon some of my fat off into you!"

Claudia made a prune face. "What a distasteful idea."

"Yes, well, I can alter your skirts for you if you'd like, or I'll run out and buy you some new things after we've got you settled. In the meantime, I'll fetch some safety pins and we'll fasten you back together."

"Never mind the safety pins. I'll keep hold of my skirt. I want to go downstairs."

"Okay, then. Let's go." Polly backed down the stairs, one step at a time, and Claudia came forward, with painful slowness.

Once they were in the living room, Claudia lowered herself onto her chaise. Polly gently laid a plaid blanket over her legs, then fetched Claudia's tea and breakfast, which she ate with infinite slowness while watching television. It was time for Polly to go out on her round of errands. Pad and pen in hand, she stationed herself on a chair near Claudia.

"Now," Polly said, "tell me where you'd like me to buy your skirts, and how many you'd like and what colors? Or, if you'd like, I could buy just one, and we could order some from a catalog."

"Brooks Brothers." Claudia set her teacup into the saucer with a slightly trembling hand, as if even that delicate object were heavy for her now. "One skirt will do fine. Brown or gray."

"Okay. Good. And I'll pick up some groceries. Anything you're hungry for? Chocolate? Pickled ginger?"

"I'm ill, Polly, not pregnant. No, chocolate doesn't appeal to me. Nothing appeals to me."

"How about some pâté?" Polly tried to tempt Claudia with the most fattening foods; she ate so little these days that every bite needed to be loaded with calories. "And a lamb shank for dinner?"

"That will be fine." Claudia shifted slightly on her chaise.

"Um, Claudia, I'm wondering . . ." How to approach this in a dignified manner? "I'm wondering whether or not you're becoming—just *slightly*—um, incontinent?"

Claudia glowered. "Absolutely not!"

Polly persisted. "It's not so unusual for women over forty to have this little problem occasionally. I mean, I do, whenever I laugh or sneeze. I wear pads—"

"I really do not need to hear the details of your personal hygiene."

"Of course not, but my point is that many women—"

"I will not wear diapers!"

"No, no, I didn't say diapers. I said pads. Like sanitary napkins. They're very light and slender, and they come with strips now that attach to your panties. I tell you what, I'll buy a package and if you want to try them, you can."

Claudia presented Polly with a dark, enigmatic glare. Placing the smallest crust of croissant on her tongue, she gazed into space, as if she'd taken a psychedelic. After a while, she said, "Have you spoken with Carolyn Sperry today?"

By now, Polly was used to Claudia's hairpin conversational curves. "No, not yet. We'll meet at the spa after yoga on Friday night."

"I see." Claudia hesitated, studying her rings, sliding them up and down her fleshless fingers. They were too large for her now, so she sat with her hands curled to keep the rings from falling off. Addressing the ruby on her right hand, she said, "While we're on the subject of physical functions, I suppose I should mention a slight problem I'm having in my elimination system."

Polly waited for clarification.

Claudia turned her rings in silence.

Okay, Polly thought. A little challenge for her skills of interpretation. "Elimination. Um—are you constipated, perhaps?" When Claudia didn't flinch, offended, Polly ventured further. "I remember Dr. Monroe mentioned that one of the possible consequences of your illness might be constipation. If that's becoming a problem, there are lots of solutions. Laxatives by mouth, and suppositories."

Claudia sniffed. "I suppose I'd better phone Dr. Monroe to ask what he recommends." She shook her head. "I'm sure he'll be glad to see the end of me."

"Are you making a pun?"

Claudia looked startled. Then she allowed Polly the slightest sliver of a smile.

Thursday afternoon, the family went to visit Heather's brother, Harry.

Aubrey drove Heather in his Jaguar, while Carolyn and Hank went together in Carolyn's Mercedes, because afterward Aubrey was taking Heather out shopping while Carolyn was going back to work at the paper company, dropping Hank at home on the way. A fresh crisis with the sales reps for Sperry's had taken all of Carolyn's attention over the past twenty-four hours, so much so that now, as Hank drove into Arlington, Carolyn lay back in the passenger seat, trying to still the busy voices in her head and catch a nap, or at least a moment's peace.

"We're here," Hank said.

Carolyn opened her eyes.

The street was pleasant, rows of double- and triple-decker homes tucked behind covered porches, the small yards delineated by mature trees and bushes. The yellow clapboard house needed a fresh coat of paint, and the yard was brown and mucky from melted snow, but the house seemed sound. Hank came around to open the car door for Carolyn, then took her arm as they made their way over the soggy grass to the front door where Heather and Aubrey waited.

An enormous male with a pockmarked face, black ponytail, and forearms like Popeye's yanked the door back. "Yeah?" Before they could speak, he grinned. One gold tooth glittered among the gray. "Oh. Yeah. Youse must be Harry's sister an' all. Come on in."

As they crowded inside, Carolyn sent silent apologies to her baby for the noxious air she'd be sending her way, for the room smelled of nicotine, beer, and males desperately in need of baths. This was the house Heather and Harry had grown up in, and the décor reflected her parents' taste, overlaid with Harry's accessories of girlie magazines, crushed beer cans, filthy ashtrays, and unapologetic stacks of videos about Scandinavian stewardesses and horny teenagers. The front room had bronze walls and a gold shag carpet. A thirty-six-inch television loomed in one corner. A gold and avocado plush sofa faced the TV, and next to it, in a wheelchair, sat a man, glowering at them as if he were the giant and they were a collective Jack, having just climbed up the beanstalk.

"Hello, Harry!" Heather kissed the top of her brother's head and gave his shoulders a little hug. "How are you feeling, sweetie?"

"Been better," he growled. In jeans and a black T-shirt with a Metallica logo, his shaggy, dark hair curling down into an unkempt beard, Harry exuded the rude power of a buffalo.

Heather beamed, as if he'd just said

something brilliant. "Harry, honey, I want you to meet my husband and his family."

Aubrey crossed the room and bent slightly, extending his hand. "Nice to meet you, Harry. Sorry about your accident."

"Orgh," Harry replied ambiguously. When he shook Aubrey's hand, the tattoos spiraling up his arm rippled over his muscles.

Hank stepped forward. "I'm Hank Wellingell, Aubrey's son-in-law. This is my wife, Carolyn. We're glad to meet you." Carolyn didn't try to shake his hand; Harry didn't seem all that thrilled to be meeting them, but she could understand how frustrated a man this obviously physical could be, confined to a wheelchair.

"I'm Bruce." The man who'd answered the door had a tad more personal proficiency. "I hang out here to help Harry, now that he's injured an' all."

Everyone said hello to Bruce, then Heather asked him to bring in a couple of the kitchen chairs, and they all settled into an uneasy circle. "Tell me about your injury, Harry," Aubrey invited. "I hope you're not in any pain."

Harry grunted, his lips curling in disdain. "Water heater fell on my back. Idiot I work with let go when we were trying to take it out of a house and install a new one. Crushed a vertebra and stuff."

"That's terrible," Hank commiserated. "What's the prognosis?"

Harry's mouth hung open.

Heather rushed to help her brother out. "Do the doctors say you'll walk again?"

"Maybe. Got to let it mend. See what happens. May need an operation."

"Are you satisfied with your physician?" Aubrey leaned forward, hands on knees. "Because I have a cadre of excellent physicians and I'd be glad to arrange for them to look at you, to see if there's anything else that can be done, or if—"

"My doc's fine." Harry folded his arms over his chest. Even in a wheelchair, he looked like a bouncer.

"It's always good to get a second opinion," Hank observed.

Harry didn't answer but stared mulishly at the ceiling.

Aubrey persisted, "If there is anything we can do, let us know. If you need money for doctors, medication, nurses, anything at all . . ."

A light gleamed in Harry's black eyes. He

looked at Heather. "I don't need charity. My sister's helped me enough."

"Well, I respect your attitude, but I wouldn't want you to think of any financial help we can offer as charity. You're part of the family now, after all."

Harry's lips curved in a private smile. "Think not."

Aubrey glanced at his wife as if seeking interpretation.

"She's ashamed of me," Harry clarified, glowering. "She's too good for me."

"That's not true, Harry!" Heather objected, clenching her fists.

"She's right." Aubrey hastened to back up his wife. "In fact, Harry, we've been talking. If it would make things easier for you, we'd be glad to have you come live with us for a while. We've got a big house, lots of room, a housekeeper during the day."

Harry's smile had an oddly demented quality about it. "Nice of you to offer." The look he cast his sister seemed strangely threatening. "I'll think about it."

"Is there anything else we can help you with?" Aubrey asked. "I assume your health insurance is covering most of your medical expenses. Are you receiving disability pay?"

"Yeah, yeah." Harry's momentary good humor fell away, his face sullen again.

A silence fell over the room. Carolyn glanced at Hank, and back at Harry, who slumped in his chair.

"Time for his pain pill," Bruce announced, adding, "he'll probably fall asleep when he takes it."

"Of course. We don't want to stay too long." Aubrey rose. Once again he shook hands with Harry, and this time, with Bruce. Heather kissed her brother on top of his head again, receiving a growl in return. Carolyn and Hank nodded good-bye and gratefully escaped into the fresh air.

25

Friday night, Alice left the Jacuzzi and headed into the locker room just as the yoga class ended. She'd planned the timing precisely. She was here as a kind of casual Hot Flash Club spy, trying to get a sense, just for the fun of it, of how the four new kids were bonding.

The locker room sounded like an aviary as women of all ages, shapes, and states of undress chattered and called as they changed into or out of street clothes. Alice pulled on sweatpants and sat on a bench to tie her sneakers.

A pregnant woman sat down next to her, heaving a sigh.

Alice smiled. "Hello, again. I remember you from the Jacuzzi last month. How are you?"

In response, Carolyn cracked an enormous yawn, hurrying to cover her mouth with her hand. "Sorry! Don't mean to be rude! I'm just *so* wiped out by the end of the week. I don't know how I'm going to find the energy to take care of a baby and do a decent job at work."

"Don't worry. You'll manage, I promise. I did. I raised two sons, as a single mother, while working full-time." She smiled, remembering. "Damn, I was busy! But it was fun. You know, I felt like Wonder Woman."

Carolyn looked skeptical. "What line of work?"

"I was in charge of personnel for the TransContinent Insurance Company which recently became TransWorld."

"Really." Impressed, Carolyn studied Alice more closely.

"Yes, and you know what? My two jobs—mother and administrator—complemented one another. I found myself using the same skills for both."

"*Really.*" Carolyn looked thoughtful. "I'd like to—"

"Okeydoke, slow poke!" Julia bounded up. "We're all ready to go!"

"Yes, and I'm starving," Beth added, pulling on her fleece vest.

"I'll just grab my coat and purse." Carolyn pushed herself up off the bench. "Nice talking to you."

"I'm Alice." She held out her hand.

"I'm Carolyn." They shook.

"We'll see you at Leonardo's!" Polly called.

Carolyn waddled off after the other three women.

Alice smiled.

———

They drove in their own cars but arrived at the same time, hurrying through the cold night into Leonardo's.

While they scanned the menus, Beth said, "Can you believe how busy The Haven is?"

"It's winter," Polly pointed out. "Everyone's desperate to get out of the house and get some exercise."

"Enough chitchat." Carolyn rapped her knife on the table like a gavel and pronounced in her chair-of-the-board voice, "I'm calling this meeting to order. So, ladies, any progress to report?"

The other three all spoke at once.

"I've moved in with Claudia!"

"You've got to check out the bruise Sonny's mother gave me!"

"Agnes made one of her Stealth Raids when Tim was out of town and found me and Belinda alone with—Beth!"

"Order, ladies, order." Carolyn tapped her Evian bottle. "I have some juicy news, too, but I think Beth's bruise should be the first order of business. Beth, what happened?"

Polly sat back in her chair, enjoying the contentment of loose, warm muscles, the satisfying swell of endorphins exercise produced, and not the least, the satisfaction of having once again done something healthy. Beth and Julia alternated in a dramatic recitation of the Saga of Sonny's Malevolent Mother and the Ice Skates. Polly responded at appropriate moments with exclamations of shock or censure. But she couldn't help stepping back a bit in her mind, so that she took in not only the tale that was unfolding, but also the dynamics of the friendship between Beth and Julia, developing right before her eyes. They glanced at each other for the right word, filled in and clarified, built and embroidered, transforming the events of that Sunday into the kind of stories that would become part of the legend of their lives.

"—so Beth and Belinda and I had just settled down on the guest bed to eat some grilled-cheese sandwiches," Julia said now, "when I heard a knock on the door, and I thought"—she put her hands to her face like the person in Munch's *The Scream*—" 'Oh, no, not now!' "

Polly laughed along with the others, while in her heart a new kind of sensation unfolded, a sort of bittersweet leaflet, with the present on one side, with a faded, blurred facsimile from the past on the other. If love could be ranked, then she would put her son, David, number one, followed closely by her husband, Tucker. But love didn't really fall into such limiting hierarchies. As Julia and Beth collapsed with laughter about the dreadful Agnes, and Carolyn looked on indulgently, Polly envisioned that confrontation, remembering in the same moment all the times she and her best friend, Franny, had groaned, gagged, and chortled about Claudia's snotty façade. As much as she had loved Tucker, and he had been her best friend as well as her lover, she just couldn't have made it without Franny's friendship.

For one thing, even though Tucker complained thoroughly, colorfully, and often
about his mother to her, Polly knew she
couldn't do the same to him. It was too
close. It broke an unwritten rule, like the one
that dictated that you could criticize your
own child, but when your best friend criticized hers, the best course was to champion that child. Polly could refer to Claudia
as that dried-up piece of beef jerky to
Franny, never to Tucker, and in turn, Franny
made fun of her own mother-in-law. Not to
mention, occasionally, her husband.

Franny had moved to Tucson a few years
ago because her husband's allergies and
Franny's arthritis required more sun and
heat than New England could provide.
They'd kept in touch by phone and e-mail,
but it really wasn't the same as sitting down
at the kitchen table over a cup of tea or curling up on the sofa with a bottle of red wine.
Oh, and the shopping they'd done together!
Polly sometimes found herself standing in
Filene's Basement, a bargain garment in her
hand, stunned by the shock of loss of
Franny's companionship and guidance.

It was a mystery to her how Claudia had
managed to live her life without a best

friend, or at least a few close friends, but Polly reminded herself how Claudia had been raised, how appearances were primary, how, in her world, you never let down your guard to expose your faults. Too bad, for friends loved you, faults and all.

"Want to know something amazing?" Julia's face was flushed, her eyes sparkling. She was beautiful, Polly thought, almost like a cartoon heroine with her short black hair and brisk motions. "Last fall, when I got stressed, my hearing crashed. This time, with Beth there, I didn't even have a momentary blip. So it's got to be psychosomatic, which is an enormous relief."

"Then we're all making progress," Carolyn said, nodding at Polly.

Polly pulled her mind into the present. "Yes, I've been asked to move in with Claudia, thanks to Carolyn."

"That's good?" Julia pulled a skeptical face.

"Yeah, I thought she was a horrible old bitch," Beth said.

"She is. But she's ill. She's dying. She's also proud, terribly private. If she had her way, I think she'd just crawl off beneath the house like a dying cat. And who knows, when I get to that point, I might feel that way, too. Anyway, she refuses to go into a hospital or care facility. She doesn't want strangers in her house. She didn't even want me around, because in her warped mind I'm not good enough to so much as clean up her vomit."

"*Eeeugh.*" Beth shuddered.

"But once she knew I was friends with Carolyn *Sperry,* I went up in her estimation."

"*And,*" Carolyn leaned forward, taking over, "she actually was very helpful to me."

"*Claudia* was?" Beth blinked in surprise. "How?"

"She suggested that Heather might have been pulling a scam with the antiques."

Polly watched Carolyn describe the events that unfolded. Carolyn became animated, less stiff, almost girlish in expression and gestures, drawing Julia and Beth closer, entranced. Carolyn's closer to their age, not mine, Polly thought with a twinge of melancholy. Polly was twenty-five years older than Carolyn, almost as much older as Claudia was than Polly. The other three women had so much of their lives ahead of them, especially the core of most women's existence: childbirth and raising children.

They were having periods while Polly was having hot flashes. Polly imagined that after Carolyn had her baby, she'd find her life too full to have time for yoga or leisurely conversations.

"Are you kidding?" Julia sat up straight, waving her hands. "You're just going to leave it there?"

"What else can we do?" Carolyn asked.

With a snap, Polly brought her attention on the present.

"Keep investigating," Julia declared. "I mean, come on, are you sure her brother's not faking it?"

Carolyn gnawed on her lip, thinking. "We'll find out eventually. My father wants to give Harry some financial support without making Harry feel like a charity case, so he's trying to find some kind of job for Harry at the paper mill."

"Okay, if that works out, *then* you'll know whether Harry's faking it or not, but how long will it be before Harry's back is better? It could be months." Julia shook her head. "I don't like this. I don't trust it. I'll bet Heather called her brother, told him to rent a wheelchair and do a Tiny Tim. Because come on, even if Harry really is injured, two hundred thousand dollars is a hell of a lot of money to hand over."

"Most of it was spent on antiques, don't forget," Carolyn said. "Well, a lot of it. Polly saw the furniture, too. There's a ton of it." She shifted in her chair to get more comfortable. "I don't see what else I can do. I can't just plant myself outside Harry's window to spy on him."

Julia grinned mischievously. "No, but we can."

"What do you mean?"

Julia lowered her voice conspiratorially. "What if Harry is faking the injury? Or what if it's not really as bad as he says? What if he can walk? He's a young man, right? He won't want to stay in that house all day. I could park outside his house. He wouldn't recognize my car. I could take my video camera. If I see him walking, I could shoot him so you'd have proof for your father."

"Cool." Beth breathed. "A stakeout. I'll come, too."

"I don't know." Carolyn looked worried. "Wouldn't that be kind of underhanded?"

"Isn't it *kind of underhanded* if Heather and Harry are cheating your father out of money?" Julia pressed her case. "Look.

Heather's already got a history of sneaki-ness. She bought furniture, said it cost two hundred thousand dollars. When you con-fronted her about the checks made out to cash, *then* and *only* then did she remember to mention her brother. Smells fishy to me."

Carolyn looked at Polly. "What do you think?"

"I think Julia's right. Think how relieved you'll be if Harry really is injured. If you don't do this, you might spend the rest of your life suspecting Heather."

Carolyn capitulated with a giant shrug. "Oh, good grief, all right."

Julia screwed up her mouth, thinking. "We'll need a camouflage car. Something that won't make Harry suspicious if he no-tices a strange vehicle parked on his street all day."

"I'll borrow one of Sonny's family's trucks!" Beth laughed with excitement. "One that says Young's Construction on it."

"Great idea!" Julia gave Beth a high five. "We've got to do it when Belinda's in school."

"How about Monday morning?" Beth asked. "I've got a class in the afternoon, and I work at the library in the evening."

"Morning's good," Julia said.

Carolyn was not so thrilled. "It's cold outside, in case you hadn't noticed. You two will freeze."

"We'll dress warmly," Julia promised.

"We'll bring Thermoses of hot tea," Beth added.

"I'll call you with directions." Carolyn struggled to get to her feet. "I've got to go to the john and home. I think this meeting's adjourned."

"We'll phone you the minute we know anything," Julia promised.

"Let me know, too," Polly urged.

"We will!"

26

Beth wore all black. Even though she didn't plan to get out of the truck, black seemed appropriate for a stakeout, and when she honked the horn in front of Julia's house, she saw that Julia had chosen to wear all black, too. Of course Julia usually did.

She swung up into the cab of the truck, setting a bag on the floor. "How are you, Nancy Drew?"

"I'm great!" Beth said. "Where's your camera?"

"Here." Julia bent over and brought out a compact silver box.

"It's so small!"

"Tiny size, great power. Zoom lens." Julia pressed a button, demonstrating for Beth how the lens whirred out for long-distance shots.

"Cool." Beth put the truck in gear. It had

turned out to be surprisingly easy to drive. "I brought coffee, chocolate, and two empty glass jars in case we have to pee."

Julia laughed. "Good thinking."

"Ready?" Beth pulled the truck away from the curb. "Carolyn said to take Route 2 to 16 to Mass. Ave. to Martin Lane."

"Yeah, those are the directions Carolyn gave me, too. Okey-dokey." Julia leaned back, looking out at the passing scenery.

The sun was out, strong and hot, melting snow off the curbs into thousands of miniature rivers trickling toward the drains. People were out enjoying the brief mild spell, walking dogs, pushing baby strollers, chatting in front of dry cleaners and pharmacies.

Julia folded her long legs and propped her feet on the dashboard. "What did you tell Sonny about what we're doing today?"

Beth groaned. "You know what? I told him the truth. I don't want to have any secrets between us, so I thought that would be the best course, but I'm afraid I shocked him a little bit. He's worried that Heather's brother might be dangerous."

"Can't be too dangerous if he's stuck in a wheelchair," Julia pointed out sensibly.

"I know. I'm not scared. Well, maybe I am,

just a little. I feel kind of apprehensive, and also, just a tiny bit wicked. I really do think I shocked Sonny."

"I'm glad you told him the truth because I told Tim the truth, too."

"And?"

"He reacted like you said Sonny did. Shocked. Amazed, really, as if he thinks what we're doing is bizarre."

"Well, isn't it?" Beth giggled. "I never imagined that I, mild-mannered grad student of ancient English literature, would ever stake out a man's house!"

"I'll bet it's not so unusual in Carolyn's world. Families with the kind of money the Sperrys have probably do this sort of thing all the time."

"You could be right. I wouldn't know. I've never known anyone as wealthy as Carolyn. I don't envy her."

"Me either." Julia leaned forward. "I think the next street is the one."

"Roger." Beth flicked on her indicator and made the turn. "Number 32?"

"Right." Julia removed her feet from the dash and sat up straight. "There. I think that's the house."

"I'll drive past, make a U-turn, and approach it from the other direction."

"That's it. The yellow clapboard."

Beth slowed as they drove past. The house sat innocently in its muddy yard. A striped tabby cat ambled across the yard, beneath a shrub, and into the next yard, where it sat with its head cocked, as if waiting.

Julia had her binoculars out. "All the windows are covered with blinds or curtains."

"He's probably sleeping. Don't invalids sleep a lot?"

"I know. We probably should have waited until the afternoon, but I have to be home for Belinda then."

"How's this?" Beth brought the truck to a stop next to a high privet hedge. "Can you see?"

"Perfectly." Julia scanned the neighborhood. "Sleepy little street."

"Now what?" Beth asked.

"Now we wait."

Two hours later, Julia stretched as well as she could in the enclosed cab. "This is killing my back. I'm not accustomed to so much sitting. What time is it?"

Beth checked her watch. "A little after eleven."

"Not a flicker of movement for two hours."

Beth made a face. "I've got to pee."

"Well, you brought the jar."

"I know. But now I'm not so keen on the idea."

"Want to stop for the day? I could arrange things with Tim and we could come back tomorrow afternoon. Can't do it in the morning; I've got a retirement luncheon to videotape."

Beth looked wistfully at the house, so still in the sunshine it seemed like a stage set. "Okay. Let's do that."

"Dr. Monroe is coming to tea."

Polly let the bags of groceries slide onto the end of the sofa. Claudia didn't like it when something as plebeian as a brown paper bag made contact with any of her fine furniture, but Polly, already puffing from hauling everything in from the car, gasped at Claudia's announcement and collapsed next to the groceries.

"Excuse me?"

"You need to have your hearing checked, Polly. Mine is perfect, but that's unusual."

Yes, yes, you're one rare and superlative specimen of humanity, Polly thought crankily. She looked over at Claudia, seated on her chaise, clad in her new brown Brooks Brothers skirt, sweaters, and pearls. Claudia was continuing to shrink just like the witch in *The Wizard of Oz* when Dorothy tossed water on her. She glanced at Claudia's breakfast tray. Perhaps two sips of tea had been taken, and the tip of the croissant, but the orange juice glass was untouched.

"Would you like me to warm up your croissant?" Polly asked.

Claudia waved a lethargic claw. "Why would I want you to do that? I've finished my breakfast. Take those things away and I'll tell you what I want served for tea."

Polly unbuttoned her coat. "What day is Dr. Monroe coming?"

Her voice crackling with irritation, Claudia snapped, "What is wrong with you, Polly! I told you already. He's coming today!"

"Oh." Polly thought for a moment. "Would

you like me to help you shower before he comes?"

"I performed my ablutions before I dressed this morning," Claudia retorted.

Polly doubted that, since Claudia could hardly stand up. Her progress down the stairs this morning had been painfully slow. Claudia had leaned heavily on the banister and paused at every third step to suck in one long, labored breath. But she had refused to take the supporting arm Polly had offered. Claudia's hair, always before her illness so beautifully coiffed, was dry and thin, bent at odd angles and sticking up in back. Furthermore, the heavy veil of perfume Claudia wore could not camouflage any longer the aroma of urine and her general lack of hygiene. Claudia's senses were obviously dulled, but was her mind? Claudia was too weak to shower or bathe herself, but did she realize that? What were Polly's responsibilities at this juncture? Should she force Claudia to shower? How could anyone force Claudia to do anything?

Polly put the groceries away and dutifully returned to the living room, where she found Claudia asleep, head lolling to one side, mouth open. Polly's entire body contracted with pity to see the elegant woman so shrunken and vulnerable. What little flesh and fat Claudia had ever carried had disappeared weeks ago, but now her muscles had also vanished, leaving her shoulder bones sticking up like knobs, allowing her cheeks to sink in so that her face was merely a skull with a thin sheet of skin over it. Claudia was experiencing no pain, but she was starving to death before Polly's eyes.

With a twinge of shame, Polly realized her own clothes were becoming too tight. Caring for Claudia had not caused Polly to lose any weight, in spite of all the stairs she was climbing and trays she was hefting these days, because every night she rewarded herself with a box of chocolates and a glass of Baileys Original Irish Cream—and she didn't use one of Claudia's delicate little thimble-size aperitif glasses, either.

Eating had always been Polly's private path to comfort. Better, she assured herself, than alcohol or drugs. And wasn't it all right to give herself these treats? She missed her own home, her own bed. The guest bedroom had such an Edward Gorey air about it, it kind of gave Polly the creeps, and she had great trouble settling down to sleep every night. The spool bed's ancient mattress sagged, as corrugated as a muddy road in springtime. The entire room seemed pervaded with an irrevocable kind of pale damp that seeped through the hand-embroidered, age-worn, threadbare linen sheets. The bedside lamp held only a twenty-five-watt bulb, so Polly had sneaked her own lamp into the house, because if she couldn't read, she'd really lose her mind. But that light made the rest of the room seem darker and dingier, and the disapproving faces of the pinch-lipped ancestors glaring down from their framed portraits hanging around the room stirred within Polly's breast guilt for sins she had never committed.

Perhaps, Polly thought, she might sleep better if the intercom between Claudia's bedroom and the dining room were hooked up between their bedrooms at night. When Polly did manage to fall asleep, the slightest noise woke her—she'd sit upright, heart thudding. *Was that Claudia? Had she called?* Fears of Claudia lying alone in her bedroom, perhaps choking, perhaps suffering, perhaps dying, poked at her nerves and made her heart race. She'd brought over a framed photograph of Tucker to put on her bedside table, so she could look at his face when she needed comfort.

Back in the kitchen, Polly started a chicken simmering—Claudia liked the broth—and organized the tea things. Claudia still slept; she spent the better part of her days sleeping. What else could she do? Polly wondered. She knew it was important to focus on the here and now, to help the dying, as well as the living, take pleasure in the present. But what could that be?

A few days ago, Polly had lifted one of the portraits off the bedroom wall and carried it down to where Claudia sat on her chaise.

"Tell me about this woman, please, Claudia. She looks so interesting." The request had been heartfelt. Polly knew little about Claudia's life.

Claudia had only lifted a weary hand. "Pull a duck trolley."

Polly had gaped while a thrill of fear raced through her: was Claudia going mad? Then she realized Claudia had her teeth out and probably meant "Put it back, Polly." She'd climbed the stairs and rehung the picture.

Yesterday, she'd asked Claudia if they

could look at old photo albums together. She wanted so much to see pictures of Tucker when he was a boy. And she thought Claudia might enjoy living, for a few moments, back in the days of her youth, but Claudia had only shaken her head and closed her eyes, as if simply listening to Polly's request had depleted her.

What else could Polly do? How do you help someone die without intruding? Claudia was offended when Polly offered to help her shower or wash her hair. She refused to let Polly enter her bedroom to change the sheets and air it out. As much as she accepted from Polly, she still kept her from doing all she could to help. Was Polly doing the right thing, helping the older woman to retain as much control and privacy as possible? Or was she neglecting her?

It seemed to Polly that whatever else Polly had ever been to Claudia, now, during this final stage of her life, during the days and weeks of Claudia's dying, Polly was Claudia's final audience. More than she needed a housekeeper, cook, valet, maid, or nurse, Claudia needed someone to see her as she saw herself, to respect her as a beautiful, refined, powerful, independent woman. Polly wanted to give Claudia that much, for as long as possible.

Still, she needed some guidance. Somehow, she had to find a way to speak with Dr. Monroe alone.

Claudia woke at three thirty. "Bwingee eye purth, pauwee."

Polly brought Claudia her purse, then stepped out of the room to allow her a moment alone to install her false teeth. When she returned, she found Claudia with her hand mirror in one hand and a tube of lipstick in the other. Claudia squinted.

"Would you like me to turn on a light?" Polly offered. The winter afternoon was almost as dark as night.

"I would not." Claudia patted her hair in gestures Polly had seen hundreds of times before over the years, but today this filled Polly with a madhouse sadness, for Claudia's action did no good. Claudia's hair spouted up at the back of her head like a clump of dried grass. "Is the tea ready?"

"It is." The doorbell rang. "That must be Dr. Monroe." Polly hurried through the hall.

She opened the door. The physician stood there in a handsome black wool overcoat, a black briefcase in his hand. "Hello, Polly." He looked so sane, so reliable.

"Hello, Dr. Monroe," she said in a loud voice for Claudia's benefit. Urgently, she whispered, "Dr. Monroe, I'm so glad you're here. Claudia's incontinent but refuses to admit it, she can't bathe herself but won't let me help her, she scarcely eats anything, she's lost so much weight! God, I know I'm babbling like someone out of Dickens, but I don't know what to do."

"Polly!" Claudia called imperiously. "Don't dawdle!"

Hugh Monroe put a calming hand on Polly's shoulder. "I understand."

Polly wanted to throw herself at his feet, clutching his ankles. Instead, she calmly led the doctor into the living room.

"Good afternoon, Mrs. Lodge." Dr. Monroe executed a handsome little bow and held out his hand.

Claudia touched her fingers to his briefly in a queenly imitation of a handshake. "Good to see you, Hugh." Gesturing him to a chair, she ordered, "Polly. Tea."

Blocking an impulse to curtsy, Polly took

herself off to the kitchen. She took her time, wanting to allow Claudia plenty of privacy with the doctor, then carried the heavy silver tray into the living room. She set it on the coffee table. Following Claudia's orders, she poured tea for Claudia and the doctor and handed the cookies around, then sat down, preparing to pour her own tea.

"That will be all, Polly," Claudia said.

"Um, perhaps I should stay, to hear what Dr. Monroe suggests . . . ?"

Claudia turned to the doctor and waved her hand, as if sweeping away a gnat. "One of Polly's qualities is a remarkable intransigence."

Polly started to object, but Dr. Monroe threw her a wonderful smile. "It's all right, Polly. I'd like a little time alone with Mrs. Lodge, and we'll tell you what we've decided."

Polly nodded, rose, and went into the dining room, shutting the door firmly behind her. She sat down at the dining-room table and stared at her sewing machine. On impulse, she grabbed a piece of extra fabric and sewed tidy seams in it. A weird thing to do, perhaps, but the work calmed her, it always did, and she hoped the sound of the little purring motor would assure them that she wasn't listening in.

"Polly?" A tap came at the dining-room door and Dr. Monroe stuck his head in. "Could you join us, please?"

"Certainly." Polly flicked off her machine.

Claudia seemed to have grown even smaller in the past half hour. Perhaps it was the way she was sinking down into the chaise.

"Would you like me to puff up the cushions behind your back?" Polly offered.

"I'd *like* you to sit down and *listen,*" Claudia retorted, as if Polly had been skipping around the room with her fingers stuck in her ears.

"Polly," Hugh Monroe said, "Mrs. Lodge has insisted she does not want to go into a hospital, but she has agreed that she would be more comfortable with a hospital bed. The pharmacy will deliver one and set it up. A bedside commode, as well. Also, we're going to ask Home Health Services and Hospice to get involved now. I'll contact Martha Wright, who's head of hospice.

She'll be here to do an initial interview, and then someone will come, at least once every day, to help Mrs. Lodge with various personal procedures."

Polly nodded and smiled at the physician, while beneath her bosom the oddest feeling bloomed—not relief, not at all, but instead a kind of ice-cold terror. *Shit!* she thought irreverently. *A hospital bed! Once you get in a hospital bed, you don't usually get out. I hate this!* she wanted to cry. *I'm scared!*

"Polly," Claudia said. "Find a pad of paper. You'll need to write down these names and phone numbers and instructions."

"Yes, Claudia." Polly rose, although at the moment she wasn't even certain what a pad of paper was.

27

Another Sunday had arrived, which meant another delightful meal *en famille* at the Youngs' house. Today Beth's culinary offering was two loaves of homemade whole-wheat bread and a plate of homemade chocolate chip cookies. She'd considered bringing brownies—she had a great recipe—but even brownies would be easy to sabotage. A little vinegar drizzled over the top, or any liquid really, would sink into the chewy chocolate, making it look even moister and taste disgusting, providing Sonny's family with another reason he should marry Robin instead of Beth. Cookies were a little more foolproof, as was the bread, wrapped in foil, ready to be heated. Beth had them tucked carefully in a book bag and had just pulled on her coat and hat, when suddenly she couldn't stand it anymore.

"Sonny, I have to ask you something."

Sonny was buttoning his jacket. "Shoot."

"How do you feel about Robin?" *There.* Embarrassment and terror sent her body temperature into the danger zone.

Sonny looked at Beth. "What do you mean?"

"Are you still attracted to her?"

Sonny shook his head and gently cuffed Beth on her shoulder. "You're kidding me."

Beth kept silent.

"Beth, come on!" Seeing that she was serious, he put both hands on her shoulders, pulling her to him. "I love you. I want to marry you."

"And Robin?"

"Robin's like another sister. Part of the family."

Quietly Beth said, "She was your first love."

Sonny rolled his eyes. "I was a *kid* then. Come on, Beth, have I ever given you any reason to think I'm attracted to her?"

Beth thought about this for a moment. "No." In a small voice she added, "But she's always touching you . . ."

"So's the dog." Sonny tilted her chin up so she had to look him in the eyes. "Robin's a babe, I'm not denying that. She was my first girlfriend. But I don't lust after her, and I don't love her, although I suppose I do care for her, in pretty much the same way I care for my sister. You're the one I love, Beth. Trust me, okay?"

"Okay." Beth closed her eyes in relief as Sonny engulfed her in a giant hug.

"Go, Pats!" the family roared in greeting when Sonny and Beth entered. The Sunday afternoon the family had watched the Super Bowl, Beth had thought she'd go deaf when, in the final few moments, the Patriots won, and the Young household exploded with cheering.

"Go, Pats!" Sonny and Beth yelled back.

"You're late!" Sonny's brother, Mark, yelled from the refrigerator as he lifted out a handful of beers. "Dad and I got first call on the Corona, so it's Miller Lite for you."

"Sonny!" His sister, Suze, was opening a bottle of red wine, so she motioned to the table with a jerk of her head. "Mom's gone mad!"

In the kitchen, pots and pans clattered, steam billowed, people yelled as they cut back and forth across the room, bumping each other like billiard balls. Every single person wore gray hoodies with the navy and red New England Patriots logo on the front. The sweatshirts had been Merle and Bobbie's presents to their family on Christmas— and they had even given one to Beth, who had been so pleased to be included that she hadn't pointed out that they'd given her a size large. She wore it now. It hung down to her knees and weighed heavily on her shoulders. She had to roll the sleeves up several times, and the thick bunch of fleece cuffing her wrists was a nuisance.

"What's cookin', Mom?" Sonny kissed his mother on her cheek. "Something smells great."

Bobbie smiled indulgently at her oldest, favorite son, whose thick black hair, deep blue eyes, and profile were a carbon copy of hers. "I thought we'd try something a little different this Sunday and have a Mexican meal. You boys always loved tacos so much." She set a large bowl of chopped onions on the table. "Hi, Beth. Hope you like spicy food."

Robin was here. Of course she was here, standing at the stove, stirring a pot. *Her* sweatshirt fit as if it had been custom-tailored to accentuate the expanse of her bosom against the narrow curves of her waist.

"Scoot over," Sonny told Robin. "I want to put this bread in the oven to heat up."

"God, we don't want *bread,* Sonny." With a tilt of her slender hip, Robin nudged Sonny away. "Not with tamales, tortillas, beans." She cooed the words in Sonny's ear in a low, suggestive voice, as if describing sexual positions.

Beth glanced at Sonny's mother. When Beth had phoned Bobbie on Friday, Bobbie had told her she was roasting a leg of lamb she'd gotten a good deal on at Stop & Shop, and Beth had said she'd make a loaf of homemade bread. Instead, Mexican food? Bobbie bared her teeth at Beth in a smile that would have frozen Cruella De Vil in her tracks.

Beth held her platter high. "I brought cookies for dessert." Her voice was lost in the general commotion. The whole yelling thing she hadn't quite managed to acquire. She set the platter at the back of the counter.

Merle hunched at the head of the table looking unhappy. "All these vegetables and beans will have me gassed up like the *Hindenburg*," he grumbled.

"Oh, go on, you need more greens for your cholesterol," Bobbie told him, placing a platter of tamales covered with melted cheese before him. Her husband reached out with a fork and she slapped his hand. "Hang on! Let the others at least sit down. Honestly." She patted his head with absent-minded affection as she looked around the room. "Mark? Take the burritos from the oven and put them on the hot pad here in the middle of the table. Sonny? Grab the bowls of chopped peppers and tomatoes. Suze, got the shredded cheese? Oh, and, Robin, are the beans ready?"

"Ready," Robin called, bringing the earthenware bowl to the table.

Beth swallowed. Quickly she counted the places set at the table. Seven. Okay, so at least Bobbie hadn't cut her completely out of the group. This was the first time Bobbie had so openly ignored Beth. Was it because she realized Beth wasn't going to go away, that Sonny really loved her and intended to marry her? Whatever, it was becoming more and more clear that Bobbie meant war.

Everyone settled at the table, and as always conversation faded to a mutter as the food was passed around.

Beth rose.

Bobbie glanced up from her plate. "Is everything okay?"

"Sure," Beth answered with her sweetest smile. "I just want to get a wineglass, I think I'll have some of that merlot." And she went right to the cupboard where the wineglasses were kept.

"We shouldn't be drinking wine, we should be drinking tequila," Suze told the group as she reached across the table to pour wine into Beth's glass.

"Oh, yeah, tequila in the middle of the day, that would be *sweet,*" Mark said, laughing.

"Hey! Remember the time we all had a contest to see who could drink the most margaritas?" Robin laughed so hard her breasts bobbled beneath her sweatshirt.

"I do not," Bobbie said emphatically.

"Oh, Mom, not you," Sonny told her. "Of

course you and Dad weren't there. It was the year Suze turned eighteen, so she wanted to get officially drunk, so Mark and Robin and—who were you dating then, Mark? Oh, yeah, right, the delectable Kathy."

"Please," Suze cut in, "that Kathy was such a slut."

"We're at the dinner table if you don't mind," Merle growled.

"Anyway, we were at that dive over on Spring Street—"

"Best margaritas on the East Coast!" Mark yelled.

Even their conversation is a team sport, Beth thought as her eyes flew from one face to the other, her own face held in an expression of fascinated interest she'd had plenty of practice achieving. Sonny's family never asked her how her week went, what kind of work she was doing, what she was reading for her degree.

Next to her, Sonny's father belched loudly. "Excuse me," he said with pride.

"Robin put ground coriander in the beans," Bobbie told them.

"What's coriander?" Sonny asked. "I don't think I like it."

"You're thinking of fennel," Robin told him, turning to him and holding out her fork. "Just take a little taste; you'll like it." She leaned toward him, her beautiful face rosy from the heat of the kitchen, her gorgeous pink lips moist with grease.

But Sonny turned away from Robin and put this hand possessively on Beth's thigh. "Have you ever used coriander in any of our meals?" He couldn't have said more clearly, *I'm with you.*

"I don't think so." Flushed with happiness, Beth felt charitable. "But, Robin, these beans *are* delicious."

"Sonny," his mother called from her end of the table, "guess who I saw last week."

"Diga me," Sonny said.

"What?" Bobbie reared back a little, frowning.

Sonny translated, "That means 'tell me' in Spanish. Since we're eating Mexican food and all."

"How do you know Spanish?" Bobbie asked, flashing a quick glance at Beth, as if she were responsible.

"Mom, come on. I had it in high school. I still remember some of it."

Bobbie rolled her eyes. "So, anyway, I saw Karen Renfro."

"No way!" Robin cried. "I thought she'd moved to California."

"She had, with that stupid hippie Dan or Dave or Doug or something—"

"Dimwit," Merle interjected.

"But she left him, moved back here, and she's getting married to—wait for it!" Bobbie was nearly choking with laughter. "Gregory Malone!"

The table exploded.

"No!" Robin screamed. "Stop! I can't stand it!"

This must be what Princess Di felt like when she took meals with the queen and the rest of the family, Beth thought. Except Beth knew Sonny loved her. Oh, poor Princess Di, who didn't even possess her husband's love! And who was hungry all the time, too. It had truly stunned Beth when Princess Di's marriage had fallen apart. For Beth, as for many women everywhere, it was like watching the shining mirror of a shimmering fairy tale that reflected all women's lives fade into tarnished glass, then shatter. Many times Beth found herself hoping one of the two royal sons would rebel, champion his dead mother's cause, and reject the entire family, after first giving Prince Charles a nice fat fist in the mouth—

"Beth?" Sonny nudged her. "Want some ice cream?"

"Oh! Sure! And I brought cookies." Beth jumped up to help the others clear the table, brew the coffee, and dish out the vanilla ice cream. When she returned to her seat, she could sense a tension in Sonny simply by the way he held himself, a little more rigid and alert, as if he were about to bungee jump. Knowing what he was about to announce, Beth held her breath.

"Guess what?" he began, then stopped himself and began again. "Actually, none of you would guess this. I've decided something. I'm going to go back to school to get a degree in architecture."

For the first time that day, dead silence fell over the room. His father continued to spoon ice cream into his mouth, as if he hadn't heard a thing, but Beth caught the look that passed between Bobbie and Robin.

Undeterred by the lack of support, Sonny continued. "I took my College Level Examination tests last week and did pretty well.

I'm taking College Writing Two at Bunker Hill Community College this semester, while I check out programs in the area." He paused, waiting for any kind of reaction. When none came, he went on, "I'm thinking of the Boston Architecture College; they take transfer students, so I'd have two years credit to start with—"

"Oh, please, Sonny!" From the end of the table, Bobbie looked toward her son, an expression of gentle disappointment on her face. "Honey, you don't need all that academic stuff! You've got Young's Construction! What more could you want?"

Sonny put his elbows on the table and faced his mother. "I'm interested in design. Don't ask me why, I just am, I always have been. I'd like to be able to design houses, oversee the entire project from the word *go,* read blueprints—"

"You want to be better than us, that's what you mean." Sonny's brother, sitting across the table, shoved his chair back and crossed his arms over his chest.

Sonny turned scarlet. "Oh, stuff it up your a—"

"Sonny." Bobbie's warning was one low word.

"He's right, though." Sonny's sister, sitting on his left, entered the fray. Her face flushed with anger, she leaned forward to point an accusing finger at Beth. "Ever since he's been dating *her,* he suddenly thinks he's too good for us. *We* didn't go to college."

"Don't be ridiculous," Sonny snapped.

"I'm not being ridiculous!" Suze had her father's coloring, but in anger her jaw worked just like Sonny's did. "You never do things with just the family anymore. You moved out of the house—"

"Hey!" Sonny was furious. "Look. One, I *started* college, I always wanted to go to college, I wanted to be an architect, but I didn't have the money for tuition. Two, I moved out of the house before I met Beth, remember? Three, Beth and I have eaten here every Sunday for the past few months, which some people would consider pretty unusual. It's not like we're the goddamned Cosa Nostra or something!"

Silence fell again, and then Robin spoke. "Well, I think it's wonderful that Sonny's going back to school." The entire Young family stared at Robin, astonished. "When we were in high school, he always talked about becoming an architect—"

Bobbie looked shocked. "He never discussed it with me!" She studied her husband's face. "Or with any of the family."

Beth couldn't stop staring at Robin, who was looking at Sonny with melting eyes. She was so softly beautiful, a dream woman, and when she spoke her voice was a caress. "No, I don't suppose he did. You don't tell your family everything when you're a teenager. You keep your dreams private."

Beth took a sip of wine, glad she still had a bit left in her glass. She wished it were pure vodka. Sonny had warned her to expect some kind of scene, but she hadn't counted on Robin weaseling in like this. She couldn't decide whether it was better to feel ignored, as she usually did during Sunday dinners, or blamed. *Blamed,* she thought, because then at least Sonny's family admitted he shared a connection with Beth.

Merle brought both hands down on the table with a heavy thud. "Just how are you proposing to pay your tuition?"

"I've got some savings. I plan to work two jobs this summer. I'm going to move in with

Beth, so we'll have just one rent to pay. And I'm going to apply for scholarships."

"So you're planning to continue working with us?" Merle's eyes seared Sonny's face.

"Absolutely, Dad, of course."

"Don't expect any breaks from me because you're in school. You won't get a lighter load. I won't stand for any shoddy workmanship. No excuses. No special treatment."

"I understand."

"Then I don't know what all the fuss is about," Merle said. "I'd like some more ice cream."

Three of the women—Bobbie, Suze, and Robin—but not Beth, rose to fetch it for him. Since no one else would, Beth passed the platter of cookies around, nearly crying with relief when everyone took a few and ate them.

28

Alice's candidate, Glen Wells, had suggested that he and Faye meet at the Museum of Fine Arts, one of Faye's favorite spots in Boston, so as Faye drove toward her appointment, she was optimistic.

Plus, she'd been dieting for six weeks, and she'd lost six pounds, which had brought her down from 164 to 158. The day that little red arrow on her scales quivered *beneath* 160 had been so satisfying! Her clothes felt less tight, and she no longer looked nine months pregnant. Encouraged by her Hot Flash Club friends, she'd also changed her hairstyle, forgoing her usual tidy chignon, and weaving her white hair into a loose braid, letting wisps of hair drift free around her face. She thought it made her look a little more youthful, and even, perhaps, a bit bohemian. Why not? After all, she was an artist.

She parked in the lot and hurried through the cold morning air to the art museum. She left her coat at the coat check, dropped the plastic, numbered button into her purse, and took the stairs to the second floor. She and Glen had agreed to meet in the Monet Water Lily room. She was a few minutes late, so she assumed he'd already be there—and when she arrived in the gallery, a man stood in front of the picture, studying it. She took a moment to study him.

He wasn't tall, but he wasn't short. Not fat, not thin. He wore casual chinos and a blue denim shirt. So far, so good, if this was Glen Wells.

"Glen?" Faye asked quietly.

He turned. "Hello."

When she saw his face, she had an immediate reaction—unfortunately, a negative one. It wasn't so much the peculiar shape of his head that bothered her, although it was a bit unsettling, the way his forehead protruded. His baldness accentuated his bulging brow. He was not a handsome man, but worse, his eyes seemed flat, judgmental.

Hoping her disappointment didn't show, Faye quickly held out her hand. "It's nice to meet you," she said politely.

"Well, we'll see about that, won't we?" Glen responded without a smile to take the edge off his words.

Unsure whether he was joking, Faye gave a faint laugh. "Um, I'm sorry I'm late. The traffic—"

Glen looked at his watch. "You're only eleven minutes late. That's not unacceptable." He glanced at the water lilies. "However, I've spent as much time with this old thing as I'd like. Let's move on to the Picassos."

"Certainly." Faye loved the water lilies and would have liked to spend a few moments gazing at the canvas—it lifted her up, somehow. But she *had* been late, and she could always come back.

As they strolled through the galleries, Glen said, "Alice tells me you're a painter."

"Yes. Although I haven't painted since my husband died."

"She told me your husband died. I'm sorry." For a moment, his eyes rested on Faye with a genuine warmth.

"Thank you." Faye swallowed the lump

that always rose when she talked about Jack. "He had a heart attack. He was very young. Only sixty-four."

Glen gave a small laugh. "Funny, how we get to the age where sixty-four seems young." He stopped in front of a Klee and cocked his head, studying it. "What kind of painting did you do? Abstract?"

"Oh, no. Contemporary impressionist. Still lifes, mostly."

"Ah. Pretty pictures."

"Yes, pretty," Faye echoed, adding defensively, "Some even called them beautiful. The Quinn Gallery on Newbury Street shows my work."

"Very impressive." He moved down toward an enormous Jackson Pollock. "I like Pollock. I like edgy art that makes me feel uncomfortable. Perhaps because as an accountant, I'm always working with numbers, everything precise and rigid and inflexible. I like the energy of modern art."

Faye's interest perked up. How nice to be with a man who not only knew about art, but actually thought about why he reacted to it as he did. "Yes, I like some modern art, as well."

"I've always wanted to go to Spain to see

Gaudi's architecture. The pictures I've seen of his work make it look like nothing else in the world."

"I've seen some of his work," Faye told him. "I went to Spain between junior and senior year of college."

"Ah, you were fortunate. I got married my junior year. Had to. My girlfriend was pregnant. We had two remarkable children, who are the light of my life. No, I wouldn't undo those years." He looked over at Faye with a smile that made his homely face much more attractive. "But I am envious of people who've been able to travel."

As they moved into the gallery hung with Warhol and Kandinsky, Faye said, "Alice told me you're divorced."

"Yes, for some years now. But Loni and I are still friends. When we divorced, we agreed to do everything we could to keep our children from suffering. They were both in their twenties, but we didn't want them to feel they had to choose sides or be peacemakers. When our daughter was married last year, both Loni and I gave her away."

"How lovely." Faye was warming to this man. "Your children are fortunate."

Now he gave an embarrassed little shrug. "I hope so."

"If you like modern art," Faye offered, "you might like driving out to Mass. MoCA in North Adams. It's a fairly new museum, with some exciting exhibits."

"Where's North Adams?"

"Over in the northwestern corner of the state, almost in Vermont."

"Hm. Might make a nice autumn trip," Glen said thoughtfully. "That's a great leaf-peaking area."

"Yes, and you could visit the Clark Art Gallery, too. Although they have mostly Impressionist art. But Williams College has a fine art museum, too, and Williamstown's right next door to North Adams."

"Isn't that near Stockbridge?" Glen asked. "What's that place—they have concerts there, outdoors, the Boston Pops often plays there—"

"Tanglewood."

He snapped his fingers. "Right. I wonder how far into the fall they have concerts. I've always wanted to go there."

"I've been there a few times," Faye said. "It's heavenly on a warm summer night. People bring blankets and picnic dinners and wine and lie under the stars listening to the music. The last time I was there, I went with my husband and my daughter for the Fourth of July. It was fabulous."

"Yes, Alice told me you have a daughter."

"Laura's just moved to California with her husband and baby girl."

"That's tough for you," Glen said sympathetically. "You must miss them."

"You have no idea."

Glen checked his watch. "It's almost noon. If we went across the street to the restaurant now, we might be able to beat the rush."

"Sounds good to me."

As they entered the restaurant, Faye once again experienced a slight sense of pleasure simply from being in the company of a man. It made her feel *chosen;* it made her feel a little more *complete.* She hated this about herself, really. Theoretically, she didn't believe a woman without a man was inferior or lacking or incomplete. But she couldn't help the way she felt. It was so nice the way Glen put his hand lightly on her back as they moved in the line up to the hostess's stand.

"Two for lunch," he said.

The hostess walked swiftly through the crowded room. Faye hoped Glen wasn't looking at her bottom. She thought her long silk tunic disguised the width of her hips, but she'd spent enough time checking herself out in a mirror to guess that when she walked, her buttocks probably shifted like a pair of piglets in a bag.

At the table, the hostess said, "Someone will be right with you," and hurried away. With excellent manners, Glen came around to seat Faye. He pulled out her chair. Faye sank into it, smiling up at him. "Thank you," she said, just as something creaked and dislodged. The chair collapsed beneath her, letting Faye crash to the floor.

She landed right on her bum, her legs sticking out in front of her, four wooden chair legs poking out from beneath her, and something stabbing her in the hip.

Everyone in the restaurant looked her way. Someone laughed. The hostess and two waiters rushed over to Faye. A bonfire hot flash ignited Faye's body, turning her face crimson. She truly did want to sink through the floor and vanish.

Glen bent to offer her a hand, which she refused, shaking her head. It was bad enough to be so heavy she'd broken a chair. She didn't want him to strain his back trying to haul her up off the floor.

"Are you okay?" the hostess asked.

Faye scrambled to extricate herself from the jumble. Setting her hands firmly on the floor on either side of her, she pushed herself to a standing position, sending a silent prayer to the gods that she'd been taking yoga and had worked up enough strength to get up by herself. She felt, momentarily, something stuck to her behind, and then the chair seat, which had somehow attached itself to her, fell to the floor with a thud.

The hostess told the waiters to gather up the parts of the broken chair and take them away. She quickly lifted another chair over to Faye's place. "I'm so sorry. It's all this frigid weather. It dries out the glue in the wood that holds the bits together. It's happened here several times, we're not sure what to do about it. Please, sit here."

Gingerly, Faye lowered her rump onto the chair. Keeping her eyes on the table, she prayed fervently that this chair would hold. It did.

Glen settled cautiously into his own chair.

"Are you all right?" the hostess asked Faye again.

"Yes. Embarrassed, but intact."

"Could we treat you both to a glass of wine?"

Faye said fervently, "That would be wonderful." She wouldn't mind getting drunk right into oblivion right now.

For the next few minutes, as they chose their wine and ordered their lunches, Faye managed to appear lucid—at least she hoped she did. But the shock of the fall, the humiliation of it, buzzed around her like a force field, separating her from reality. She could see Glen's mouth move, hear his words, but they didn't really signify. She tried to look fascinated, but he could be telling her he enjoyed wearing women's underwear for all she knew. She shifted on her chair, which held firm, feeling a slight ache near her coccyx. She doubted that she'd hurt it much, not with all the padding around it. No, it was her pride that had been injured.

The only possible good thing about it was the way Alice, Shirley, and Marilyn would laugh when she told them. Thinking of that cheered her up. By the time their food arrived, she was almost back to normal.

"Do you miss working at TransWorld?" she asked.

"Sometimes," Glen answered. "I enjoy accounting. I like solving complex problems. I run a private operation out of my home now, helping small businesses with their financial records."

"Really," Faye said, infusing interest into her voice.

Encouraged, Glen regaled her at length with sagas of his adventures in bookkeeping. Faye listened, appearing rapt. What had her fascinated, in a creepy way, was how Glen, before taking one bite of his chicken Caesar salad, carefully cut up every sliver of chicken and every leaf of lettuce into bites of exactly the same size. He was extremely precise. Not only were the bits of lettuce the same size, they were also the same shape: square. When he finally began to eat, he did so with great deliberation, forking a bit of chicken, then a bit of lettuce. He chewed like a beaver, crunching his food audibly, swallowing with a slurp. His teeth, Faye couldn't help but notice, were a mixture of gray and yellow. She almost shuddered. She had a thing about teeth.

When Glen ran out of chicken and still had lettuce on his plate, he put his fork down. "Would you like dessert?"

Right, she thought, a few more ounces and she'd break *this* chair. "No, thank you."

The waiter brought the bill. Glen reached into his pocket, took out a pen, and scribbled numbers swiftly on the check. "Your share comes to twelve dollars and twenty-three cents. That's adding a tip of fifteen percent."

"All right," Faye said agreeably, although she thought perhaps his math was slightly off.

"Your meal was more expensive than mine by twelve percent," Glen informed her, "so your share of the tip was proportionately higher."

Faye choked back a childish urge to point out that it was because of her that they were given free glasses of wine.

They said good-bye outside the restaurant. Glen had parked on Commonwealth Avenue, Faye over by the Isabella Stewart Gardner Museum.

"Thank you for a pleasant day," Faye said formally to Glen, holding out her hand.

"Thank you," he said, and to her surprise, leaned close to kiss her on the cheek.

It was a gentlemanly gesture, almost a courtly one, and spoiled, unfortunately, by his bad breath.

29

"Good to go, Hercule Poirot!" Julia climbed up into the truck, her snazzy little digital camcorder hanging from her shoulder in its leather case.

"Julia!" Beth shrieked. "You're letting your hair grow! I thought it looked a little longer the other day, but now I can see you're doing it on purpose, aren't you?"

"Yep." Julia flipped down the visor. No mirror. She tugged on the ends of her hair. "I don't know why, but I'm all into a feminine kind of mode. Must be your influence."

Beth blushed, surprised by the compliment. "You do look prettier with some color near your face. Is that shirt from the J. Jill catalog?"

A passionate discussion of clothing catalogs carried them from Julia's house through the winding roads and crowded highways to Arlington, and Heather's brother Harry's house on Martin Lane. Beth parked the Young's Construction truck in front of the house next door to Harry's.

"It's a beautiful day." Julia held the camcorder to her eye, scanning the yellow clapboard house. The blinds were all drawn, curtains all closed. "*Drat.* After the bitch of a winter we've had, I'd think Harry'd want to get out in the sun."

Beth reached behind the seat and brought out a brown bag. "Cookie?"

"Sure." Julia grabbed a couple and munched. "Yum."

Julia listened to Beth babbling on about Sonny, while her own interior voice continued to blip in her brain like a computer glitched on a page. The yoga and other programs at The Haven had pretty much taken care of her headaches and hearing loss, but she still experienced occasional nausea. Probably just nerves. Because this week was Belinda's school's winter break, Julia and Tim had packed up the little girl's suitcase and driven her out to western Massachusetts to spend five days with Annette's parents. The pleasure of having the house to herself, of being able to make love with

Tim anywhere, anytime, was offset by the totally weird fact that Julia missed Belinda. And she really hated herself for wondering whether Belinda missed her. For God's sake, that poor traumatized little child had had enough tragedy in her life without a possessive stepmother wringing her over-protective claws!

"So I don't know," Beth was babbling, "and I wish I didn't care."

Julia forced herself to tune in to Beth.

"I mean, it *is* their fortieth wedding an-niversary, after all, and that's a very big deal. It's going to be a surprise, as if anyone could keep a secret in that family, a big blowout at the local Marriott. *Robin's* order-ing the cake. The three sibs are giving their parents tickets to Acapulco for a week."

"What are you going to give them?"

"That's just what I'm saying. What *can* I give them? Suze, Mark, and Sonny planned everything. Then Suze told Robin, who got first dibs on ordering the cake."

Julia studied Beth's face. "Look. Have you discussed this Robin thing with Sonny?"

Beth turned to face Julia. "Oh, of course I have! He says he doesn't love her anymore, doesn't feel attracted to her, although how that can be possible when she's a walking sex machine, I don't know. He says she's like a sister."

"And you believe him?"

Beth was silent for a moment, giving the question her full consideration. "Yes, I do. I trust him."

"Then you're going to have to learn to accept Robin. She's part of the package, right? She's like a sister, right? So no more pouting because she's glued to the family. You're the new kid on the block. Suck it up."

Beth saluted. "Yes, *mein Kommandant*."

"Plus, I have a totally awesome idea for a present you can give them."

"You do? What?"

"A video of their anniversary party."

Beth shook her head. "I couldn't afford that."

Julia snorted with impatience. "Idiot. I'll do it for free, for you."

Beth shook her head passionately. "No way. You told me last week you make three or four thousand dollars for something like this. I couldn't—"

"You could and I will!" Julia's spirits lifted; she got excited. "It will be fun! I mean, come

on, think about it! I'll photograph you and
Sonny looking dreamy together, and I'll
catch Robin when she's got cake stuffed in
her mouth or her finger up her nose!"

Beth giggled. "That's terrible."

"It's brilliant! This way, they'll have a me-
mento that will last them forever. Longer
than the cake or their hangovers!"

"That's true. But I—eeek!" Beth slid down
in the seat. "Someone's coming out!"

Julia turned her attention back to
Heather's brother's house. The front door
opened. A Goliath with a ponytail lumbered
out, pulling on a black leather jacket covered with dragons, bones, and emblems as
he walked.

"Could that be the male nurse Carolyn
mentioned?"

Julia adjusted the zoom lens. "Doesn't
look much like a nurse to me." Just for the
hell of it, she shot Ponytail clomping over to
a beat-up old Toyota. He got in and drove
away. "I'm surprised he hasn't sprung the
shocks," Julia said.

Beth sat up, then sunk back down. "The
door's opening again."

Julia trained her camera on the front door.

A bleached blonde in tight jeans, high

heels, and a foxy little fur vest over a plunging T-shirt stepped outside, looked up at the
sky, and shivered.

"Who's that?" Julia asked.

"Don't know. Never saw her before.
Maybe another nurse?"

Julia snorted. "Yeah, baby, that's a nurse
if I ever saw one. Hang on. Someone else is
coming."

A man joined the blonde on the sidewalk.
He, too, wore a down vest over a T-shirt,
and jeans and cowboy boots. His block-
shaped head was too big for his body, an
effect exaggerated by his ragged dark mop
of hair and scruffy dark beard.

"Oh, my gosh, that must be Harry! Carolyn said he had a beard," Beth hissed.
"He's not in a wheelchair! He's standing on
his own! Is the camera on?"

"You bet." Julia focused and zoomed.
"He's one ugly hombre."

As they watched, the blonde reached up
to smooth his hair. The man jerked his head
back in irritation. Blondie pouted. Harry
stared at her for a moment, then grabbed her
by the waist and kissed her so hard her head
was forced backward. Blondie pressed her
body up against his. Harry released her with

a slap on her bum. She laughed and took his arm. Together they went to an ancient Thunderbird. Harry got in the driver's seat, Blondie snuggled down into the passenger seat, the car roared and shuddered to life, and off they went.

"Did you get that?" Beth asked.

Julia clicked off her camera. "Every enchanting moment."

"Do you know what this means? We've got proof that Harry's not confined to a wheelchair." Beth sighed. "So they *are* pulling a scam on Carolyn's dad. Oh, this is bad news. I'm glad we did it, but I feel awful."

Julia slid her camera into its leather case and took out her mobile phone. She hit a button, waited until she heard Carolyn's voice, then said, "We've got something to show you."

It was a bit like having a baby in the house, Polly thought. A scrawny, cranky, ill-tempered, irrational baby. Claudia was now installed in her hospital bed, which with its bars resembled a giant crib. Polly improvised meals to tempt Claudia—Ensure mixed with a teaspoon of applesauce, since Claudia refused Ensure on its own. Chicken broth swimming with chicken fat. Lots of tea; Polly had to be sure Claudia did not get dehydrated, and tea was all she would drink. Polly also assisted Claudia when she needed to use the commode, an appliance of stainless steel and plastic stationed next to the bed. A pack of diapers waited in the front hall for the approaching time when Claudia wouldn't have the strength to get out of bed at all.

The pace of Polly's days and the width of her world were now shrunken to Claudia's requirements and requests. Polly still slept upstairs in the guest room, with the monitor next to her on the bedside table. All through the night Polly would waken, hearing Claudia cough or snore, and wait until Claudia's breathing was steady once again before falling back asleep. In the morning, she tip-toed down the stairs to make her own breakfast as silently as possible. She took her second cup of coffee into the dining room. She no longer used her sewing machine—she was afraid the noise would prevent her from hearing Claudia call. Instead, she was knitting a sweater out of pale pinks and peaches, finding enormous pleasure in the spring-hued pastels.

Claudia usually woke around eleven. Polly would hear her stirring, but would wait for Claudia to summon her, at which point Polly would waft around like a young Julie Andrews as a novice nun in *The Sound of Music,* presenting the breakfast tray, clicking on the TV and handing Claudia the remote control, then emptying the commode bucket and washing it out with Pine-Sol and hot water. After that, she sat in the living room with Claudia, providing a sounding board for Claudia's opinions of the various guests on the talk shows or characters in a soap opera.

The highlight of Polly's day was around noon when someone from hospice knocked on the door. The same three women alternated days, and each one wore, from Polly's point of view, a halo of pure radiant gold. They were so much more knowledgeable than Polly about this dying business, and amazingly undeterred by Claudia's snappish resistance to their efforts. They gave Claudia a bed bath every day, as well as providing small amenities Polly hadn't thought of, such as mouthwash and a small stainless steel pan for Claudia to spit in when she had finished.

Later, Polly sat docilely at Claudia's side, pad in hand, as Claudia read the newspaper. A month ago, Claudia read every page, every paragraph, every word, dispensing her comments on matters to Polly. These days, Claudia read only the parts pertaining to society, and Polly took dictation.

"Delphine Harris's daughter had a baby. Go to Shreves and have them send her a little gift. Nothing over one hundred dollars. I never liked the girl."

"Would you like me to do it today?" Polly asked hopefully.

"No. That can wait. Did an invitation come for the Wendelhof's party?"

Polly picked up the teetering pile of mail Claudia kept on the table next to her. After a quick search, she said, "Yes. Here it is."

"You'll need to call with my regrets."

"Very well."

Polly so longed to have one serious talk with Claudia. She had so much to ask. *Whom do you dream of while you're sleeping here? Do you dream of Tucker, do you see him waiting for you, could you give him a message, tell him I love him? Do you know that Tucker and I were happy together? Even though I'm not whom you would have wished for a daughter-in-law, you do realize how much Tucker and I loved one another, don't you? Are you frightened? Do you believe in God? Do you believe in an afterlife? Resurrection? Why have you always behaved like such a snobbish old bat to me? What are your regrets, what are your most beloved memories? How can you not care about David? You knew him for twenty years, and he's such a funny, smart, clever guy. Do you hate me because I never had children with Tucker, is that it? Do you know how sorry I am that I never was able to give you a grandchild?*

But Polly could not ever bring herself to ask any of the questions, although she never gave up her vigilance for the slightest opening in Claudia's shuttered façade.

After reading the *Globe,* Claudia would nap, during which time Polly would tidy the house. Then, to keep herself sane, she'd curl up with a novel and a box of chocolates. Chocolate was good, one of the hospice workers had told her, it resembled the drug Atavan, which was both a mood elevator and a tranquilizer. Too bad it worked only when she ate it, Polly thought ruefully, and not during all the rest of her life as she carried it about on her hips.

In the evening, after their brief meal, Polly and Claudia watched TV together. More and more these days, Claudia slept through the programs, allowing Polly to read.

One afternoon Polly screwed up her courage and accompanied the hospice worker to the front door, where she put her hand on her arm. "I'm not certain how to ask this. I'm not even sure I should ask it. But—do you have any idea how much longer . . . ?"

The hospice worker smiled. "It's fine to ask the question. My best guess is that she'll be here for another month or two. However, Claudia's a real crackerjack. She might hang on even longer."

"Is there anything else I should be doing? I don't know how to help her."

"You're doing everything you can. She's comfortable, in no pain, and not alone. If she starts to feel pain, we might want to consider moving her to a hospital. But until that point, she seems to be more than content to be here."

Polly developed odd obsessions with the

hospice workers. They were so pretty, competent, gentle, serene. Cindy's blond braid was so tidy, her soft, plump hands so satisfactory to watch. Doreen was slightly overweight, but no more than Polly, and her loose scrubs decorated with silly prints of cartoon or circus themes were fun to see. All the women smelled good, of soap, lotion, and mint. Sometimes Polly hated to leave the house to do her errands; she was depriving herself of the hospice workers' company.

The truth was, Polly felt cut off from the rest of the world, like some kind of eccentric, depressive recluse growing fatter and fatter on chocolate. Soon she wouldn't fit out the front door. Occasionally, the phone would ring, and it would be Julia or Carolyn or Beth, calling to report on their latest exploits. Listening, laughing, gasping in surprise, Polly felt as if she were plugged into an IV of pure serotonin. Their friendship was even better than chocolate. But they were all so busy with their own lives and their work that often several days went by without any communication from them, and then Polly felt rejected, forgotten, the kid no one wanted on their team, and once again she would remind herself how much older she was than the other three. Beth, Julia, Carolyn, were all young, starting their lives, pregnant with their futures. Polly had gone through menopause, her child was grown, she was already widowed. She phoned David now and then, but hearing about Jehoshaphat was bittersweet, since she couldn't see him. Pretend you live in a foreign country, she told herself, and every day she felt that this was true, that she was in a foreign country, on a kind of floating island, and every day she drifted farther out to sea, away from those with vivid, juicy, optimistic, sociable lives.

As the days passed, the time of Claudia's newspaper analysis shortened from an hour, to thirty minutes, to fifteen. Then the day came when Claudia asked Polly to read the pertinent parts to her; Claudia no longer had the strength to hold the newspaper in her hands.

30

"Good grief, Gertrude," Julia exclaimed, as she and Beth entered Carolyn's living room. "This place is enormous! I feel like I'm in that movie *Clue.* Did you ever see it? They turned the board game into a movie, set in a house just like this one, huge, lots of old wood and old portraits. Is a butler with an Alfred Hitchcock accent and a sinister smile going to show up suddenly?"

Carolyn shifted uncomfortably, slightly insulted by Julia's remarks. "We have a housekeeper—"

"Mrs. Danvers?" Julia guessed, laughing.

"We call her Mrs. B., and she couldn't be nicer," Carolyn snapped.

"Wow." Beth stood just inside the door, gawking around as if she'd just entered the Sistine Chapel.

Carolyn scooted clumsily on the sofa, like a tugboat grounded on a sandbar. "I can—"

"You can sit still," Julia said. "Beth, you arrange the chairs to face the TV." She bent over the VCR, fiddling with the remote.

Beth crouched down in front of Carolyn. "You look tense."

"I *am* tense! I don't think my father will thank me for this." Carolyn buried her face in her hands. "I wish Hank were here, but he had to be in Washington for a conference on endangered national parks." She felt a tap on her shoulder.

Julia held out a mug. "Drink this."

"What is it?"

"Warm milk. I've heard it helps you fall asleep, so it might help your nerves. I put a little honey in it."

"Oh. Well, thanks." The milk was sweet and soothing.

A knock came at the door.

"Showtime," Julia said. Tonight she'd worn all black, wanting to look professional and formidable. She'd worn her highest boots, too, and she was glad. She hoped she intimidated Heather, the little crook. Julia wouldn't have Carolyn's life and money for anything, not when people like Heather were around to prey on her.

Julia opened the door. "Hello. I'm Julia Hathaway, and this is Beth Grey. We're friends of Carolyn's." Julia took a moment to look the couple over. Carolyn's father was as reported, distinguished and handsome. His piercing dark eyes were exactly like Carolyn's. Next to him, Heather was innocuous-looking, in a flowered dress with a matching sweater.

Aubrey raised an eyebrow at Carolyn and her friends. "What's going on?"

"I'm sorry, Father," Carolyn apologized. "This will only take a minute."

"One hundred and seven seconds, to be exact," Julia said.

"Sit down, please." Carolyn gestured to the chairs.

Heather sat, gazing around like a chick just hatched from its shell.

Aubrey stationed himself behind his wife, his hands on her shoulders. "I don't need to sit. Get on with what you have to say."

"It's what I have to show you, actually," Carolyn told her father. She nodded to Julia, who pressed the buttons on the remote control.

The television flared to life. After a momentary wiggle, the scene steadied before them: the yellow clapboard house, the winter-brown lawn, the "nurse" in his leather jacket coming out the front door.

"That's my brother's house!" Heather gasped.

"Good God, Carolyn!" Aubrey roared. "What are you up to?"

A loud squawking noise interrupted him. Heather was leaning forward in her chair, emitting tormented noises, like someone being choked. "Cherry!"

Carolyn looked at the television. Harry and Blondie were standing on the front stoop, locked in their rapacious kiss.

"Cherry!" Heather croaked.

"Harry?" her husband asked.

"Cherry! He's with Cherry! That bastard! I'll kill him! That bastard!" Heather rose, throwing off her aura of sweetness as if it were a veil, revealing a face suffused with angry blood. Her eyes bugged from her head, her fists were clenched, her mouth twitched. "That conniving son of a bitch, I'll *kill* him!"

Exploding through the room, she knocked over a side chair on her way, yanked open the door, and stormed out into the hall.

Carolyn looked at the television. Harry and Blondie had finally stopped kissing.

"I don't understand," Aubrey said.

"I do," Julia told him. "Let's go." Pointing a commanding hand at Carolyn, she said, "Not you. You stay here and rest. Beth will stay with you."

"Beth will?" Beth cried in frustration.

But Julia and Aubrey had already left the room.

The television screen went blank as the tape ended. Carolyn looked at Beth. "She's not our boss. We don't take orders from her."

Beth wrung her hands in indecision. "Oh, but, Carolyn, we're worried about your health. Your blood pressure. Your baby."

"I'm worried about my father, too. I want to be there for him." Stamping her feet on the floor, she hauled herself up off the sofa. "I've *got* to be there for him."

"I'll get your coat."

They raced through the long halls, finally exiting onto the porte cochere, where they paused to get their bearings. It was a dry, crisp winter night. The moon was bright enough to illuminate the various vehicles parked in the drive.

"My father's Jag is gone," Carolyn said.

Beth pulled her gloves from her shoulder bag. "So is Julia's Volvo. Heather must have taken Aubrey's car, and Julia is driving your father. I'll drive you in my car."

Carolyn eyed Beth's modest blue Camry nervously. "I'd appreciate it if you drove. I'm too bulky now to do it easily, but would you mind driving my Mercedes? I'd feel safer."

"I'd love to. Let's go."

Carolyn was anxious as Beth steered them through the sleeping town of Sperry and onto Route 2 east. But Beth seemed to be a competent driver, quickly angling over into the fast lane, keeping them at a steady sixty-five miles per hour, speeding up when she had to pass an eighteen-wheeler. Carolyn's heart skipped around in zigzags, and her breathing was irregular. She forced herself to lean back against the headrest and close her eyes, telling herself she was enclosed in the shelter of the Mercedes, while her daughter was enclosed in the shelter of her own body. The hum and shush of passing vehicles seemed like sounds of an invisible river rushing them into the future.

Next to her, Beth hummed quietly. Carolyn couldn't quite make out the song. What was it? Oh, yes. Queen's "We Are the Champions." Carolyn smiled.

Finally, they reached the suburb of Arlington.

Carolyn asked, "Do you see their cars?"

"No, but they left a good five or ten minutes before we did. Doesn't matter. I know where the house is."

Beth gave herself a mental pat on the back for sounding so cool and collected. Carolyn still terrified her, just a little, partly because she was from a wealthy, significant Massachusetts family. Partly because Carolyn was eleven years older and carried herself with an air of absolute authority, making decisions like the competent, experienced businesswoman she was. Partly because Carolyn had such startling coloring, that pale skin accentuating her striking dark eyes—it made all her judgments seem more harsh. And that house! It was more than a mansion, it was an estate, nearly a castle! Beth couldn't imagine ever inviting Carolyn to her own modest rented apartment. Now, Polly was easy to like even though she was so much older, because she was so warm, so easy with her laughter, so kind.

But it was Beth who was driving this expensive car with its two valuable passengers, mother and child, and as she drove, Beth felt as if she were passing a kind of rite-of-passage test, as the knights did in ancient times, except, of course, she was female. It had surprised her when Carolyn had allowed her to drive, as if Carolyn trusted Beth to be a careful, competent driver. So Beth kept alert as she drove. She was proving something to Carolyn, and to herself.

Beth said, "This is the street."

Carolyn sat forward as they turned onto Martin Lane. Streetlights burned white, spilling light over the neighborhood.

"I see their cars. The Jag and Julia's Volvo."

Beth brought the Mercedes to a stop behind the other cars. Carolyn unfastened her seat belt and swung her legs out of the car. From the next yard came a dog's alarm, a shrill, annoying little yap. Beth hurried around to take Carolyn's arm, helping her make her way over the sidewalk, still rutted with old snow and ice.

When they reached the front door, they found it unlocked and slightly open. Carolyn glanced at Beth. They went in.

It took a moment for Carolyn to make sense of the scene unfolding before her. In a living room thick with shag carpet, plush furniture, alcohol fumes, and cigarette smoke, her father was reaching out, attempting to catch hold of Heather's arms, which were flailing like propellers as she hit out at a bearded man trapped on the sofa. It had to be Harry—it was hard to tell, because his arms were lifted up over his head, warding off Heather's blows.

"You filthy, scum-sucking, lying piece of shit!" Heather screamed. "I'm going to kill you!" Her whole body jiggled as she swung her arms.

Julia stood against one wall, arms folded like a bouncer's, chewing her lip, watching anxiously. In one corner of the sofa next to Harry, a cluster of pillows repositioned themselves. After a moment, Carolyn realized the shape was a skinny blond woman curled up in a defensive ball, clutching a pair of throw pillows to her face as shields against the blows Heather occasionally aimed her way.

"Aaargh!" With a roar, Harry suddenly grabbed Heather by both wrists and shoved her away with such force she fell backward. In a domino effect, Aubrey, just behind Heather, fell, landing in a cone-shaped wicker basket chair. Harry stood up, his fists clenched, his face furious. "You stupid bitch, you've ruined it!"

Heather scrambled to her feet. "Don't blame it on me, you piece of shit," she spat. "I'm the one doing all the fucking work! All you had to do was hang out here, drinking beer with your buddies. But, no, you couldn't keep your pecker in your pants!"

Veins stood out like ropes on Harry's neck as he shouted, "Why should I? Don't tell me you weren't getting poked regularly by Old Father Time over there."

Carolyn rushed to kneel by her father, still collapsed in the chair. "Are you all right?" His knees high, his hips sunk into the bottom of the basket chair, Aubrey struggled to stand, a vein standing out frighteningly on his forehead.

The blonde, taking advantage of the momentary lull in the brawl, scooted off the sofa and tried to run to the kitchen, but Julia grabbed her by the shoulders. "Harry isn't Heather's brother, is he?"

The blonde's laugh had the raucous rasp of a gull's. "God, no! He's her boyfriend!" Looking at Heather and Harry shouting at each other, she added, "Or he was."

Aubrey went very still, his full attention riveted on Heather. His face was white. Carolyn grabbed his wrist. Was he going to have a heart attack? Caught in the chair like a lump of ice cream in a cone, he was like a struggling insect. She couldn't bear the indignity of it for him. She took his wrist. "Let me help you stand."

Aubrey nodded at her and heaved himself forward. Carolyn pulled with all her strength, feeling her own body tighten fiercely in her effort. As her father stumbled to his feet, Julia grabbed Aubrey's other arm, steadying him. Heather struck out at Harry, who bobbed and weaved like a boxer, laughing and taking up most of the space in the small room, his swinging elbows nearly hitting Aubrey, Carolyn, and Julia.

"Let's go, Father," Carolyn implored.

Aubrey looked at his wife. Heather was collapsed on the sofa, wailing like a fire engine siren.

Aubrey straightened his shoulders. "My lawyers will be in touch."

The blonde laughed wickedly, letting her head fall back, aiming her laughter at the ceiling.

"Where's a goddamned beer?" Harry puffed, his eyes scanning the room.

"Father," Carolyn said again, "let's go."

Beth pulled the door open. Julia and Carolyn, on either side of Aubrey, led him away from his sobbing, cursing wife, or tried to. A contraction gripped Carolyn so fiercely she stopped dead in her tracks, bending over from its force.

"Carolyn?" Julia shot a worried look her way.

"I'm fine," she panted. "Give me a minute." Was she supporting her father or leaning on him?

"The old dude's not gonna hurl, is he?" Harry looked fascinated. " 'Cause I'm not cleaning it up."

Beth rushed to Carolyn, wrapping an arm around her shoulders. "Lean on me."

The blonde had left the room. She returned, a glass of water in each hand. She handed one to Aubrey and held one out to Carolyn. "Take a sip."

Aubrey drank. His spine straightened. His shoulders leveled, his head rose high. "Thank you, young woman," he said to the blonde. "Good-bye, Heather." He left the house.

The glass the blonde held toward Carolyn had naked women on it, not to mention greasy fingerprints. Accepting the glass, she took a sip of cool water. Her contractions eased. Nodding to Beth, she said, "Okay. Let's go."

Together Beth and Carolyn left the house. They caught up with Julia and Aubrey, who were consulting next to the Jag and the Volvo.

"I'm perfectly fine to drive," Aubrey was saying. "Besides, I don't want to leave my Jaguar here. Who knows what they might do to it."

"Then I'll drive your car home, and Beth can bring me back to pick up my Volvo." Julia's voice was mild, but firm. "You've just had a terrible shock. No way will I let you drive."

"I'll drive Carolyn," Beth said. "We'll meet you there."

Julia looked searchingly at Carolyn. "Are you okay?'

"I'm fine. Just a momentary cramp. Yes, you two go on, and we'll meet you at home." She looked at Aubrey. "I'm so sorry, Father."

Aubrey nodded and made a gesture with his hand, as if waving a brief farewell. Julia went around to the driver's side of the Jag. Beth and Carolyn got into Carolyn's Mercedes.

"Are you really okay?" Beth asked, fastening her seat belt.

"Yes," Carolyn said, but at that moment another contraction gripped her. "Oh, no," she whispered. "Don't do this. Please. It's too soon." She looked helplessly at Beth. "I think I'm starting labor. I think you'd better take me to the hospital."

31

It was as if the essential Claudia were dis-
appearing right before Polly's eyes. As if,
had Polly the aid of just one more grade
of vision, past ultraviolet, past X-ray, she
would be able to watch Claudia's very
atoms detach and drift away from her, up
into the warm air.

Now Claudia slept almost all the time.
She lay still in her hospital bed, supported
by pillows so that she wouldn't choke on
her saliva, eyes closed or, sometimes, eyes
open, but so glazed and gazing into a far
distance that she was unaware of Polly in
the room with her.

Perhaps three times a day, Claudia would
awaken. During these lucid moments, Polly
would hold a cup of tepid tea with a straw
to the older woman's mouth. Claudia would

drink, then she would say, primly, "Thank you."

"Are you comfortable?" Polly would ask.

"I am."

"Could I get you anything?"

"Turn off the television. It distracts me."

"Of course." But how curious, Polly thought. The television distracts her? From what? Was dying like taking a kind of test, needing one's full concentration? Was Claudia drifting in her memories, were they as vivid as headlights of passing cars against the windows?

Now when the hospice worker arrived, Polly was free to leave for the entire hour, because Claudia wouldn't know she was gone. Somehow, though, Polly didn't feel relieved or sprung. She'd developed an odd sense of responsibility for Claudia, as if she'd been entrusted with taking someone else's child to their first day at kindergarten or to a station to wait for a train—as if she had to *be* there to see Claudia safely off on her journey. So Polly rushed to the nearest grocery store to gather the necessities and rushed back home again, scarcely noticing the weather, the other people, the traffic, the expanse of the ordinary, busy world.

In the same way, during the long hours she sat with Claudia, Polly could not summon the kind of intelligence it took to do alterations for customers, or even to sew on a button. All she could do was knit. Baby blankets, shawls, mufflers. She kept the lights low throughout the house, except for one lamp behind her chair, which bathed her and her work in its warm illumination. Knitting was so ancient an art, she imagined the scores of years of women keeping bedside vigils during illnesses and deaths, hunched as she was, knitting a blanket, tugging the yarn like time through her fingers. As she sat in the large old house while Claudia slept, Polly did not feel alone.

But at times Polly grew restless from so much silence. She was grateful for the morning arrival of *The Boston Globe,* curled and wrapped in plastic, on the doorstep. It helped lend an order to the day. Whenever during the morning Claudia awoke for her sip of tea, Polly would read aloud the society bits she thought Claudia would like. The Boston Ballet's new performance reviewed. A marvelous exhibit of Gauguin at the MFA. She read all the wedding and engagement announcements, as well as the obituaries, not knowing who might be important to Claudia. Besides, it made it seem almost as if there were conversation in the room.

Every so often, the telephone would ring, the shock of the unexpected noise nearly ejecting Polly out of her chair. Occasionally it was an acquaintance of Claudia's, asking about her health. Polly would do as Claudia had instructed her: she would tell the caller that Claudia could not come to the phone right now, but would return the call when she could.

Sometimes, Julia or Beth or Carolyn phoned—when that happened, Polly's entire body lit up. For a few moments, she was part of the world of the living. And their news was so dramatic.

"Claudia!" Polly said after one conversation. "You'll never guess what happened! Carolyn found out that Heather's 'brother' is really her boyfriend. She's been scamming money off Aubrey. Aubrey's having the marriage annulled. Plus, they insisted on doing a paternity test, and Heather's pregnant, but the baby is Harry's, the horrible boyfriend's, not Aubrey's. Isn't this wild?"

Claudia showed no signs of hearing.

Sometimes, for comfort, Polly read aloud

from books of poetry: Tennyson. T. S. Eliot. Emily Dickinson. Auden.

Sometimes, she simply babbled.

"It's wonderful, how Julia and Beth and Carolyn are becoming friends, don't you think? It cheers me up to think of their collaboration to save Carolyn's father from the dreadful Heather." Knit one, purl two. "You know, recently, the English language has adopted the German term *schadenfreude,* which means the happiness you feel when someone you dislike is miserable. Well, I think we should have a term like *freuden-freude,* too, don't you? The happiness we feel when someone we love is happy is such a gift, isn't it?"

Claudia slept on.

"I wonder if my bird feeders need refilling at home. I ought to check. They depend on food being there. Recently I've noticed a squirrel trying to get into the feeder." Knit one, purl two. Silence. "And in the spring, there's a rabbit who eats my fresh new plants." Knit one, purl two. "Just think, if the squirrel mated with the rabbit, they'd have a squabbit." Polly laughed aloud at the word, then laughed more at herself. She knew she sounded just slightly demented. And maybe she was.

Late evening was the hardest time for Polly. The night seemed darker at ten than it had at nine, even though Polly knew this wasn't logical. Polly still slept in the upstairs bedroom, with the intercom on, but her sleep was broken, uncomfortable, and full of turbulent dreams. She came to dread midnight, when she climbed the stairs to bed. Loneliness loomed at her from the shadows of the room like a faceless creature with a dark cape.

———

"Jehoshaphat is five months old today," Polly announced one morning. "I wonder if he's sitting up by himself yet. Probably not. Amy probably has the poor child bound to her body with ropes woven from her own hair. I never thought David would end up working on a farm, eating twigs and berries, and especially I never thought he'd be so, well—*submissive*—to a woman. Of course, I'm sure you never dreamed your son, Tucker, who attended all the best private schools, including *pre*school, would end up married to a plump Irishwoman who takes in sewing. Yet Tucker and I were so happy together. I do hope you know that, Claudia. I want to believe David's as happy with Amy as I was with Tucker. I *have* to believe that." The needles spinning out a new baby blue blanket went still in her lap. "I wish I could see my grandson." She glanced over at Claudia, who slept on, oblivious. With a little sigh, Polly picked up her needles and went back to her knitting.

Saturday night, Sonny said, "Wow, Beth, you look great!"

Beth twirled. She'd bought this turquoise silk dress with the short froufrou chiffon skirt especially for the Youngs' anniversary party at the Marriott. "So do you!"

"No," Sonny grumbled, "I look like a Las Vegas pimp." He and his brother, Mark, and his sister, Suze, were going to sing a medley of romantic tunes for their parents, and Suze had insisted the men wear tuxes in harmonizing variations of blue. "But if I refuse to wear this thing, that will give them even more proof that I'm a snob."

"I think you look absolutely dashing," Beth teased, "in a camp, Johnny Depp in *Pirates of the Caribbean* kind of way."

Sonny rolled his eyes. "Come on. Suze insisted we get there early."

The party wasn't to start until eight, but at seven thirty, when Beth and Sonny walked into the ballroom at the Natick Marriott, they found Suze, Mark, and his girlfriend, Barbie, already there. Suze was setting little boxes of chocolate at each place at the table. When she saw Sonny and Beth, she raced up to them.

"How does it look?" The little beads of perspiration on her forehead sparkled more than the sequins on her sapphire blue dress.

"As great as it did two hours ago when I helped you hang the streamers," Sonny said.

Beth wanted to kick him in the shin. She wished she'd had a sister as softhearted and generous as Suze. "I think it's just dreamy."

"Do you really?" Suze clasped her hands and looked around the room. "What do you think of the color scheme?"

"It's heavenly," Beth told her honestly.

Shades of pale blue twined with silver on the balloons, tablecloths, napkins, and streamers. Great masses of dried blue hydrangeas served as centerpieces for the main table and filled silver pots around the room. "Can I help you do anything?"

"The band's coming and I want to be sure they're set up all right. Sonny, you could help with that." Suze turned to Beth. "Would you finish putting the party favors around?" She handed her a white paper shopping bag filled with small boxes.

"Sure." Probably, Beth thought, it would be inappropriate if she fell to her knees and kissed Suze's feet in gratitude. She tried to act as if she found it perfectly normal that Suze had for once included her in the family's duties. She went around the room, putting the little blue and silver boxes at each seat, then drifted to the main table to read the place cards. She found one with her name on it, next to Sonny's. It was at the very end of the table, but someone had to sit at the end of the table, and at least she was included. One giant step forward, she thought, laying her evening bag on her chair.

Near the head table stood an easel holding an enormous cardboard panel covered with photos of Merle and Bobbie Young in all the phases of their life together. As Beth studied it, she felt her spirits lift as her eyes filled with sentimental tears. Such a passage of years, so many smiles. A black-and-white snap showed Bobbie as a seventeen-year-old in a Dairy Queen uniform, grinning at Merle, who had a full head of thick brown hair pomaded into a kind of Elvis Presley pompadour. Next came a photo of Merle and Bobbie leaving the church on their wedding day, laughing and bending their heads beneath a rain of rice, and then the shots were full of babies. The years paraded past as the children grew. To Beth's utter amazement, no photo of the beautiful Robin was on the panel, probably because there was so little room. Of course, neither was there a photo of Beth, but she hadn't expected there would be. Except— she bent closer—in the final snapshot, taken this past Christmas in the Youngs' living room, she spotted one brown boot, which she was certain belonged to her.

She turned away from the photographs. The room had filled with people. Julia was over by the bandstand, holding her camcorder on her shoulder, nodding diligently as Suze gave her instructions. Although the band had begun to play soft rock, no one was dancing; they were all gathering at the open bar or loading plates from the buffet. Laughter floated through the air like balloons.

Beth searched for Sonny in the crowd and found him surrounded by several people his parents' age. Mark was with them—and so was Robin. Her blond hair swept up in a French twist, her dress was a long sheath of ice blue. She looked like a princess.

Someone touched Beth's shoulder. Julia put her arm around her. "You look gorgeous, kid."

"Not as beautiful as Robin," Beth whispered. "Did you see her?"

"Yes, I did. No doubt about it, she's a beauty. But Sonny's engaged to *you,* remember? Listen, I won't hang out with you much tonight, we don't want them to think we're too close. I just wanted to say hello."

"Okay," Beth agreed. "Hey, look, Robin has a date!"

"Yeah, I noticed. Tell you what. Every picture I get of her, I'll be sure she's with him. Subliminal advertising, okay?" Julia checked her watch. "It's almost eight. I've got to be by the door to catch the guests of honor when they come in. Have fun!" She shouldered her camcorder and went off.

"Hey!" Sonny pushed through the crowd to grab Beth's hand. "It's almost time. Let's get up front!"

The crowd was swarming toward the main door, faces flushed with anticipation. Men dressed in tuxes and suits and women resplendent in dangling earrings and glittering dresses made way for them, some of the men patting Sonny on his shoulder as he passed, the women covertly scrutinizing every square inch of Beth's clothes and body. All these people had known Sonny's family *forever.* Carpenters, schoolteachers, plumbers, Little League coaches, Little League kids grown up with their own little kids riding their shoulders as if at a parade, they all loved Merle and Bobbie Young.

They reached the front. Mark yanked Sonny toward him. Sonny kept his hand on Beth's, pulling her into the row of family members just as Merle and Bobbie entered the ballroom.

"Surprise!" the crowd roared.

Merle stood stock-still with his jaw hanging open, and Bobbie burst into tears.

After that, the evening passed in a blur. They feasted and sipped champagne while people rose to toast the Youngs and relate their favorite anecdotes. Beth worked on memorizing their faces, names, and other relevant facts. Harold with the bulging belly and bawdy humor had been Merle's best friend since kindergarten. Eloise with the rabbit teeth and aggressively blond hair had been Bobbie's maid of honor at the wedding. Lovely red-haired Ethel, who looked at least ten months pregnant, told the crowd about being Sonny's first girlfriend, in sixth grade, and how she'd thought the best part of it had been Bobbie's coconut-chocolate-chip cookies.

After the toasts, the dancing began. As Sonny squired Beth around the dance floor, she noticed Merle dancing with his wife, his daughter, Mark's girlfriend Barbie, and Robin. *I will not take it personally if he doesn't dance with me,* Beth told herself, girding herself for disappointment, but when Merle approached Sonny to cut in, she nearly fainted with gratitude.

By the end of the evening, Beth was euphoric. The only Young who'd not made her feel totally welcome was Bobbie. Bobbie had allowed Beth to kiss her cheek, but she pulled away quickly. When Julia gathered the immediate family together for a group photo, Bobbie had insisted on having "her girls" near her and Merle: Suze on Merle's left, Robin on Bobbie's right. Mark stood where his parents directed him, to Suze's left, with Barbie on his own left. That meant Sonny had to stand on Robin's right. He pulled Beth into the frame, putting his hand firmly on the front of her gown at waist level, making their union clear. Beth put her left hand over Sonny's, hoping the engagement ring would show up and that Bobbie wouldn't have her excised from the final photos.

32

Marilyn, Alice, Faye, and Shirley gathered in Faye's condo Friday evening, after the board meeting. While Faye prepared drinks—red wine for Alice and Marilyn, seltzer for Shirley and dieting Faye—Shirley scribbled notes in her lavender notebook.

"Before we get to the important stuff," Shirley said, "let's just finish up about the open house. I've had the secretary send out announcements and paid ads to all the newspapers. Jennifer and Alan are set to cater. Faye, how's the art exhibit coming?"

"Everything's good to go." Faye handed Shirley a glass tinkling with ice and garnished with a sliver of lime. "I just need to experiment with the walls in the lounge to find a way to hang the art without leaving marks in the paneling."

"Let me know when you do," Shirley told

her. "Justin's planning to have some of his poetry students print their poems out in large type on handsome paper so they can be hung for people to read." She snapped her notebook shut and stuck it in her bag. "This is going to be so much fun! Our first open house wasn't all that well attended, but we've had a year plus to build up a nice body of clients. They'll come, their friends will come, and so will their families."

Alice took the other end of the sofa. "So, Faye, have you heard from Glen?"

Faye set a platter of fresh vegetables and a hummus dip on the coffee table, then sank into her easy chair. "I have not."

Alice grimaced. "Ouch. It's been how long since the MFA?"

"Three weeks." Faye shrugged. "It doesn't break my heart, Alice. I was *so* not attracted to the man. But I was prepared to go out with him again, simply to keep you all happy."

"There's a silly reason to date a man," Alice scoffed.

"Perhaps not," Faye argued. "It's like Shirley said, we don't want to curl up like dust bunnies in the corner of our lives."

"But," Alice insisted, "that doesn't mean you have to date a guy you don't like!"

"I agree!" Faye said triumphantly. "Therefore, I have fulfilled my Hot Flash Club duties. I've dated three new men, which proves I'm not depressed, cowardly, or pessimistic. Now I intend to prove to you all that it's perfectly possible to live a happy, fulfilled, fascinating life without having a man in it."

"The problem with planning the rest of our lives," Alice said slowly, "is that we don't have any role models. Our age group is the first to be living so long, in such good health"—she knocked the wood of the coffee table, and so did the others—"with so many opportunities."

Marilyn agreed. "True. We've accomplished a lot. We've had children, and husbands, and lovers. We've had friends, houses, and careers. Now how do we decide how to live the rest of our lives?"

"Are you talking about retirement?" Shirley asked.

Marilyn shook her head thoughtfully. "No . . . it's more that, even if we eat well, exercise, and take good care of ourselves, we're not going to live forever. What I'm trying to figure out is—how do I decide what to do with the rest of my life when I don't know the variables?"

"I know exactly what you mean," Alice said. "It's what I've been thinking. Given the fact that we all have a finite amount of money—some of us have more than others, sure, but only Marilyn has real wealth—"

Marilyn objected. "Not really. Remember, my ex-husband made the money and he fought like a fiend to keep every penny he could."

"Okay, then," Alice continued, "given that we've got a finite amount of money—"

"How do we plan the rest of our lives when we don't know how much longer we have to live?" Faye finished for her.

"Exactly!" Marilyn said. "Time. The variable we can't control."

"I mean"—Alice held out her hands as if she were weighing objects—"should we live frugally, in case we live for thirty more years, or go wild now because we could die in five?"

The four women sat in silence, considering the question.

"I think," Faye said slowly, "if there's anything enormously important to us, something we've wanted to do all our lives, I think we should do it now and hang the costs."

"But you're financially independent," Shirley pointed out. She looked around the table. "So are all of you, more or less."

"Is there anything you've longed to do all your life that lack of money's preventing you from doing?" Marilyn asked Shirley.

"Well, duh, *yes!* I wish I'd had a nicer house, a nicer car, and there've been about a million dresses I haven't bought because I couldn't afford them, not to mention eating in restaurants."

"Okay," Alice said, "but what about *now*? You can't change the past. Is there something you want to do now that lack of money's preventing you from doing?"

Shirley took a sip of seltzer as she considered. "Well, I guess not. I mean what I've longed to do all my life was have my wellness spa, and I have it!"

Faye admitted, "I'd like to travel a bit. I've always wanted to spend time in London, Paris, Florence."

"Well, gad, Faye," Shirley said, "you've got the money. What's stopping you?"

"I'm not sure. I suppose I was afraid to go off and leave Laura, even after she was married. I've wanted to be near, in case she needed help."

"I understand," Marilyn agreed. "It's a kind of superstition held over from when our babies were little and we had to leave them with sitters. As if having fun independent of them might mean they'll get hurt."

"But we agreed we're not going to let fear rule our lives!" Shirley reminded her.

"Shirley's right," Alice said. "Look. Here we all are, in our fifties and early sixties, and I'll bet we've all lived in fear of something that hasn't happened."

"True," Faye concurred. "I was always afraid something terrible would happen to my daughter. That she'd have sudden infant death or get hit by a car or try drugs and become addicted."

"And none of that happened, right?" Alice asked.

"Right." Faye laughed. "Of course, now I worry about the same things, only for my granddaughter."

"My fear," Alice confessed, "was professional. I was always afraid I'd be at our annual board meeting, and Melvin Watertown, my immediate supervisor, would say, 'Alice, on page seventy-nine of the personnel

handbook, you left out the word *not,* cost-
ing this firm millions of dollars in compensa-
tion.' "

"I totally get that." Shirley worried about
similar things during her meetings with the
spa board. "Did that ever happen?"

"No, thank God. Because I read and
reread the fine print like someone with
OCD."

"Well, you see," Shirley said, brightening.
She always liked finding silver linings.
"There's an example of our fear actually
helping us. Like it helped me. My greatest
fear has always been that I'd start drinking
again and start the downward slide to perdi-
tion. But I haven't had a drink in years, and
at this point I'm feeling pretty optimistic that
I won't ever."

"You should be proud of yourself, Shirley," Faye said. She turned to Marilyn.
"What's been your greatest fear?"

Marilyn shifted uncomfortably in her chair.
"Um, I'm not sure . . ."

Alice pounced. "You're not evading us
that easily! Come on, out with it!"

Marilyn blushed. "To tell the truth, I've always been afraid I'd die before I found out

whether or not the Loch Ness monster exists."

Alice snorted with laughter. "You are so weird."

"Marilyn," Faye said, "that seems a really odd fear from someone with a scientific mind like yours. I mean, even I know the Loch Ness monster is a hoax."

For Marilyn, those were fighting words. "Not necessarily. Nessie very well might be a plesiosaur, an ancient reptile who lived at the same time the dinosaurs lived and probably died when they did, about sixty-five million years ago. Recent sonar tests have located large moving targets, but the loch is so long, and so deep, it's easy for a large creature to evade detection."

"Have you ever gone to Loch Ness?" Alice inquired.

"Oh, no." Marilyn shook her head. "I've been so busy with my lab, my classes, my research articles, my home."

"You should go," Shirley decided. "Definitely. You don't have to worry about money, Marilyn. You could even rent a boat and cruise the lake, loch, whatever. Maybe Nessie would appear for you."

"Don't be silly." A wistful expression crossed Marilyn's face.

Shirley pressed her point. "I'm not being silly. Miracles happen!"

"Well, it's true, I never thought of going there," Marilyn murmured.

"I could go with you," Faye offered. "We could spend some time in Edinburgh and London."

Marilyn's face lit up. "Wouldn't that be fun?"

"Yes," Faye's face clouded. "But Laura—"

"—is in San Francisco!" Alice bluntly reminded her.

Shirley added, "She wouldn't want you to sit at home just waiting for her to phone you! She'd want you to be happy."

"Not to mention, you're still a role model for her," Marilyn said.

"You know something?" Shirley pointed her finger at Faye. "You need an attitude adjustment."

"Where do I go to get it?" Faye joked.

"Well," Shirley proposed, thinking aloud, "how about this? We have so many celebrations in this culture to mark passages of life. Weddings. Funerals. Baby showers. Birthdays. Graduations. Bat and bar mitzvahs.

Confirmations. Retirement parties, like the one where the four of us met. Wouldn't it be great if there were a kind of 'You're Officially off the Hook' celebration?"

Alice nodded enthusiastically. "Yeah, I totally agree! The next part of our lives can be so rich. Now we have time to take courses we didn't take before, learn about the world, travel, or play bridge."

"On the subject of enjoying life . . ." Shirley straightened in her chair, lifting her chin defiantly.

"Oh, boy, here we go." Alice arched an eyebrow. "Justin again. I'd bet my teeth."

"You're right, of course, Alice." Shirley glared. "It does involve Justin, but it also involves the three of you."

"You're not getting married!" Alice croaked.

"No. But Justin's moving out of his condo and moving in with me." Seeing their expressions, she glared. "Look. You've been grumbling about the fact that Justin lives in his condo and doesn't pay rent or utilities—"

"We have not been grumbling!" Alice objected.

"This way, we'll have the condo free,"

Shirley argued. "Star, the yoga instructor, has been looking for a place to live nearer the spa, and this will be perfect for her. And she'll pay rent."

"Oh, Shirley," Faye said, trying to placate her, "our concerns aren't about money. We're just afraid you're—" She bit her lip, trying to think of the right words.

Alice didn't mince words. "We're afraid you're thinking with your crotch."

Shirley shook her head impatiently. "Justin wants to write a novel. He's wanted to write one all his life, but he's always had to work, he's never had the time and stability to write. I want to give that to him. I want him to live with me for a year, and he'll teach his courses in journal writing and poetry, and you know those have huge enrollments. And he'll write, and when the year's up, we'll go from there."

"What if he's using you, Shirley?" Alice kept her voice affectionate, worried.

"What if he is? Look. I know he's twelve years younger than I am. I know he could easily fall for another woman. I know he's handsome, charming, and seductive. But we've been talking about what we really want for the rest of our lives, and about fear not getting in the way, and this is what I want. And if he's just using me, fine. I've never had so much fun as I am now. I'm happy. And if he leaves me in a year, well, I'm willing to pay that price."

The three other women exchanged glances.

"We don't want you to get hurt," Faye said gently.

Shirley gave a little shimmy. "Hey, ladies, remember, I'm sixty-one. My heart is so battle-scarred there's not much room for another cut. Besides, he might actually love me. Hell, he could even get his novel published and dedicate it to me! Whatever, it's a risk I'm willing to take." When the others didn't respond, she said, "I thought our first rule was not to let fear control our lives."

"You're right," Marilyn agreed. "So I say do it."

"I agree," Faye said.

They all looked at Alice. "Oh, hell. All right. Go for it, Shirley."

Shirley smiled radiantly. "Thank you. Thank you, all!"

Faye rose. "Now. Time for dinner."

They all rose and helped set the table. Faye took a casserole from the oven while

Shirley tossed the salad. When the other three were seated, Faye reached into a cupboard, brought out a gorgeous chocolate layer cake, and set it in the middle of the table for them all to admire.

"What's this about?" Alice asked. "Not that I object."

"I just felt like it," Faye said. "I look forward to these evenings so much, and I've lost ten pounds, so I feel like I deserve a treat."

"You're absolutely right, honey," Shirley said.

"True," Marilyn agreed. "After all, the third rule of the Hot Flash Club is 'Celebrate every chance you get.' "

33

On Friday evening, Carolyn lounged on the living room sofa with her belly rising beneath her peach silk caftan like a two-ton pumpkin. A week ago, when Beth had rushed her to the hospital, she'd discovered she was only having Braxton-Hicks contractions, painful but not true labor. The experience had frightened her. She didn't want to give birth to her daughter prematurely. She'd hated the way the nurses had humored and babied her, as if she were some cute dumb thing too thick to spot the difference between false and real labor. She felt like such a novice at this childbirth thing, so inept, it made her cranky.

"They're here," Hank announced. He opened the door.

Julia, Beth, and Polly came in, nearly

skidding to a Keystone Kops stop when they saw Hank.

"I'm Hank, Carolyn's husband." Hank shook hands with them all. "I've had orders to vacate the premises for a couple of hours, so I'm off to the gym. Have fun, ladies."

The moment he left, Carolyn's friends went wild.

"Oh, my god, he's so cute!" Beth squealed.

"True," Carolyn agreed smugly.

"Sure he wouldn't want to watch the videotape with us?" Julia asked.

"Quite sure," Carolyn assured her.

"Hello, Caro." Polly bent to kiss the top of Carolyn's head. "Sorry to drive away your gorgeous husband. Maybe these home-made sugar cookies will make up for it. I didn't make chocolate because the caffeine might be bad for your heart. I'll heat water for coffee. Herbal tea for you, right?"

Julia bent over the VCR, slipping in a video. "Carolyn, how's your father?"

Carolyn sighed. She was sighing like the rain forest in a typhoon these days, with the baby using her lungs as punching bags. "Depressed, to put it mildly. The lawyers are working on the annulment, Heather's moved back into her house with her boyfriend, and Aubrey's gone down to a resort in the Bahamas for a couple of weeks. He's hoping sunshine will cheer him up."

"Is he going to take any legal action against Heather and Heinous Harry?"

"No. He'd rather take a loss on the money than have this turned into a public spectacle. I think what hurts him the most is that he feels like such a sucker, getting taken like that."

"Love can make the smartest person foolish," Polly observed, as she and Beth carried in the trays. "Have a cookie." She held the plate out to Carolyn.

Sugar, butter, and a hint of vanilla melted in Carolyn's mouth. "Yum."

"I can't wait any longer!" Beth cried. "I want to see the tape!"

Polly looked surprised. "You mean Julia hasn't told you what's on it?"

"No. She's been torturing me."

Julia rubbed her hands together gleefully. "Just you wait, my pretty." She gave a wicked-witch cackle. "Everyone ready?" She hit the remote control.

The screen flickered, then steadied. A

camera scanned a hotel ballroom where a party was in full progress. A band played a soulful rendition of "The Twelfth of Never." The dance floor was crowded with couples of all ages dancing in every kind of mode except the minuet. The camera focused for a moment on a handsome guy in a baby blue tux with a pretty brunette in his arms.

"That's Mark," Beth told the room. "Sonny's brother. And his girlfriend, Barbie. She's nice."

The camera panned over the crowded floor, coming to rest on a tall, lean, dark-haired woman who kept pushing her hair with her hands as she danced.

"That's Suze," Beth said. "Sonny's sister. She's nice, too. She's a real jock. *So* not frilly. She had her hair done for the party and they sprayed it stiff. It drove her crazy all night! That's her father, Merle, she's dancing with."

"Oh, look, there you are!" Polly cried. "Beth, your dress is delicious!"

"Thanks." Beth's voice softened. "Isn't Sonny handsome?"

"Only in a Mel Gibson/George Clooney kind of way," Julia joked. Pressing a button, she fast-forwarded through the next few seconds, stopping the tape at a shot of a black-haired older woman in a navy blue dress standing close to a beautiful blonde wearing a sheath of pale blue.

"Oh, my gosh," Beth squealed. "You guys, there's Sonny's mom talking with Robin! Isn't she beautiful?"

"Only in a Gwyneth Paltrow with big boobs kind of way," Carolyn said.

"You're as lovely as she is," Polly loyally assured Beth.

"Sssh," Julia said. "Listen."

They all listened as the camera left Bobbie and Robin. It panned around the room, and they could tell Julia was walking now, the camera on her shoulder just slightly jiggling. When it steadied, it was focused on a back view of Sonny's mother and Robin.

". . . admit it's just hopeless," Robin was saying. "I mean, look at Sonny's face. He's in love with her."

"Turn up the volume," Carolyn said.

"It's at the max already," Julia told her. "This is the best I could do for sound."

". . . not hopeless." Bobbie put her arm around Robin. "Come on, honey, you know Sonny's just having a little fling before settling down."

Beth screamed. *"A little fling!"*

"Quiet," Julia ordered.

". . . not so sure."

"Well, I am." Bobbie's face set firmly. She looked like a general surveying her troops. "See this crowd? They're our friends. They're our world. Sonny doesn't want to lose all this. He's just sowing his wild oats before he settles down."

"Wild oats," Beth whimpered.

On-screen, Robin shook her head. "Bobbie, that girl is wearing Sonny's engagement ring."

"So what? They haven't set a wedding date yet. If I have my way, they never will. You're part of our family. You are meant to marry Sonny."

Robin shook her head. "I'm not so sure."

"I am. This is my *family* we're talking about. I don't like that girl and I don't want her in it. I wish I'd pushed her harder when we were ice skating. I wished she'd cracked her head and died instead of just falling—"

A sixtyish man with a bulbous red nose stumbled up, interrupting them. "Where's the bride?" he bellowed, holding out his arms. "Haven't had a dance yet!"

"Yeah, Stan, but you've had enough to

drink, that's for sure." Bobbie rolled her eyes at Robin, but allowed Stan to lead her to the dance floor.

The screen went staticky, then blank. Julia clicked the VCR off. "How 'bout them apples?"

Beth looked stunned. "This is terrible."

"The woman's a bitch." Julia was mad. "But now you've got evidence that she's *aggressively* trying to undermine you. It's not just a matter of you being some oversensitive little neurotic whining, 'Your mother isn't nice to me.' "

"That's right," Carolyn agreed. "Wait till Sonny sees this tape! My God, she actually *pushed* you when you were ice skating!"

"She's a monster," Julia agreed. "I mean, I know Agnes hates me, but that's kind of logical. I'm in the spot where her own daughter was, where her own daughter should be, and it's just damned unfair. So I can deal with it. But Bobbie has no reason to be so antagonistic toward you, Beth. It's not like you've tied Sonny up with ropes and drugged him. Fact: he doesn't love Robin. Fact: he does love you. Bobbie should be grateful her son's so happy. This kind of behavior, well, it's just *nuts!*"

"Julia's right." Carolyn shoved another toss pillow behind her back. "You're going to have to show Sonny this tape, and you're going to have to find a way to get out of his mother's range of attack."

"But how?" Beth quavered.

Julia offered, "Well, you and Sonny could move to another state."

Beth wailed, "Move? Oh, I don't know. Sonny's so close to his entire family—"

Carolyn interrupted, *"Enmeshed* is the psychological term. That kind of closeness is pathological. Sonny's mother, what's her name . . . ?"

"B-B-Bobbie," Beth stuttered.

"Bobbie's not allowing her children to grow up. It's creepy, those three grown children having dinner every single Sunday of their lives at their mommy's house. They should get a life. *She* should get a life. Doesn't Merle ever want to take Bobbie off to a romantic restaurant, just the two of them?"

Julia was nodding. "You're right, Carolyn. Absolutely right. You know, Beth, you might want to take notes. These are good points Carolyn's raising."

Beth looked perplexed. "But *you* live in the same house as your father!"

Carolyn shook her head impatiently. "That's different. We seldom share meals, we lead very separate lives. Hey, my father got married without even mentioning it to me first. And he certainly didn't have a thing to say about who I married. Although, thank heavens, he likes Hank, always has." She was in executive mode now. "Look. Here's what you have to do. First, you have to draw up a plan of attack."

"Right," Julia agreed. "Think it all through. Even write down what you have to say so you won't forget it in the heat of the moment."

"Good idea," Carolyn continued. "Second, arrange a time and place when you and Sonny won't be interrupted. Take the phone off the hook. Tell him you two need to have a serious discussion. Third, show him the video. Fourth, be ready for a brawl. Allow him time to vent. But finally, be ready with some positive suggestions, like moving."

Beth looked shell-shocked.

In the momentary silence, Polly reached out, poured more tea in Beth's cup, and handed it to her. "Drink some of this, Beth. And eat some of the cookies."

"You've been awfully quiet, Polly," Carolyn noted.

Polly's smile was sad. "Well, I'm just so terribly sorry to see this video. I find it heartbreaking, how miserable human beings make life for the ones they love, because of their lack of tolerance or simple human kindness."

"Yeah, it's sad, but it's an unavoidable fact," Julia argued. "I mean, look, your own daughter-in-law won't let you see your grandson," Julia reminded Polly.

"Oh, believe me, I think about that every day of my life," Polly said. "It breaks my heart. But Beth's situation is different."

Carolyn was frustrated. "You're not saying Beth shouldn't show the video to Sonny?"

"I think she ought to give it a lot of thought before she does," Polly replied. "Bobbie may be a difficult old troublemaker—"

"Troublemaker!" Julia shouted. "She's a malevolent, controlling, conniving old witch with the morals of a hyena!"

"Even so, she's still Sonny's mother,"

Polly said. "Beth, I don't think you want to try to cut Sonny off from his family."

"Oh, come on, Polly," Julia sputtered.

Polly held up a restraining hand. "You really should try talking to Bobbie privately, first."

Beth looked as if Polly had suggested slicing her own wrists.

"Take the video," Polly advised. "Show it to her. Tell her you don't want to show it to Sonny, you don't want to be a divisive element. Ask her to help you figure out a solution to her problem."

Beth wrung her hands. "Doing that would be really hard, Polly. It scares me to think about it."

"Yeah, and I don't agree," Julia argued. "Your theory is sweet, Polly, but your basic premise is flawed. Not everyone is nice."

Polly continued calmly, "I agree. And Bobbie is controlling and manipulative. She'll probably be a terrible thorn in Beth's side—"

"More like a giant pain in her ass," Julia muttered.

"—during Beth's entire marriage to Sonny. I'm not advising that Beth just lie down and take it. I'm suggesting that she try to find a way to compromise with Bobbie. I really do believe she's got to make a good attempt at solving this problem if she's going to have a happy marriage with Sonny."

Julia made a small harrumph sound, and then all four women sat silent, letting their thoughts churn.

"What you're saying," Carolyn said slowly, "is that if the person we love comes with a toxic relative attached, we've got to accept it."

Polly considered this. "Yes. Accept it, yes. Change it somehow, if possible. Deal with it for sure."

"Oh," Beth moaned, "I know you're probably right, Polly, but the thought of confronting Bobbie terrifies me."

"You can do it," Polly assured her.

Beth looked around the room. "I wish you all could be there with me."

"We can't do that, but I know something we can do," Carolyn told her. "We can role-play. I learned to do this when I was in my early twenties, trying to learn how to negotiate and supervise people older than I was. Each of us can be Bobbie, and you can go through the entire scenario with us, and

we'll be nasty, bitter, confrontational, accu-
satory, hurt, and heartbroken, the entire
spectrum. We'll do it over and over again,
and when you're really doing it, it will be like
sliding down a hill."

"What a good idea!" Polly said.

Beth brightened. "Yeah. Yeah, that would
help. Do we have time to do it now?"

Carolyn checked her watch. "Sure. We
can start, at least."

"You're sure you feel up to it?" Polly
asked. "We don't want to tire you out."

"I'm fine," Carolyn promised.

Polly rose. "Then I'll go make a fresh pot
of tea."

"Yeah," Julia said, "and if I'm going to
play Bobbie, I'll go sharpen my fangs."

34

"Here we are, superstar." Julia kept tight hold of Belinda's hand as they left the Volvo and threaded through the rows of parked cars, heading across the parking lot toward the new cement-and-cedar structure attached to Theodore Roosevelt High School.

The high school auditorium seemed an overambitious and perhaps daunting venue for the midwinter ballet recital, since it seated eight hundred and only about forty little girls would dance today. Julia wished the recital could have been in the evening, when Tim and a lot other parents could have come, but this wasn't the enormous extravaganza that would take place at the end of May. This was more a kind of rehearsal, giving the children a chance to experience the full joy/trauma of performing in front of an audience, or as the teacher pre-

ferred to say, providing them with the opportunity to feel like real ballerinas for a day.

As they walked into the room backstage
where all the other little girls and mothers
were, Belinda's grip tightened. A swarming,
buzzing, pastel hive of tutued girls from
seven to thirteen filled the room, bending to
tie on their ballet slippers and pull up their
tights while their mothers made fussy last
adjustments to their hair. Some of the older
girls were stationed at the wall of mirrors,
gliding lipstick over their mouth or mascara
over their lashes. Belinda, usually entranced
by older girls, was too wired to pay them
any attention today.

Kneeling down, Julia helped Belinda out
of her parka and boots. Julia fitted on the
soft, pink leather ballet slippers. She fluffed
up Belinda's tutu and retied the pink ribbons
on her French braid.

"Oh, wow! You look just like a princess! A
princess ballerina!"

Carter, a diminutive redhead in a matching tutu, twirled up. "Hi, Belinda!" Belinda
beamed. The girls joined hands, bobbing up
and down together.

Baylor, Carter's mother, joined Julia.
"Could they be any cuter?"

"Not possible."

"All right, parents!" The ballet teacher, Judy Preston, a slim, young woman with dark hair sternly skewered back in a bun, clapped her hands. "It's time! Please take your seats!"

Julia leaned forward to whisper into Belinda's ear. "Good luck, Daffy Duck."

Baylor and Julia trailed the other parents out of the room, through a door, and down a set of steps to the auditorium. A pair of mothers handed out programs printed on pale pink paper. As they seated themselves, Baylor leaned over to whisper, "I'm so nervous, I wish I had a Valium."

Julia laughed. "I know. I had a glass of wine." She took her small camcorder out and focused it.

"Oh, wow, I wish I'd brought mine. Will you make me a copy?" Baylor pleaded.

"Sure." Julia scanned the program. The classes would appear according to age, the youngest first. Belinda's group had to lead off. Julia crossed her fingers, saying a private prayer.

The houselights went down, the stage lights came up. From the backstage stereo system, an overture burst into the air. The curtain rose. Nine little girls in pink and white tutus pranced out onto the stage, their arms, cuffed in white chiffon, beating up and down. They were ponies. Pink princess ponies, and their parents nearly melted with adoration to watch them.

They paraded around the stage twice, then formed a line at the back, trotting in unison like a chorus line of pink pixies, as each little girl detached herself from the front of the line, trit-trotted up the center stage, pranced in a circle, then trotted back to the line.

When Belinda's turn came, Julia's heart banged away inside her chest like a drum. Belinda was so sweet, so vulnerable, so proud! She made a perfect circle, while Julia wept behind her camera. Next came Carter, also giving a flawless performance.

"A star is born!" Baylor gasped.

Carter clip-clopped back to the line. The next little girl hesitated. The child behind her nudged her, then gave a little shove. The girl, a tiny brunette with an angular frame, inched toward the front like Marie Antoinette toward the guillotine, not keeping in character or in step with the music. When she reached center stage, she pranced once, reluctantly, then faltered, staring out at the audience as if they'd all grown monster heads. She stopped moving. Hands at her side, she burst into tears.

"Oh, the poor thing," Baylor whispered.

The chirpy CD music continued, a bouncy counterpoint to the child's frozen terror.

"The teacher should help her get offstage," Julia told Baylor. "Someone's got to do something!"

Suddenly, a little girl left the line. Still prancing, in sync with the music, Belinda trotted to the front of the stage, took the weeping pony by her hand/hoof, and led her back to the line, all without missing a step. The audience watching breathed such enormous sighs of relief the noise blew through the auditorium like a breeze, and spatterings of applause broke out.

"That's the cutest thing I've ever seen in my life!" Baylor said. "Did you get that on tape?"

Julia nodded. Tears were streaming down her face and her throat was so choked she couldn't speak. She felt Baylor looking at her. They were not close friends, they only saw each other at ballet and school occasions, but now Baylor reached over and took the hand not holding the little digital camera.

"Belinda is so brave! She wouldn't have been able to do that if you hadn't been such a good stepmother. You should be proud of yourself."

Julia bit her lip, *hard.* Those kind words made her nearly break down and blubber.

The rest of the recital passed with the speed of a tortoise as far as Julia was concerned. The other groups were older, more graceful and accomplished, but *none* of the other girls could compare with Belinda.

Finally it ended. All forty-three ballerinas came out onstage, arranged by height, so Belinda and Carter were in the first row. Julia couldn't clap while she was filming their bows, so she stomped her feet, hooted, and slapped her leg with her left hand. The curtain fell, the audience rose, the parents rushed backstage. As Julia and Baylor filed back with the crowd, several other parents, people Julia didn't even know, came up to her to tell her how adorable, clever, brave, Belinda had been.

"I feel like a stage mother," Julia told Baylor. "The scary thing is, I like it."

They found Carter and Belinda against

the wall near their coats, holding hands and jumping up and down, still jazzed from their performance.

Julia knelt to face her stepdaughter. "Belinda, you were *wonderful*! You danced beautifully, and you were so good to rescue that other little girl! I got it on tape, I can't wait to show your father, and we'll make copies to send to your grandparents. Oh, I'm so proud of you!"

"Shall we go get some ice cream to celebrate?" Baylor asked.

Julia looked at Belinda. "Want to?"

Belinda nodded. Loosening her grip around Julia's neck, she turned back to Carter, grabbed her hands, and the children went back into Mexican jumping bean mode.

At home that evening, they couldn't stop watching the video.

"I'm going to bring dinner in here," Julia said.

Belinda remained glued to the TV. Tim followed Julia into the kitchen, where she bent over the oven, taking out a casserole she'd prepared earlier in the day. He put his arms around her. Julia leaned back into his embrace.

"I love you," Tim whispered.

"I love you." Julia turned in his arms and nestled against him.

They kissed, agreeing with their eyes to continue this particular conversation later that night. Julia spooned the casserole onto plates and filled water glasses while Tim carried the plates in and set them on the coffee table. Belinda knelt on the floor, eating with absentminded hunger, her attention still focused on the ballet recital.

"That little girl behind Belinda?" Julia pointed with her fork. "That's Carter. She's Belinda's friend. Her mother, Baylor, sat next to me. She's a good little dancer, isn't she, Belinda?"

Belinda nodded her head enthusiastically, not taking her eyes from the screen.

"Here she comes!" Julia cried, as excited as if this were the first instead of the fifth time they'd seen it. "Look, Tim. Belinda is *perfectly* in step. Just perfect. What a little ballerina."

"You're the prettiest girl there," Tim told his daughter.

"Now, look!" Tears welled in Julia's eyes again. "That poor little child! Now watch! Belinda to the rescue! Just as if she's been doing it all her life! And she never once got out of step! Look at her, prancing while she leads that little girl back to the line. You know what, Belinda, we've got to phone your grandmother to tell her about this!"

After dinner, Julia rose to take their empty plates back to the kitchen. "Tim, would you like an apple or some cookies? Belinda and I already had our dessert, we had ice cream with Carter and her mom."

"An apple would be great." Tim picked up his daughter and cuddled her next to him.

Julia set the three plates on the counter and took an apple from the bowl. Her hands were under the running water when a thought struck her. Her head whipped to the side. She stared back at the plates. The three empty plates.

Three empty plates.

Tonight, without her even noticing, so many things had changed. Belinda had eaten without a fuss, even though for the first time ever, they hadn't sat at their routine places at the dining room table. *Plus,* Belinda had eaten *all* her food, even though

Julia had forgotten to pick out the broccoli or separate the rice and the chicken; she'd intended to, when she made the casserole. But she'd forgotten in the heat of the moment.

So had Belinda.

It was a tiny miracle.

Winging a silent prayer of thanks, Julia carried the apple and the portable phone into the living room. They watched the video another time, then Tim froze it on Belinda at center stage. He punched in Agnes and George's phone number.

He handed the phone to Julia. "You should tell them. You were the one who saw it."

With Belinda watching, Julia had to disguise her emotions as she took the receiver. Belinda's grandmother answered. "Agnes? Are you busy? I've got such a wonderful story to tell you! Do you want to get George on the extension?" Tim had left the room, returning now with another portable phone, which he handed to Belinda. "Belinda's listening, too. Hi, George. Oh, my gosh, you have no idea how amazing Belinda was at her ballet recital." Julia described the entire affair second by second, prance by prance.

When she'd finished, the line was strangely quiet. For a moment, Julia thought they'd been disconnected.

Then Agnes spoke, her voice choked with tears. "I wish I could have been there. I would have been there if I'd known the date three months ago. We couldn't cancel George's colonoscopy appointment."

Julia braced herself for battle, but managed to keep her voice sympathetic. "Agnes, we didn't *know* the date of the recital three months ago. We only found out two weeks ago, and we told you then."

Agnes sniffed.

"How is George?" Julia asked.

"Oh, he's fine. He had some blood in his stool a while ago, but it turns out it was probably from a hemorrhoid."

Thanks for sharing, Julia thought with an inward grin. "What good news. We're all so glad!"

"George and I have been talking." Agnes blew her nose, then continued, "I hate being out here in the Berkshires, with my little grandchild so far away. We've decided. We're going to move. We're going to start looking at houses in your area."

"*Oh!*" Julia's stomach lurched. She

glanced at Belinda, who looked as if a bug had just crawled out of the handset. "But, Agnes, won't you miss all your friends? And your wonderful house?"

"Not as much as I miss seeing my grand-daughter every day."

"Um, here, why don't you tell Tim about your plans!" Julia thrust the handset at her husband. Her dinner was on an internal elevator, rising up from her stomach to her mouth. She smiled brightly at Belinda, then raced out of the living room, down the hall to her bedroom, and into the bathroom, where she knelt on the cold tiles and delivered the casserole into the toilet.

35

At four in the morning, Polly stood in the front hall of Claudia's elegant house, saying good-bye to Martha Wright, the Home Health nurse, who had come immediately, as she had promised, to note officially Claudia's death. They had phoned Claudia's mortician of choice. When he and his assistant arrived, Martha had led Polly into the dining room, a practice, Polly assumed, to protect the living from observing the physical transfer of a person, now a body, out of the house.

Martha's face was puffy from lack of sleep. "Will you be okay?" she asked Polly as she pulled on her wool cap and gloves.

"Yes, of course," Polly replied automatically.

"You do realize you're crying, don't you?" Martha asked gently.

Polly touched her cheeks, her fingertips finding wetness. "Oh. I am."

"Yes, you were crying when I came to the door. You've been crying steadily for about two hours now. Quietly, of course. Like a British rain."

Polly chuckled. "Claudia would have approved."

Martha adjusted her heavy shoulder bag. "Tell me, what are you going to do now? I mean right now, after I leave?"

"Um—" Polly rubbed her eyes. "I'll lock up the house and drive home."

"It will be nice to be in your own home, won't it?"

"It will."

"Do you have anyone waiting for you? Or a friend you could call to come be with you for a while?"

"Oh, I'll be fine," Polly assured the other woman. "I'm just very tired."

"Will you be able to sleep?"

"I think so. I have some Ambien my doctor prescribed. I doubt if I'll need that, though."

"Remember, you're in a gentle kind of shock. It's never easy, when someone dies."

"I'll be fine," Polly said again. "Thank you for everything."

Martha folded Polly into a warm hug, then went out into the darkness. Polly shut the door.

The house was silent. The lights glared harshly. The hospital bed where Claudia had taken her last breath loomed in empti- ness. Martha had helped Polly remove the soiled sheets, blankets, and pads and stuff them into a large plastic bag, which tilted sideways next to a table littered with glasses and cups, tissue boxes, bottles, and a kidney-shaped stainless steel pan. Polly's knitting needles protruded from her canvas bag, a spot of bright color. Claudia's teeth, floating in a water-filled glass, seemed oddly alive.

"Well." Polly's voice sounded loud in the empty room. "I guess I'll go home."

She walked through the house, checking to be sure the back and side doors were locked. She turned off the lights. She put on her coat, hat, and gloves and picked up her purse. She went out into the dark night.

Driving home, she made a mental list of things to do: visit the funeral home to make the arrangements Claudia desired; that would be easy enough, because Claudia had written them down, just as she had written the obituary Polly would send to the Boston papers. There were no acquaintances to phone; Claudia had explicitly forbid Polly to phone anyone. She would call Robert Gershong, Claudia's lawyer, who would probate the will. Who would write the check to the Historical Society? Polly wondered. Who would handle the sale of Claudia's house? Polly had to phone the pharmacy to tell them to come take the hospital bed and commode. Fairly soon she needed to ask Pearl to help clean the house. What about all of Claudia's antiques? Her clothes? Her silver?

Polly's head swam. Her eyes burned.

By the time she reached her own house, it was almost five in the morning. She hadn't left a light burning, and when she entered, Roy Orbison wasn't there to greet her. She'd call the Pecks later, to ask them to bring her good old dog home.

The house was cold. Polly adjusted the thermostat, then walked through her house, still wearing her coat. In the kitchen she paused. Did she want a cup of tea? Weren't you supposed to drink tea when someone died? Or perhaps a drink? She was too tired to know what she wanted.

"Oh, Tucker," she said aloud. "I miss you so much."

Down in the basement, the oil-fired furnace clicked on, rumbling companionably. Slowly, as if each foot weighed a ton, Polly climbed the stairs to her bedroom. For a moment she just sat on her bed, staring at the wall. What next?

———

At ten o'clock, Polly woke with a start. At some point she'd simply fallen over backward on her bed. She still wore her coat, but her wool cap had slipped and hung from one ear.

Outside, rain poured down. Had she ever lived through a winter with so much rain? But the house was warm, and it was her *home.* Her stomach rumbled. She wanted breakfast, a shower, and her dog.

Shower, first. The pounding hot water relaxed her body and invigorated her spirits. The fragrance of her citrus and honey shampoo made her take deep, grateful breaths. Wrapped in her favorite old terry-cloth bathrobe, hair turbaned in a thick towel, she slid into her slippers and hurried down to the kitchen to make coffee. After she'd savored a cup, she picked up her phone and dialed her son.

Katrina, David's mother-in-law, answered. "Oh, hello, Polly. How are you?"

"I'm well, thank you. I'm calling to speak to David, if I could."

"Sorry. He's not here now. Could I take a message?"

Polly would not let her son hear of Claudia's death through Katrina. "Please just ask him to phone me as soon as possible."

Putting the phone back in its cradle, she turned to make breakfast, but instead sank into a chair, overcome with weariness. Never had she felt so all alone. She missed her husband, she missed her son, she even missed her mother-in-law. Whatever else Claudia had done, she had claimed Polly, in her own tyrannical way, at least at the end of her life. Polly knew she was only kidding herself to think that now Claudia was gone, David would be part of her life again. It was not what his wife, Amy, wanted. Polly couldn't understand why, but really, that didn't matter. Polly had to face it: the largest chunk of her life belonged to the past. She'd already had most of the allotted three score years and ten, and who knew when death's irrevocable grip would reach for her? Cancer, heart disease, plane crashes—there were so many ways to die. She had lived a wonderful life. She shouldn't be greedy. Glancing around the kitchen, she wondered for the first time if she should sell her house now while the market was good. She could buy a place in a retirement community, put the rest of the money in a money-market account, so her savings would carry her through her senior years. She wanted to be cautious, while still allowing herself the luxury of doing, at last, all the things she'd dreamed of over the years. One problem—the things she'd dreamed about had been centered around her family. Taking her grandchildren to Disney World, that sort of thing.

Well. Time for a new plan.

She hoped she'd enjoy a long life, and if so, she needed to be careful. What if she developed a long-term illness, even a minor, only slightly debilitating one? She could not expect David to help her, and certainly not Amy. Never had she intended to rely on her son in her old age, but after this interlude with Claudia, Polly was even more determined. She was alone in the world. She had to prepare for her death, and for the rest of her solitary life.

———

Beth had invited Bobbie to her apartment for lunch, hoping to gain some slight psychological advantage by removing her from her home territory. But Bobbie declined, saying that she had to stay home to make lunch for her husband or to take messages for Young's Construction. Beth was welcome for lunch, Bobbie had said. Beth had replied that she didn't really want lunch, she just wanted to talk.

Sure, Bobbie had said. Anytime.

So here Beth was, driving to the Youngs' house, just as if she were sane. She parked her car behind a red Ford truck, walked to the back of the house, and let herself into the kitchen.

Bobbie was at the counter, in jeans and a teal blue sweatshirt that set off her dark blue eyes. "Hi, hon. Good timing, I'm just about done icing this cake."

Framed by tied-back blue gingham curtains, the kitchen windows were steamy. A pot bubbled on the back burner of the stove, filling the air with the rich aroma of herbs. Tinkerbelle, snoozing on a rag rug, opened one lackadaisical eye, thumped her tail to greet Beth, then continued snoring. Beth hung her coat on the rack near the door but kept her handbag, with the cassette inside, in her hand.

"Pour yourself a cup of coffee, hon." Bobbie motioned with a jerk of her head toward the coffeepot, kept fresh and full all day.

Beth obeyed, taking a mug from the cupboard, milk from the refrigerator. She leaned against the counter, watching Bobbie ice the cake. The older woman was deft with her knife, scooping up the final clumps of icing from the sides and bottom of the bowl, swirling it onto the cake with swift, practiced gestures.

"Looks delicious," Beth said.

Bobbie smiled at her handiwork. "It does, doesn't it? Sometimes I try a new recipe, but this old devil's food cake is their favorite. I've made it so many times, I don't need to read the recipe. I think I could make it in my sleep." She held the bowl out to Beth. "Want to lick the sides?"

"No, thanks." Coffee, Beth felt, was neutral, eating icing too intimate right now.

Bobbie set the bowl in the sink and ran hot water in it. "Okay, I guess I can sit down for a few minutes." She poured herself a cup of coffee and sat at the table. "What's up?"

Beth swallowed. She took a minute to force air into her lungs, as deeply as she could get it to go, at the same time summoning up the spirits of Julia, Polly, and Carolyn for moral support.

Still, when she began her prepared speech, she felt her face turn scarlet. "Bobbie, this is difficult for me to say. But—I think you and I have a problem."

"Oh?" Bobbie leaned back in her chair, lifting her feet to the seat of another chair, getting comfortable.

"What I mean is—I know you don't like me. Or perhaps you like me, but you don't want Sonny to marry me. You want Sonny to marry Robin." Beth reached into her purse. "I know you do, because—" It was now or never, Beth thought, her nerve failing her. If Bobbie wanted to sabotage Beth before now, how would she feel after discovering Beth had taped a private conversation?

Bobbie arched an eyebrow. "Because I make it obvious?"

Beth hesitated. Perhaps it wasn't necessary to use the tape. Perhaps they could just talk it out. "Well, yes, partly. I—"

"I won't stop, you know." In an instant, Bobbie's voice rang with steel. Her face changed; with just a few muscles, her smile turned threatening.

"But why?" Beth cried, leaning forward. "I'm not so bad! I'm good! Plus, I love Sonny, and he loves me, and—"

"You don't fit into my family. You never will. You don't belong. Sonny still loves Robin."

Now Beth was fighting mad. "You are *so* wrong! Sonny loves *me*. We're going to get married. We're going to have a life together, and we're going to have children. What you have to decide is whether or not you want to see your grandchildren, because believe me, I'm not bringing them around here for you to insult me."

Bobbie slammed her mug on the table so hard it cracked. "Get out."

"Not until I'm finished." Beth whipped the cassette from her purse. "Before I go, I want you to see just a few minutes from the tape taken at your anniversary party."

Bobbie frowned. "What are you talking about?"

"I'm talking about the conversation you had with Robin. When you said Sonny was having 'just a little fling' with me. When you said you'd pushed me when I was ice skating."

Bobbie's face was ashen. "You little bitch."

Julia and the others had called Beth that during their role-playing session. Now Beth didn't even flinch. The word actually triggered a prepared response. "Oh, I could be worse than that! I could show Sonny this tape, and I could cry, and I could ask him to move to another state with me, I could say he has to choose between me and you, and you'd better believe it, Sonny would choose me."

Bobbie almost growled. The tension in the room and the anger in their voices woke Tinkerbelle, who rose, looking from Bobbie to Beth with alarm. "Don't be so sure."

Beth relaxed her voice. "The point is, Bobbie, I don't want to be a divisive factor. I want Sonny to remain part of this family. But he needs his own life, too, he needs independence, he needs to try to get his architect's degree, because that's who he is. I know you think he'll be different if he marries me and goes to college, and he will be, but why can't you love him if he does? Think of him as challenged or something! Furthermore, what about Robin? I could tell from the tape that she's not in love with Sonny anymore. She has no illusions that he's in love with her. Anyway, she doesn't want to be your daughter-in-law, Bobbie, she wants to be your daughter! She loves this family, she needs this family, it's the only family she really has. She doesn't want to offend you by hooking up with someone else, and that's terrible. That's just plain sad! Why not let Sonny marry me, and let Robin fall in love with some other guy, and let *him* be part of this family, too!"

Bobbie held up her hand like a stop sign. "Enough. I'm not listening to any more of this. You have no right to tell me what to do." She rubbed her forehead, looking older now, and tired. "You're just a snotty, conniving, little—"

"Conniving, yes. Snotty, no. Little physically, yes. But psychologically, Bobbie, I'm *huge*."

The kitchen door flew open. "Anybody home?" A large woman in OshKoshes and boots stomped in. "Oh, good, Bobbie, you're here. I need to borrow your spring-form pan."

Bobbie stood up. "Hi, Milly. What are you making?"

"I've got a new recipe for a flourless chocolate cake."

"Got time for coffee?" Bobbie asked.

"Sure do." Milly threw her coat over the back of a chair. "Am I interrupting something?"

Beth held her breath.

"Not at all." Bobbie looked as if she were chewing glass, but she said, "We were just gabbing. This is Beth. Sonny's fiancée."

"Oh, I've been dying to meet you! I didn't get to at the party, it was so crowded." Milly held her hand out to Beth. "I'm Milly, an old friend of the family."

Beth gave Milly her sweetest smile.

Driving away from the Youngs', Beth let out a Cherokee war whoop. She'd done it! She had to tell Julia!

"Hey, girlfriend! What a nice surprise. Belinda, look who's here!" Julia gave Beth a big warm hug. "Coffee?"

Beth shook her head. "Oh, I think I deserve champagne. At least some white wine!"

"You did it? You confronted the old bat?"

"I did!"

"Do tell all, doll!" Julia hooked her arm around Beth and drew her back into the kitchen, just as Belinda came running toward them, a spoon in her hand.

"Wow, what have you got there?" Beth squatted down to kiss the little girl. Belinda held the spoon up for Beth. She took a lick. "Mmm. Lemon icing!"

"Today is Belinda's grandmother Agnes's birthday. We're having her for dinner and we've just finished icing the cake. Come see the dining room. Belinda made it look so pretty!"

Beth followed Julia and Belinda around the dining room, admiring the place mats Belinda had colored, the presents Belinda and Julia had wrapped, and the bouquet of flowers and net Belinda had chosen at the florist's to set at her grandmother's place. Julia had gained a bit of weight, Beth thought silently, and it looked good on her.

In the kitchen, Julia poured them each a glass of wine and gave Belinda a wineglass filled with apple juice.

"Wow! What a cake!" Beth marveled at the four-layered masterpiece, thick with lemon-flavored icing. "Agnes ought to like it. Looks like the entire thing's made out of Marshmallow Fluff."

Julia grinned. "Method to my madness, baby!" Turning to Belinda, she said, "Want to go watch a little *Nemo* before your dad gets home?"

Belinda shook her head vehemently and planted herself at the kitchen table.

"How about making your grandmother a special birthday card?"

Belinda nodded. Julia gave her a stack of

white paper and a box of watercolor paints. She turned to Beth. "Now. Tell all."

Beth didn't have to be asked twice. "Oh, gad, Julia, I was so scared, I thought I was going to faint! When I walked into her house, I felt like Jack from the beanstalk about to confront the ogre. I mean, it felt *mythical* to me, you know?" She recounted the conversation with as much accuracy as possible.

"So." Julia tapped her lip in thought. "Bobbie didn't actually surrender. She didn't say, 'All right, Beth, I'll stop being such a gnarly old witch and be nice to you from now on.' "

"No, because Milly arrived just then. But I never assumed this would end in a Kodachrome moment, with Bobbie and me falling into each other's arms, swearing eternal devotion. I just did what I could. You know I've always lived my life through books. I always loved the whole fairy-tale thing with the knight on the white horse rescuing the fair maiden, and I guess I thought that's how my life would be. That I'd be like Sleeping Beauty or Snow White, just lying there looking pretty, you know, while my troubles were solved and the prince came to kiss me and make everything all right. I don't think I've ever had to face any monster in any den before. And you know what, no matter what happens, I'm glad I confronted Bobbie. I'm proud of myself."

"I'm proud of you, too, girlfriend."

"Well, I couldn't have done it without you," Beth said honestly. "You and Polly and Carolyn—gosh, that role-playing was fabulous! When she called me a 'conniving little' "—Beth glanced at Belinda, whose head was bent over her watercolor masterpiece—" 'witch,' it didn't even faze me. I just shot back with all the stuff we'd practiced." Beth spread her arms wide. "I feel like a new me! The new, improved Beth! The grown-up, capable, dare I say *powerful* Beth!"

"Congratulations, champ!" Julia toasted her.

Beth checked her watch. "You have to get ready for Agnes, don't you?"

"Yeah. First, let's schedule a date to get together with Carolyn and Polly and share some bubbly to celebrate."

36

On a platter in the oven, the fried chicken was kept warm while Julia stirred the gravy. This was not a meal Julia had prepared before, and she wasn't thrilled about the fat content her family would be ingesting, but this was Agnes's favorite meal, and Julia wanted to do it right, even though her stomach churned. Damn, Julia thought, I must be getting an ulcer.

Tim came into the kitchen. "Can I help?" In honor of the occasion, he still wore his suit and Belinda's favorite tie, covered with flying pigs.

Funny how he always offered to help in the kitchen when Agnes and George were here, Julia thought wryly. "Sure." She nodded her head toward a pot. "Put the peas in that bowl. The carrots in another bowl, the flowered one."

She poured the gravy into a gravy boat and carried it to the table. Tim brought in the vegetables and the mashed potatoes. Julia lifted out the warm platter of fried chicken and bore it triumphantly into the dining room, setting it before Agnes.

"This looks very nice," Agnes mumbled dutifully. Her expression said, *I'll be lucky if it doesn't choke me.*

"Your favorite meal!" Julia said, sliding into her place at the table. She lifted her wineglass. "Happy birthday, Agnes."

Agnes nodded reluctantly. "Thank you." *I'll eat it but I won't enjoy it.*

Julia passed the vegetables and rolls to George, while Tim prepared Belinda's plate, carefully keeping the carrots from touching the chicken, and making a well of mashed potatoes to pour the gravy in.

"How's the house-hunting going?" Tim asked when everyone's plate was full.

George was too busy chewing to reply. Clearly he found Julia's cooking good enough.

"Houses are so expensive here." Agnes cut into her chicken, inspecting it closely, as if expecting an alien to pop out.

"We like the Realtor, though," George

added cheerfully. "We've seen a few places that might do."

"Nothing as nice as we have," Agnes muttered. "Nothing with a yard like we have at home."

Agnes and George's house in the Berkshires had a large garden. Julia thought George found great comfort in his riding mower and toolshed. "Doesn't it depend on the suburb?" she asked. "I think the farther you get from Boston, the less expensive land prices are."

"Oh, right! So we should stay out in the Berkshires!" Agnes snapped. *You want us as far away as possible, don't you, you fiend!*

"That's not what I mean," Julia hastened to say. "I'm just suggesting you look to the west of the city."

"Suburbs like Marlborough," Tim chimed in. "Southborough, Milford, Medway."

At that, Agnes seemed pacified. The rest of the conversation centered on suburbs and the kind of place George and Agnes would want.

As they talked, Julia glanced at everyone's plate: Tim and George went through three helpings of everything, and even Belinda ate every bit of her food. Agnes alone refused a second helping and left much of her first untouched.

Julia rose to clear off the table. Tim grabbed some bowls. "Belinda, could you help us, please?" Julia asked.

In the kitchen, Belinda climbed up on a chair. Julia put the cake in front of her, and Tim lit a match and handed it to Belinda, who solemnly touched the flame to the wicks of sixteen candles. Julia wasn't sure how old Agnes was, so she let Belinda decide the number, and for whatever reason, sixteen was what Belinda had settled on.

"Okay!" Julia whispered. "Tim, turn off the dining room lights." She lifted Belinda to the floor. "Sure the cake isn't too heavy for you to carry?"

Belinda shook her head fervently.

"Okay, then." Julia set the cake in Belinda's outstretched hands. "Here we go." She grabbed her digital camera, following behind Belinda, filming their little parade. Tim and Julia started singing "Happy Birthday."

Tim helped Belinda set the cake on the table. Julia knelt to film Agnes blowing out the candles, then turned on the light. She brought the dessert plates and cake knife to the table and set them before Agnes.

Agnes pulled her granddaughter to her. "Oh, sweetheart, this is the most beautiful cake I've ever seen in my life! Did you decorate it?"

Belinda nodded her head.

"Then you deserve the biggest piece!" She sliced into the cake.

Julia returned to the kitchen to start the coffee brewing. Returning, she settled back at the table just as Agnes had finished passing around cake for everyone, and she couldn't help admiring her creation, the pale yellow cake, tinged to daffodil perfection with food coloring, bits of lemon zest glittering like citrines in the cake and icing.

"Where's the ice cream?" Agnes inquired.

"Oh, I didn't think we'd need any, not with this cake," Julia said, staring down the length of the table at Belinda's grandmother. "Actually, the recipe book we used said the flavor of this cake is so delicate, it would be overwhelmed by ice cream."

Agnes put her fork down. She gave her plate a little push away. "I don't believe I want any, in that case. I don't like cake without ice cream."

"Grandmother," Belinda said in a clear, high voice, each word as distinct as a chime from a bell, "why are you always so mean to Julia?"

Everyone at the table gasped. Julia's entire body broke out in goose bumps. Tim smiled from ear to ear. Agnes looked as if she'd just swallowed a live frog.

"Belinda," Agnes quavered when she could find her breath. "Oh, honey, Belinda, you can *talk.*"

Tim and Julia exchanged terrified glances. Would Belinda continue talking? Had a miracle occurred, or simply a momentary blip?

"I know," Belinda said matter-of-factly. "I could always talk, in my head."

Julia thought she might explode with joy. Tim gulped and blew his nose on his napkin. "Well, Belinda," he said, trying to sound unruffled, "it's wonderful to hear your voice again. It's just wonderful."

"Yes," Julia said. "And how perfect, to hear you speak on your grandmother's birthday."

Agnes choked as if she were being strangled. "Your stepmother's right, Belinda. This is the best gift anyone could ever give me.

Thank you." Bending forward, she pulled her granddaughter to her in a hug. Then, looking at Julia, she said, "And, Julia, thank you. Thank you for making this amazing cake."

"You're welcome," Julia said. "We made it together, didn't we, Belinda?"

"Yes," Belinda said. "We made it together."

Julia looked around the table at her family. "Well, good golly, Miss Molly."

Something awakened Carolyn just after she fell asleep. She lay alone in the king-size bed, not apprehensive, but alert.

Hank was at a brainstorming environmental retreat in the Adirondacks. He'd be there for almost a week, his last major trip. After that, he'd refused all meetings outside a one-hour radius of Boston, so he'd be able to be with Carolyn when the baby came.

As if reading her thoughts, the baby stirred. The invisible drawstring inside her belly pulled and tightened. Braxton-Hicks again, she thought, glancing at the clock. It was only midnight. She'd been asleep for perhaps an hour. Grunting like a sow on a National Geographic special, she managed to turn onto her side, pulling a pillow between her legs for support.

Was that a sound? She strained, listening. The house must have mice. No one else was here tonight. Mrs. B. had gone home at five. Her father was still in the Caribbean, visiting with friends, playing golf, recovering from the shock of his costly, inconvenient, abandoned marriage.

Lying on her side was less comfortable than lying on her back. When the contraction came, she couldn't get her breath. *Ouch.* It was unrelenting, like a cramp in her foot. She rubbed her sides, trying to ease the constriction.

When she could move, she struggled to the side of the bed and sat up. Panting, she pushed herself to a standing position. She could tell she wouldn't be able to sleep, not for a while. Well, she'd use this insomnia. The newly revised personnel policy needed reviewing; she'd make a cup of chamomile tea, settle down at the kitchen table, and get some work done.

She headed for the kitchen, turning on lights as she went. As she reached the sink, a contraction gripped her so fiercely she bent in half, clutching the counter.

"Oh, no, no," she pleaded when she could catch her breath. "Not yet."

Still, she'd better time these contractions. Lowering herself onto a chair, she sat looking at the clock, waiting. She felt light-headed and faintly queasy.

Four minutes. The contractions were coming every four minutes. So? Certainly they seemed much stronger than the contractions she'd had earlier, but still they probably were false alarms, weren't they? The baby wasn't due for a month. What should she do? By now it was one in the morning. She couldn't phone her doctor or labor coach. She didn't want to wake them for another false alarm. Oh, God, why wasn't Hank here? Suddenly, her lonely state frightened her. What if she really was starting labor? How did a woman ever know? The first baby was supposed to be *late.* How peculiar the body was, to be so uncommunicative to the conscious mind, especially about something as important as this. Perhaps, if she got to work on that personnel policy, it would take her mind off these cramps. Fine, she would do that. She would make herself a cup of tea—she looked over at the stove. No, she hadn't started the water boiling yet. Her mind was all over the place.

Another contraction. This one hurt so much she heard herself yell.

Think sensibly, she commanded herself when it ended. But she couldn't. She sat in her own kitchen like a lost refugee in a train station who didn't know this language. *Stop panicking,* she told herself. She was an adult, a perfectly capable woman. She'd taken the childbirth prep classes. She might actually be starting labor—perhaps she should get the book and read the chapter on labor again, to compare it with her present state.

She stood up, intending to go find the book, when a contraction clamped itself around her and would not stop.

Call an ambulance, she told herself.

Don't be such a baby, another part of her mind scolded. *Don't embarrass yourself again!*

I'm scared! she thought. *I need help! I don't know what to do!*

Her mind said, *Call Polly.*

It took Polly thirty minutes to get to Carolyn's house, which was fine, since it took Carolyn that long to get from her kitchen to the door. Through the leaded glass, Carolyn saw the headlights of Polly's car flash like a lighthouse beacon, and then Polly was hurrying up the walk, her car coat unbuttoned, flapping like wings.

"Carolyn! This is so exciting!" Polly's naked face was puffy, her eyes swollen and red, but her smile was genuine. She wore no makeup and had fastened her red curls back in a slapdash ponytail.

"I'm so sorry to get you out of bed in the middle of the night. I'm sure it's just another false alarm."

Just then, a warm gush of liquid drenched her legs and feet.

"Okay," Polly said, "that's your water breaking. I'm thinking it's the real thing."

"Probably—" A contraction almost brought Carolyn to her knees.

Polly grabbed Carolyn by her elbows and supported her as she stood, half-squatting, almost blind with pain.

When it subsided, Polly looked at her

watch. "Two sixteen. Is your hospital bag all packed and ready?"

Carolyn nodded. "In the bedroom."

"I'll get it. You wait here. If another contraction comes, put your hands against the wall, let the wall support you." She took off down the corridor, then stopped, turning back. "Have you phoned Hank?"

"Not yet."

"We'll do it in the car." She rushed off.

When Polly finally came running back, Carolyn had had another contraction and was in the grip of another.

"This house is too damn big!" Polly's hands were full. She dropped Carolyn's bag on the floor next to her purse and helped Carolyn into her coat. "I've phoned the hospital, they're expecting you. Let's get you in the car."

Polly opened the door. Outside, the night was dark and cold.

"I'm scared," Carolyn whispered. "Fucking damnation, I'm so scared!"

Polly wrapped Carolyn in an awkward hug. "Of course you are. Everyone is. But you'll do fine, I promise."

A sob broke from Carolyn's throat. "Polly,

my mother died when she was thirty-seven!"

"Well, *you* are *not* going to die," Polly told her firmly. "I won't let you." She gripped Carolyn's shoulders. "Got that, Carolyn? I mean it. You're not going to die. So stop thinking that way. Think about your little girl, she's almost here! Relax, let your body do what it was designed to do. And don't worry. I promise, you'll be okay."

In the dark of night, they wound through the sleeping streets of Sperry and raced along the Mass. Pike. Carolyn's contractions, coming every two minutes, were so painful she couldn't help crying out.

"Polly. I'm afraid I'll have this baby in your car!"

Polly patted Carolyn's hand. "Don't worry. You could continue labor for hours yet."

"With contractions like this? Coming every two minutes?" Carolyn felt her eyes bug out of her head in horror.

Polly laughed. She handed Carolyn her cell phone. "Call Hank, tell him to get home fast."

Carolyn waited until a contraction passed, then punched in the numbers. The phone rang and rang and rang. Finally, Hank answered, his voice groggy with sleep.

It was so good to hear his voice, she nearly sobbed. "Hank. I'm having the baby."

"You're sure?"

"I'm sure."

"Where are you?"

"In Polly Lodge's car. She's taking me to the hospital."

"I'll leave now. I'll get there as soon as I can. I love you, Carolyn."

"I love you."

By the time they arrived at the hospital, Carolyn was sick with pain. She lay with eyes closed against the passenger door, trying to breathe as she'd been taught. The attendants helped her into the wheelchair. She vomited all over herself.

"Sorry," she panted. "Sorry, sorry."

The pain was making her nutty. The admitting clerk took so long Carolyn wanted to rise up out of her wheelchair and shake her.

"You have all that information already!" she groaned.

"Your husband isn't here?" the clerk asked.

"He's out of town."

"Is your labor coach here?"

"Yes." Carolyn nodded her head toward Polly. "Right here."

In the labor room, Carolyn was dressed in a johnny, helped up onto a table, and examined.

"Good girl," the nurse said. "Already eight centimeters. You've been busy."

"How much longer?" Carolyn asked.

The nurse shook her head. "We don't know, hon. Not much longer. Maybe an hour or two."

"Polly!" Reaching out, Carolyn grabbed Polly's arm. "I can't do this anymore!"

"Oh, sure you can." Polly smiled. "I'm right here, and I'm going to help you." Leaning close, she stroked Carolyn's hair back from her face. "You're doing really well, you know. Eight centimeters dilated, that's great. I'm sure it won't be much longer. Try to relax, sweetie. Breathe with me."

"I hate this!" Carolyn wailed. "I really hate this! I feel trapped!"

"Okay, let's get you some control. Are you comfortable?"

"Jesus Christ, *no,* of course I'm not comfortable!"

"Let's try sitting up, then." Polly looked over at the nurse, who pushed a button, and the head of the bed rose.

That did help. Carolyn felt less nauseous, and also less like an invalid, flat on her back like a fish out of the water, gasping for breath. The room was cheerful, paper with a floral print. Polly was hanging their coats in a little closet. A rocking chair sat next to the bed—

"It's starting again," Carolyn whimpered.

Polly came to her side, took Carolyn's hands in her own, and said, "Okay. Focus on me. Breathe with me, the way I breathe."

"How can you remember?" Carolyn demanded. "Your son is what, thirty-four years old?"

Polly smiled. "Believe me, once you've learned this kind of breathing, you never forget."

Carolyn tried so hard. She wanted to do this right. She wanted to have the baby without drugs because it was best for the baby. And Polly was helping. She puffed along with Carolyn, and in between contractions she rubbed Carolyn's back or fed her spoons of ice. Nurses came to check her dilation, blood pressure, the baby's heart tones, then went away. Carolyn felt as if she had the worst case of flu in her life, while at the same time being backed over by a Greyhound bus.

Suddenly the pain changed. No longer a controlled ebb and flow, it became a raging, searing, tectonic eruption, so powerful, so agonizing, she screamed.

"Something's wrong! Help me!" Carolyn was dying, she was going to die!

Nurses buzzed around her. Polly smoothed her hair. The doctor was at the foot of the bed. He said, "Push."

Carolyn pushed. He said, "Again." She pushed again. He said, "Take a breath." She was shaking, sobbing, shivering. She saw Polly's radiant face. Realization surged through her: she was having her baby *now*.

She was here, where she'd longed to be so many years, here at the birth of her child.

"Push," the doctor said.

This time when Carolyn pushed, she was fueled by such amazing energy, it was not pain, it was power, power as she'd never known before.

"Push," the doctor said, and Carolyn pushed, and she saw Polly's face shine with tears, and the doctor lifted a squalling, red-limbed little girl, bald and wrinkled like a giant cranberry, onto Carolyn's stomach.

"Hello, little girl," Carolyn whispered. She couldn't take her eyes off the baby. "Oh, Polly, isn't she beautiful?"

"She's the most beautiful little girl in the world," Polly said.

37

Julia lay on the sofa, just waking from a nap. Tim would be home soon. She had to dress. A group of her photographs was part of the art exhibit at the open house tonight. She should be nervous. Instead, she felt a bone-deep contentment, like a retriever who, after a long run in the cold and a hearty meal, had lain down in the room with his family on a rug in front of a fire.

It was no wonder she was thinking of dogs. At her feet, their new powder puff of a puppy, Sweetie, perked up, gazing hopefully at Julia with her round, black button eyes. When Beth had told Julia she wanted to give Belinda a shih tzu puppy, Julia had at first demurred. Not that she didn't think a dog was a great idea, but now that Belinda was talking, singing, and acting like any normal kid, wouldn't a bigger, less frivolous dog be better for her? Wouldn't a tiny, fluffy, yipping little varmint no larger than a chrysanthemum keep Belinda in "princess" mode? But Beth had persisted, pointing out that a small dog would be easier for Belinda to care for, and easier, for that matter, for Julia to deal with, which was important, now that so much was changing in her life.

Julia rolled on her back and tickled the puppy with her toes. "Come up here," she invited.

Sweetie pranced daintily along the edge of the sofa, then mounted Julia's chest with the pride of Hillary achieving Mt. Everest, the tip of her lollipop-pink tongue sticking out.

Damn, but this dog was cute!

"I wish I had some of your energy," Julia told Sweetie.

Sweetie wagged her tail.

Julia looked around the room. The move had happened so quickly, she still couldn't believe it. She still woke surprised to see these walls instead of the ones she'd lived within for over a year. She liked this ordinary split-level ranch, and someday, when she'd managed to get all the cardboard boxes un-packed and chosen colors for paints and fabric for curtains, she knew she'd make it into a comfortable, attractive, even charming home. Until then, she was happy just to be here. She liked the way the sun slanted in the windows, the way the house sat on its spacious lot. She liked the white picket fence surrounding the large backyard, with its apple tree already hung with a rope swing and a shaded area just meant for a sandbox and jungle gym.

"Okay, cream puff," Julia said, holding the little dog to her chest. "Time to rise and shine." She swung her bare feet to the floor and padded over the cool wood floors. Later, she knew, they'd think about rugs and carpets. With summer on the way, bare floors were fine. She had so much to get ready.

She had the baby's room to get ready.

Leaning in the doorway, she smiled. The walls of the empty room were papered in a football motif, and along one wall ran wooden shelves that had once held about a zillion sports trophies. The woodwork and closet door were scuffed, scarred, and marred, testimony to the boy who had grown up here and was now married, with a home of his own. Julia grinned, imagining the kid wrestling with friends, knocking a lamp into the door, or tossing a ball against the wall on a boring rainy day. She could imagine her own son doing that someday in the future.

For her baby was a boy. She patted her belly. "Have a nice nap, tadpole?"

She still awoke astonished that she was pregnant, amazed that she hadn't realized it before. She'd been so engrossed with the whole Agnes thing, so certain that nerves, suppressed anger, and her concealed, guilt-provoking deep resentment toward the interfering old hag was what was making her throw up all the time. Instead, she was pregnant. She was already four months along.

Sweetie, manic after her nap, skittered around on the bare floor, her tiny toenails clicking as she raced down the hall and back again, then zipped into Belinda's room. Julia followed, sinking down onto Belinda's bed and looking around. It was the only room they'd had time to decorate, exactly as Belinda wanted it, with a pink carpet, ballerina wallpaper, twin beds with ballerina bedspreads and sheets. The first few nights there, Belinda had awakened, crying, and Tim had had to sit with her until she fell back asleep. Now she slept through the night. Recently, she'd asked to put up posters of the Powerpuff Girls on her walls.

And when she went to stay with her grandparents, she would sleep in her old room, with its lavender walls and girlie-girl everything, because Agnes and her husband had bought and moved into the house where Belinda and Tim and Annette had once lived. When Tim, Julia, Agnes, and George had arrived at this solution, they'd felt like geniuses: Agnes and George would be nearer to their granddaughter. Tim, Julia, and Belinda could live in a larger house, one with space for another child—and perhaps even more. Belinda wouldn't be traumatized by losing her old house, because she could visit it whenever she wanted.

And Agnes and George could of course visit them in their new home, which just happened to be in a suburb over an hour's drive away. That had been one of Julia's secret qualifications for buying their new home. She didn't want Agnes dropping in every moment of every day. The location had the more obvious advantage of being closer to Tim's office.

Belinda was with her grandparents now. She'd spent the day with them, and they were bringing her to the open house and the art exhibit at the spa this evening.

Art exhibit. Julia snorted, rose, and set off for the bathroom, Sweetie scampering along at her heels like a sand crab in the wake of a seal. Tossing her clothes in the hamper, she stepped into the shower. Her feelings about the art exhibit were mixed. These photos weren't what she'd intended to do with her life and skills. They were all of Belinda in ballerina costume. They weren't cutesy proud-mama shots, although Belinda with her curls was a natural for that kind of thing. Instead, she'd done black-and-white studies: Belinda sitting on a hard wooden bench, brow wrinkled in concentration as she fit her foot into a ballet slipper. Short, slightly bowlegged Belinda, watching with awe as her tall teacher performed a perfect arabesque. Belinda just risen from a plié, one arm arching over her head, her face strained with determination. Julia thought she'd captured something of the spirit of the little girl, her willingness to work, to struggle, to change herself, and what she was doing in her ballet class was a kind of microcosm of what she was doing in her life—bravely going forward, trying to trust her teacher, her own body, and the rules of the mysterious world that had taken her mother away.

What others looking at her efforts would discover, Julia didn't know. If the guests at the exhibit smiled and passed by, that would be fine. Julia was content to please her private audience. Once she'd intended to save the world. Now she was more realistic, more humble. Now she wanted to celebrate the world, one little girl at a time.

In a little black dress and strappy high sandals, Beth was ready for the open house. She couldn't wait to introduce gorgeous Sonny to her friends.

"Sonny? We should go pretty soon."

From the bed, Sonny groaned ambiguously.

Beth sat next to him. "What's wrong?"

He covered his eyes with his arm. "Maybe you should go by yourself."

"Why?" She touched his chest. "Don't you feel good?"

He shrugged. "I don't know how much fun I'm going to have at this thing. They're your friends. And I don't know anything about art."

"You don't have to know anything about art! This isn't some heavy intellectual occasion, Sonny. It's just a party."

He removed his arm and gave her a look. "What do I have to say to Carolyn Sperry. 'How does it feel to own half of Massachusetts?' "

Beth was shocked. "Sonny! This isn't like you at all! In the first place, Carolyn Sperry isn't as wealthy as you think she is—"

"She's still fifty times as wealthy as I am."

"So what? She's nice! Just say hello. Maybe congratulate her on having a baby. What do you think she's going to do, converse with you in rhyming verse?" That made him grin, so she persevered. "Come on, Sonny, we won't stay there long, and I really really want my friends to meet you. It means a lot to me." She moved her hand suggestively along his body. "Please come, please, please, please. I'll make you really glad you did."

"All right." Reluctantly, Sonny rose. "But I won't wear a tie."

"You don't have to wear a tie." As he dressed, Beth absentmindedly redid her lipstick, thinking how unreasonable Sonny was. How many hours had *she* spent at Sonny's family's house, trying to fit in, trying to make them like her, trying to please them? Because her own parents were dead, Sonny was free from the obligation of reciprocating. He was being totally unfair, making her beg!

"Ready?" Sonny wore khakis and a blue cotton shirt that set off his dark hair and blue eyes.

A wave of lust washed over Beth, a surge of desire spun through her body. She was profoundly in love and superficially irritated with the same person, and it made her body feel as if it contained a swarm of bees.

38

One month after Claudia's death, Polly was invited to see her grandson again. The first time, eight months ago, just after Jehoshaphat's birth, had been in Amy's parents' house. Today would be Polly's maiden voyage into David and Amy's home in the renovated barn down the hill from the main house on the Anderson land.

As she stepped from her car, Polly patted her silver-red curls in an effort to calm them down; the spring humidity sent her hair into crazy corkscrews and she *so* did not want to look flippant around this earnest family.

Sheltering maples leafed out all around the converted barn, and the air smelled of mown grass and hyacinths. In the distance a tractor purred, cresting one tidy green hill. She had to admit, she thought, as she knocked on the door, it was peaceful out here.

"Hello, Polly, come in." Amy wore a long, patchwork cotton dress, and her brown hair was held back with a scarf.

The door opened to a large kitchen. The room was charming, in a time-warped kind of way, with wide board floors, rag rugs, caned chairs, curtains of natural hemp, and bunches of dried herbs hanging upside down from the ceiling.

"If you don't mind," Amy said.

Confused, Polly followed Amy's eyes. Next to the door, a rough wooden box held a pair of clogs. Amy's feet were bare. Awkwardly, Polly slipped off her molded black loafers, which with their corrugated soles seemed as anachronistic here as truck tires at a medieval fair.

"Oh!" Polly spotted the baby sitting in a wooden playpen. He wore a diaper and a cotton undershirt and was gnawing on a wooden block. Letter *C.* "Oh, Jehoshaphat is so *big!*"

"Yes," Amy agreed placidly. "Would you like some tea?"

"That would be lovely." Polly knelt at the playpen, feeling like a jeweler spotting the most perfect diamond the earth could offer. "Hi, Jehoshaphat. I'm your grandmother Polly."

Jehoshaphat squealed in reply, grinned, and held out his block, glistening with drool.

"He has a tooth!" Polly said. "And his hair is darker now, almost auburn. And he has David's blue eyes. Oh, could I hold him?"

Amy set two pottery mugs on the table. "Perhaps after our tea. He's so wiggly right now, I like to keep him away from anything hot."

Well, Amy, Polly wanted to say, *screw the tea. Let me hold my grandson!* She swallowed her reply, but remained on the floor, conversing with Jehoshaphat, who crawled across the playpen and reached a chubby hand out to touch her nose.

The front door flew open and David stomped in, halting on the mat to kick off his clogs. "Hi, Mom." He'd gained a lot of weight, at least thirty pounds, and grown a shaggy beard, which, with his sunburned face, straw hat, and suspendered linen trousers, gave him the air of an Amish farmer.

"Hello, David," Polly answered faintly.

David kissed Amy's cheek. He bent over the playpen. "Hey, big guy."

"Would you like some peppermint tea?" Amy asked her husband.

"No, thanks. I've got to get back out to work. Just wanted to say hello." He started to lift his son from the playpen.

"David," Amy said. "Hands."

"Right." David washed his hands, *then* picked up his son and sat down to bounce him on his knee.

Polly got up off the floor, settled in a chair, and drank her tea, her eyes on the little boy. Vaguely she listened to David and Amy's conversation, which centered around lambs, compost, and the prospect of rain. She studied her son and his wife as they talked. They were completely involved, intense, connected. David looked happy, devoted, *complete.*

Polly felt as if her heart were cracking open. As if her heart were an eggshell, and the life struggling to break out were something huge, foreign, and undeniable, like, say, a gorilla. It didn't make sense. She could actually feel her heart laboring to expand inside her chest. It hurt.

This little family worked well, that was obvious. David, once a banker, *thrived* as a farmer. Was there some kind of twisted dynamic at work here? Was he rebelling against the kind of life his mother and step-father had? Was he hurting Polly intention-ally, in retribution for her marrying Tucker when David was only a boy? She didn't think so. David looked purely happy. Did he even know he was hurting Polly by leaving her out of his family life? She doubted it.

In the end, did it matter? Children grew up and went away. Some went off to live in faraway lands; David was geographically near but spiritually in another time zone, if not on another planet. Polly had to open her heart and accept her child's choices for a life completely different from what she would choose for him. This was as painful as the physical labor of birth. No one told her that when women give birth, they do it first with their body, and then with their heart, over and over.

Jehoshaphat began to fuss. Amy made agitated motions. Polly started to rise from her chair. "Perhaps I should go . . ."

"Nah," David replied. "He fusses a lot these days—he's teething. Want to hold him?"

Surprised, Polly nodded and held out her arms. David handed the baby over.

Jehoshaphat stared wide-eyed at Polly as she settled him on her lap, his woes forgotten in the midst of this adventure.

"Oh! What a nice solid bundle you are!" Polly smiled at her grandson, then made popping noises with her lips. Years ago, David had loved this, and sure enough, it worked magic on Jehoshaphat, who broke into a grin and wiggled his fat arms in delight. Was there anything sweeter than a baby's smile?

Engrossed, totally infatuated, Polly progressed to making bubbles, and through her laughter and Jehoshaphat's, she heard her son say to his wife, "You see? I told you. He'll be fine."

Polly braved a questioning glance at David.

"We were wondering if you'd ever want to come out to babysit for an hour or so," David said. "Amy would like to catch up on some work."

"I'll just be in the other room," Amy hastily interjected. "Or out in the garden."

Probably, Polly thought, it would alarm David and Amy if she fell on her knees, babbling with gratitude. So she simply answered, "I'd love to!"

A few moments later, Jehoshaphat began to fuss in earnest, and Amy carried him off to nurse, and David returned to his fields.

As Polly drove away from the farm, she couldn't stop smiling. Funny, how sometimes life could turn on a dime. Odd, how days and weeks could pass by in a monotonous blur, and then suddenly, everything would go right. She'd held her grandson today. She had a date to babysit him tomorrow morning—and she had a grown-up date tonight!

———

Carolyn adored her one-month-old daughter, but she was exhausted deep down to the bedrock bottom of her muddy soul.

Because Elizabeth was premature, she was slightly underweight and needed almost constant feeding. For three weeks, Carolyn nursed her baby, but her milk didn't seem to satisfy the child, and Carolyn didn't really enjoy the experience, which caused her agonies of guilt and mortification because she knew *real* mothers, *natural* mothers, *good* mothers, loved nursing. So she tried Elizabeth on a formula, and the baby liked it, which really made Carolyn feel like some kind of natural freak, a maternal failure, physically less capable than a goat or a cow.

She was just tired, she reminded herself. Even though Hank diligently popped up whenever Elizabeth cried at night, Carolyn hadn't gotten more than two hours of consecutive sleep in the past month. Her head buzzed, the joints of her body ached like those of an ancient arthritic.

And as if some kind of malicious sprite were hovering around her life like a fat bumblebee, a week ago, their trusted housekeeper, Mrs. B., had come to tell Carolyn she needed to retire. She knew, Mrs. B. said, it was the worst possible time for Carolyn, but her husband's health was such that she just had to be home with him full-time now. Furthermore, this house was too much for her at her age. It needed two full-time people really, at least.

Carolyn understood. She asked Mrs. B. to try to find someone to take her place, at least temporarily, but so far they'd had little luck. Women wanted to work in malls and businesses around other people, not alone in this enormous, dark, dust-generating, historical mound.

Plus, her father was depressed. So depressed that during the five or six minutes in the day when Carolyn wasn't weeping herself, she considered asking him to get professional help, provided she could ever find the energy to drag her dripping, sagging, throbbing, used-up body through the endless rooms and corridors to his wing. Aubrey was pleased at the arrival of his granddaughter, and he often came to look in on her, but each time he arrived, he looked just a little bit older. Sometimes, alarmingly, this man who had always before been immaculately groomed to the point of seeming a dandy hadn't bothered to shave, and his clothes looked dingy even, from time to time, stained and spotted. He dressed well when he went to work, but apparently, once there, he was incapable of making necessary decisions, which meant that his secretary and some of the other executives were phoning Carolyn several times a day for her advice and input.

Through her windows, she saw the trees leafing out, thousands of tiny perfect leaves gleaming lime green in the April sun. The television weatherwoman forecast the temperature in the high seventies. She wanted to take Elizabeth outside. She wanted to be outside herself, to feel the sun on her slumped shoulders.

But she didn't know whether she had the energy to push the baby carriage through the corridor, down to the back hall, and out the door onto the porte cochere. Could she lift the carriage down the steps without bursting into tears? And what about the wind? Here at the summit of the hill overlooking the town, the wind always blew, having nothing to obstruct it. Didn't the wind make babies colicky?

Hank came in, his arms full of grocery bags. "Got the diapers," he said. "Got everything on the list." He disappeared into the kitchen. Carolyn heard the cupboard doors opening and closing. Returning to the living room, he gazed at his daughter, in Carolyn's arms, falling asleep as she sucked a bottle. "She's sleeping. Good. I want to show you something."

Carolyn yawned. "Okay."

"We have to go for a little ride." Hank looked mischievous.

"Oh, Hank, I can't go out like this, and I

don't have the energy to change." She didn't have the energy to walk across the room.

"Sure you can. You look fine." He lifted his daughter from Carolyn as easily as if he'd been doing this all his life, easing the nipple, with a pop, out of Elizabeth's rosebud mouth, nestling the tiny, hot head in the crook of his arm. The baby didn't cry but slumbered on.

"Really," Carolyn protested. She wore a pair of stretched-out sweatpants and one of Hank's old blue button-down shirts. "I can't."

"Really. You can." Hank went out the door, carrying his daughter with him.

Carolyn shuffled behind him, muttering curses. Once outside, she sighed. The fresh air was so sweet! Hank buckled the baby into her car carrier in the backseat. Carolyn collapsed into the passenger seat. They drove down the hill and through the town. Carolyn kept the window down, to feel the sunlight on her face. They passed Main Street, the post office, library, and pharmacy. Just past the medical complex, they turned off onto a road angling up a hill past riding stables. David turned off onto the drive of a handsome modern house built of glass, cedar, and stone.

"What I want to show you is inside." He lifted the baby carrier out and went up the slate walk.

Groaning, Carolyn followed. The house was empty. It smelled of fresh new wood and paint. The honeyed oak floors unrolled before her with pristine glossiness. The rooms were full of light.

"What?" Carolyn asked.

"I want us to move here." Hank kept walking just ahead of her, from room to room, his footsteps echoing in the emptiness.

"Move? Here?" Carolyn stopped dead in her tracks. "But it's so small!"

"No, it's just *normal.* It's got five bedrooms, Carolyn, plus a suite off the kitchen for a live-in nanny. It would be easier to take care of, and a damned sight less gloomy. It's elegant, new, in perfect condition, it's just a few minutes from the paper mill. It's got a great backyard that borders the forest. Look, where we live now, there's no place for a child to play."

"But . . . but . . . my family's always managed to raise its children there."

"Those were different times. And different women." Hank turned to face Carolyn. "Don't start comparing yourself to your ancestors. That's crazy. They had a horde of servants, which we don't want. We want to make our lives easier, we want to do more things faster, we need efficiency, and we don't need so much space."

"But what about my father? Where will he live?"

"Wherever he wants! He might want to move into a condo. He might want to move to Florida or the Bahamas. It might shake him up to move, get his blood running again. Carolyn, it's time for a change for us all."

Carolyn's heart hurt a little, as if it were tough, root-packed soil, with green shoots pushing through. The kitchen at the back of the house was large and bright, with a fireplace at one end and a handsome array of cupboards and shelves at the other. The windows here streamed with rivers of light. She took a deep breath. This room made her want to do that, it made her want to *breathe.*

She walked through the upstairs. From the bedroom window, she saw through the trees the windows and yards of other houses. Another room looked down on a pasture where a colt kicked his heels, showing off for his placid chestnut thoroughbred mother. How neighborly it felt here, how good to be among people, rather than looking down on them from her isolated bastion on the hill.

Back downstairs, she returned to the kitchen, opened the sliding door, and stepped out onto the deck. They could fence the yard, so that someday Elizabeth could run in and out of the house, tracking mud, giggling at her puppy, kidnapping the pots and pans to use as an imaginary spaceship.

Hank came up to stand next to her. "Do you like it?"

"How long have you been thinking of moving?"

"I haven't been. I just drove past this place yesterday, and it caught my eye. The entire location." He held out his arms. "So I phoned the Realtor this morning, and the moment she opened the door, I knew it was right. Doesn't it seem *right* for us, Carolyn?"

Carolyn looked up at her husband, realizing how she hadn't really paid attention to him for a month now. He'd been a kind of blur in the background, separated by a moat of baby's cries, her body's complaints, the fuzz of sleeplessness. Specks of gray salted his hair, and his eyes, like hers, were puffy. He had always accepted Carolyn's weird family situation without objection. He'd behaved with affection toward her father, with courtesy toward the employees they occasionally and dutifully entertained, he'd accompanied her willingly and in good spirits on their journey through life, without asking for much at all. He was an intelligent, sensible, even sensitive man. She trusted him. She loved him. She liked it that he had been creative enough, open enough, to consider the idea of moving from her family's elephantine residence. Like this house, he was young, full of light, cheerful, easygoing. Elizabeth slept soundly in his arm, as at home there as a baseball in a glove.

"Wouldn't this be a kind of, oh, I don't know, *impulsive,* thing to do?" she asked.

"Yeah," Hank said easily. "Probably would be."

Impulsive. The thought of it—the sheer audacity of moving out of the house that had sheltered her mother, grandmother, and great-grandmother! It made her feel daring. It made her feel young. It made her feel optimistic. "Let's do it."

39

Dazzling weather favored the open house with lingering light and a bright blue sky.

Under Shirley and Faye's direction, the lounge of the old building was transformed. The casement windows were cranked wide, letting the spring air sweep in and the evening sun mingle with the electric lights, every single one on. In the lounge, the hearth of the marble fireplace held a huge urn spilling with forsythia, japonica, and wild-cherry branches. Smaller vases of tulips, daffodils, and hyacinths shared the various tables with platters of edible delicacies. Exhibits were set up in the four corners: paintings and photos in the art section; poems calligraphed onto handsome handmade papers in another; quilts in the third. In the fourth, the masseuse had set up a massage chair and was giving free, brief demonstrations.

The place was hopping. Cars were parked chockablock on the drive, in the back lot, and along the road. Clients of the spa, present and prospective, passed between pansy-wreathed stone lions into an entrance hall with its double set of French doors opening to the crowded lounge. They stopped to take a glass of wine or sparkling water, then moved around the room, studying the art on the walls, fingering the silky handmade quilts, lining up for a brief back and neck massage, reading the brochures and other literature placed around the room.

In the far corner of the entrance hall, mats had been laid out for Star, the yoga instructor, who was giving an informal demonstration. Alice watched, magnificent in a turquoise wrap skirt, white shirt, and a small fortune in heavy turquoise and silver jewelry. Gideon was with her. Next to them stood Marilyn and Faraday, both their red heads glowing like flames, although Marilyn, in her taupe silk trousers and a matching silk sweater, looked like a female cardinal next to Faraday, who was decked out in a nearly fluorescent tartan blazer of lime, yellow, and navy.

"Hello, gorgeous." Shirley, sleek in a long, lavender tunic over violet trousers, sidled up next to Alice. "Thinking of taking yoga?"

Alice shrugged. "Maybe."

"You should. Hello, Gideon." Shirley leaned past Alice to kiss his cheek. "Hey, you know what? We're thinking of offering a couple's yoga course." She turned to Marilyn. "Hi, guys. How about you and Faraday?"

Faraday leaned forward to receive Shirley's air kiss. "It might not be a bad idea."

Marilyn's face went as red as her hair. "It might not be a good idea, either," she said softly.

"Why not?" Shirley was pumped with adrenaline tonight, ready to champion every course offered at her spa.

"I don't think so, Shirley," Alice said.

"But," Shirley persisted, "as we get older, we need to stretch more. It's good for our muscles, our hearts, our brains. Yoga can—"

Alice gripped Shirley's elbow, steering her backward until they were out of hearing range of the yoga demonstration. Curious,

Marilyn followed. The three women bent toward one another.

"Sometimes," Alice said to Shirley, "you're as dense as paste."

"Why?" Shirley demanded.

"Because I don't want Gideon to see me in such revealing postures." Alice glanced over at Star, who sat on the mat with her feet in her hands, balanced on her bum, her Lycra-covered crotch tilted toward the sky.

"Not to mention," Marilyn added in a whisper, "in that position, I'd be backfiring like a rhino on a rampage. *So* not romantic!"

Shirley laughed. "Listen, you two, in yoga class, everyone makes all kinds of sounds and they're all acceptable. In fact, there's even a position in yoga called the full wind-relieving pose. You lie on your back, wrap your arms around your knees, pull them into your sternum, and press your back to the floor."

"Yeah, that would do it," Alice said drily.

"The thing to remember is that your partner won't be looking at you. It's an inward focus. Each person is communing with his own body. There are gazing points, and sometimes your eyes are closed. Or you're looking at the teacher."

Faye, seeing the other three members of the Hot Flash Club, came across the lounge. "What's going on?"

"She's trying to convince us it's okay to pass gas in front of our lovers," Marilyn said, rolling her eyes at Shirley.

"Oh, dear." Faye laughed. "Random acts of flatulence! Yet another of the glories of growing old. I was in the grocery store the other day, getting a can from the bottom shelf. When I stood up, I sounded like a fireworks display. I couldn't stop myself, and a really cute young man was walking by. I wanted to sink through the floor. But what can I do? It's all these vegetables I'm eating!"

"Keep it up," Shirley advised. "You look really fabulous tonight."

"I've lost twelve pounds!" Determined to be cheerful, Faye wore a new *red* dress to show off her new figure.

The four older women laughing together caught Polly's eye as she came in the door with Hugh Monroe. She wished she knew them. They were having so much fun.

"Oh, there's Star, my yoga teacher!" She led Hugh toward the demonstration.

This was her second date with the charming physician, and Polly couldn't figure out whether she was more excited or terrified. On their first date, he'd taken her to dinner, beguiling her with his easy humor and intelligence. At the end of the evening, he'd walked her to her door, declined coming in for coffee, yet bent down to brush his warm lips briefly against hers, provoking a swell of lust Polly hadn't known she was still capable of experiencing. She'd stumbled into her house as giddy as a schoolgirl.

Hugh had phoned her every day after their date, and now, a week later, he was accompanying her to this event. What would happen afterward? What if he did come in for coffee, or for brandy? What if he wanted to—*make love*? She broke out in head-to-toe goose bumps at the thought. She'd already cleared the idea with her conscience. She would not feel unfaithful to Tucker, not when she'd met Hugh through Tucker's mother. In a weird way, it seemed almost meant to be. And she had no rational reservations. She was old enough. Certainly her senses provided every sign of approval.

It was her vanity, and her fear, that held her back. She was sixty-two. She was *old,* wasn't she? Her once curvy body was downright plump after her self-tranquilizing by chocolate during the weeks she had been with Claudia. Worse, she might not even *know* just how bad she looked.

Tonight as she was putting on her bra, she was shocked to notice wispy hair sticking out from her armpits. How could that be? She'd only just showered and shaved under her arms. Returning to her bathroom, she picked up the little pink plastic disposable ladies' razor from the soap dish where she'd dropped it a few minutes before. Turning it this way and that in the light, she could see, now that she had her glasses on, that she hadn't removed the clear plastic safety cap from the blades. She made a sound that was half-laugh, half-moan. So this was how old age began! Underarm hair one minute, food on the bodice the next, and soon you were wandering through the streets in your nightie? A thrill of fear raced down her spine. This was kind of funny in a horrible way, or horrible in a funny way. She needed to laugh, so in spite of prime-time rates, she dialed her best friend down in

Tucson. But Franny was off hiking with some women's group, her husband told Polly, and Polly had hung up the phone feeling even lonelier. This wasn't the sort of thing she could discuss with Carolyn, Beth, or Julia. They were all too young. Perhaps, if she and Hugh became close, perhaps someday she could talk with him about it? After all, he was aging, too, especially around the belly, and thank heavens for that, otherwise she'd be too self-conscious to go out with him.

At her side, Hugh watched the yoga demonstration. "I should try this sometime," he said. "I know it's supposed to do marvelous things for the body."

"It's made me more limber," Polly told him.

"Really?" Hugh smiled wickedly. "How interesting."

Blushing, Polly looked away. From the corner of her eye, she spotted Julia coming into the building, holding hands with a china-doll child whose other hand was linked with a tall, gangly man. "Oh, there's Julia. Let's go in the main room and see her photographs."

Shirley nodded hello to Polly as she headed for the main lounge with a stream of other guests. Turning to Marilyn, Faye, and Alice, she observed, "We should mingle."

"Oh, right. I should be with my students' exhibit." Faye whirled off.

Shirley left Alice and Marilyn with their dates and went off into the main room, greeting people as she walked, at the same time checking on a thousand little details. Jennifer and Alice's son Alan glided around offering drinks and canapés. Across the room, Justin chatted to a couple, both of whom had taken his poetry writing course; later on tonight, they'd read their poetry.

Justin was so handsome! Shirley sighed with pleasure at the sight. His silver hair was tied back in a ponytail, accentuating his narrow face. He'd been using the tanning machine a lot recently, and now his bronzed skin made his blue eyes glow like aquamarines. In jeans, a white dress shirt, a navy blazer, and black boots, he looked younger than his forty-nine years, and much younger than Shirley's sixty-one. She understood how Alice, Faye, and Marilyn could doubt his love for Shirley, but even though he was always surrounded, as he was now, by women of all ages batting their eyelashes, presenting their bosoms, and laughing seductively, Justin spent every night with Shirley. She trusted him. She understood that all his careless charm tonight, the way he smiled into the eyes of other women, was for the benefit of her spa, to entice more women to join.

———

"Oh, these are marvelous." As Carolyn complimented Julia, she hoped she sounded sincere. Actually, these photos of a little ballerina weren't really Carolyn's thing. She'd never been interested in all that little-girl stuff. She'd preferred sports to ballet, jigsaw and crossword puzzles to dolls, playing store to playing house. She'd never wanted to be the princess bride. She'd always wanted to be queen.

Julia introduced her to Belinda, cute in a flippy black skirt and Powerpuff Girls tee.

Carolyn crouched down to her level. "I like your high-top sneakers!"

Belinda grinned. "Thank you. Julia bought them for me."

Carolyn rose awkwardly, grateful for Hank's supporting hand. Her body still hadn't snapped back to normal after Elizabeth's birth. "I think we'll go sit down for a few minutes," Hank told Julia.

Carolyn found a sofa and sank gratefully into the cushions while Hank went to get her a glass of sparkling water. Tonight they'd left little Elizabeth home with a bottle and the new nanny, who'd come with a mile of references and such a mild manner that even the fretful baby settled down in her roly-poly arms. Too bad she couldn't get a nanny for her father. She looked around the crowded room, searching for her father, whom she'd convinced to come out with them tonight.

Earlier, when Hank had brought up the subject of moving, Aubrey confessed he'd wanted to have his own place for years. He wanted to live in Boston, closer to the clubs, concert halls, and museums. He'd obviously given it a lot of thought, because he suggested giving the Sperry mansion to the town of Sperry to use as a historical museum, which would give them a great tax

break. Thank heavens Hank thought so creatively, as well as being her Rock of Gibral-
tar.

"Carolyn?" A fabulous-looking black
woman settled on the sofa next to her. "I'm
Alice Murray. One of the spa's board members."

"Oh, yes," Carolyn replied. "I remember
talking with you in the Jacuzzi." Who could
forget this woman? Carolyn thought privately. She'd looked imposing in the
Jacuzzi; dressed, decorated with her magnificent turquoise jewelry, she looked absolutely regal.

"I'm trying to put together a seminar, for
the Spa Club, focusing on women's leader-
ship. I wonder whether you might be interested in helping me design and organize
it?"

"Oh," Carolyn started to object. She'd
just had a baby. She was so tired. Yet the
thought of collaborating with Alice Murray—
who had been an executive, Carolyn remembered, because her mind retained
such things, for TransWorld Insurance—was
oddly energizing. "Well." She felt herself
wake up as she spoke. "Well, *yes*. I would
be interested."

"Great. I'll be in touch."

Just as Alice rose and left, Beth appeared out of the crowd, looking svelte and sexy in a sleek black dress and high black heels, towing behind her a handsome man in khakis and a blue cotton shirt. "Carolyn! I've been wanting you to meet Sonny."

"Hello." Sonny was handsome but aloof.

"Where's Hank?" Beth asked, joining Carolyn on the sofa. Sonny stood staring around the room like a captain on the deck of a ship searching for land.

Perhaps Sonny was uncomfortable around her. People often were, it was one consequence of being a Sperry. "Off getting me a drink. My father's around here, too, somewhere."

"Good for him!" Beth said exuberantly. "Did you see the new brochures? They're starting several new courses geared for seniors. A yoga course, a memoir course— that reminds me, are you going to come back to yoga?"

Carolyn groaned. "I don't know, Beth. I don't know if I'll have the time or energy to drive out here for class."

Hank arrived with the water for Carolyn and was introduced all around.

"Where do you live?" Hank asked Sonny.

"In Methuen," Sonny said. "My family's lived there for decades."

Hank said, "That's on the Spicket and Merrimack rivers, right?"

Sonny's face brightened. "Right."

Jennifer offered a tray of canapés to Marilyn and Faraday.

"Thanks." Marilyn took a bacon-wrapped scallop, then whispered, "Do we have enough food for this horde?"

Jennifer laughed. "Just barely. Alan's thawing out some more cheese straws and slicing up more veggies. Isn't this a great turnout?"

"Fabulous."

Jennifer disappeared in the crowd.

Faraday nodded toward the therapist. "You know, maybe I'll give polarity a try. It's a little alternative, but my leg's been bothering me so much not even eight aspirin a day completely relieve the pain."

"Perhaps you should try acupuncture, too. And a beginner's yoga class."

"If I sign up for all these things, I won't be

able to travel this summer," Faraday pointed out.

"No," Marilyn responded reasonably, "but if you don't do something, you might never be able to go on a good hiking trip again."

"But I thought you really wanted to go to Scotland this summer."

"I do." Marilyn munched her canapé thoroughly, using the time to gather her thoughts. The truth was, she'd prefer to go to Scotland by herself, or with Faye, if Faye could get over her fear of flying, rather than with Faraday. Indecision tormented Marilyn these days. She knew, because her friends told her so a thousand times a day, how rare a straight, decent, pleasant, intelligent man was. She knew she was fifty-three years old, divorced, never a sex goddess at her best, and obsessed with prehistoric biology, hardly a tantalizing, man-tempting topic. Did she want to be alone in her old age, shuffling around in a retirement home with a bunch of cackling old crones when she had the opportunity to be with this kind, good man who actually shared her interests?

"Perhaps," Faraday was saying, "if I had therapy, I could get my leg in shape by September. Scotland's beautiful in the fall."

"Um," Marilyn responded, not wanting to be tied down. The thing was, she had *settled* when she married Theodore, linking her entire life to his because he was the only one who showed any interest in her. Now that she was divorced and had learned how much fun sex could be, she certainly wasn't ready to strike it out of her life forever, and with Faraday, sex was so brief as to be non-existent. But she wanted to be kind to Faraday. What should she do?

Across the room, Faye was taking photos of her art student Julia, her husband, and her stepdaughter, posed in front of the photos of Belinda in ballerina guise.

"I'd like my photo taken alone with Belinda," honked a woman as bossy as a goose, with about as much charm.

"Certainly, Agnes," Julia said.

Faye gave Julia back her camera, then strolled away to look at the other art.

A handsome older man scrutinized an oil painting of a budding cherry tree.

Faye asked, "What do you think?"

The man looked at Faye. His smile was

rather wonderful, showing off a handsome set of white teeth and lighting up his dark eyes. "I think it's quite good. So good that if it were for sale, I'd buy it."

Faye laughed from sheer pleasure. "You have no idea how pleased I am to hear you say that. That's one of mine."

"You painted that?" He looked at her more closely.

This allowed her to study him in return. He wore a white shirt, navy blazer, and striped red tie. She liked it that he wore a tie; men so seldom did these days. "I did," she told him proudly. "But I must confess, I've painted all my life and exhibited in Boston galleries. I'm *teaching* this course, so perhaps I shouldn't have put this painting up . . ." Her voice trailed off as she tried to edit her very personal thoughts. Although . . . this man might understand. He might even be glad to hear what she had to say. "But I wanted to show it off because it's the first decent thing I've painted since my husband died."

The man nodded. "I'm glad you did. It's very fine." His voice was deep and smooth, like brown velvet. "And now that I know the story behind it, I like it even more, the way

most of the painting is the dark, rough tex-
ture of the bark and twigs, with only the
palest blush of pink showing. Optimism after despair."

A sensual shiver raced up Faye's spine.
She loved the way this man talked!

"Yes, that's what I meant *exactly*." She
held out her hand. "I'm Faye Vandermeer."

He took her hand. "Aubrey Sperry." An
electric charge jumped between them, so
powerful Faye was surprised not to see
sparks.

He didn't take his hand away, nor did she.
They stood there smiling at each other like a
pair of teenagers.

After a moment Faye pulled herself together. "You don't have a drink."

Aubrey nodded at her glass. "Is the wine
any good?"

"Yes. Not expensive, but pleasant." A hot
flash ran through her. "It's a little warm in
here, isn't it?"

"It is, indeed. This place has beautiful
grounds. Why don't we go out for a stroll?"

"Good idea. Let's get you a glass of wine
on the way."

As they made their way through the
crowd, Aubrey freed Faye's hand. But he

put his hand on her elbow, and he kept it there.

They passed Jennifer, coming around with another tray of canapés. Alice had just sunk onto a sofa, grateful for the opportunity to get off her feet, which ached, in spite of her compromise shoes—low-heeled, wide-toed, instead of the flirty high stilettos she used to adore. Gideon was across the room, reading the poetry taped to the walls. Alan slid through the crowd toward Jennifer, who was working so hard beads of sweat glinted on her face. The two young people bent toward each other, conferring urgently, no doubt about whether the delicious munchies they'd concocted for this evening would suffice for the unexpected crowd. Alice studied her son and his girlfriend. Her handsome black son and his white girl-friend.

Shirley bustled up to Alice, flounced down on the sofa, and grinned. "Successful evening, don't you think? We've already had a ton of new people signing up!"

"It's great," Alice responded absentmindedly.

"What's up with you?" Shirley followed Alice's eyes. "Don't tell me you're sitting here stewing about Alan and Jennifer! Oh, *please.* Alan and Jennifer have been together now for over a year. They've built up their catering and bakery business, they've dealt with the stress of satisfying clients who wanted Emeril food at McDonald's prices, and look at them, they're still madly in love!"

"I just don't want Alan hurt," Alice said gloomily. "A black man and a white woman—"

"Hey, they're grown-ups. They know the score. Maybe you're the kind of mother who won't approve of *any* woman your son marries," Shirley challenged.

Alice rounded on Shirley. "That's a terrible thing to say!"

Shirley didn't back off. "Well, think about it. You told me you never liked Alan's ex-wife, what was her name, Genevieve Lee?"

"Genevieve Ann. She was a scrawny, arrogant, pretentious little phony. *But,*" Alice hastened to add, "I never once told Alan I thought that."

Shirley snorted. "Yeah, I imagine you were a masterpiece of deceit."

Alice looked away guiltily.

"Okay," Shirley reminded her, "and then they get divorced and Alan shows up as despondent as a stray dog lost in the rain, and you were so worried about him! Remember? And when did he start perking up? *When he met Jennifer.* And he's been stable, happy, healthy, he's been really good ever since he hooked up with her."

Alice pressed her lips together.

"You know, Alice, I think you're forgetting the number one rule of the Hot Flash Club. *Don't let fear rule your life!*" With an emphatic nod of her chin, Shirley rose to her feet in one lithe movement. "I'd better get back to work."

"Good." Alice folded her arms defensively over her chest. Sometimes Shirley made her so damned mad.

But she couldn't deny it; Shirley had a point. Alice's son *was* happy with Jennifer.

Gideon came over. "Can I get you a drink?"

"No, thanks." Alice patted the sofa and Gideon sank down next to her. God bless the man, he had a weight problem equal to hers. "The crowd's beginning to thin out. That greasy little con artist Justin is going to hold the poetry reading at a quarter till eight. That should drive people away in droves."

Gideon chuckled. "You're in a charming mood."

Alice couldn't help smiling. "Sometimes I feel retirement doesn't allow me to use the full range of my critical skills."

"You're just cross because we missed bridge to come here tonight."

"You're right." Alice was grateful for the charity of his thoughts. She leaned against him, enjoying the warmth of his massive, comforting body. She did want this for her son, this sense of belonging, of being cared for. And he seemed to have it with Jennifer. "Alan and Jennifer are working their asses off. Let's invite them out to dinner some night this week. Let's choose a really swanky place, too. Give them a little treat."

"Woman," Gideon said, putting his substantial arm around her shoulders, "you are full of surprises."

Alice nestled against him. "I certainly hope so."

In the middle of the room, Shirley clapped her hands loudly. "Excuse me! Excuse me, everyone! I'm delighted to inform you, it's time for our poetry reading." She gestured toward the corner where Justin was placing a metal podium. Six of his students awaited, notebooks in hand, while Alan, Jennifer, and Gideon set up folding chairs facing the group.

A small crowd strolled over to the poetry corner, but most people sped out of the room as if Shirley had announced that alligators were loose in the building, a common reaction to poetry readings, and one Shirley had counted on to end the evening. Glancing over, she assured herself that Marilyn and Alice were both on their way to the front door, to say good-bye and hand out brochures. They'd agreed on this beforehand, so that Shirley wouldn't have to miss Justin's big event.

Faye and Aubrey ambled into the lounge, flushed from their walk in the fresh spring air, and as they sat down, Aubrey angled his entire body toward Faye, who leaned in his direction. Faye caught Shirley looking at her and threw her a sparkling smile. Three rows behind, Carolyn and Hank noticed and raised questioning eyebrows at each other.

Out in the foyer, Marilyn and Alice said good-bye to the last departing guest, then leaned in the open doorway, catching their breath. From the lounge came the soft murmur of a woman reading her poetry. From outside came the chirps and peeps of birds settling down for the night.

"What a successful evening!" Marilyn sighed.

A pretty middle-aged woman with silver-red hair and green eyes slipped quietly out of the lounge and hurried toward them. "Excuse me. I wonder if you could help me. I'm Polly Lodge, I take a yoga course here. There's a restaurant nearby I'd like to go to, but I can't remember the name. It's Italian, it's got fabulous bread . . ."

"Leonardo's?" Marilyn suggested.

"That's it! Thanks." Polly tapped her temple. "Sometimes my brain seems as full of holes as a moth-eaten sweater."

"I hear you," Alice said warmly.

"I've got the same problem," Marilyn added.

"Do you?" Polly's face lit up. "It hasn't really bothered me, but tonight I'm on my second date with a man I really like, and I *know* he'd like this restaurant. But I fell into one of those circular mental traps. The more I couldn't think of the name, the more flustrated I got."

Alice laughed. "Do you mean *frustrated* or *flustered*?"

Polly looked baffled. "Excuse me?"

Marilyn told her, "You said *flustrated.*" Looking at Alice, Marilyn said, "Actually, that's a pretty good word, we ought to add it to our lexicon."

Polly's face fell. "Oh, no. I *am* getting senile."

Alice took pity on her. "No more than the rest of us. The other day, when I was worried because Gideon wouldn't go to the dentist, I told him sometimes he made me feel depissed."

Polly snickered. "Depissed is what I get when I laugh too hard."

"My mother used to make malapropisms," Marilyn said musingly. "I remember once, when she was in her eighties, I took her out to lunch, and she ordered a grilled sneeze sandwich."

"Gross!" Alice moaned. "Oh, Lord, is this what we have to look forward to? Our urethras leak while our brains clog up?"

"That's better than the other way around," Polly observed with a grin.

Alice chortled. "You're right about that." She cocked her head, looking Polly over. She liked this woman. "How old are you?"

"Sixty-two," Polly answered truthfully.

"And you're on your second date with a guy?"

Polly nodded.

"Have you slept with him yet?" Alice asked.

"Alice!" Marilyn said. "Don't be so pushy."

"Oh, I don't mind," Polly hastened to assure them. "I've been *dying* to talk about this with someone my age. No, I haven't slept with him yet, and I'm downright terrified about it. I'm so afraid he'll be disgusted by all my sags, stretch marks, and molds."

"Molds?" Marilyn repeated.

"Did I say *molds*?" Polly slapped her forehead. "I meant *moles*. All these little skin bumps . . ."

Alice grinned. "We know what you mean.

We've got them, too. You're seriously *flustrated,* honey."

Shirley and Faye peeked around the lounge door, then hurried on tiptoe to join the other three.

"Here you both are!" Shirley whispered, looking curiously from Alice to Marilyn to Polly. "What's going on?"

Marilyn and Alice exchanged glances. Alice nodded.

Marilyn smiled. "I think we're in the process of initiating a new member of the Hot Flash Club."

ABOUT THE AUTHOR

NANCY THAYER is the author of thirteen novels, including *Custody, Between Husbands and Friends, An Act of Love, Belonging, Three Women at the Water's Edge,* and *Everlasting,* which was a Main Dual selection of the Literary Guild. Her work has been translated into nearly a dozen languages. Her first novel, *Stepping,* was made into a thirteen-part series for BBC Radio, and her ghost novel *Spirit Lost* has been optioned and produced as a movie by United Image Entertainment. In 1981 she was a Fellow at the Breadloaf Writers Conference. She has lived on Nantucket Island year-round for nineteen years with her husband, Charley Walters.

**Visit the author's website at
www.nancythayer.com.**